FIFTY FIFTY

FIFTY
FIFTY

JAMES PATTERSON
AND
CANDICE FOX

Little, Brown and Company

New York Boston London

Little, Brown and Company
Hachette Book Group
1290 Avenue of the Americas, New York, NY 10104
littlebrown.com

First North American Edition: February 2018
Originally published in Australia by Century Australia, a division of Penguin Random House Australia, July 2017

Little, Brown and Company is a division of Hachette Book Group, Inc. The Little, Brown name and logo are trademarks of Hachette Book Group, Inc.

The publisher is not responsible for websites (or their content) that are not owned by the publisher.

The Hachette Speakers Bureau provides a wide range of authors for speaking events. To find out more, go to hachettespeakersbureau.com or call (866) 376-6591.

ISBN 978-0-316-44976-2 (Costco ed.)
LCCN 2017909799

10 9 8 7 6 5 4 3 2 1

LSC-H

Printed in the United States of America

FIFTY FIFTY

CHAPTER 1

SHE WAS PERFECT. And so rarely the perfect ones came, fluttering out of the darkness like moths into golden light. Swift and uncatchable.

He had wandered the third floor of the car park for a couple of hours now, risking it all for his ideal victim. A number of young women had crossed the little grassy field below where he stood as classes at the university ended and new ones began. He watched them toting shoulder bags and the occasional paper coffee cup, blinking in the warm daylight. Then the place was deserted again, and he waited.

It was bright out, leaving a dark shadow in the corner of the parking lot, to the right of the fire stairs. He'd watched a potential girl enter the stairwell, his heart thumping, but she was only halfway up the concrete steps toward him before he realized she wasn't right. She had a friend on the phone. Cackling laughter. No. He'd know her when he saw her. Big doe eyes. Frightened, down-turned mouth. Thin wrists he could squeeze and twist.

The desire to flee picked at him. It was risky, hanging around too long. The university campus was on high alert after the police had found his previous works. Marissa. Elle. Rosetta. His brunette beauties mangled, ruined. Tragedies laid out on the sand. As news of the Georges River Killer spread, girls across campus had started dyeing and cutting their hair, walking in groups at night, having the security guards take them to their cars. It wasn't about the hair for him—although he hadn't failed to notice their striking resemblance to his first, many years ago. No, his university girls had simply been the right kind of innocent. Content, confident. He looked for the forthright stride, the high chin, the captive excitement of rosebuds just before they bloom.

He told himself to be patient. The plan had gone so well so far. His finale was worth the risk. A few more minutes. He wandered into the stairwell as he heard footsteps.

Then he saw her, her hand on the rail, gripping, pulling as she ascended. A slice of her soft cream brow and high cheekbone as she turned the corner.

Oh, there she was. His perfect girl.

CHAPTER 2

SHE EMERGED FROM the stairwell door and he swept an arm around her throat, yanked her backwards. The sickening rush of chemicals through his veins threatened to knock him off balance. She didn't make a sound at first. The breath left her instantly. Her bag fell. Then the clap of his palm over her mouth, her heels dragging as he turned and pulled her toward his vehicle.

"No!" a muffled wail. "Stop! Stop! Stop!"

She bucked, twisted, tried to sink out of his arms. He was ready for the movement, knew the victim's dance by heart. He sank with her, gripped tighter, pulled her body hard against his. Never letting her think for a moment that she had a hope of escape. Hope was a dangerous thing.

He had no idea where it came from. She was totally under his control. But hope *had* infected her, as tangible in her body as an electric pulse. Without warning she stiffened, let go of his hands and swung her fists over her own head at his face.

A fumbling blow. The shock of it. He let her go. She hit the ground and the scream erupted out of her, rapturous, like a song. He punched her in the stomach, tried to gather her up. This wasn't the plan!

She twisted and scrambled against a car. He swiped at her. Missed.

She was up and running. And as she ran, she almost knocked over another girl standing there watching, mouth hanging open, phone in hand.

"Run!" his victim screamed at the girl, already disappearing into the fire stairs. "Run!"

He righted himself. The new girl was too shocked, appalled by what she'd witnessed, to take a step back out of range. Big brown eyes, dark skin, the slowly opening and closing mouth of a woman feeling paralyzing terror wash over her.

She wasn't his perfect girl, but she was a delightful surprise.

He seized her wrist.

CHAPTER 3

SHE FIRST BECAME aware of the television in the corner, its robotic noises, bleeping and zooming and piercing jingles, the crash and tumble of advertisements. Caitlyn shifted her face against the mattress. She was sweating badly, or bleeding, she couldn't tell. She tried to speak and found her lips were sealed by tape. Panic shot through her. A spike of pain that reached from the heel of her bare foot to the crown of her skull. She turned, struggled against the tape on her wrists. Her nose was broken.

A damp concrete room. A bare mattress, a blanket bunched at the end. Rusty beer kegs and wooden crates, a pile of trash in the corner waist high. Mop heads and buckets and a milk crate full of bottles, a vacuum cleaner covered in an inch of dust. Caitlyn reeled, tried to get her bearings, scrabbled against the wall. Her ankles were bound. The terror was so loud in her brain that for a moment it blocked out all sound from the television. She saw him standing before the screen, turned away from her, his hands hanging by his sides.

The university. The car park. She'd been on the phone to her mother in California, fending off her ridiculous warnings about the killer on campus. It had been bright. Sunny. Afternoon. Then, in a snap, a different picture altogether, the curtain sailing closed and sailing open again on a horror-movie scene. The girl fighting with the hooded figure between the cars, rushing past her, a blur of heat. *Run! Run!* Caitlyn hadn't run. Hadn't done anything. And then he'd been right in front of her, impossibly fast, his fist swinging down toward her face.

Every story she'd ever heard of abduction and death and rape rushed through her mind, a whole catalogue of atrocities collected since she was a child and her teacher first taught them about Stranger Danger. True crime novels she'd browsed in airports. Macabre, late-night episodes of *SVU,* young girls being dragged out of sex dungeons, recounting atrocities, shivering in the witness stand. *Now you are one of them,* Caitlyn thought. *Now your nightmare begins.*

The man in front of the television was angry. His broad shoulders were high. She watched, wild-eyed, as he gripped the back of his shaven skull, ran a hand down his neck and back again, scratched hard. Caitlyn looked at the television screen just beyond him, the police leading a cuffed, black-haired man toward a waiting paddy wagon.

"*...the arrest of Samuel Jacob Blue over the murders of three young women abducted from the area surrounding the University of Sydney campus. Police say Blue was apprehended in...*"

"This wasn't the plan," the man with the shaved head murmured. He turned and glanced at Caitlyn where she sat huddled against the wall. He seemed to be assessing, his mind churning with decisions. "Fuck. Fuck!"

The rage rippled through him. She saw it creep up his arms until his neck tightened, the thick jugular standing out against sweat-sheened skin.

He turned and watched the screen and gripped his head again. "It wasn't finished yet!" Caitlyn watched as he knelt, almost shakily, before the screen. His fingers twitched, inches away from the glass, as Samuel Jacob Blue appeared, glancing fearfully at the crowd as the paddy wagon doors closed on him.

"I need you," her captor said, his eyes locked on Blue. "I need you, Sam."

FOUR MONTHS LATER...

CHAPTER 4

FOUR MONTHS. ONE hundred and twenty-seven days, to be exact. That's how long my brother had been in prison for a crime he did not commit. I stood on the steps of the courthouse, ignoring my partner, trying to decide if my math was correct. It was. As I waited, staring down at my ridiculous high heels, listening to the shouts of the crowd nearby, another day of Sam's life was being lost. I drew hard on my cigarette, clutched the stupid pink handbag into my side. The passing seconds were agony. Waiting for the court to open once again on the circus that was the Georges River Killer case. Another day I would fail to bring him home.

I am a Sex Crimes detective with the Sydney police. I used to think I was pretty good at my job. Versatile. Adaptable. I had a keen sense for bad men, and I wasn't afraid of bending the rules to make them admit what they were. A cracked tooth here, a broken finger there. I made men tremble in their seats. Harriet Blue: Terror at Five-Foot Two. While I was the natural enemy of the caged rape suspect, I could also be soft and gentle enough to coax a tiny, bruised child into revealing what his or her abuser had done, when no amount of coddling and bargaining by trained psychologists had struck pay dirt.

But, four months earlier, my own colleagues had left the police station where I worked on their way to make the biggest arrest of their careers—a man they believed was a vicious serial killer who had tortured and murdered three university students. No amount of intuition, or skill, or training had prepared me for the fact that that man was my own flesh and blood.

Sam's case was all the nation was talking about. The newspapers were calling him Australia's worst serial killer, and that was no small claim—every article compared him with the fiends who'd taken up the mantle before him. Ivan Milat, the Backpacker Murderer. Arnold Sodeman, the Schoolgirl Strangler. Eric Edgar Cooke, the Night Caller. Now came Samuel Jacob Blue, the Georges River Killer, responsible for the prolonged, brutal deaths of three beautiful, young students.

For four months, I'd been determined to do everything right to help my brother go free. He was innocent. I was sure of it. The man who abducted, raped, tortured and strangled the three women I saw every night on the news was not the man who'd once been a boy snuggled beside me in the temporary beds at the offices of the Department of Children's Services. He was not that terrified boy, whispering to me in the dark, wondering which foster home we were going to be shipped to next. He was not the teenager who'd defended me at various high schools when the kids came to pick on the shabby interlopers. The one who made me birthday cards when our new families forgot. Whoever he was, he did not have my brother's soulful kindness. His never-ending generosity.

On the footpath nearby, the usual gathering of gawkers and court ghouls waited for the doors to open. One caught my eye and spat on the ground, spoke loudly to his friend in the queue.

"She knew what he was up to," he said. "How could she not?"

"Don't listen, Harry." My partner, Detective Edward Whittacker, tried to take my arm and turn me away from the crowd. "You'll only make yourself madder."

"I'm not mad," I lied, shrugging him off. "I'm cool. I'm calm. Today's going to be the day. We'll find it today. The key."

I'd been talking about the "key' to my brother's case since his arrest. The thing that freed him. A piece of false testimony. A surprise witness. Something, anything. I'd been looking into Sam's case, and I hadn't found the key that proved he wasn't the killer. But I had high hopes. Hell, my hopes got so high sometimes I had fantasies of the killer himself walking into the courtroom and confessing. Giving up was far from my mind.

I spotted my brother's prosecutor, the enormous, broad-shouldered Liam Woolfmyer, strolling toward us with a colleague beside him. Whitt had my arm again, his other hand fumbling at his necktie.

"Don't say a word," he growled.

"You keep pawing at me and it'll be more than words you have to worry about."

"I'm warning you, Harry." Whitt glared over the top of his glasses at me. The gentle, fastidious detective had been mortified to hear me sneer a stream of obscenities at Woolfmyer the first morning of my brother's hearings.

Sometimes there's a wild Harriet in me, a woman I can't control. She rears her ugly head without warning. The comment from the queue already had her twitching. But then I stole a glance at Woolfmyer, and the worst of all things happened. He locked eyes with me, smiled, and leaned over in mock confidence to his companion.

"Samuel Blue won't last a single night in Long Bay prison," Woolfmyer said. "He's far too pretty. Someone will make him their bitch."

The bad Harriet in me swelled, like white-hot steam, blinding and painful behind my eyes. As Woolfmyer passed I was already taking steps to catch up with him. I barely heard Whitt's call.

The few meters between Woolfmyer and me closed in an instant. I was behind him. My hand reaching up, completely beyond my control.

I tapped him on the shoulder. Woolfmyer stopped and turned.

I punched him as hard as I could in the temple.

CHAPTER 5

I'VE ALWAYS BEEN a fighter. It's necessary, when you have a child-hood like mine, to know how to defend yourself physically. I was a scrappy, dirty fighter before my police chief taught me how to box. He made the mistake of honing the self-taught craft of a brutal, remorseless combatant. Size means nothing when you know what you're doing. I swung up and to the left with a hard, balled right fist and smashed the prosecutor with all the force in my arm, shoulder and hip.

The only sound was the dull thump of his body on the pavement, the whisper of his settling robes, a big bird brought down out of the sky by a rifle blast.

My regret was instant. I looked around. Woolfmyer's friend stagger-ing back. Whitt nearby, his hand still out, reaching, desperate. The crowd, a huddle of journalists. Horror and guilt rushed up through my body. Cameras flashed.

I felt a bizarre impulse to reach down and help the unconscious lawyer to his feet. To brush him off, slap him on the back, pretend it was all going to be OK.

But everything was far from OK. The police officer who had been guarding the front doors of the courthouse began to march toward me, taking his cuffs from his belt.

CHAPTER 6

I STOOD IN the entrance to the holding cell and stared at the women there. They were like lazy, uninterested cats lounging on the steel benches. One girl was lying on her belly on the floor, a magazine spread out before her. There were more magazines in a stack on one of the benches, trashy celebrity rags. An adult slumber party in a concrete bedroom. A gaggle of arrested shoplifters, prostitutes, drug runners. I went to the nearest bench and sat down, put my face in my hands as the steel door slammed shut.

I guessed a lot of women who ended up in a cell at the Parramatta Police headquarters thought what I was thinking in that moment. That their lives were over. That they'd had some fuck-ups in their lifetime, sure, but this was a whole new level of idiocy. Holding cells are where mistakes are offered up for evaluation. This is it. This is where all a person's chickens come home to roost.

Detective Inspector Nigel Spader was at the door to the holding cell now as I sat cracking my aching knuckles. He leaned on the wall and looked through the bars at me, folding his hairy ginger arms.

"Harriet," he said. "What a mess you've got yourself in."

Spader had spearheaded the case against my brother. During the active investigation, I'd fought hard for entry onto the Georges River Task Force team, annoyed and confused as to why I was being kept away from what was possibly the nation's most important case. I had the skills. I had the enthusiasm. I'd had no idea that I was being shut out because the main suspect was Sam. I'd always hated Nigel anyway, had got into a few fistfights with him in the past.

"What's the word?" I asked.

"Mr. Woolfmyer's going to be fine. He's got a mild concussion."

"Is he going to go for an assault charge?"

"Of course he is," Nigel snorted. "You knocked him out cold."

"Woolfmyer, the lawyer?" the girl on the ground broke in. "You punched a lawyer?"

I turned toward Nigel and tried to signal that my conversation with him wasn't for public consumption. But the other women in the holding cell were watching me with interest now.

"If they're going to lock me up, I want my notes on Sam's case," I said. "They're in my handbag. I'll still be able to work on his defense."

"Harry." Nigel shifted closer to the bars. "Your brother is a killer. You're going to have to move past the denial phase and wake up to what's happening here. I know you and I have had our differences. But we didn't lock him up to spite you. We locked him up because he murdered three girls."

I grabbed a handful of the magazines from the stack beside me and hurled them at the bars. Nigel flinched. The girls in the cell around me cheered. I was shocked by the noise, brought suddenly out of my fury. I realized my jaw was clenched so tight that my teeth were clicking as they ground together.

"I reckon you forced that confession out of him," I told Nigel, giving my fellow inmates a warning look. "There was a lot of pressure to catch the killer."

Nigel shook his head. "Harry, you and Sam are violent people. I've experienced your family's violence personally." He touched his brow, an old scar I'd given him about the seventh or eighth time he'd parked in my designated spot.

The girl on the floor had shifted closer to me, her grin spread wide.

"Wait a minute," she chirped up. "You mean, you punched this guy, too?" she said, flicking her chin at my colleague.

"I did," I said. I looked at Nigel. "And he cried like a baby."

CHAPTER 7

I WAS TEACHING the women in the cell how to land a left hook without fracturing their wrists when I noticed Pops standing at the door, waiting for the guard to unlock it.

My chief. My friend. My boxing trainer, a man who'd also seen the hair-trigger aggression that thrived in the very marrow of my bones. Pops said nothing as we walked down the sterile hall toward the offices. I tottered on my ridiculous heels. Eventually I stopped, reached down and pulled them off. We were standing between the row of holding cells and the doors to the bullpen where my colleagues worked, a corridor between two worlds. My brother existed in the world we'd just walked through, the criminal world. My own life, until then, had been ahead of us, in the swirling blue universe of police and their struggle against evildoers. Here I was, balancing on the tightrope connecting the two.

"I had a private chat with Judge Steiner," Pops said. "We went ahead and held the assault hearing in your absence."

"What?" I said. Suddenly, I could hardly find words, which was unusual for me.

"Woolfmyer agreed not to push forward with an assault conviction, but he applied for an AVO, and Steiner granted it."

Still no words came.

Pops raised his bushy eyebrows. "Yeah. You're banned from the trial. You're banned from the entire courthouse, in fact. You're not allowed to come within five hundred meters of Prosecutor Woolfmyer. Which means anywhere he regularly goes is off limits to you. The prison where your brother is, for example. Sam's lawyer's office."

"This is..." I was shivering with rage.

"This is perfectly reasonable." Pops shrugged, angry. "Judge Steiner could have recorded the conviction *and* granted Woolfmyer the apprehended violence order. But he didn't. Because I convinced him you were going to get your arse out of town."

A young probationary constable was walking up the hall with my handbag, confiscated from me when I was arrested. I snatched the stupid pink bag off him and started rummaging through it for cigarettes.

"I told Steiner I'd find you a case. Send you off into the desert again for a couple of weeks so you can cool down."

"I'm not going back out there," I snapped. "I'm going to sit on the front steps of the courthouse. If I can't go inside, I'll still be there. I'm not leaving Sam."

"That's exactly what Judge Steiner said you'd do." Pops shook his head. "He wanted to lock you up instead. I said you're not going to be on the courthouse steps. You'll be out in the desert, out of trouble, just like you were after they picked Sam up."

"Nope," I said. "Not happening."

I couldn't find my cigarettes. My hands were shaking too badly.

"Blue," Pops called as I walked toward the door, following at my heels. "This is not up for discussion. You get out of here or he'll reverse his decision. And then you'll be no good to Sam at all. You want to try working on his defense from a jail cell? You'll be lucky if they give you paper and a pencil in there."

I stopped by the big glass doors.

There was a certain appeal to what he was saying. I could go back out into the Australian badlands, out among the tiny towns where people who didn't want to be recognized fled. I could run away from the horror of my brother's situation. Blessed denial.

"When does the order expire?"

"Nine days."

I bit my lip. I wanted so badly to cry. But I was not a crier. I was not weak. I squeezed the door handle, trying to hold on to some semblance of control.

"You fucked up, Blue," Pops said. It was rare that he swore. I looked at his eyes. "You're a hothead. And I love that about you. It's half of what makes you a good cop. Your fearlessness. Your fire. But you need to get away from here before you do some real damage. This?" He flipped the frilly collar of my blouse. "This is not working. When you're not bashing prosecutors you're standing around pissed as hell and doing a bad job hiding it. The princess getup makes you look about as harmless as a hired assassin."

I exhaled. I wanted a hug. But I was not a hugger, either.

"It's only nine days," he said. "How bad could things go in that time?"

CHAPTER 8

I LEANED MY head against the car window in the dark.

Beyond the glass, New South Wales desert rolled by, barren and hard. I was out here again. In exile for my own good, for the good of Sam's case.

I was six hours from Sydney, four of them by plane, two of them by car, on the straight edge of the western border of New South Wales. Red dirt country. We were headed to a tiny, dim star in a constellation of sparse towns, most notably White Cliffs to the south of us (population 103) and Tibooburra to the west of us (population 262). My driver, a plump and pretty blonde woman wearing a dusty police uniform and standard-issue baseball cap, shifted uncomfortably behind the wheel. She'd been jibber-jabbering since we left the airstrip, about the region, its history, seasonal precautions about snakes. I was so angry at myself, so distracted, I'd hardly been answering her. I sighed quietly. She was gearing up to take a run at me about why I was there. How could I possibly explain what I'd done? I could feel it—the curiosity.

"So the papers said…" She licked her lips, hesitated, as most people do. "They said that the lawyer made some derogatory remark toward you?"

"My brother," I answered. "He made a joke about my brother being raped in prison. I work in Sex Crimes. Rape jokes aren't funny."

"Struth! You're right, they're not. Plus, it's your brother," the cop sympathized. "I mean, it doesn't matter what he did. He's still—"

"He didn't do anything. He's innocent," I said.

I realized miserably that I didn't even know this officer's name. My mind was so tangled up in my personal life that I'd completely forgotten it as soon as she'd introduced herself. I reached down for the case file at my feet and pretended I was shifting it to the backseat so it wouldn't get damaged. I glanced at the name on the cover. Senior Sergeant Victoria Snale.

"I've got to say"—Snale's voice was irrepressibly cheerful—"it made an amazing picture for the front pages. You standing over the lawyer. Him all splayed out on the concrete. It must have really been some punch."

I felt microscopically uplifted. "It doesn't have to be hard if it's on target."

"And now you're here," she said brightly. "I can't say I'm sad about that. It's pretty lonely out here, to be honest. It'll be good to have some more cops around. Someone who can relate. You know?"

"How many cops are there in town?" I asked.

"Active officers? I mean, we have one retiree…"

"Active officers."

"Just me." She looked over, smiled. "Just *us*."

I didn't want to burst Snale's bubble, but I didn't plan on being out in the desert long. *Nine days* of "us." Then it'd be back to Victoria Snale: Lone Ranger.

The moment Prosecutor Woolfmyer's AVO expired, I'd be back—

back in that jerk's face, fighting him and the state's crack team of lawyers about my brother's innocence.

The empty desert around me was familiar. I'd been shoved aside when Sam had first been arrested, shipped out into the middle of nowhere, away from the public eye, away from my distinctly uncomfortable colleagues and their guilty looks after months of lying to me. Back then, I'd succumbed to the journey. I'd felt such shameful pleasure at having something to think about that was not Sam and what he was facing. Now was no different.

I squeezed my folder of notes on Sam's case against my chest. A thick binder of papers detailing all the leads I'd tried to chase down. Most of the work I'd done was hopeless, dead ends I'd pursued over the months searching for something, anything, that might set my brother free. The binder was battered and bruised, but it was my lifeline. I wasn't leaving it behind. I wasn't putting it in my bag. I was hanging on to it. As long as I had the binder, I wasn't abandoning Sam.

CHAPTER 9

"LET'S CHECK OUT the view before we go down," Victoria Snale said, beaming. "You'll love it."

The officer pulled the four-wheel drive off the side of the highway and let it rumble to a stop. I climbed out and breathed the desert air, felt the warm wind ruffle my hair. The great domed sky was heavy with stars. I felt so far from where I belonged. Wonderfully small.

"Come this way," Snale beckoned me, kicking up dust in the car's headlights. "This is it."

I stood with her on the edge of a rocky cliff in the dark. "This is Last Chance Valley," she said.

She swept her hand dramatically across the landscape, indicating a less-than-impressive collection of gold lights clustered at the bottom of a moonlit rise. I nodded, made an interested noise. I felt bad for being so distant for the whole trip toward the town.

"You can't see it very well right now, but the town is actually at the bottom of a massive crater." She pointed to the curve of the rise we stood on. "Biggest crater in the Southern Hemisphere. This ridge is just the edge, it runs all the way around. It's sort of egg-shaped, with the town right in the center and properties spreading out around. The first family settled down there two hundred years ago. There are seventy-five residents now."

"Uh-huh."

"They're not sure what formed the crater, but it may have been a volcano. A meteorite. Every now and then somebody comes out and runs a study on the place. Very exciting stuff. I usually get to brief the town on their visits, tell everybody to behave themselves."

"Sounds great."

"I guess the settlers thought the crater might shelter us from the desert dust storms," she mused, rolling a rock under her boot. "It doesn't. In fact it makes things worse. We get about ten centimeters of dust when the summer winds roll in. It also floods real bad, and the floodwaters hold beneath the earth. When it floods, we get green grass. We can grow wheat here. There's plenty of cattle. But, being the only grass around for thousands and thousands of kilometers, it brings locust plagues."

I was glad Snale was the local cop and not the tourism director. I tried to maintain a serious face.

"Locusts?" I said.

"Yeah, we're just getting over the last plague. Here's one right now, in fact."

She reached out toward me, and I realized a creature was walking up my biceps, an enormous brown grasshopper covered in the patterns of the desert, spots and stripes in red and brown. I didn't scream. But it wasn't easy.

Snale plucked the creature from my shirt and tossed it into the wind. It fluttered into the dark.

"Oh great," I said, brushing off the place where the thing had been. "This is great."

"They bite, but it's not that painful."

"And what exactly will I be working on out here?" I asked.

"Well," she said cheerfully. "Turns out somebody's planning to kill us all."

CHAPTER 10

WE SAT IN the car together and Snale took a package from the glove compartment. It was a notebook secured in a police evidence bag, a sheaf of photocopies, which she handed to me. She started the car but kept the overhead light on so I could read as she drove.

"A trucker found this diary in a backpack on the side of this highway, at a rest stop." She pointed over her shoulder. "Back the way we came, about five kilometers. He spotted it sitting there when he stopped to pull a dead roo from his front grille. Brought the diary into town and handed it in to me. It contains detailed analyses of spree killers, weapons, massacre plans. We think someone is, or was, constructing a plan to kill as many people in Last Chance Valley as possible."

"When was this?"

"Two days ago."

"And you vetted the truck driver?"

"Yeah, I let him go."

I felt the hairs on the back of my neck stand on end as I looked at the photocopied pages before me. My eyes breezed over the tight, small writing and fell upon the hand-drawn images, sketches of a person in a hood running toward fleeing groups of people, mowing them down with a huge rifle. There were diagrams of the layout of the town below, lists of names and addresses. I examined the notebook in the evidence bag, turned it over. Of course, there was no name on it. That'd be too much to hope for.

The thing that struck me immediately about the pages I was looking through was the sheer weight of preparation that the diarist had gone to. Every page was filled on both sides with either illustrations or notes, or with excerpts from books that had been copied and pasted onto some pages. It was all very calm and methodical. Where there were illustrations, they were very well done. More like scenes of war than the macabre scribblings of a maniac. There were photographs of buildings, I assumed areas of the tiny town below us from different angles. This was more than a speculative work. This was serious.

Snale drove us over the edge of the crater and down toward its depths. I looked up at the other edge of the valley, rocky and pointed against the burnt-orange light.

And as I looked across the crater I saw the explosion.

The sound it made took seconds to reach us across the distance. A bass thump I felt in the center of my chest.

The sky lit up with a fireball directly across from us, on the steep rise.

"Oh my God!" Snale swerved, gripping the wheel.

I shoved the papers aside and sat bolt upright. "Get there. Get there *now!*"

CHAPTER 11

THE EXPLOSION ON the other side of the town seemed to have ignited the brush there in flames. I kept my eyes on the dim glow as we raced up the main street and between the fields beyond. Small houses. Fences. Snale's jaw was set. She squinted at the dark rise before us.

"Might have been kids with fireworks," she murmured. "The kids around here, they're pretty feral."

"Those are some pretty big fireworks," I said.

We took the winding road up the slope at a roaring pace. I gripped the door of the vehicle as Snale took the corners. Country driver. She'd been taking these roads at breakneck speed since girlhood.

We could smell the blast zone from the side of the road as we parked. Snale was no athlete but she bounded into the bush ahead of me, agile as a rabbit, her gun drawn. I had no flashlight, but followed the bouncing white light of hers, razor-sharp desert plants slicing at my jeans. The fire was burning itself out in the tough grass and the oily leaves of the eucalypts above us.

The smoke seared my eyes. We split up. I almost tripped over a plastic chair, or what remained of it. Three of its metal legs were buried in the dirt, and the back had melted to a black husk, sharp, sticking upwards like a dagger. Snale came back to me, huffing, winding her flashlight beam across my face, then to where I was crouched, examining the chair.

"May I?" I grabbed the light and swept it over the chair, found the crater where the bomb had gone off. There were bodily remains here, tangled in the dirt and grass. The blackened and burned slivers of flesh of something or someone blown to bits.

"Oh no," Snale was saying gently, following close behind me. "Oh no. Oh no."

I zeroed in on a shiny object—a hand wheel valve. There were splinters of metal shining in the dust. Entrails, blood everywhere. Hair. An animal? I nudged the valve with my boot, didn't have evidence bags with me.

"Propane gas bottle," I said.

"Oh man." Snale gave a frightened shudder, taking the light from me with her cold fingers. "Oh maaaaan!"

I followed her. She'd noticed something hanging from a nearby branch, swinging gently in the breeze. It was a man's hand and forearm, blackened and charred, held there by the remains of a shred of melted duct tape. The tape wrapped around the wrist seemed burned to the flesh.

I was just beginning to wonder how on earth it was still hanging on when it fell, slapping to the ground at our feet. Snale yelped in terror. She grabbed at me as a new fear rushed through her: the sound of a large vehicle leaving the roadside back near where we'd parked.

We could hear it crashing through the undergrowth toward us.

CHAPTER 12

DEER-HUNTING LIGHTS. Eight of them. They pierced the night around us, blasting through my vision, making me cower behind my arm. It was like an alien ship landing. Snale cocked her weapon, but in seconds she seemed to relax.

"Oh. It's only Kash," she said. There was a slight upward lilt to her voice, like she'd just been given good news. I was still blinded. I stumbled forward, grabbing the back of her shirt to guide me through the painfully illuminated blast zone.

"Jesus, those lights!"

"Hands up!" someone bellowed. "Identify yourselves!"

"It's me!" Snale put her hands up. I didn't bother. "It's us. Vicky, and my new friend Harriet."

I thought "friend" was going a bit far.

An enormous man emerged out of the light like an overexcited dog, a flurry of hard breath and wild gesturing. Incredibly, he had a flashlight in his hand.

"Vicky. Right. Have you seen the suspect? Where's the suspect? Any signs of where he went?"

"The what?" I tried to see his face, glimpsing a chiseled jaw, black curls. "What suspect?"

"You"—Kash pointed at me—"head down the hill and sweep southeast in a standard second-leg search pattern. Snale and I will take southwest. Give it a K, maybe a K and a half. We'll meet back here in twenty."

"A search?" I yelled. "Using what? I'm not sure I'll ever see again."

"Double time! Let's go!"

The muscled goliath took off into the bush, crashing over plants and shrubs like a tank. I jogged, confused, in the general direction he'd indicated.

There was nothing to indicate that a suspect was on the loose. But the big man in the dark had overcome my decision-making abilities with his barking voice, like a slap to the side of the head. I was annoyed and bristled, but I did what he said. There was no one south or east of the blast zone.

Snale and the big man, Kash, were there when I returned. She was searching the remains again with her flashlight beam. Kash was standing uselessly with his hands on his hips, looking generally "in charge" of whatever might have been about to happen. In the light of the enormous truck I saw an action-figure body and Clark Kent glasses on a head as square and thick as a sandstone block. When I came back into the light, he walked toward me, hand extended.

"Elliot Kash, Counter-Terrorism Task Force, Islamic Fundamentalism Division, ASIO."

"Of course." I nodded. I understood all the dramatics now. This guy was in national security. I'd come across his type before. "Of course you are."

"You've heard of me then? Good. That'll save time. Let's secure the entry to the blast zone, erect a checkpoint on the road. We'll do hourly sweeps of the search grid to see if the suspect comes back. They often return to film their work for their online campaigns."

I noticed Kash hadn't asked me for my name, or a long-winded explanation of my position within the police. I let it go.

"Who exactly are you talking about?" I asked. "We've got a dead guy and a bomb. How do you know who else was involved?"

"You've seen the diary?"

"Barely," I said.

"Well, you're behind." Kash sighed. "You can get a debriefing once we've established a secure boundary. We need to act now and ask questions later. Get going. I'll take charge here."

I suffered the same verbal slap to the head, the phenomenon of compliance sweeping over me like a spell. I found myself walking back toward the road, thinking I'd move Snale's truck, put lights on the road, see if she had some traffic cones in the back to guide any passersby onto the shoulder so we could question them. I didn't further analyze Kash's resolve that a dangerous suspect was behind this, and that it was possible he or she was somewhere around here.

The spell wore off before I hit the roadside. I stopped, frowned, tried to get my thoughts in order. Snale bumped into me from behind. She'd been jogging up the path behind me.

"Sorry." She sniffed. "I've got to get to the radio and call in the team from the next town over. We need more people. This is bad. This is really bad."

"It's OK." I jogged alongside her. This was probably the most terrible crime to ever happen in Last Chance Valley. Maybe the only serious crime they'd ever had. "Agent Dickhead's got it all under control."

"You don't understand," she said. "I just found the victim's head. I know who he is. He's my chief."

CHAPTER 13

HE CAME EVERY second night when the temperature began to sink, at what Caitlyn assumed was sunset outside her concrete room. The first few times, she tried to brace herself for what was about to happen. She visualized it for hours on end, her skin crawling and stomach turning, trying to decide how she would endure the rape or torture or prolonged death he had planned for her. But after a week, when none of those things had happened, a deep, sickening confusion set in. And then there was the rage. Caitlyn sat on the mattress in the dark and boiled with a quiet, dangerous rage.

The man with the shaved head came and unlocked the door, walked down the steps and put her supplies on the floor. Two packaged sandwiches, one chicken and one roast beef, the kind a person buys at the service station. Two bottles of water. Two chocolate bars. One roll of toilet paper for the bucket in the corner. He wouldn't look at her. The ritual was always the same. He came, he dropped the supplies, he changed the bucket and he left, locking the door securely behind him.

Caitlyn had tried everything she could think of. She'd waited by the door and swung a wine bottle she'd found in the crates at his head, missed her target by centimeters. The wine was expired and tasted foul, but after breaking a couple of bottles she'd come up with a good, shiny dagger that she came at him with the next time, again to no avail. He'd shoved her hard down the stairs, and she'd lain crying, the back of her head bleeding on the cold stone floor.

The next time, she'd been a bit trickier. Caitlyn had pulled lengths of fabric from the old mattress and woven them into a strong trip-wire, pulled this across the doorway. He'd tripped, and she'd launched herself at him, clubbed him hard in the back of the skull with a lump of wood broken from one of the crates. She'd got through the doorway and looked down the dark hall that led to wherever she was before he'd grabbed her ankle and dragged her back into her prison room. Down the hall she'd seen a long concrete walkway, stairs to the upper levels, and plenty more heavy trash that he dragged in front of the door after he locked it. Caitlyn glimpsed flyers on the ground, warped and yellowed, a box of molded brass numbers, the kind a person would screw to a door or the front of a house. An old hotel? The power must still be turned on for her television to work. Why couldn't anyone hear her cries? Was she underground?

Caitlyn didn't know if her captor was just unusually strong or if the rations and the lack of sleep had left her weak. She was no match for him. As the days passed, it became harder for her to wake. Harder to think. Harder to cry. In the daytime, she screamed for help. At night she sat and watched the television in the corner, pulling at strands of her hair.

Caitlyn recognized this for what it was. A holding pattern. Something had gone wrong with his plan, whatever it had been. Now he was simply keeping her alive. Uninterested. Out of ideas. If he didn't want sex from her, and he didn't want to torture her, and he didn't want to talk to her, why the hell was he doing this?

When the news came on, it was more often than not about the Georges River Killer's arrest. Sam Blue had featured in the media for months.

She sat chewing her nails and remembering the first night in the concrete bunker, one of the only times she'd seen her captor show overt emotion. Surprise and rage at the image of Samuel Blue on the screen. He'd said it wasn't finished yet. That this wasn't the plan.

What wasn't the plan? Caitlyn knew she hadn't been her captor's planned victim. That the girl she'd interrupted him trying to abduct had been the one who was supposed to be here now. But was it more than that? Caitlyn remembered the man standing before the television screen, running his fingers up the back of his skull, gripping at the muscles in his neck as they locked, rock hard, with anger. Sam Blue's arrest. Did that have something to do with it all?

Was this man the Georges River Killer's partner?

CHAPTER 14

EDWARD WHITTACKER STRAIGHTENED his tie in his reflection in the courthouse windows, smoothed down a cowlick at the side of his narrow head. He felt strangely lonely without Harriet, although she'd been so detached since the beginning of the Blue hearings that sometimes he'd forgotten she was there beside him, fidgeting in her "pretty sister" getup.

She'd been impossible to talk to in the weeks since their return from the desert, when Whitt decided he'd leave his home in Perth and come to Sydney to support the new partner he'd learned to admire. She was a hard creature, Harriet Blue. Unpredictable and sharp edged. When he'd met her on their case in Western Australia, her brother had just been arrested, and she'd been stripped bare of the minimal friendliness she managed to maintain in order to get on with others. But in their time in the Outback, fleeing a sniper who was hunting young men and women like dogs, the Sex Crimes detective had grown on him. She was a good person, even if that goodness was buried deep under plenty of bad behavior. He wanted to help her. And now that she'd gone and got herself banished from the courthouse altogether, he had no choice but to be her representative. It was what good friends did.

Whitt now stood watching at the edge of the crowd gathered around the New South Wales Police Commissioner on the courthouse steps, a tall, broad man wearing a uniform laden in red and silver buckles and stars. Microphones bobbed and swayed as Commissioner Sorrell moved his head. A petite journalist at the front of the crowd was trying not to be pressed against the man by the bigger journalists behind her shoving forward to catch quotes.

"We have faith that Caitlyn McBeal will be located safe and well," Sorrell said. "We know that she has not fallen victim to the Georges River Killer, because our primary suspect in that case was under surveillance the entire day she disappeared. At the approximate time of Caitlyn's last confirmed sighting four months ago, Sydney police detectives already had Samuel Jacob Blue in custody. That's all I can say right now."

Whitt knew some of the inside information about the Caitlyn McBeal abduction. The supposed incident at the University of Sydney hadn't even made the news right away. Television screens across the country had been flooded with images of Sam Blue's arrest from that morning. But way down the list of items on online news sites, a vague story was emerging. A young student from the university, Linny Simpson, was claiming someone had tried to abduct her from a car park and she'd managed to escape, passing an African American girl as she ran to safety. That African American girl fit the description of the now-missing Caitlyn McBeal.

Whitt had been exhilarated. Was this the Georges River Killer, trying to nab another victim only hours after Sam had been arrested? If it was, then surely Sam would go free! The nightmare for his friend and her brother would be over. All they had to do was find Caitlyn McBeal.

Then problems started to emerge with Linny and her tale. Linny admitted she'd fainted after reaching the bottom of the stairs of the car park, terrified by her ordeal. She'd hit her head and suffered a concussion. Details of her ordeal were inconsistent across her interviews with police. Her abductor had tried to get her into a white van. No, a green van. He'd been tall. Maybe not so tall. There had been another girl in the car park. Caitlyn and one other. Two others, maybe.

Then Linny's history was exposed. Her teenage drug use. A stalking report against an ex-boyfriend that had been entered and then withdrawn. The police were still searching for Caitlyn McBeal, and were heartened by reported sightings of her in Queensland. Maybe she'd just run off. That was the solution in most Missing Persons cases. The stress and struggle of daily life simply got too much. They dropped their belongings and fled, started again somewhere new. Whitt had seen it plenty of times during his career. He'd seen mothers lock the front door on their children and simply wander off, turning up years later with a new name, a new job, halfway across the country. Caitlyn was young and alone on the opposite side of the planet from her life back home. She had no serious commitments. Disappearing, even just for a while, would be easy.

Whatever had happened to Caitlyn, Linny Simpson's explanation for it wasn't anyone's favorite lead, because she was inconsistent. Confused.

But if she was right, even somewhere *close* to the truth, it meant two things that no one on the Georges River case wanted to admit.

That Sam Blue was innocent.

And that the killer was still out there.

CHAPTER 15

I STOOD BY the side of the road, watching the sun rising on the distant edge of the crater, a depthless black in silhouette against warm pink. The temperature was coming up fast. Soon the town below me would be swirling with gossip about the explosion in the early hours. Already, local farmers who had heard the bang and become curious had started to line the roadside, eyeing me cautiously as they met with Snale to get the lowdown.

The town's only police officer was barely keeping it together. Snale's chief, a man in his sixties named Theo "Soupy" Campbell, owned the bloodied, dirt-clodded head she had found about ten meters from the center of the blast zone. I assumed he'd owned the arm we'd seen hanging from the tree, and the various other bits and pieces of human that had been strewn about the bush. We hadn't done too much more wandering around in the crime scene. It was best to leave it for Forensics, who would soon be boarding a helicopter back in Sydney. The entire police force from the nearest town, Milparinka, were on their way to help us secure the scene and the dead police chief's truck, which we'd found parked in the bush on the opposite side of the road to the blast. Milparinka's force comprised two officers, bringing our total to five. I felt drastically out of my depth. I was used to securing crime scenes with the help of dozens of people, patrollies covering doorways with tape, chiefs standing about looking important before the cameras, forensics experts donning their gear.

I went to Snale's truck and sat in the front passenger seat with the door open, brought out the photocopy of the diary and began reading through it again. I didn't want to leap to any conclusions about the connection of the bomb to the book. Yes, what had happened to Chief Campbell looked like murder. The duct tape on the wrist was a sure sign, even if one accepted the highly improbable idea that he'd chosen to commit suicide by bomb when he likely had a perfectly good gun in his possession. I needed to find something in the diary that connected the idea and the crime.

The first pages were all about guns. I spread a page over my knee and looked at the photocopied pictures of two handsome teenage boys.

The page was a study of the Columbine killers, Eric Harris and Dylan Klebold, who'd gone on a shooting spree at their local high school in Colorado, killing twelve students and a teacher and injuring twenty-four others. I knew the story, had read a couple of true crime books about it. The diarist had made a list, beside a doodled sketch of the wolfish Harris, entitled "Successes."

1. Kept the circle of conspirators small.
2. Surveillance of victims for maximum impact.
3. Covert weapons purchases.

What was this? A list of the things the Columbine killers had done right in their evil plan? Was the diarist comparing and contrasting the massacre plans of high-profile shooters to come up with the perfect kill plot? I flipped the page. More about the Columbine killers' work, excerpts from the boys' diaries and maps of their school. There were five pages dedicated to the Columbine shooting in the diary. A sickly feeling was creeping up from the pit of my stomach. I ran my fingers over a note at the bottom of the last page on Columbine.

Thirteen victims, it read. *I can beat that!*

CHAPTER 16

ELLIOT KASH CAME to the open door of the car and leaned on the window, folding his thick arms on the sill. I reached for a cigarette. I figured I was going to need one.

"I've had a chat with Victoria about our operations, but I really want to sit down with you before this thing kicks into high gear so you can download my concerns," he said. "The priority right now needs to be security. I want maximum operational confidentiality throughout this case. We need to keep covert information tight. This is a small town, and we know there's a lone wolf or, possibly, a terrorist sleeper cell hidden within it. We cannot afford unplanned leaks right now."

I exhaled smoke into the thin morning air. "I have so many problems with what you just said, I don't even know where to start."

"Oh really?"

"Yes, really." I looked at the town in the distance. "You want to sit down with me so I can download your operational concerns? Who the fuck gave you authority over this case?"

"I did," he scoffed. "I'm Federal. Did you miss that?"

"How could I? *Maximum operational confidentiality?* Who talks like that?"

"I do."

"Yeah, you and G.I. Joe."

"Well, you know I'm the Fed in this relationship. So I'm in charge."

"You'll be in charge when we establish this is radical Islamist terrorism," I said, flipping the pages of the diary. "Which, if this diary gives us any indication, is going to be *never*. There's nothing even mildly Islamic-looking in here. All I can see thus far is praise for dickhead white-boy school shooters."

"That diary is pure terrorism, and I'm the terrorism expert, so I have jurisdiction," he said.

"Nope."

"Yes!"

"Nope," I repeated. "You can have jurisdiction when the Attorney General flies his big golden helicopter into the middle of nowhere, waddles his fat arse up the hill to where I'm sitting and tells me you have jurisdiction." I put my feet up on the dashboard. "Until then, it's a three-way partnership. You, me and Vicky."

Kash laughed, leaned in. "Officer Snale's experience is in chasing down lost cattle dogs and wrangling drunks out of the local pub. She'll be useful for local intel only."

I ignored him. "My next concern is with your presumption that I'd leak operational information even if this *was* a federal case. Are you serious?"

"Of course I'm serious," he said. He reached into his back pocket and pulled out a folded sheet of newspaper. I couldn't stop a grimace rising to my face at the image of me on the front page of the *Telegraph*, my legs splayed over the body of Prosecutor Woolfmyer. I looked like a pint-sized Wonder Woman action figure, my breasts straining against the ridiculous blouse. I tried to contain my fury.

"Is this not you?" Kash gave a crooked, patronizing grin.

"Oh, fuck off."

"No one told me I was going to have to babysit an insubordinate, dangerous state cop while I was posted here," he said. "This was supposed to be a very exclusive task force. Me, advising the local authority." He jabbed a thumb in Snale's direction. "That's how it works with this type of case. You get an expert in, and he infiltrates, taking the suspects down when they show themselves. If I have to have you along, I don't want any of this kind of behavior."

He thrust the newspaper page at me. I let it slide to the floor of the car.

"Maybe you're feeling hostile because of your brother's situation," Kash said. "Maybe you're always like this, and that's some indication of why Samuel did what he did. I don't know. But I don't want you going off half-cocked and hurting someone on my watch. I'm going to need you to keep it contained while you're out here, Officer."

"I'm going to need *you* to call a dentist." I put my legs down, leaned into his face. "Because the next time you talk to me like that, I'm gonna kick you in the mouth."

We watched each other. Only Snale drew our eyes away, approaching the car, her notebook still in hand.

"We've got our first lead," she announced. "A suspect. It's not good news."

CHAPTER 17

A GROUP OF men in slouch hats had assembled by the edge of the road, talking animatedly, now and then pointing toward the town. Angry, and unable to look at each other. This didn't bode well. Snale had managed to rein in her grief but she had the sunken look of someone who had much crying to do yet. She stood beside the passenger-side door with Kash, looking in on me.

"Chief Campbell retired about six months ago," Snale explained to me. "I'm the only cop on active duty in the town. It was a long hand-over, and sometimes Soupy would help me out if I needed it. He got special approval to keep his handgun and cuffs for that very reason. Everything's been fine. You know, the usual sort of stuff. Drunk driving is my main problem around here. But I have been having some troubles with this kid named Zac Taby and his little crew of misfits."

"How old's Taby?" I asked.

"Fifteen," Snale said. "One of our senior students."

"You guys have got your own school down there?" I looked at the tiny town below us. It hardly seemed to have enough buildings.

"Of the town's seventy-five residents, twelve are kids," Snale said. "There's a little schoolhouse behind the post office. Two teachers."

"And those guys reckon this Taby kid's written the diary?" I said. "Makes sense. The book's full of praise for idiot teens. So they think they're looking for an idiot teen. Who are they, anyway?"

"They're just local farmers." Snale glanced back at them. "They say they've seen Taby around the junkyard over in Tibooburra playing with engine parts. He's basically everybody's first suspect when anything happens around here. I have questioned Zac but I wasn't convinced he had anything to do with the diary."

"What made you so sure?"

Snale shrugged. "He's been in and out of the station a lot, and I've always had him write statements of what's occurred. Zac hates writing. Why would he spend hours upon hours constructing a handwritten diary?"

"If a kid's interested in something, they'll put in the effort," I said.

"What's Taby's religious background?" Kash asked.

"Oh, I'm not sure. If you want to go to church around here you've got to drive all the way to Fowlers Gap. That's Catholic. There are no mosques out here."

"So he might be Muslim?" Kash had perked up, like a dog catching a scent.

"I don't know." Snale shrugged again. "He's Pakistani. His is the only nonwhite family in the valley. People have always given the Taby family a hard time. Problem isn't just whether the Taby kid is responsible for this. It's that people *think* he is."

"What do you mean?"

"Once things get reported as fact in small towns, they remain fact. And people decide facts for themselves out here. There was a rape over

51

in the next town last year. Everybody decided it was the local plumber who did it. He had an alibi and everything, and the DNA didn't match. But once people had decided, that was it. They ran him out of town." Snale already looked stressed. She walked back toward the men on the side of the road.

Kash beckoned for the diary on the seat beside me.

"Probably better give me that," he said. "It'll be safer in my custody. I'll do an analysis of the content and draw up a report."

I didn't move to hand him the diary. He raised an eyebrow, his hand out, waiting.

"I'm not playing this game," I said.

"What game?"

"This one." I pointed to his chest, mine. "This territorial crap. This stupid dance, where you tell me to step off, wave your dick around, puff your chest out. That shit doesn't work on me."

"It doesn't?"

"Nope," I said. "And I'll tell you why. I'm looking at you and I'm guessing you're about . . . what? Thirty years old?"

"I'm thirty-three."

"Right." I nodded. "I'm thirty-six. My brother and I were removed from my mother's care when I was two years old. She was a prostitute. A drug addict. I spent sixteen years in foster care," I said, watching his face. "I don't know how many homes we were shuffled through. Sometimes Sam and I were together. Sometimes we were apart. We never stayed anywhere for more than a year. But in each and every family, the kids would tell me the same thing as soon as I arrived. *This is my house. Those are my parents. You don't touch my toys. You don't hug my mum. You don't belong here.*"

Kash's defiant frown had softened a little, if only with confusion at my candor. I leaned forward so that he could see that I meant every word I was saying.

"People have been telling me to fuck off out of their territory since before you were born," I said. "And for all those years, my answer's been exactly the same."

He waited.

"This is my house now," I said.

CHAPTER 18

WHITT SQUEEZED ALONG the packed aisle and settled near the middle of the row of spectator seats to the left of the courtroom. Above him, the press gallery were all looking at their phones, updating their editors before the morning's session began.

As Harriet's brother was escorted into the huge space in his crumpled suit, a hush fell over the crowd. Whitt tried to catch the man's eye, but Sam's stare was on the back of the courtroom.

Today, expert witnesses would testify about Sam's mental capabilities. The frail, big-nosed Doctor Hemsill had taken the stand, and avoided eye contact with Blue as he read from his report.

"We can infer that much of Samuel Blue's troubling history is directly attributable to developmental issues caused by his mother's use of illicit substances during her pregnancy," Hemsill said. "His tests show low patterns of stimuli reaction in the prefrontal cortex and amygdala, which we know are areas of the brain affected by substance abuse in utero. The prefrontal cortex controls a lot of our civilizing, inhibiting behavior. It's what stops you lashing out or acting violently, for example, when you're experiencing rage."

Whitt thought about Harry as he made notes. The times he'd seen her kick down doors, throw things, charge forward with her fists balled when the stress of her situation became too much. He tried to shake her out of his head.

"Impulsivity is something we see often with these kinds of brain activity patterns." Doctor Hemsill sighed. "Reactions to emotion, rather than logic. Blue's social abilities are also greatly hindered by his neurological patterns. He has trouble with empathy. He can be abrasive. Hard to relate to. He naturally finds it difficult making friends at all, but when he does make them, his loyalty endures beyond reason."

Whitt had accidentally written "Harry" instead of "Sam" in his notes. He crossed out the name, but circled the word "empathy," tapping his pen thoughtfully on the page. Harry shared her brother's wild, unpredictable personality. She was abrasive and hard to relate to. But she did not lack empathy. Whitt had spent a couple of weeks in the desert with her, watching her toss and turn in her sleep, watching her struggle under the almost physical weight of her worry for whomever the Bandya Mine Killer would target next. She'd been brokenhearted after a spider in their cabin had been found unceremoniously squished. She felt things for others. In fact, sometimes Whitt thought she felt them too keenly. She would take the crusades of others on as her own responsibility, fight for people who didn't want or didn't deserve it.

Whitt had lost himself in dreaming. He rubbed his eyes, looked around. At the end of his row, a man with a closely shaved head was sitting with his hands on his knees. Whitt didn't know what it was that drew his focus to this man. Perhaps it was his attentive presence in the distinctly sparse seating area reserved for supporters of the accused. Whitt and the man were alone on the bench, and the bench behind them was empty. But no, it was something more. Whitt realized that almost every set of eyes in the courtroom was focused on the large screen behind the witness stand, where Doctor Hemsill was pointing at parts of the human brain lit up with different colors.

But the shaven-headed man's eyes were on Samuel Blue. The man was not just staring; his gaze was *locked* on Blue, like a cat with its attention fixed on a bird. The hairs on Whitt's arms were beginning to stand on end. Something told him to commit this man's face to memory. He looked at the notebook before him. Perhaps he could make a sketch. He took up his pen. But when he turned back to examine the man again, he was gone.

CHAPTER 19

I SAT AT Snale's kitchen table with my head in my hands, listening to the officer rattling around the kitchen, scraping food together for her two city guests. It had been a long day, and when Snale showed us to our accommodation, my space a single fold-out bed at the end of her large enclosed porch, I felt the desire to fall into the sheets and bury my face in the pillow. It was a struggle to keep my mind on the diary that lay open in front of me. Snale came to the table with her notebook in her mouth and two wineglasses in her hands.

"Don't drink it all at once." She put a glass down before me. "Wine's expensive out here. They only do a supply run every two weeks."

Without warning there came a grunting, scraping sound. I almost spat out my first sip of wine when an enormous gray creature emerged into the narrow hall from the front room. The pig was at least a meter and a half long, covered in a fine black fur and a smattering of speckles. It trotted lazily into the room, looking me over with little interest.

I felt the first smile of the day crack my face. "What the fuck?"

"Look." Snale sighed. "There are thirty-three adult men in this town. Thirty of them are married. One's seventy years old. And the other two aren't interested. It gets lonely out here."

I laughed. "You could have got a dog."

We watched the enormous pig sprawl out on a blanket by the door, giving a long, guttural groan as it flopped onto its side.

"Jerry is a real presence in the house," Snale said. "His footsteps are heavy, and he snores really loud all night long. It feels like there's someone here."

Kash finished a phone call and joined us.

Forensics had arrived that afternoon and completed a onceover of the diary for DNA and prints, so we could touch it now. We'd also handed off the plain red backpack the book had been found in. The backpack looked new, and nothing else was in it. That was odd. Why not just carry the notebook by itself? Was the red backpack meant to attract attention from the roadside? Did the diarist want the book to be found?

I perused the pages quietly while Kash and Snale chatted. The writer had indeed done some extensive investigation of bomb-building options, focusing on explosives that could be made from everyday household objects. The idea seemed to emerge out of Dylan Klebold and Eric Harris's failed attempts to blow up their school cafeteria with gas-bottle bombs before they went on their rampage.

"Let's get the handwriting analyzed against all the handwriting samples we can collect from the town," Snale suggested.

I made notes, a list of to-dos.

"So this is the preliminary breakdown of the Campbell scene from Forensics today?" I asked, pulling Snale's notebook toward me.

"Yes, classic propane bomb," she said. "Seems to the team that Theo would have been sitting with the gas bottle either between his legs or wedged under the chair when it went off. He was sitting facing the town." She sighed long and deep. "His wife, Olivia, is in tatters. Just beside herself."

"Does she have any ideas about suspects?"

"She wasn't very coherent," Snale said. "Says Theo was over in the next town fixing a mate's roof—someone called David Lewis—and then was going to stay for dinner. When he didn't answer his phone she figured he must have stayed the night. I'll go back to her for suspects in a day, maybe. Give her time to get over the shock."

"Let's go talk to David Lewis. See if Theo was acting weird."

"Right."

"Any sign of someone else at the crime scene?" Kash asked.

"Maybe," Snale said. "There were footprints. Smeary, hard to tell the tread, but looks like an ordinary old workboot. Size seven men's, nine women's. Looks like a person pacing back and forth not far from the blast site. But they can't really date the prints. Could have been a day or two before. Theo's service weapon is missing, so someone must have got hold of it, used it to coerce him into the chair."

"Where did the chair come from?" Kash asked. "Surely the killer didn't bring it with him."

"There's a bunch of junk up there on both crests, on the roadsides in and out of town," Snale said. "Kids go up there and smoke and throw things off the cliffs. Every Saturday night I go and do a sweep through the bush there and down in the gully, make sure they're not doing anything too naughty. The chair was probably from one of their little campsites. The duct tape, I don't know."

"Yes, the duct tape. Where were Theo's handcuffs?" I asked.

"I'd be surprised if he had them with him. Neither of us has ever really bothered with them," Snale said. "I haven't cuffed anyone in the ten years I've been out here. Things never really get that out of control. And I know every single person who lives here. There's nowhere to run, so why try to get away?"

I turned to Kash, who was staring at the wineglass in my hand. "Propane bombs. Are they hard to make?"

"Not at all. They're the terrorist-in-training's favorite improvised explosive device," he said. "Simple design, easily obtainable ingredients. Any idiot can make one. You get a gas bottle from a backyard barbecue, duct tape a can of petrol to the side of it. Take the cap off, put a wick in, light it up and run away. Boom." He threw his hands up.

"So we could literally make one right now?" I scoffed. "With Snale's barbecue gas bottle?"

"You could make a bunch of different bombs with stuff lying around here." Kash took out his mobile phone, showed it to me. "I could crack this open, find the wire that connects to the ringer, expose it so that it'll spark. Dump it in a bottle of something. Make a call to it. There you go. Mobile phone–activated bomb."

"But where does a person get the knowledge to put these things together?"

"The internet," Kash said.

"Surely people send up red flags with your agency when they search for stuff like that," I said.

"If every teenage boy in the country who ever searched for how to blow something up earned a file with ASIO, the department would cease to be operational." Kash was eyeing Snale now as she drank her wine. "We don't identify terrorists by their Google searches. That's amateur hour."

"Let's get all the IP addresses in town anyway." I made a note. "Check everyone's internet activity."

"Why Soupy?" Snale's lip quivered. She sipped her wine to cover it. "Why pick him? He was an absolute doll. Someone's pacing back and forth. They've got him taped to a chair with a bomb between his legs. Facing the town. It's a good view from up there. You can see everybody. All the houses."

"Everybody can see you, too," I said.

"It's very . . . showy," Snale said. "A demonstration. Either for Theo or for us, down here. A spectacle. Only the timing wasn't great. No one awake to see it. Was it a practice shot? Or was *Theo* the audience— was he supposed to see the town spread out before him just before he died?"

I liked Snale's musings. I wanted her to continue, but Kash spoke up.

"Look, I don't mean to interrupt. But are we going to be making drinking a part of our ongoing investigative practice? Or is this a one-off drinking session?"

Snale and I looked at each other.

"Don't get me wrong. You've both had interesting lines of inquiry so far. But we're shooting the breeze about this case over a bottle of red in a dining room like a bunch of old ladies."

"Would you like to move to the garage?" I snorted. "Should we ap-point a chairman? Let me guess. It should be you."

"There is a violent terrorist in this town." Kash took the diary from in front of me and waved it in my face. "Is the seriousness of the situa-tion escaping you?"

"We are taking it seriously," Snale huffed. "We're just cooling off, that's all. It's been a long day. I had to go tell a woman her husband was blown to pieces all over a hillside today."

"Well, I'm sorry." He shrugged. "I guess I'm just not on the same page as you two. When I was on assignment gathering intel in Afghanistan, I was seeing guys being blown to pieces all over hillsides every day. And it only toughened my resolve. I think we shouldn't drink on the job."

He got up and traipsed away into the living room. I let my eyes wander to the shell-shocked Sergeant Snale.

"That was hilarious." I took a sip. "I think my wine actually tastes better now."

"Let's look through this diary." She pulled the book toward her. "We're going to catch this killer, with or without him."

CHAPTER 20

MY SLEEP WAS thin. The diary had disturbed me deeply. There was a detailed profile of Seung-Hui Cho, the Virginia Tech shooter, who'd killed thirty-two people on campus in Blacksburg. Once again, there was a list of the elements of the massacre plan the diarist seemed to find useful for this study.

1. *Chained doors, trapping victims.*
2. *Made detailed manifesto video, so reasons would be known.*
3. *Low personal profile, maintained non-threatening reputation before attack.*

Cho had acted out of a seething rage, making a rambling video manifesto while kitted up for the massacre. His cap turned backwards, the sullen, dark-eyed young man talked about a fiery demise for his enemies. I lay in the dark, his words bouncing around my brain, visions of his victims running for their lives flashing against the backs of my eyelids.

I was starting to get a mental picture of the diarist. If he—it was unlikely to be a she—had decided these were the attributes of a successful killer, then surely he'd be putting these behaviors into place in the lead-up to his own plan, whatever it was. He'd be maintaining a low profile, keeping quiet and resisting the temptation to bring collaborators in on their mission. He'd be trying to obtain weapons without raising any eyebrows. It wouldn't be hard out here. Every farmer in the town would have a gun. It would only be a matter of amassing them on or just before the day, once the killer had worked out where they could all be found.

I tried to tell myself to sleep. Without sleep, I'd never catch this guy. I was drifting in and out when the sound of grunting broke through my consciousness. I thought at first it was the pig. I climbed off the end of the bed and went to the porch screen door. Kash was out there in the barren dirt yard, a barely visible black streak against the rise of the distant ridge. I pushed open the door, still mussed from sleep. He was shirtless. A rippling, sweat-glistening torso lit up as I switched on the backyard light.

"What the hell are you doing?"

He was jogging back from the end of the property. He ignored me, dropped and did ten seamless, perfect push-ups. The muscles in his triceps looked surgically carved.

"Are you nuts?" I continued. "It's ... What time is it?"

"It's two am."

"Why are you working out at two in the morning?"

"If you want to bring down the enemy, you've got to think like the enemy," he said. He'd huffed rhythmically through ten jumping jacks, dropped for more push-ups. "Think, act, live like them. This is a classic training regime used by the Taliban for their frontline fighters. They conduct sessions at early morning hours to train the brain out of its circadian rhythm. They can eat, sleep and access high levels of physical energy whenever they need to."

I watched, bemused, as he took off again toward the back of the property. He sprinted back and dropped to complete a set of sit-ups.

"You're a bit of an addict of this stuff, aren't you?"

"What stuff?"

"The terrorism gig."

"Don't knock it just because you're incapable of it."

"Incapable of it?" I squinted. "Of what, exactly?"

"Of the lifestyle. Of the kind of commitment it takes to work in national-level human security. I mean, there's a reason you're a cop. You want to protect people. But if you were capable, surely you'd do it at *this* level." He gestured to himself with one arm as he did push-ups with the other. "Not *that* level." He pointed at me.

"You know, I've met some colossal douchebags in my life, Kash. But you're slowly climbing the ladder to number one."

"Number one," he mused. "Sounds like me."

"You're not even doing those properly," I said. "Your chest is, like, ten centimeters off the ground."

"Is that a challenge?" he asked.

"I'm just saying, if you're going to run around training like a lunatic in the middle of the night, there's no point in doing a half-arsed job."

"A half-arsed job?" He stopped working out for the first time since my arrival. "Are you serious?"

"I don't joke about push-ups."

"You wouldn't last to the end of this workout," he said. "I guarantee it."

"Right," I snapped. I went back inside, slamming the door, dragging my bag from where it lay at the end of the bed to search for my shoes. Agent Kash had no idea what I could withstand. In a life like mine, full of darkness and pain, a tough workout was child's play.

CHAPTER 21

THE WORKOUT WAS invigorating, my quiet exhilaration heightened when he announced ruefully that I'd completed it. My body screamed through dozens and dozens of burpees, joint-grinding squats and panicked sprints to the end of the yard and back. When I knew he was looking, I scratched my nose with one hand during the push-up sets, the other arm continuing on through the exercise with what I hoped looked like effortlessness. I finished drenched in sweat. There were no congratulations from my new partner. He trudged off toward the house in silence.

I sat in bed making a list, light beginning to creep under the curtains drawn closed around the glassed-in porch. The porch was creaky, and when Jerry the pig came out to join me at sunrise the whole thing rattled like an old wooden wagon. The huge animal stood snuffling at me for a while, its big brown eyes searching mine, then flopped to the floor by my bed with an exhausted sigh.

Snale was right. The snoring was oddly comforting. I lay on my side and watched the animal's ear flapping now and then as it dreamed. Its body warmth made my corner of the porch cozy. I fell asleep to thoughts of Sam's case.

I had so much that I wanted to do to help my brother, but all of it was out of my hands. There was so much evidence against Sam. Not least his confession.

I walked up behind her. I was quiet. I swept my arm around her neck, pulled her backwards toward my car . . .

Sam confessed to all three murders. But less than an hour after leaving the interrogation room, he said the confession was coerced. I didn't want to believe that my own colleagues might have psychologically tortured my brother, exhausted him and threatened him until he simply surrendered. Maybe they'd beaten him. I'd been known to get a little rough with suspects myself, inside and outside the interrogation room.

But I also didn't want to believe that Sam was guilty. So I tried not to believe anything.

Marissa Haydon was last seen on the university grounds, in a small car park behind the campus bar on a quiet Tuesday afternoon. My brother's credit card records showed he had been in the bar that same afternoon.

Elle Ramone was last seen on a street three blocks away from the university, in the residential area behind the main street of Newtown. Sam usually walked home that way at around the same time she had gone missing, from his graphic design business in Marrickville, where he worked the three days a week that he wasn't teaching.

Rosetta Poelar was last seen on a side street off of Parramatta Road, near the university's veterinary science building. CCTV inside a bicycle shop captured Sam walking through the area just fifteen minutes before Rosetta was last seen.

Sam had been at the right place, at the right time, for all three abductions. Police had been watching him, and they didn't like what they saw. He was single. He was antisocial. He had a history of juvenile crime. If he was as violent as his sister when he lost control, he might be deadly. The task force had jumped in and made an arrest even if the evidence was flimsy. The media had been hounding them for progress. Even a false arrest at that point would have been *something*.

That night, things took a turn. The police had found worrying evidence inside Sam's apartment—some violent porn, a rape dungeon–style setup in his back bedroom. Those things were circumstantial. There was no evidence of any of the girls at Sam's place, and no evidence of Sam on any of their bodies. But the prosecution could physically place him near all three abduction sites. What were the odds?

I woke from a sweaty half-slumber and slid my notebook out from under my pillow. I flipped through the crime scene photographs of the girls' bodies sprawled on the banks of the Georges River. I looked at the trees on the opposite bank, a blur of pale eucalypts in the photograph. Fine gray sand and murky brown water. This place meant something to the killer. What had it meant to us?

My childhood had been full of rivers, fields, national parks. Often, Sam and I found ourselves in large families with multiple foster children lumped together with biological children. When child services found a willing foster carer, someone who was reliable, they sent them as many kids as they could possibly handle. Sam and I, two moody, aggressive white kids, would become part of an odd collection of youngsters all under the care of one foster couple. With so many kids in tow, traditional means of entertainment were off the cards. Going to the movies was too expensive. The families would take us to parks, rivers and long, empty beaches. Sam and I had spent time at the Georges River, but that time hadn't been any more meaningful than time spent anywhere else. At least, it hadn't to me.

Maybe there were things about Sam I didn't know. We'd been separated now and then, sometimes for up to a year, when families wouldn't take us both. Maybe there was another Sam, a brother grown out of those blank spaces in his life, the ones I hadn't witnessed.

An evil Sam.

CHAPTER 22

THERE WAS LITTLE to say to Kash and Snale when I arrived in the kitchen in the morning. Kash was reading the *Herald* on his iPad, a two-page spread about my brother.

"We've got to go," I said, drawing on my cap.

As we started walking into town, Kash lagged behind us, talking on his phone. I eavesdropped on his conversation, trying to distract myself.

"You can't take that. I bought it. You—But, Tenacity, baby, let me talk for a second, will you?"

Tenacity. I'd heard that name before. When I first learned Tenacity Bridge's name, I thought she'd probably had a mother who'd thought she was cool landing her daughter with a moniker people would cringe at for the rest of her life, like mine. My secret shame, "Jupiter," was at least my middle name and not my first, and I'd been able to hide it for most of my life.

The Tenacity I knew had been a victim I met in my work in Sex

Crimes. A young man named Alex Finton had climbed in through her bathroom window one night and sexually assaulted her in her bed. I wondered silently if the woman Kash was talking to on the phone was the same one. How many could there be?

I was drawn out of my daydream by the crowd gathered out front of the town pub, squinting in the sunlight. They turned angry faces on Kash and me. A sneer twisted the lips of the nearest person. It was only then that I noticed almost all of them were carrying rifles.

"There they are," said one man, advancing toward us.

CHAPTER 23

"WE WANT TO know what the hell's going on." The man jutted his chin at me, turned and sized up the much larger Agent Kash. "We're hearing the whole bloody town's about to be attacked, and we're seeing Sydney's sent exactly *two* coppers to protect us. This is bullshit!"

"Whoa, hold up." Kash put a hand out. "I'm not a cop. I'm a trained federal agent specializing in counterterrorism."

"Terrorism?" The group glanced nervously at each other, shifted their rifles. "Is it a terrorist?"

"No." I stepped between them. "There is nothing to suggest right now that—"

"Them Muslims," someone seethed. "I knew it'd only be a matter of ti—"

I didn't have the patience for this. I was about ready to snap when a man broke into the group, short and potbellied with thinning ginger hair.

"Let's keep this under control, huh, Jace?" He put a hand on the rifleman's shoulder. "I'm sure these officers know what they're doing." The man turned to me, offered a hand. "I'm John Destro. Everybody calls me Dez."

"Dez is the mayor," Snale told me.

The man laughed, showing teeth so straight and white they could have been dentures.

"Well, technically Last Chance is too small to appoint a mayor. I call myself that but I don't get the salary." He smiled warmly. "I run the post office. So I'm the most powerful guy in town."

He gestured to a two-story building diagonally across the road from where we stood. It occurred to me exactly how powerful a postmaster could be in a situation like this. He literally had a monopoly on the essentials of life out here—food, alcohol, tools, farming supplies. It paid to be nice to the people who controlled your supplies, particularly when it was a two-day drive to anywhere with a population above five hundred.

"I'm here to help in any way that I can."

"Of course," I said. "Thanks. You can start by telling everyone to put their guns away. There is no evidence of an imminent threat to the people of this town. And this many people running around with rifles and frayed nerves is going to get someone killed."

I walked inside the pub, where the tables surrounding a large stage were packed with people, some of them already halfway through breakfast beers beside plates of toast. There were people on the upper floor, arms hanging over the railing, watching. This is what people do in country towns when there's trouble: go to the local pub, gossip, get a hold on the situation, regardless of the work to be done that day. The place was the beating heart of the town. There was a sweaty bartender standing behind the long, polished counter, holding a pint of beer to his lips. The glass featured a brass nameplate with "Mick the Prick" engraved on it. I guessed drinking on the job was acceptable here, at least.

I walked to the stage and thirty sets of eyes followed me. Literally half the population of the valley was here.

"My name is Detective Inspector Harriet Blue," I said loudly. "I'm from the Sydney Metro police department. I've got a few things to say."

I drew a long breath. How many of these people would recognize me from the front page of yesterday's paper? Snale was watching me from the doorway, with "Jace" and the hostile group of farmers.

"Last night, your former police chief Theo Campbell passed away," I said. There was no rumble of voices, no gasps of surprise. "We're still investigating the circumstances, and whether they are linked to the diary Sergeant Snale questioned you all about some days ago. At this stage there is no reason to believe that anyone else in town is under any further threat. I advise you to go about your business. Those people we want to question about the case will be contacted shortly. If you think you've got relevant information to share with us about Mr. Campbell's death, or the diary, then please do so."

I tried to leave the stage and almost ran right into the solid wall of human muscle that was Kash. My stomach sank.

"Ah, actually"—he shifted past me to the center of the stage—"it might be helpful, Detective Blue, for us to provide a deeper understanding of what information might be relevant."

"What the fuck are you doing?" I whispered. He ignored me.

"My name is Special Agent Elliot Kash. I'm a highly trained counter-terrorism expert, specializing in Islamic terrorism and insurgency. I've spent years in Iraq and Afghanistan gathering surveillance and intel on lone-wolf and sleeper-cell development."

The crowd stirred. The bartender slammed a pint glass down.

"Because of my specialist experience," Kash said, "I can tell you the kind of thing we're looking for. You need to keep an eye out for someone you know who's been acting strange lately. Maybe spending more time than usual on their own or on their computer. Ask yourself if someone in your household has gained a sudden interest in organized religion, particularly Islam, or if they've been making aggressive political statements. Have they withdrawn from their circle of friends? Are they making or receiving private phone calls in the middle of the night? Hypervigilance is the key here, people. Be aware, and if you see something, say something."

"Terrorists," someone at the back murmured. "I bloody knew it."

"That Taby kid's always on that laptop," someone else said. "You see him around town with it. That's how they radicalize them. The internet. The videos. The chat rooms."

I all but yanked Kash off the stage as he tried to wrap up. He seemed confused by my fury. I pushed him out the pub door and into the shade of the awning.

CHAPTER 24

"YOU ARE GOING to panic the people of this town." I shoved his chest. "There is no evidence of organized terrorism in this case so far. *None!*"

"Maybe not to your eyes," Kash said. "You don't have the training, or the experience. This is how lone wolves operate. They hide out in small regional towns where their activities don't raise suspicion, and they experiment, honing their skills, until they can move on to bigger targets."

I tried to breathe evenly. Snale exited the pub, shoulders hunched, embarrassed by the public display of antagonism. I had to salvage this situation, if not for the case, for the town's perception of city law enforcement. Threatening Kash, shouting at him, wasn't working. His skull was too thick, trapping messages outside his tiny brain. I needed to be calm. Reason with him.

"You know," I said, "my training is in Sex Crimes. I live it. I breathe it. I spend my every waking moment dealing with it. So when a victim or a witness comes to me and tells me their story, my natural instinct is to believe what I've been trained to believe—that a crime has occurred."

"I don't see where this is going," Kash broke in. I took a moment to visualize myself punching him in the face, then closed my eyes and carried on.

"But sometimes," I said slowly, "very rarely, a crime hasn't occurred. Someone is lying, or they're mistaken. I have to make sure that I approach every situation with an *open mind,* and look at the *evidence,* before I form any conclusions."

"So?" Kash shrugged.

"So you've assumed there's a terrorist in this town without any evidence to support that. And worse, you've just warned these people to look out for someone acting strangely, who's withdrawn, moody, and who gets phone calls late at night. You know who that sounds like? It sounds like every fucking teenager I've ever met."

"Radicalists often target teens," Kash said. "They're usually already despondent, disenfranchised. Vulnerable to the ideas of terrorist organizations."

I turned to Snale, who was watching Kash with the kind of confused awe reserved for audiences of the truly mad.

"Find me Zac Taby," I said. "We need to get to him before someone else does."

CHAPTER 25

I STOOD FUMING while Snale went back to the house to get the four-wheel drive. I couldn't so much as look at Kash, who was now talking to Mayor Dez, probably giving him a rundown of covert surveillance tactics in the rural environment. I was steadily becoming exhausted. It seemed the further I got from the city, my home, the harder it was to breathe. Already the midday sun was baking the air, making it feel like steam in my lungs. *Seven days*, I thought. *It's only seven days.*

I noticed the farmer Jace standing nearby when he spat on the ground. He was watching me from the shadows beneath his hat. All of him was browned by the relentless sun, black freckles and moles standing up on his arms like cracked pepper. He had a foot propped on the stone front step of the farming supply store next to the pub.

"Was there much of Soupy Campbell left?" he asked.

I considered the question. It was odd. Not only deeply inappropriate, but slightly voyeuristic, too.

"It was a terrible scene," I said. "I can't imagine why you'd want to know."

"Well," Jace said, shrugging, "out here we have pretty simple beliefs about justice. The blackfellas, they have their ways. They'll have the elders sing to the spirits about you. Bring down some bad luck. Sometimes they'll have a ceremony. Spear you in the legs. Depends on what you done."

He looked me up and down, as though assessing my life's worst deeds.

"Then there's the white man's bush justice," he said. "An eye for an eye. Sounds like Soupy's woman won't have much left to bury. Whoever did this, it should be the same for their family."

"Look." I let my head loll. "That's very impressive and scary, and believe me, I understand your way of looking at things. I've encountered a number of predatory scumbags in my particular line of work who I'd have loved to torture slowly with a barbecue fork. But that's not the way the world works."

I was mildly uncomfortable at my own words. I had, in my time, tracked down and beaten a couple of sex offenders who had escaped justice. I had relished in hearing that violent child-sex predators got the old "Long Bay Welcome Tea"—a bucket of scalding water thrown over them on their first night in prison. That was the violent part of me. The beast inside. But this man didn't need encouragement to go out and punish Theo Campbell's killer with his little band of sunburned cronies. The men I'd punished had endured full, fair trials. I'd known they were guilty. The farmer before me was itching for a suspect to hurt. And there was no way he was going to wait to make sure he had the right guy.

"Any suspects yet?" he asked, as if on cue.

"No. But if we find some, and anything happens to those suspects before we can get them locked up, I'll be looking at you." I pointed at Jace's eyes. "So take your white man's bush justice and fuck off."

He laughed at my bravado, gave me another long visual assessment, his eyes wandering right down to my boots, back up to my face. I stood sweating in the sunlight as he wandered away.

CHAPTER 26

ZAC TABY WASN'T hard to find. Snale picked us up in her four-wheel drive and drove us, not to the school but away from the town. Along a dirt track that rattled the car windows almost out of their frames, we came to a shaded gully at the foot of a tall cliff face covered in spray-painted tags. I got out of the truck and stared at the peppering of cigarette butts at my feet. Somewhere in the shady brush someone was playing music, a whiny peal from phone speakers.

A large black-and-gray dog rushed to the car to intercept us, barking in a decidedly unfriendly manner. Its stride jangled with the string of Coke cans tied to its tail. Snale sighed, exasperated.

"Digger," she snapped. "Come here. Come *here*, girl."

The dog gave up its vicious charade and allowed itself to be freed.

"Whose dog is that?"

"It's the town dog." Snale ushered the dog up onto the back seat of the four-wheel drive. "No one really owns her. Everybody feeds her. Which is probably why she's so fat."

A stringy, dark-skinned teenager emerged from the brush. I noticed others scuttling off through the trees, a couple of girls and a tall, lanky young man in a huge black trench coat that was ridiculous in the heat. Zac must have known we'd come looking for him after hearing about Theo Campbell's death. There was laughter on the wind as the teens took the back route into the bush, a couple of defiant cries of "Fuck the Po-lice!"

Zac had a practiced surliness well beyond his fifteen years. I might have wondered what it took to become this angry at life so young, but I had been exactly the same kind of kid. I never slept. I smoked like a chimney. I swore at strangers and hung out in the wrong places. One of my foster dads had nicknamed me "bitch face" because he said I always looked like I wanted to scream at someone. This kid thought nobody cared about him, and he was probably right.

"You got some friends, Vicky?" the teen asked, eyeing Kash and me. "That's a first."

"We need you to come with us, Zac," I said. "We've got to get your parents so we can chat about an incident yesterday morning."

"I'm not going anywhere."

"Oh yes you are."

"Suck my dick, bitch," he snapped at me. "I don't know anything about what happened yesterday. So you can go and annoy someone else, because I ain't no terrorist, and I don't keep a diary. Diaries are for little girls."

"We just want to talk," Snale said. "Maybe you can tell us something that will help. You and Soupy were... well acquainted. You might know someone else who had a major grudge against him."

"Whoever it was deserves a fucking medal." Zac drew a cigarette packet out of his jeans. "Dude was an A-grade fucktard. I heard the bomb blew his head right off. Is that true?"

"We don't have time for the tough-guy games." I strode forward. "Get in the car."

"Should I resist?" He jutted his chin at me, grabbed a handful of his junk. "Would that be exciting for you?"

"That's it," I heard Kash mutter as he came up behind me. He pushed me aside and grabbed Zac, slamming the kid into the dirt.

"Stop! Stop!"

Zac was squealing with terror, all his bravado gone. Kash had a knee in the kid's back and both hands in his pockets, scooping and dumping detritus on the ground around us: cigarettes, joints, condoms, a pocketknife, scraps of paper. Kash got the boy's phone and let Snale and me drag him off the wailing teen.

Zac rolled in the dirt. "Fuck you! Fuck you, po-lice piece of shit!"

"Let's have a look," Kash was saying, swiping through Zac's phone. "Recent photos."

"Stop, Kash." I grabbed at him, just missed the phone. "This is an illegal search. Anything you find on there is going to be tainted."

"Says who?" He held me back with a massive arm, worked the screen with the thumb of his other hand. "I see...naked teen girls. I see kids sucking on bongs. What's this?" Kash showed me the phone screen. I glimpsed a mess of wires and tools and glass jars on a sprawling, cluttered table. "Bomb-making in progress?"

"Give me the phone," I told Kash. "Or I'll take it from you."

He was trying to zoom in on the photographs, backing away from me. I gave Kash a few seconds to comply, then strode forward, lunged and grabbed the hand that held the phone. He was fast, catching my other wrist as I went for an open-handed slap to the side of his head. I dropped and hooked a leg around his, pulling him off balance. He let go of my wrist to save himself from hitting the dirt and I got my slap in, wrenching the phone from his fingers as he was distracted by the blow.

"Oh shit!" Zac was laughing, pointing at me. "Bitch has got some moves!"

I threw the phone at the boy, who only barely caught it against his chest. "Call me bitch one more time," I seethed, "I'll shove that phone so far up your arse you'll be able to Skype your spleen."

Kash watched the teen run off into the bush. His face was slowly flushing with color, one hand steadying himself against the ground.

"That was a big mistake," he told me. "Assaulting a federal agent is a minimum two years' prison."

"Conducting a search without a warrant is a serious service violation," I said. I was rolling up the sleeves of my shirt. "But neither of us is going to make a report."

"We're not?"

"No." I set my feet apart, cracked my knuckles. "We're going to sort this out right here, *right now.*"

CHAPTER 27

"OH, COME ON," Kash snorted, rising to his full height. "Don't be ridiculous."

"Harry." Snale put a hand on my arm. "This isn't a good idea."

"Victoria, our special agent friend here thinks in very simple terms." I kept my eyes on Kash. "He's not a complex man. He understands strength and weakness. Good and evil. Winning and losing. He needs to be shown that he isn't the alpha dog here, and when he knows that he can fall the fuck into line."

Already I could see Kash's interest in my challenge piquing, the way it had the night before when I ragged on his workout. A smile was playing about the corners of his mouth.

"I don't hit women," Kash sneered. "So you can back down right now before you overexert yourself."

"You don't have to hit me. You just have to pin me."

"And what exactly will that achieve?" he asked.

"Whoever gets their face pinned against the dirt loses all jurisdictional authority over this investigation."

"Oh, bullshit," Kash snorted. "I'm SAS–combat trained, sweetheart."

"Then this should be over quickly."

"I'm not involved in this." Snale backed off toward the truck, her head down.

"I need you as a witness!" I called.

"So, what? I pin you against the dirt, and I'm the boss." Kash's eyes wandered over my body, measuring, underestimating, the way everybody did. "And you'll fully accept that. It's my investigation to run from start to finish."

"It's got to be the face."

"Right," Kash said. "I put your face in the dirt and your arse is mine."

"You put my face in that dirt and I will trawl this town for Islamic terrorists until the cows come home." I put my hand on my heart. "I will speak operational jargon so pompous and ridiculously over-official that not even you will be able to understand me."

He didn't even ask me what I wanted him to do if I won. The possibility never entered his mind. He rushed toward me, huge hands out, ready to break me.

CHAPTER 28

KASH FAKED LEFT, swept to my right and gathered me up in a chokehold, his hairy arm wrenching me backwards. I let him take me, pushed off the ground and rolled over him, shocking him with how fast I had him on his back.

We both twisted, righted, kicking red sand. His glasses had been knocked off. He ignored them. My heart swelled with a sick kind of joy. I liked to fight. I'd been fighting since I was a kid. Trying to claw some corner of existence for myself in houses where I was the cuckoo invading the nest.

Kash was eyeing me, trying to decide his next move. I didn't give him time to go on the offensive again. I rushed at him, caught his arm and tried to twist it as we danced in the dirt. He grabbed the back of my neck and shoved me downwards, using my own momentum as I'd used his. I was pinned on my back, the wind knocked out of me. Most people panic when they can't breathe in a fight. But I knew the air would slowly return. I kicked out and he overbalanced, fell on me. I shoved his jaw upwards.

Snale was watching us from the truck. I locked eyes with her, my neck and shoulders and arms on fire as the incredible weight of Kash's body came down upon me. She grimaced as Kash leaned on me. It was clear who she was rooting for.

I kicked again, got him in the hip. I twisted and scrambled out from beneath him, got him in my own chokehold, a knee in his spine. He stood and I went with him, absurdly hanging off him like a monkey trying to wrestle a bear. He tried to shake me off, gripping at my arms, but I locked my legs around his waist. And then he did what I hoped he'd do.

Kash sank to his knees and fell backwards, trying to crush me against the ground. I slid sideways before I could hit the dirt, let go of his neck and scooped up his arm. I wrenched it high against his back. He yowled, shocked by the sudden pain, and I shoved the back of his head down so that his cheek hit the red earth beneath us.

"Yes." I stumbled off him, wiping sweat from my eyes. "Yes. Yes. Yes!"

The giddy exhilaration of my win lifted the weight of the Last Chance case, of my brother's case, right off my shoulders in an instant. For a second I felt free. When I fought, I felt strong. I felt that I could take care of myself. I was a warrior.

Kash was dusting sand out of his ear when I came back to myself. Back to the shitty hole in the desert, the middle of nowhere, far from where I needed to be. My smile faltered, as with painful clarity a little voice in my head reminded me that though he was clearly an idiot, a stubborn and ignorant being, this man was supposed to be my partner. We were supposed to be working on this thing together.

I offered my hand to Kash, but he didn't take it. He gave me a hateful look and walked off toward the car.

CHAPTER 29

WHITT TURNED THE page of the psychologist's report before him, the clatter and crash of the prison visitors' center pushed back in his mind until it was only a dull hum in his ears.

Beyond the Plexiglas, a door opened at the end of the small corridor. Samuel Blue was shuffled to the chair before the detective. Whitt put the psychologist's report in his briefcase and pulled out his notebook and pen.

"How you going, Edward?" Sam gave a tired smile. The two had met in the courtroom briefly the day before, exchanged a phone call.

"Oh, you know. How are you? That's the more important question."

"I really need that money you were talking about on the phone." Sam leaned forwards so that his mouth was centimeters from the speaker holes in the glass. "I'm hot property in here, and the only thing that's going to keep the other cons off my back is protection money. I've used up the cash Harry gave me."

"Are you still receiving threats?" Whitt asked.

"Daily. Staff and inmates now."

"Jesus."

"Yeah." Sam sniffed. "I know the drill—Harry told me. Protection money in prison is a lifetime deal. You pay once, you have to keep paying. But I need to at least keep drip-feeding these guys some cash or I'm not going to survive to see the rest of the hearings."

"I'll move some money into your account this afternoon." Whitt made a note.

"I don't know how to fight." Sam seemed distracted, rubbing his palms together hard. "I'm a fucking graphic design expert. I haven't been in a scrap since I was a kid. Harry's the fighter."

"I spoke to her this morning. She's desperate to get back here."

"She should stay as far away as she can." Sam locked eyes with Whitt. "I never wanted her here in the first place. Whoever's doing this to me, they'll be after her next. Someone's got to want to see me suffer big-time to put this much effort into a frame-up. I'd suffer pretty badly if anything happened to Harry, right?"

Whitt tapped the side of his page thoughtfully with his pen. He worked through his words before he spoke. Tried to keep them diplomatic. Supportive.

"So you still think someone is framing you?"

"It's the only explanation," Sam said. "They went into my apartment. They planted those things. Someone abducted those girls when I was in the same area. They must have been following me."

"It's . . ." Whitt cringed. "It's a lot of effort to go to. To do this to you."

"You're telling me, mate."

"I mean, you have no idea who it is?"

"No clue."

"How can someone be that angry at you, and you have no idea who they are?" Whitt asked. "Whatever you did to them must have been a supreme betrayal to warrant this. Something really, really bad."

Sam's lips twitched. Whitt could see a hidden anger flickering there, pulsing like a heat behind the man's eyes.

"You don't believe me?"

"I never said that."

"Because Harry said you were on our side."

"I'm on Harry's side." Whitt swallowed hard. "And Harry's on your side."

"Right." Sam nodded, his jaw ticking with barely contained fury. "Well, mate, you're correct. Whoever is framing me has gone to an awful lot of effort. They must hate me really bad. And it would be ridiculous for me to have no idea what it was, *unless of course I never knew how angry they were in the first place.*"

"OK." Whitt nodded. "I see your point."

"What if it's an ex-girlfriend?" Sam shrugged. "Someone I broke up with, who I thought was OK, but who really wasn't? You know, people can get these crazy stalker women. What if, all these years, she's hated me for leaving her. And I never knew it. And the hate has just been festering and festering."

"Hmm," Whitt said.

"Imagine how many sick and twisted people I might have offended in my ordinary everyday life who I have no idea have harbored this...this *vendetta* against me. I've had students over the years who have plagiarized assignments for my classes. They were expelled because I caught them out. Because I brought their work to the Dean, and he canceled their enrollment."

"Right."

"There was a guy..." Sam was almost rambling now, his eyes wandering over the scratched surface of the glass between them. "Another applicant for the position at the university. Maybe he blames me for not getting that job. Maybe this goes back further than that. Maybe it goes all the way back to when I was a kid moving around in and out of care.

What if someone got placed in a family, or *didn't* get placed in a family, because of me?"

"Sam—"

"What if—"

"Sam, I think you're winding yourself up now," Whitt said, touching the glass where the prisoner's knuckles rested. "You're right. If it's a frame-up, it could be anyone. This person is sick. Why they're doing it to you may not be as logical as we're expecting it to be."

Sam tapped his wrist on the table before him, making the cuffs clatter rhythmically on its surface. He was panting. On the edge of losing it completely. Whitt made notes in his notebook, glancing up now and then at the frightened man's eyes. It was all very convincing, Whitt thought. If Sam's distress wasn't real, it sure was a good act.

CHAPTER 30

HE DIDN'T EVEN feel the impact. Whitt was walking across the darkened car park toward the elevator of his apartment building when suddenly it seemed that the lights went out. He only realized he'd been hit when he tried to move and felt the oily, wet surface of the asphalt beneath his face. He shifted and the pain in his head made itself known, a huge, thumping ache.

Terror sparked through him. He saw blood on the hand by his face, his own hand, numb. Whitt tried to rise and a voice stopped him.

"Not so fast," a gravelly voice said. "You'll make yourself yack."

Whitt slid carefully into a sitting position, propped himself against the wall by the elevator. There was a man leaning against the hood of someone's car just meters away, a slice of pizza in one hand and a cardboard pizza box balancing on the flat of his other palm. Unkempt blond hair. A dusty leather jacket. Big boots. Whitt took the details in slowly, his mind refusing to come to full consciousness all at once.

He did, indeed, feel like "yacking." He felt the back of his skull tentatively with his fingers, noted the blood soaking his hair. His briefcase, wallet, phone, gun. It was all gone. He found his glasses and slipped them on.

"Did you do this?" Whitt asked.

"Heh! No. I'm not a fucking coward. I use my fists."

"I was . . . hit with something?"

"You been slocked," the man said. "Congratulations."

The man rolled a lump of asphalt he'd been toying with under his enormous black boot across the space between them. It came to a stop near Whitt's knee. He picked up the chunk of rock and looked at it, dazed.

"Whoever it was that hit you, he was an ex-con." The man took a bite of his pizza, chewed while he talked. "You learn to slock a guy in prison. Back in the day, you'd do it with a padlock. In a sock. Hence, "slock." Plenty of locks around prisons. Makes a convenient, disposable weapon. Take your sock off, load it up, swing it up, over, and down on the guy's head. Dump the lock, put your sock back on."

"I see."

"You know any ex-cons?"

"Just current ones." Whitt dragged himself to his feet. "I didn't catch your name."

"Tox Barnes."

"*Tox?*" Whitt squinted.

"Yup."

"I'm—"

"Edward Whittacker. You're the reason I'm here. I expected to find you upstairs in your apartment, sippin' a chardonnay or browsing an IKEA catalogue or some shit. Nope. Looked in the windows there and saw you face-planted on the garage floor. Who'd have thought."

Whitt struggled to comprehend. One minute, he'd been walking from his car to the elevator, dreaming of home, worn out from the day in court, visiting Sam in prison. Now a strange, disheveled man was schooling him on prison fight tactics. Whitt dragged himself up. He reached for his phone. Remembered it was gone.

"I'm with Harry," Tox said.

"Oh." Whitt watched the man finish the crust of his pizza, then chuck the empty box on the floor of the garage with a soft *whump*.

"Yup. I'm here to help out with the thing with her brother."

"Oh," Whitt said again.

"So, you're on your feet." Tox looked his new partner up and down. "Let's roll."

CHAPTER 31

IT WAS A long, awkward ride back into town, Kash in the front seat, me in the back. Snale tried to make light, cheerful conversation to cover the silence. The dog sat staring at me as though my pockets might be full of treats, a long string of drool hanging from her tongue. She started barking as we came into sight of the town.

"Oh, shit," Snale said as we pulled into the main street.

At the end of the row of ten stores, comprising the entirety of the town center, was the tiny police station. It was crowded with people. The gun-slinging group from the front of the pub had Zac Taby bailed up against the front doors. Digger and I jumped from the car before Snale had time to shut the engine off.

The dog ran toward the group, her tail wagging so hard her hindquarters were swaying back and forth. She certainly was a friendly thing. I could see why the town was so attached to her.

"We've had enough!" A man had Zac by the front of his T-shirt, pushing him into the glass. "You're going home to pack your shit, and then you're outta here."

"Murderer!" someone cried. "Terrorist!"

"Break it up!" I pushed the men aside. "I will arrest the lot of you if I have to. Back the fuck up."

One of the farmers pointed a gnarled finger at Zac. "He's murdered our police chief. If you let him keep going, him and his kind will kill us all."

"He's dangerous," a woman said. Suddenly the number of people around me had doubled. "We want him out of our town. We know he's behind this."

"You don't know shit, bitch." Zac spat in the dirt. "Suck my fat di—"

"That's enough from you." I shoved Zac into the police station. He stumbled deliberately against the front counter, clutching his elbow. "Argh! My arm! Police brutality!"

"You are going to see some brutality in a minute." I frogmarched the boy through the empty station and into the interview room. Zac flopped into the chair, sunk low, so that his head looked straight across the tabletop, his legs spread beneath its surface. Snale and Kash shut the doors on the crowd and followed me into the darkened room, flipping on lights.

Kash leaned on the table, taking up most of its space with his huge arms, forcing Zac to back off into his chair.

"You probably deleted all those photos," Kash said. "But they'll be easy enough to get back."

"No shit," Zac said.

"You're in a real mess, boy-o. Tell me about those pictures."

"These ones?" Zac took out his phone and swiped through the photos Kash had talked about at the gully. Naked girls. Kids at a party, huffing dope. "I didn't delete them. I'm not an idiot, dude. I know you can get them back. That's my ex-girlfriend. Those are her tits. You want a closer look?"

He shoved the phone at Kash's face. I took the phone from between them, looked through the pictures.

"She's eighteen. I like older women, and they like me." Zac winked in my direction. "And for all you know, those bongs are full of green tea. Try to prove otherwise. I fucking dare you."

"I bet those joints we pulled out of your pockets aren't full of green tea."

"You came all the way to this shithole to charge me with possession of weed?" Zac sneered. "What a bunch of pretenders."

"The picture that concerns us is this one," I said, finding the picture among the collection.

The photograph was of a cluttered table in the middle of a dark shed. Tools, wires, buckets of screws and nails. In the background, a rusty gas bottle sitting on a shelf.

"That's my mate's dad's shed," Zac said lazily. "We build shit in there when we're bored. That lump of metal in the middle of the table is a half-built go-cart."

"You ever built anything that goes bang?" I asked.

Zac didn't answer, stared at his fingernails.

"There was a spate of low-level mischief involving explosives about two years ago." Snale sighed from where she stood in the doorway. "A student teacher doing his internship came out to Last Chance Valley in the second school term. He was being supervised by one of our teachers, Greg Harvey, but one morning Greg let the intern take the class by himself. The young teacher thought he'd endear himself to the kids. It was a science class. He taught them about different types of explosives."

"Oh, great," I said. Kash and I looked at each other.

"It was nothing as complex as what we saw up on the hillside," Snale said. "So it sort of slipped my mind until now. He taught them about gunpowder, basically. How to make their own fireworks. So some of the kids got together and made their own mini-firecrackers."

"Bungers," Zac said. "You can make them as small as a cigarette. About two seconds' fuse. Chuck them at old ladies. Fuckin' hilarious."

"Not you, though. You wouldn't do anything like that." I rolled my eyes.

"No, no. Not me."

"How many kids were in that class?" I asked. "The one about explosives."

"'Bout five of us." Zac smiled, sat giggling to himself, the only sound in the room as Snale, Kash and I quietly despaired about the four other kids we now had to interview. Kash slapped the table soon enough, shutting Zac up instantly.

"This is all very hilarious, I'm sure, but the number one suspect as far as the rest of the town is concerned is you, mate," he said. "I've worked in villages outside Johannesburg where suspicion of a serious crime is all it takes to get you dragged into the bush and hung from a tree."

"*I've worked in villages outside Johannesburg...*" Zac waved his hands, his voice a buffoonish imitation. "Dude, you're such a try-hard. You're not impressing anyone."

Kash looked like he wanted to leap across the table and strangle the kid. But he met my eye and I shook my head. I was in charge now. If we were going to do any roughhousing of the suspects, it was my call. And if we spent too much time knocking innocent people around, the people of this town would clam up on us. Small towns were full of secrets, and if we became their enemy, they'd hide the killer in their midst just to spite us.

CHAPTER 32

KASH WALKED OUT of the interview room, veins beginning to creep up from beneath the skin near his sweaty temples. Snale followed. I went to sit in the chair Kash had vacated and put my feet up on the table.

"Is that tosser your partner?" Zac asked.

"At the moment." I took an intake form from beside the recorder and tossed a pen at the kid. "Fill in this form." I would take the paper and compare Zac's handwriting against the diarist's. The kid sighed and began writing.

"So that guy's your boyfriend, then," he said eventually.

"Certainly not."

"I thought that was the whole deal, though." He snorted. "When dude and lady cops work together they get into dangerous situations. Have to save each other's lives. Then they *fuck.*"

"I'm no lady," I told the kid. "And you should be less concerned with who's fucking who and more concerned about the townsfolk lynching you the moment they get a chance."

"The townspeople can blow me." He sat back in his chair. This kid had a real fascination with fellatio. "You ask me, it's the Old Man you lot should be looking at."

"Who's the old man?"

"The dude," he waved vaguely behind him, in a westerly direction, "I don't know his name. Us kids just call him the Old Man. He lives out there in the never-never. His people and Dez's people had some drama back in the day, when Last Chance was first settled. He won't be friendly, join the town. But won't fuck off, either. You'll know him when you see him. He's scary and old."

"Scary and old," I said. "Right. I'll make a note of it. Until then you're going to have to stay low. People around here want your blood."

"What else is new? Everything around here falls on me. You get used to it. I'm too big for this joint. They won't know who to pin shit on when I bust outta here."

"You've got plans to leave?"

"End of the term, I can legally leave school," he said. "I'm getting out of here and I'm *never* coming back. I don't care if I have to work at a McDonald's and sleep under a bridge. You've gotta start somewhere, man."

"Is that what people do?" I asked. "Take off as soon as they get the chance?"

"No way." He put his arms behind his head. "Around here you take over your family farms or you go work for the mines and send your money back here. That's the only reason people have kids in this town—because if they don't, their farms will close down. If everybody leaves, the whole town closes down, so anyone who makes plans to go hasta keep it secret or people will start calling you a traitor, talking about how you're abandoning the place. It's supposed to be one for all, all for one. So people keep having kids, and their kids take over the farms, and then *they* have kids. It's an endless, meaningless cycle of bullshit."

"So what happens if you're a kid around here and you don't want to be a farmer?"

He made a gun with his fingers, put it to his head. "Bang!"

"Don't they try going into the cities?"

"How are you gonna leave and start again in the big city when you grew up your whole life in a hole in the earth? You got no money. No friends. No family backing you. No work experience. You don't know the city ways. You try to climb out, it just sucks you back in."

"But you're not going to get sucked back in."

"No way." He stretched, reached for the ceiling. "I've got a plan."

"Oh yeah? What's that?"

"None of your business."

He settled back in his chair and knitted his fingers over his skinny chest like he was planning on going to sleep. I knew that kind of calm. The emotionless resolve that comes with knowing you've reached rock bottom, that there's no more trouble that you can get into. No expectations. Maximum ostracism. I'd been that kind of teenager. Wandering around the city at night on my own, spray-painting trains, breaking windows, lighting rubbish bins on fire.

It was actually while I was sitting in a holding cell at Maroubra Police Station, listening to the goings-on in the office, that I'd found my calling. An old lady had wandered in bleeding after being knocked down only a couple of blocks away, her handbag stolen. I'd watched through the bars as two female officers brought her to a chair by one of the desks, tended to her, soothed her, made her a cup of tea. They were like two daughters caring for their frightened, befuddled mother. And the old lady's eyes wandered over their immaculate blue uniforms, their faces, with awe and joy. I'd imagined someone looking at me like that one day. Like I was their hero.

Zac Taby needed to decide how he wanted to be looked at. Right now it was only me looking at him, seeing myself. But I knew what he was in the eyes of the people here. Their runt. The enemy in their midst.

"You're going to go home and stay there," I said. I shoved the kid's phone back toward him. "Play Xbox or something until this whole thing blows over. If I hear or see you around town before I leave, I'll kick your arse."

The kid took his phone and gave a dismissive laugh. He didn't know how serious I was.

CHAPTER 33

THERE WAS A slender, beautiful Pakistani woman standing in the police station's main room with Snale and Kash when I emerged, shutting Zac in the interview room to cool his heels. Zac's mother. Kash still had his interrogation stance on, arms folded and head bowed, eyes narrowed as he took in her face, her figure, as though he could see cruel intentions written on her very countenance. I didn't see anything but a worried, tired woman fed up with her son's antics.

"Is he in there?" She pointed toward the door as I closed it. "I am going to absolutely nail that kid."

I laughed. Her words were much feistier than her appearance.

"Your son hasn't done anything wrong, Mrs. Taby," I said. "Not lately, anyway. Not that we can see."

"Yeah, not that anyone can see," she scoffed. "Half the trouble he gets into, I only hear about it three weeks later when someone makes some snide remark to me about their dead cat or their burned-out shed. He didn't kill Mr. Campbell, Officer, but I can tell you he hasn't been out there collecting funds for charity. I haven't seen him in three days. He needs a smack on the behind."

"Well, after you've smacked his behind, we'd appreciate it if you locked him up for a couple of days," I said. "Just until everything settles down."

"Where is Mr. Taby?" Kash said.

"Mr. Taby doesn't have time to be running around after our little monster." Zac's mother rolled her eyes. "He works remotely for Ektor Corp. His hours are strange. He has to be up all night sometimes talking to his divisional partners. He's locked to that computer sixteen hours a day."

"Ektor Corp." Kash nodded. "Huh."

"Your son's in a lot of trouble, Mrs. Taby," I said. "We're going to need you to keep an eye on him. There are people in this town who would just love to get their hands on him."

"They'll have to wait till I'm done with him first," she said, marching toward the interview room.

CHAPTER 34

"I REALLY THINK I ought to seek medical attention." Whitt touched the back of his skull tenderly as he sat at the bar Tox had taken him to, looking at the blood on his fingertips. Tox put two shots of Scotch on the counter before them.

"I hate working with people," Tox said. "Don't make me work with a pussy."

Whitt drank the Scotch greedily. His mouth was dry, his nerves rattled. And this "Tox" person was doing little to settle his apprehension. Nothing about the man he was sitting beside convinced him that he was as he said: an active police officer, someone who had worked by Harry's side on a major case.

"Harry has been responsible for most of the hard work on Sam's case," Whitt said. "In my briefcase, I had a copy of her notes. Whoever hit me might have been someone working for the press. Someone looking for fresh story angles on Sam's case."

"I don't think so," Tox grumbled. "I think it was whoever framed

Sam, trying to get ahead of our game. Trying to know what we know."

"So you think this whole thing is a frame-up, too?"

"Yep."

"But why on earth would someone do this?" Whitt shifted closer, intrigued. "Kill three innocent girls, just to get revenge against Sam?"

"Whoever this is, they were going to kill those girls anyway." Tox waved a dismissive hand. "All three girls were the same type. White, young, ambitious brunettes. No, that was someone's fantasy. It was ritualized. Same kill technique. Same dumping ground. Whoever murdered those girls, he's done it before."

"That doesn't fit Sam Blue." Whitt sipped his Scotch. "He's got a record, but none of it's violent or sexual. Petty theft and drug charges in his teens. He's been good as gold for a decade at least."

"Mmm-hmm," Tox grumbled. "But Harry's got the violent streak, so the public will assume Sam's just better at hiding his."

The two men watched their drinks.

"You ask me," Tox said, "we're looking at two possibilities. The killer has decided to pin his crimes on someone, and he's chosen Sam Blue, whether it's for vengeance or whatever the hell. That, or the police investigating the killings have decided they need a patsy, and Sam Blue's it."

"The police?" Whitt scoffed. "Now you've lost me."

"You know the guys on the task force? Nigel Spader and his team?"

"No," Whitt said.

"I knew them way back when. In the academy. They're cowboys. I got a bit of a history myself." He glanced at Whitt. "You'll learn about it soon enough. So I've seen these guys with their claws out. It might be that they came upon Sam by accident. It might be that they've got some beef with Harriet, and her brother naturally made a great suspect."

Whitt sighed. "What the hell are we going to do to clear this up?"

"From my understanding, Harry's been working on the girls, checking out their autopsies, the crime scenes, their abductions, trying to look for clues there. I reckon we find out what's happened with this Caitlyn McBeal girl. Find out what Linny Simpson's final version of events is. Where is Caitlyn? Why isn't she answering her phone or accessing her accounts? It's weird. And the police reaction to it is even weirder. The cops just don't want to admit something's wrong there because it fucks with their Sam Blue theory."

"OK." Whitt sat up. He felt tingles of exhilaration rush through him. Hope. Dangerous hope. "We can do that. We can find her."

"Don't get too excited." Tox sipped his drink. "We want to find her alive. We find her dead and all we've got is more unanswered questions."

CHAPTER 35

"THE VIDEO CAMERA they found at Sam's. That's weird, too," Tox mused.

"It is," Whitt agreed. "The task force found the camera just sitting there at the end of the bed on a tripod. No files on it. Totally blank. And there isn't a single fingerprint on it, or trace of DNA. How does the guy use the thing for a prolonged period of time without leaving a trace of himself on it? It didn't have *anyone's* prints on it. It had been wiped clean. Why wipe your prints off it if you're just going to leave it sitting in your apartment?"

"It's a prop," Tox said. "It's been planted. For sure. The magazines, too."

"And where are the video files?" Whitt shrugged. "Nothing was found on either of Sam's computers at home. Nothing on his work computer. Why take all the time to record your deeds and then destroy the files?"

The two men considered the glasses on the countertop some more.

Whitt fiddled with the gash in the back of his head. He wasn't sure what would happen now. The man beside him looked tired, ragged, almost bored with the whole thing. But something told Whitt that he might be the kind of man who always looked that way, a sleepy old python not easily aroused into showing its fangs. Whitt wasn't sure if this man was a police officer or a private investigator. He was itching to call Harriet and check out if he even was who he said he was.

"It might be that we're completely wrong about all this," Tox said. "Maybe there is evidence to convict Blue. Lack of prints, lack of DNA—it doesn't mean they're not there. It just means the Forensics guys haven't found them. Maybe Blue wasn't acting alone. And whoever he was acting with, that's where all the pieces lie. That's how it all fits together."

"What makes you think a partner might be involved?"

"Look, it doesn't make sense that Blue's the killer and he left that evidence in the apartment the way it was," he said. "Innocent or guilty, Sam Blue did not leave a setup like that on purpose. No way. Maybe Blue is innocent, and the whole thing has been planted on him by someone. Or maybe Blue is guilty, and he has a partner. And his partner knew the two of them were going to go down. He sacrificed Blue so he could go on killing. Make a fresh start."

"How would he have had time to plant the evidence?" Whitt asked. "Surely Nigel's team went straight to the apartment after arresting Blue on his way to work."

"Nope." Tox smirked. "They arrested Sam at eleven am. They didn't get into the apartment until six that night. Nigel's team. Bunch of excited schoolgirls. Everybody wanted to be in on the Blue interrogation. Only dragged themselves away when they started hitting a wall. Could be someone snuck into Blue's apartment after the arrest but before the raid. I don't know."

Whitt thought about the shaven-headed man in court. The image of him suddenly popped into his mind, a flash. He dismissed it. His battered brain playing tricks, speculating.

"Blue had scratches on him that the team photographed after the interrogation," Tox said. "Nigel tried to say they were from the girls trying to fight Blue off. But Blue was in that interrogation room for twenty-two hours. I reckon he might have copped them in there. No one photographed him at intake. That's dodgy. We gotta figure out what's going on here, one way or the other."

"I guess we're looking at two very interesting possibilities," Whitt said. "Blue's either completely innocent..."

"Or he's a very dangerous psychopath," Tox said. "The kind who wears sheep's clothing."

CHAPTER 36

IT WAS MIDNIGHT. I sat at Snale's kitchen table, listening to the sound of Jerry's snoring coming from the room nearby. Photographs of Theo Campbell's various remaining body parts had been emailed through to us from the morgue in Orange. Was Theo Campbell's death indeed a part of some grander plan? Were there more bodies to come?

Kash had tried to convince me all evening that Adeel Taby, Zac's father, was a worthy avenue we needed to be looking into. Ektor Corp, the company he worked for, had its hands in oil and gas extraction in the Middle East, and there were rumors of the company's interest in arms dealership. I reminded him that I was in charge. We'd made a deal. Taby's parents didn't interest me as suspects.

I pressed open the diary again and touched the tiny, fluid handwriting, ran my fingers over the printed images of mass shooters glued onto the pages. The handwriting didn't look like Zac Taby's. But I wasn't an expert on that. The diarist and Zac shared a propensity to push overly hard on the paper, dent the pages, make it difficult to read the words on the flip side of every page.

The diarist had made a close analysis of the actions of Elliot Rodger, who'd killed six people and injured fourteen others on a rampage through Isla Vista, California. Rodger had stabbed his three house-mates, then gone after young women in a sorority house nearby, punishing any women he could find for all the sexual rejection he'd faced in his life. The diarist's commentary was more critical of Rodger's killings than it had been for the other shooters. There was a list of "mistakes" on the right-hand side of the page, under a map of the killer's route of terror through the city.

1. Most victims random, not personal.
2. Undignified video confessional before shooting. Sounds desperate.
3. High-risk initiation—could have been caught after stabbing house-mates.

I made a note to check what sort of counseling services were available in the area, both to teens and adults, and what the levels of depression and suicide were in the region. The diarist seemed particularly interested in leaving a good-quality manifesto of his ideas and complaints, his reasons for doing what he was planning to do. He would only plan on doing that if he didn't see himself being around to talk about those things in the aftermath.

Eric Harris and Dylan Klebold attacking kids at their high school who had taunted them. Elliot Rodger attacking girls who had rejected him. I googled Seung-Hui Cho and watched excerpts of his video manifesto on YouTube.

You have vandalized my heart, raped my soul and torched my conscience. You forced me into a corner and gave me only one option.

These young men weren't trying to inspire people. All of them would kill themselves after their attacks. They wanted vengeance. It wasn't terrorism. It was payback.

I shifted my papers around, found my phone and looked through Whitt's email from earlier in the evening about meeting Tox. A tiny smile played about my lips. My heart had been aching to be home, and now I had a new reason to dream of myself there. The incomprehensible partnership of Whitt and Tox: a man who never went anywhere without a personal manicure kit, and a man who I'd seen walk around with blood all over his shirt for two straight days. Wherever the two went with the leads I had given Whitt, one of them would meticulously gather the tiny breadcrumbs of every possible scenario while the other walked ahead of him, kicking down doors and shoving people out of his partner's path.

When my phone rang, I expected it to be Whitt, but it was a number I didn't recognize. I walked out to the front porch and sat on the step looking at the stars.

"Harry," a voice said. "It's me."

My heart twisted in my chest.

CHAPTER 37

THE LAST TIME I had seen my mother had been on the street corner outside my apartment in Pyrmont. Her hands had been wrapped in bandages, and her hair had been a thin, burgundy nightmare. A fresh tattoo on her neck. She'd wanted to live with me. I'd had to turn her away. She'd stayed overnight with me before, but I'd awakened to find all my valuables and cash gone and my front door wide open.

I didn't know what to say to her at first, now that she was on the phone. I had tried to contact our mother when Sam was first arrested, but she hadn't responded. I'd wondered if she was dead. There was not a centimeter of the Australian landscape that wasn't saturated with the media coverage of the Georges River Killer and his dramatic capture. I looked at the stars and sighed.

"Are you there?"

"Yes," I said. "How can I help you, Julia?"

"I wish you wouldn't call me Julia," she said. "It's bad manners."

"Is there something that you need?"

"I don't need anything, baby. I'm calling to see how youse are. You and Sam."

Why don't you take a guess?

"We're fine," I lied. "Was there something else?"

"I tried to go to the courthouse today, but I was too late. They'd shut the doors. I want to visit Sammy but I'm not on his visitors list. Can you get him to put me on?"

"You're not worried you'll be arrested as soon as you walk in the door?" I asked. "You've still got warrants out." My mother's crimes of choice were burglary and car theft. She was wanted in four states.

"I need to see him."

"Well," I sighed, "you could give it a shot."

"I've been crying for days and days," she sniffed. "It's been hard to contact youse both. After I saw the headlines, I was just fucking out of it. You know? I just lost it, mate. I went to bed and I pretty much haven't been up in months."

"Uh-huh."

"I can't believe this. Any of it. How has this happened?"

"That's what we're all trying to work out."

"Well, I'm ready to do my part now, ay? I'm ready to help you both through this. It's the least I can do." She drew a deep breath, allowing me to prepare myself for the grand show of generosity that was about to come. "They've asked me to do a spread in *Her Weekly*. It's paid. I want to donate some of that money to Sam's legal fees."

"You..." I felt heat rush up into my mouth. "You what?"

"Some magazine lady called me. They want to do a four-page spread on my story. It'll be me and some photos of youse when youse were kids. Some stories about raising you both."

I was speechless.

"They're offering forty thousand dollars," she sniffed. "So I thought, you know, five or ten grand of that could go to you and Sam, help out with the lawyer or whatever."

"You can't do this," I said. I was standing now, my mouth opening and closing, the words failing to come. "You just…can't, Julia. I mean, what the hell are you going to say? Sam and I…we were practically toddlers when we left your care."

"Harry, it's not like I didn't have any say into how youse were raised. I always knew where youse were. I called. I called dozens of times."

I couldn't breathe.

"Harry, are you there?"

"Julia," I said. "Listen to me very carefully. *Her Weekly* isn't interested in how you raised us and what lovely children we were. They're not going to paint this as some beautiful tragic tale of a misunderstood woman and the perfect little angels who were stolen from her by evil Child Services. They're going to represent you as an irresponsible junkie and the two of us as institution rats with violent backgrounds."

"No they're not."

"Yes, they are." I gave an angry laugh. "Anything else would be a lie!"

She was silent. In the background of the call, I could hear a television playing, a man shouting.

"Julia, they're going to sit you down and wave money in your face and get you to confide all the awful stuff you've done over the years. And then they're going to use that as evidence to suggest Sam is guilty."

"Harry, my life is really hard right now. I don't expect you to understand, you being a fucking copper and all. You've been trained to hate people like me."

"OK," I said, "I'm hanging up now."

"I need that money, Harry. I'm going to use it to start again. I've met someone, and we're going to start a business together. This is the one, Harry. I can feel it. He's not like the others."

I didn't say anything.

"I have always loved you, Harriet." She gave a sharp, furious sigh. "I have always loved your brother. Doesn't that count for anything? Jesus Christ, I don't know how you ended up such an ungrateful bitch. I'm doing my fucking best here."

I hung up, gripped my hair. I wanted to howl into the night. It was like my brother was sinking in quicksand. Every time I thought someone was coming along to help me free him, they only kicked more sand at him. The more he struggled, the deeper he got. I knew if too many people joined the crowd trying to bury him, I'd never get Sam out alive.

CHAPTER 38

IN THE MORNING we paid a visit to Theo Campbell's friend David Lewis, to see what he thought about the former police chief's death. The younger man had seen Theo that afternoon, climbed the roof of his little farmhouse with him and accepted his help in fixing some broken tiles. Lewis had of course heard the news already and seemed bewildered. The last person to see the victim before a tragedy is often haunted by what has happened. David repeated words I'd heard often, that Theo had seemed fine, that he couldn't believe he watched his friend walk off so casually to what would be such a violent death.

The sun was high and blazing as we pulled into the Campbell driveway. Olivia Campbell opened the door to us, her hands red from wringing and her eyes puffy. She had the reserved dignity of a cop's wife, her outfit put together and her hair neatly pulled into a tight bun. A woman who carried on in the face of adversity, at least in terms of appearance, someone who never let the cracks show. There was a framed wedding photograph of the two of them just inside the door. Theo was broad-shouldered, tall and bushy-browed. I went to the doors that looked out onto the backyard, watched the family cat as it toyed with a dead locust by the edge of the lawn.

"It's drugs," Olivia said as she and Snale settled on the lounges. "People are saying it's terrorism, or it's related to the diary they found. But I'm telling you, it's some drug gang that's got him."

Snale and I exchanged glances, shocked. I didn't know what I'd expected. Some small talk about Theo, about how Olivia was coping. But she launched straight in. Kash looked skeptical. He stood at the bookcase, looking over the tattered paperbacks there. He zeroed in on a copy of the Qur'an like a hawk and seized it from the third shelf, as though he'd find the answer to Theo's demise there.

"What do you mean, drugs?" Snale asked gently. "We're on top of the drug situation in the region. We don't have any gangs out here."

"Theo said he was running an undercover sting," Olivia explained. "See, we went to bed one night, maybe a month ago, and I woke up at around midnight and Theo wasn't beside me. I went to the front windows and looked out. I saw him talking to Jace Robit and his crew. I asked him what was going on when he came back inside. He wouldn't tell me much about it. He said he thought there was drug activity going on. Ice production."

Snale shook her head ruefully, disbelieving. I came and settled on the edge of the couch.

"There *is* ice around here," Snale told me. "Softer drugs, too. Lots of weed. But any amphetamines are mostly brought through by the truckers heading to Bourke, about four hours out. Bigger town. People buy it at one of the local pubs there, we think, to keep themselves running until the next round comes through."

"It's only small amounts?"

"The kids use it recreationally. They're bored. There's nothing to do out here. We'd know if anyone in town was manufacturing it.

Something like that would be difficult to hide. And there'd be no point in making it. You wouldn't be able to sell huge amounts of it out here. Ice is made in the cities, where you've got a chance of blending in."

I remembered the wonky-toothed, narrow-bodied man with the rifle, Jace. His little gathering of similarly sun-worn types.

"Robit has a cattle property on the south side of the valley." Snale pointed.

"Was Theo sure it was drugs they were manufacturing?" Kash asked Olivia, who looked up, red-eyed. "Or was he just suspicious?"

"I don't know." Olivia wiped her nose on a well-used tissue. "I only saw them that one night, and I didn't ask for any more details. I remember them all standing out there on the road. Their headlights were all on. The forensic officers, they told me that whoever killed Theo had been pacing around near him. Had him tied to a chair." She fought back tears. "Maybe it was some sort of interrogation, see whether he'd told anyone else."

I wandered into the office while Snale comforted Olivia. This was obviously Theo's domain. There was a cracked leather desk-chair and an old, dusty laptop, a collection of brass nautical navigation equipment on the desk in desperate need of a polish, more books. I went and sat in Theo's chair, looked out the window onto the bare lawn. There were papers on his desk. A half-finished memoir of a rural police chief's life. Zac Taby had said that diaries were for little girls, but Theo Campbell had spent hours upon hours reflecting on his long career, setting down his personal history in these pages. I flipped through and caught the occasional word. *Honor. Evidence. Tragedy. Arrest.*

"He would have told Snale about an undercover operation," Kash whispered from the doorway. He was still holding the Qur'an like a much-loved teddy. I watched him go to the bookshelves here.

"I agree," I said. "If farmers were making ice out here, there'd be no need to run an undercover sting. Just go raid their properties. Ice manufacture is expensive. Complicated. And it reeks. How on earth would they hide the smell? Besides that, there isn't a big enough market for it out here. I can understand how the truckers get away with it. Some city drug dealer gives them a package and they slowly sell it off, town by town, all the way across the country. But cooking it out here? It would be stupid."

"It might have been a one-off," Kash mused. "Make one big batch, take it to the city, sell it and make a fortune. Pay off your debts. Theo found out and was trying to talk them down, so they killed him."

"And the diary?"

Kash stared at his feet.

"Maybe it was a decoy," he said.

I hadn't thought about that. That someone might have constructed the diary to throw us off. It wouldn't be hard. A few late evenings sketching, doodling, noting down tidbits from what was perhaps a passing interest in spree killers. Maybe the diary had nothing to do with Theo Campbell's death. Maybe his was a straight-up drug-related killing.

A guilty little zing of excitement ran through me. If I could wrap this case up as quickly as that, I could go home to Sydney. Sure, I wouldn't be allowed anywhere near my brother or the courthouse, but I would at least be closer to him. All of that was calling me. Conduct a raid on Robit's place. Find something. Anything. Lock up him and his cronies and be done with it all. Ignore the possibility that the town was in further danger, that someone here was planning a day of reckoning. Wham, bam, thank you ma'am—some quick arrests and the six days I had to wait to go home would become zero.

I realized I was shuffling idly through the objects in Theo Campbell's desk drawer. Pens and little notepads. I shoved the desk drawer closed and a plastic ruler wedged itself in the gap. I tried to yank the drawer back open but it stuck, the plastic biting into the wood. I threw my weight backwards and the drawer shunted open, rattling the desk, causing a flush wooden panel at the front to flop open.

Kash and I looked into the cavity the panel had revealed.

My hopes of leaving dissolved.

CHAPTER 39

I KNELT AND peered into the dark slot in the side of the desk, ten centimeters wide, crammed with black plastic. I pulled out a package. It was as big as a shoebox, wrapped tightly in duct tape to form a lumpy rectangle.

"Christ, she was right," I breathed. I took a pair of scissors from the desktop and began to carefully slit open the side of the package. "What do you think it is? It's heavy. Might be black tar."

Kash knelt beside me. I could smell the sweat on him. That morning, I'd woken to the sound of him huffing back and forth across Snale's lawn, stopping, dropping and pumping out push-ups to timed beeps from his phone. Snale had been standing at the windows to the porch, enjoying a coffee, watching the show. Kash's bare chest glistening with sweat in the new pink light of sunrise.

I slipped a small bag out of the package. A heavy, dusty brown rock about half the size of a golf ball. I opened the bag and took out the rock.

"Brown rock heroin," Kash said. "I've seen it over there in northern Africa. Dirty stuff from back-shed kitchens. Goes cheaper than black tar."

"Guess again," I said. I spat on the rock in my palm. "This rock's only brown on the outside."

I rubbed the top layer of dirt from the nugget. The gold shimmered, dull yellow and porous in the light.

"Whoa!" Kash snatched the gold from me. I rolled my eyes and took another rock from the package. "That is one massive piece of cheese!"

"That's about two ounces you're holding," I said. I crossed my legs and took out my phone, looked up a converter on Google. "A couple thousand bucks on the market right now."

We looked at the bag between us. I weighed it in my hands. I guessed I was holding about two and a half kilos, over eighty ounces. Approximately eighty thousand dollars' worth of precious metal.

"What. The. Hell." Kash looked at me. "You think it's legit?"

"I have no idea," I said. "You can't buy it like this. This is right out of the ground. So, what? Campbell's taken it out of the ground, or someone he knows has? This is not his retirement nest egg. I'm betting it's not even declared as a personal asset for tax purposes, if he's got it squirreled away like this."

"How does he have so much of it?" Kash asked. "You couldn't find this much all in one go. It must represent years, decades, of fossicking with a metal detector."

"Maybe he did find it all in one place," I murmured, losing myself in thought. "Maybe that's why it's hidden."

"We've got to put this back." Kash took the nugget from my hand and tucked it back into the package. "There's nothing to prove it doesn't legitimately belong to Theo Campbell. He might have hidden it in case of a break-in."

"If Theo found it legally, Olivia would know about it, right?" I stood, holding the package against my chest. I pulled a strip of tape from the dispenser Theo kept beside his monitor and sealed the package shut. "Olivia, can we borrow you for a minute?"

Theo Campbell's wife heard my call from the living room and came in. She'd been crying again, probably urged on by Snale's kind, accepting face, her warm hands.

I stood holding the package under my arm in full view. I even stepped aside so that Olivia could see that the secret panel in Theo's desk was hanging open.

"We were just wondering if Theo had a...a diary?" I asked casually. "A calendar or something? We just wanted to check out his forecasted appointments."

Olivia ignored the package in my arms, the door of the desk. She went, bleary eyed, to the laptop screen.

"He used the desktop calendar," she sniffed, waking the little machine with a tap of her finger. She opened the calendar and pointed. "Here."

I put the package on the desk, right beside her hand. She glanced at it, uninterested.

"What's that?" she asked.

"Oh, forensic stuff. Tools. They keep them packed up in little baggies. Keep them sterile."

"This bloody desk." Olivia bent and popped the little panel at the front of the desk shut. "It's a million years old. Theo's father's."

She sighed and made for the door.

"Well, that answers that question," I told Kash, hefting the gold off the desk again. "She had no interest in it. She's never seen it before. I'm convinced." I offloaded the package to Kash. "We're taking this with us. I'm going to make a bet Theo Campbell wasn't the only person who knew about it."

CHAPTER 40

DETECTIVE INSPECTOR NIGEL Spader was the God of Gotham. It was one of his only hobbies, constructing his dark city, a place where good and evil clashed violently over hand-painted sidewalks and green flocked grass. The sprawling table in the center of the concrete garage barely contained the complex miniature model city. Artistically warped and leaning buildings crowded over a long, narrow headland jutting into a model harbor filled with black waves. The miniature city had everything. Uptown, the narrow streets held neat brownstone town houses and apartment buildings lined with tiny fire escapes. Downtown, he had constructed the imposing city hall with hundreds of steps, homeless people glued in and around its buttressed sides with their trolleys of garbage. Men in suits with long black coats froze midstride on the sidewalk, briefcases swinging, passing the tiny models of prostitutes on the corners.

Nigel sat on a leather stool by the sprawling Wayne Manor, gluing the side of the ancient building to the front with the careful strokes of a nail polish brush. The battery-operated subway train emerged from the tunnel at the side of the harbor and wound around the corner by his elbow, then over an ornate gothic bridge that had taken Nigel four weeks to create. He felt happy. The world beyond the reach of his garage light, the wet Sydney streets, were nothing. He was the lord of this place, and at this moment, in his universe, everything was well.

The sensation did not last long. Nigel jolted as the garage door slid up just enough to allow Tox Barnes to emerge into the light. The man walked into the garage like he owned it. Nigel found his mouth was hanging open.

"Evening, Detective."

Nigel felt a splinter of pain in his brain. He knew Tox Barnes. Everybody did. The man was rumored to have murdered a mother and young son when he was a child himself, an eruption of violence from a group of boys who must have been frenzied with rage. Nigel didn't know how much truth there was behind the rumor. All he knew was that Tox Barnes was poison, and that anyone who worked with the man was stained.

"What the fuck are you doing here?"

"Oh, you know, I was in the neighborhood. I'm working on the Samuel Blue case. Understand you were head of the task force." Tox's eyes wandered over the enormous model city. He bent and looked through the windows of an office building, noting the tiny people at the desks on the fourth floor. "Jesus Christ, this is some setup you've got here. You've spent a lot of time on this. I thought you were married? You should marry someone."

"I'm not going to discuss a single aspect of the GRK case with you." Nigel looked at his hands. He was holding the glued pieces of Wayne Manor together. He could not put them down now, before the glue set, or it would be hours sanding the lumpy glue back off again. "Get out of my garage."

"Look, I'm really only interested in Sam Blue's confession," Tox said. "I know you've muscled suspects into confessions before. Did you lean on Blue?"

"I'm not . . ." Nigel was almost blind with rage. "Get . . . out . . . of my . . ."

"Huh! Look at this!" Tox said. He reached into the city, somewhere around Third Avenue, and plucked up a prostitute. Nigel heard the *snap* sound of the glue securing the model woman's feet to the sidewalk. "You've got tiny little prozzies!"

"Stop! Don't touch that!"

"Oh shit." Tox examined the figurine's stiletto heels. "Was that attached? Sorry."

Nigel put down Wayne Manor, wincing as the still-wet sides became unwed and flopped apart. He shoved Tox in the chest and rescued the miniature prostitute, looking at the space where she'd been ripped from the model.

"Did you lean on Sam Blue, Nigel?" Tox asked.

"We lean on everyone, arsehole," Nigel snapped. "This is a fucking serial killer case."

"Well, there's leaning and then there's leaning. Did you guide him into the confession? Did you drop hints about what happened to the missing girls so his story would line up?"

"We did nothing unprofessional."

"Come on."

Nigel gave an exasperated growl. "I wasn't there for the entire interrogation, OK? We took shifts. It's possible someone else dropped hints."

Tox put a finger on the train tracks. The train stopped at his finger, the tiny wheels grinding in their slots.

"Stop! You're going to break it. This is not a toy, you fuck! This is very expensive shit!"

"Did you reveal anything . . ." Tox said slowly, "that would have led Sam . . ."

"I left the autopsy photos with him, OK?" Nigel breathed. "He'd have known the girls suffered certain injuries from the pictures."

"So you forced the confession?"

"We *encouraged* it. There's nothing wrong with that. We provided him with materials to help him along. That's all."

"Did you starve him?"

"No."

"Did you beat him?"

"No!"

"Did you leave him in the custody of people who *did* do those things?"

"Get out!" Nigel grabbed a cricket bat from beside the garage door. "Get out of my garage!"

Tox took the train from the tracks, detaching the battery-pack carriage, making the internal lights flicker and die. He threw the train over his shoulder so that it crashed onto the cluttered table against the wall.

"I wasn't there for the whole Blue confession, all right?" Nigel begged. "No one was. We didn't keep a log. It was twenty-two hours. People came and went. The tape wasn't always on. It's possible Blue was leaned on too hard."

"It's possible?"

"It's possible, yes."

Tox nodded, wandered around to the harbor, making sure he was always on the opposite side of the table to Nigel. He spied the miniature model of the Joker standing on steps of the town hall, a Tommy gun in his hands. Tox snapped the Joker from his place on the model landscape, smiled at the tiny purple-jacketed figure in his fingers.

"Ah." He smiled. "My favorite."

Tox threw the Joker up and caught him in his palm, put the little man in the pocket of his leather jacket. He winked at Nigel as he ducked back under the garage door and out into the night.

CHAPTER 41

LINNY SIMPSON CUT a dejected figure at the back of the cafe, staring into a stained coffee cup as Whitt entered. He went to her table and stood there expectantly, perhaps a couple of seconds too long, before she broke from her reverie.

"Ms. Simpson?"

"Hi," she said, watching him sit. The inch of coffee at the bottom of her cup that had so fascinated her looked cold. "I don't have long to talk to you."

"That's perfectly fine. I'm grateful for you giving me any time at all." Whitt caught the eye of the waitress and ordered for them both. "I understand you've stopped cooperating with the officers you've been dealing with. Detective Spader and his team."

"They don't believe me," Linny said. Though it had been almost five months, Whitt could hear astonishment lingering in Linny's voice. Flickers of rage. "No one believes me. My own family are starting to think twice about my story. I'm getting messages online from people I don't know saying I'm lying about all this."

"Are the messages threatening?" Whitt asked.

"They're abusive," Linny said. "People think I'm making up what happened because I want to free Sam Blue. Or because I want attention. My fifteen minutes of fame."

"There are some difficulties with what you've said," Whitt said carefully. "Your story changed in subtle ways."

"Well, it was hard to remember," Linny pleaded. "I mean, in the beginning. I remember it clearly now."

Whitt nodded though his thoughts were grave. That wasn't how memory worked. The longer Linny waited after the actual event, the more degraded her memory of it would become. An inference here, a suggestion there, a few sleepless nights running the thing over in her mind, and the whole story would become unrecognizable.

"Why don't you take me back to that day?" Whitt took out his notebook, slid a collection of papers across the page. "I have your police statement here. You say you'd just finished an ethics class..."

"I walked over to the parking garage." Linny said. "Up the fire stairs. There was no one around, not on that level anyway. I think I'd seen some people before I went up, but I'm not sure. He was waiting just next to the door. When I came through, he grabbed me around my throat."

Whitt made notes. Linny Simpson was the Georges River Killer's type. Brunette. White. Slim, petite. Student of the university, a motivated, budding business undergrad. The way she described being grabbed was convincing. An inexperienced abductor might grab a woman around the middle, allowing her to scream, to throw her weight forward, her center of gravity keeping her upright. If he swept his arm around her throat instead, made a headlock, and yanked her backwards, he'd have her off balance and silent.

"He tried to drag me toward a white van parked to the right of the door," she said. "I was screaming."

"How could you have screamed when he had you in a headlock?"

"I don't remember," she said. "I was so shocked. It happened so fast."

"Was the van indeed white?" Whitt asked.

"Yes."

"Your initial police statement says it was green."

"I was mistaken," Linny said. "I remembered later that it was white."

There had been no green vans in the car park lot that day. There had been a white one, but it had come and gone well outside the times necessary to line up with Linny's story.

Whitt made a noise in his throat. It sounded more dismissive than he planned. He jumped when Linny banged the table with her palm.

"Hey," she snapped. "I thought I was going to die, you understand?" Whitt looked at her eyes, searing with furious tears. "When was the last time you thought you were going to die?"

CHAPTER 42

"I DID SCREAM," Linny insisted. "I screamed my lungs out."

Whitt glanced at the police statements lying on the page beside him. Beneath Linny's statement was one from the security guard on the boom gate on the ground floor of the car park lot that day. He had not heard Linny's screams, despite the car park making the perfect echo chamber, the building hollow down the middle through the ramps and the sides open to the buildings around it.

"You say you fought him beside the van," Whitt said. "And you got free somehow."

"I don't know how."

"Maybe you kicked him? Maybe you punched him?"

"I said, I don't know." Linny took her coffee from the waitress, hugged it with her hands as she had the other cup. "I was scared."

"Did he actually get you into the van?" Whitt asked. "Did you get in and then somehow get out?"

"The van door was closed," Linny said.

Whitt wrote furiously. His mind was churning, pumping like an engine. He dipped his shirt cuff in the coffee as he reached for the sugar, cursed himself.

"OK. You struggle, you get free, and you run, and it's then that you notice a girl watching what's happening."

"A black girl," Linny said. "Caitlyn McBeal."

"Now, I mean, we've got to be careful here," Whitt warned. "You say it was Caitlyn McBeal. How do you know that?"

"I've seen pictures of her. She's missing."

"But you didn't know her personally before you saw her there that day. You didn't say to yourself as you ran past her, "Oh, that's Caitlyn." '

"It was fucking Caitlyn!" Linny yelled. People at the tables near them stopped their conversations, stared. "This is bullshit! Yes, I was confused in the beginning. I'd hit my head. I got knocked out."

"Yes," Whitt said. "Initially you said there were two girls watching. Caitlyn and another girl. A blonde."

"No, the blonde wasn't there," Linny said. "I made up the blonde."

Whitt felt a muscle in his jaw twitch. When she was seventeen, the woman sitting before him at the cafe table had made a statement to police that her ex-boyfriend was stalking and harassing her. A couple of weeks later, she withdrew the complaint, her relationship with the boy obviously repaired. In her secondary statement, Linny had said that she'd "made up" the stalking allegation.

Linny seemed to know what he was thinking.

"I mean that my brain made it up," she said. "Not that I made it up...deliberately. Consciously."

"You fled the scene and ran back down the fire-escape stairs," Whitt said. "At the bottom you slipped, and you sustained a head injury. You believe you lost consciousness temporarily."

"Yes."

"For how long?"

"I don't know," Linny said. "It couldn't have been long, right? Someone would have found me."

"However long it was, no one found you. You regained consciousness on your own and went to the university's administration office to report what had happened," Whitt said. "And in that initial report you didn't mention that you'd seen Caitlyn or the blonde girl. You only mentioned her when police arrived, twenty minutes later."

Linny didn't answer.

"In fact, I have a statement here from one of the administration ladies, Michelle Stanthorp, who says that she and another assistant sat you down behind the counter and while they were hearing your story, she received a call transferred over from the security department. It was from Caitlyn McBeal's mother telling them she was trying to get in contact with the girl. She was concerned for her daughter's safety, worried because Caitlyn had hung up on her unexpectedly and now wasn't answering her phone," Whitt said. "Michelle Stanthorp says that while she was on the phone to Mrs. McBeal, she drew up Caitlyn's student file, including her photograph, on a computer in full view of where you were sitting."

When Linny didn't answer, Whitt looked up. The girl's head was bowed into her hands. In all his determination to find the truth, Whitt realized he had slipped into interrogation mode. This girl was not a criminal. At worst, she was a liar. He reached over and took a hand down from her face, squeezed it.

"You don't believe me, do you?" she said.

"I believe something happened to you," Whitt said gently. "Something bad. And you didn't deserve me to be so cold about finding out what it was. I'm sorry."

"It was supposed to have been me," Linny said. She was suddenly distant, staring out the cafe's front windows to the busy street. Her teary eyes wandered back to Whitt. "Whatever happened to her, whether she's dead or alive, it was supposed to have been me."

Whitt closed his notebook. Sighed.

"You've got to find him," Linny said. "Before he does it again."

CHAPTER 43

THE DAY WAS filled with interviews. Zac Taby had said that there were four other Last Chance Valley kids who sat in on the explosives lesson with the visiting student teacher two years earlier. Of those four, one, Brandon Skinner, had died of a drug overdose the year before, home alone and experimenting with meth. The remaining three were called to Snale's place, two of them with parents in tow. Snale and I sat them down on the couch and picked their brains. Had they participated in the spate of firecracker mischief that had ensued after the ill-fated lesson? Did they know anyone who had? How did they feel about the town and its people? How did their friends feel? Did they know anyone who owned a bright red backpack? The answers to our questions, from all of the kids, were a consistent no. These were the bored, hopeless rug rats of Last Chance. They got up to trouble. It was what kids did out here. None of them were going to admit anything.

Townspeople came to the door to drop helpful hints to Snale and me about locals they thought were responsible for the bombing. Most of the tips were about Zac Taby. There were a couple of mentions of a man named Jed Chatt who lived outside town, Zac's "scary old man."

Whitt started texting me at midday on a new number. I didn't ask why.

The account you set up for Sam is empty. I visited. He's nervous.

I eased air through my teeth. I'd known, as soon as my brother was arrested, that this was going to be an expensive time in both our lives. With his permission, I'd sold almost all of Sam's possessions immediately after his arrest, and taken charge of his bank account. I'd sold my apartment, my car, and some collectibles of my own, and unlocked some term deposits of my personal savings. Within a week of his arrest, the spending started. I put some money into Sam's commissary account at the remand center so he could buy snacks and sundries, toothpaste and the like. Then, like clockwork, the threats on his life began. I started feeding protection money into his account, as slowly as I could manage, just enough to keep his enemies satisfied. I knew they'd want more in time. But all I had to do was keep Sam alive until the end of his trial. I'd take out a loan if I had to. Get a second and third job. Whatever it took.

I'll deposit some more now, I told Whitt. *You and Tox OK?*

There was a lengthy pause. *I'm not sure we're the most suited of partners. He's an unsettling person with an unsettling reputation, and I worry about his actual plans for the killer if we find him.*

I smiled at that. Tox was, indeed, unsettling. Whitt had likely heard by now the rumor on the police force that Tox had murdered a mother and her son when he was a kid. I was one of few people who knew the real truth—but I wouldn't divulge Tox's secret behind his back.

I texted Whitt, tried to stem his curiosity.

Five days and I'll be home. Tox is good people. Trust me. You're safe with him.

He smells like a wet dog, Whitt replied.

CHAPTER 44

I BORROWED SNALE'S car and took a drive out into the desert to clear my head while she and Kash worked on the package of gold from Olivia Campbell's house. When I had left Snale's place the two were dissecting it, weighing the gold and using lifting tape to secure any prints from the wrapping. Kash was rambling about how the difficulty of tracing precious metals made them perfect funding for terrorism.

I understood Kash's way of looking at the world. I knew officers who had worked in Sex Crimes so long they let it divide their minds clean in half, so that all men became potential predators and all women their potential prey. To stay away from men was to be, by definition, safe.

I'd called Tenacity on the hands-free without asking myself why. I guess I was curious to see if it was indeed the Tenacity whose case I'd solved years earlier.

When she picked up, she sounded like she was clattering around the house, moving pots and pans.

"Oh my God, Harry," she laughed. "What a surprise."

"Just checking in on my tenacious friend," I said. "How's things?"

A little guilt rippled through me as she sighed and started complaining about how her mother couldn't find a job, her brother was getting sued, she couldn't keep her house clean. She told me she'd been doing great in counseling, though. I didn't know how to get around to the topic of Kash, or even if I should. I'd decided that it was totally inappropriate of me to even think of talking to her about him.

"I'm in the middle of a divorce, though," she said.

"Oh dear."

"I've been with Elliot sixteen years," she said. "We were high school sweethearts."

I made an awkward noise. Tenacity paused.

"What?"

"I think I might be on a case with him."

"Who? Elliot?" The clattering in the background of the call stopped. "Elliot Kash? Jesus!" She gave a humorless laugh. "Small world."

"I feel very ashamed," I said. "I heard him say your name, and I thought—"

"You thought, 'How many fucking *Tenacitys* could there possibly be in the world?' I get it all the time. Let me guess, you want me to drag him home and out of your hair."

My face was burning. I tried to focus on the road.

"Well, you listen to me, Harriet Blue," she said. "I don't care if you have to chain him to the front fence of the town hall. You keep him out there as long as you can. I need a break, you understand?"

"A break from what?"

"From feeling like I'm going to get held hostage every time I walk into a bloody airport!" She was ranting now. "From looking at every person on the bus like their bag might be packed with explosives! From waking up every morning to *Voice of the Caliphate* on the radio, copies of jihadi recruitment magazines spread all over the kitchen table! My friends think he's a fucking nutcase. Elliot's obsession with Islamic terrorism is driving me nuts. I thought *I* had problems."

"Well, it's his job," I reasoned. "I mean—"

"It's not his job," she snapped. "It's his *life*. When I met Ell he was a laid-back surfer type. He was a bricklayer. Hard hands. Brown as a nut. Then everything changed. He went to Bali on a surfing trip with four of his mates and they all went to the Sari Club on the first night."

My heart sank. I knew where this was going. In 2002, two hundred and two people, including eighty-eight Australians, had been killed by a suicide bombing in Kuta conducted by an Islamic terrorist group called Jemaah Islamiyah. One of the bombs had gone off outside the Sari Club, which was full of tourists having a good time.

"Three of his friends died that night," she said. "The fourth died in hospital the next day. Elliot applied for a fast-track uni degree two weeks later. International relations, security major. Before I knew it he was interviewing for a position with ASIO. And ever since then it's been *this*." I imagined her standing in her kitchen gesturing angrily around the countertops laden with stacks of books and papers, aerial shots of tiny Afghan villages. "I can't keep doing this. Elliot is not going to stop terrorism all by himself. He's going to end up as their next victim, by destroying everything and everyone he loves with his fixation."

CHAPTER 45

I'D TURNED OFF the highway onto the faint tire tracks in the hard earth that led toward the scary old man's house. The land was sparsely populated here with spiky desert plants. Inhospitable brush led to distant clumps of trees dotting the horizon like approaching armies, shimmering in the heat. Last Chance Valley seemed like an oasis compared with this endless dead zone of shadowed valleys and hazardous cliffs. There were no landmarks to guide the wanderer. Mobs of gray kangaroos lounged in the minimal shade, eyeing the car as I passed.

Snale had briefed me on Jed Chatt while she stood over the dining room table, marking out the tiny speck that was his house on his vast property in the empty space west of Last Chance. There had been a dispute between Jed's people and Dez's nearly two hundred years earlier, apparently over land within the valley that both parties seemed to want. Snale didn't know much more about it than that, but she told me that the resentment ran deep. Jed hardly came into the town at all, but when he did people shied away from him. He would be dependent on

Dez for his mail services, and on the town for his food and supplies, the occasional visits of fly-in, fly-out doctors and dentists. Jed seemed like a hovering black eagle, the townspeople in the valley uneasy mice.

The house sat perched on the side of a low hill facing back toward the valley, only the gentle slope of Last Chance Valley's crumbly ridge visible in the distance. I got out at the bottom of the hill and looked up toward the property, saw no one. The place was very bare, functional. Shutters closed against the raging sun. A porch that hadn't been painted in years. There was a small awning where a person might host barbecues, but there were no chairs suggesting anyone ever did. Instead a rusted old grill stood, propped up on sandstone blocks. There was a collection of rusty gas bottles under one table.

I walked up onto the porch. Jed was sitting so still that I must have stood in his presence for a good twenty seconds before I noticed him. The man lounged in an old mustard-colored armchair in the shade of a floral sheet nailed to the rafters, a makeshift screen trying and failing to block the sun. I was wandering along when I noticed him, the gun in his hand trained on me.

CHAPTER 46

"THAT'S FAR ENOUGH," the man said.

I'd expected someone older, more decrepit looking. But Jed Chatt wouldn't have been sixty, or if he was, he carried it well. Even from the way he sat, I could see he was a tall, slender man with broad shoulders and strong arms. Black curly hair streaked with gray, dark brown skin. The sawed-off shotgun sitting along his leg was a well-oiled thing with a duct-taped handle.

I put my hands out slightly from my sides, froze with one foot out, the heel up, midstep.

"I'm a cop," I said.

"I thought so." He nodded to a huge rifle sitting on a table to his left, pointed at my car. There was a long scope mounted on it. "I had you in my sights not long after you turned off the highway. Saw you talking while you drove."

I glanced toward the road.

"I figured you were either a crazy person talking to yourself, or a sane person talking on a phone. The only person out here so stressed they've got to talk and drive at the same time would be a cop."

"Good guess," I said. "Now put the gun down."

"You put yours down first."

I reached slowly behind me and took my pistol from the back of my jeans, set it on the ground at my feet. Jed responded by shifting the aim of his gun from my belly to my knee.

"I assume you're Jed Chatt, terror of Last Chance Valley."

"You've got the right guy."

"I'm Harriet Blue," I said. I felt a small measure of relief when he didn't show any recognition of the name. "I just want to talk."

"Is this about the boy?" he asked.

"What boy?" I said. He didn't answer. We stared at each other, neither daring to be the one to show their cards first. It was only when a thin, pealing cry sounded from inside the little house that the expression on his face changed, softened for an instant, before hardening again.

I cocked my head. "Is that ... Is that a *baby*?"

Jed put the shotgun down and emerged from his chair, even taller than I had imagined. He walked past me and disappeared into the house. I followed him and stood in the doorway. It was dark and cool inside. Pushed up against the back of the couch was a battered wooden baby's crib. There was almost no other furniture in the room. The big man took an infant from the stark cotton sheet and lifted it against his chest.

I was shaken and confused by Jed's transformation from menacing armchair spider to whatever he was now, holding the child. I stepped closer. The baby was brown-skinned as he was, gripping at the tired blue cotton of his old singlet.

"Nobody invited you in," he said.

"Is this the boy you were talking about?" I asked. Jed glanced sideways at me, said nothing. I watched as he tried to hold the baby and retrieve the child's teething ring from the crib at the same time. I bent down and got it for him. Our fingers brushed. Jed's skin was hard and warm.

"No one in the town told me you had a kid out here."

"I'd be surprised if anyone knew," he said. "It's none of their business."

"Whose…" I struggled. "I mean, you're a bit…mature…to have a newborn."

"It's a long story," he said. "If you're not here about the child, then it's none of your business, either."

The baby played with the teething ring. I sat on the arm of the sofa and watched the man taking a bottle of formula from the fridge, boiling the kettle, pouring the water into a bowl. He rested the milk bottle in the bowl, turned it slowly, the baby grizzling against his chest. The hand that held the baby's bottom tapped it gently, a soft, steady beat. This man had raised children before. But as I looked around the walls, there were no pictures of them. The baby's arrival seemed to have been an unplanned thing. There was a small bag of children's clothes by the door and not a toy in sight. The infant and the man were alone out here. There was no sign of a woman's touch about the place. I spied a handgun on the counter beside some old books full of handwritten notes.

"What are you here for?" Jed asked.

"I'm part of the investigation into Theo Campbell's death."

"His what?" Jed was testing the temperature of the milk on his hairy forearm. "Theo Campbell's not dead."

"I've got a forensics team who begs to differ."

"What happened?"

I noted the question. *What happened?* rather than *Who killed him?*, a question that might have suggested he knew Theo Campbell had been murdered. The tension in my chest was starting to ease.

"That's what I'd like to know."

"I can't help you," he said. "I stay out of the town as much as I can."

"People down there don't seem to like you."

He snorted a small laugh. Bitter, and tired. "I don't fit into the narrative."

I was beginning to think he didn't fit into my narrative either, that I was wasting my time out here. It didn't make sense that this man would have been setting up bombings, planning to terrorize a town full of people with a baby strapped into the passenger seat of his dusty old ute. I found myself hazarding a few steps closer to the man and the child, a strange desire stirring in me to see the baby's eyes.

I was knocked out of my spell by the sound of barking coming from outside the house. Jed and I turned toward the sound, and I saw Digger the dog crossing in front of my car, sniffing at the wheels.

"That bloody dog," I said. "It sure gets around."

"You can take it back to town before I shoot it," Jed said, slipping out from between me and the kitchen counter, taking the baby out of sight. "I'll give you a thirty-second head start."

CHAPTER 47

SNALE WAS WAITING for me outside John Destro's beautiful, sprawling mansion just down from the schoolhouse on the northern side of Last Chance Valley. Dez had organized the dinner with Snale—the officer agreed he had the best relationships with everyone in Last Chance, would know things about them that she didn't. Dez seemed somehow to have secured all the best grass in the small town. To the right of the double garage I could see an extensive green lawn softening to sparse fields inhabited by slow-moving cows. The animals made long shadows as the sun lingered on the edge of the valley rim.

"Where did you go?"

"I went out to see Jed Chatt," I said.

"What!" Snale slapped my arm. "By yourself? Are you crazy?"

"I don't think he's as scary as you all make out."

"He's plenty scary," she said. "It's not right, him living out there all by himself with nothing to do. Creeping into the town to buy his supplies, not talking to anybody. It's weird. I wish he'd just go off somewhere else. He gives me the willies."

I don't fit into the narrative. Jed's words came back to me. *I don't fit in.*

"Is he the only member of the Chatt family living nearby?" I asked.

Snale nodded. "All his people moved on years ago," she said, walking me to the front doors of Dez's house. "They were all scattered around, and it was tense, you know, because of the fight between the two families way back when. Some were in the town, but they didn't seem to belong. They all went their separate ways eventually, but he stayed. Making us all feel bad for the way we live down here in the valley."

"Do you know much about his family?" I asked. "The ones who moved on?"

"No." Snale shrugged. "I don't think they keep in touch."

I didn't want to mention the baby. Jed had been right to suspect that, as a non-local cop, I'd probably come out to check on the welfare of the child in his care, concerned about the inappropriateness of the environment for raising a baby. I knew plenty about child custody from my time as a foster kid. There was no way the authorities would condone the arrangement out there, Jed and the baby alone in the desert, the guns and the blistering isolation.

I thought about my mother. When child services had come and taken my brother and me away from her, we'd been covered in cigarette burns and rashes, malnourished and bruised. The one-bedroom apartment where we lived with her, her pimp and another man had been raided on suspicion of drug dealing the week before by police, the door splintered and duct-taped back together from being kicked in. A cop in the raiding party had probably reported my brother's and my condition to child services.

I wasn't going to be the cop who brought child services down on Jed Chatt. But I knew I wanted to go back, to understand what was happening out there. To discover if the man was a danger to himself, the baby, or the town.

CHAPTER 48

WE ENTERED THE high-ceilinged hall of the house. There were pictures lining the walls, framed landscapes of the sun hitting Last Chance Valley at different romantic angles, some vintage blueprints of the town pub and the post office. I stopped by a charcoal sketch of a bunch of European settlers standing by the edge of the empty valley, shovels and pickaxes on their backs, their bonneted wives hugging children nearby.

"This was done by my great-uncle," Dez said, coming up beside me. He smelled of aftershave and was dressed crisply in a stark white shirt and tie. "Beautiful artwork, right? The family camped up there on the ridge for two months while the men went down and prepared the valley."

"Hmm," I said. "It's nice."

"There are more here." He led me into the living room. "Make yourself at home. Can I get you a glass of wine?"

Kash was standing on the porch looking at the cows in the field, a small glass of what might have been Scotch in his hand. I could only see a slice of his profile, but he looked sad. I wondered if he'd spoken to Tenacity while I'd been out with Jed. He noticed me through the window, glanced a little guiltily at his Scotch. I smiled.

The girl who wandered out from the kitchen came as a surprise. A waif-like figure with long blonde hair. Dez's daughter. She'd managed to escape her father's squat, bulky frame but she had his ginger freckles snaking down her cream-colored arms. She came over and stood beside me, admiring the sketch.

"This is from the north side," she said, pointing. "They walked around the whole valley trying to find the best way in before they descended. It was treacherous. They lost a couple of horses just trying to get down."

"Harriet, allow me to introduce my daughter, Bella. She's been hearing stories of the Destro settlement since she was a kid." Dez was setting the table. I took a chair on the end, next to Snale.

"Do you live here with your dad?" I asked. Bella smirked. She was wearing a T-shirt that read "I'd wear it if it came in black" and shorts, a pair of expensive slippers. She went to a nearby chair and sat down.

"Hardly. I'm just visiting. I'm supposed to be studying for end-of-year exams. I'm at Sydney Uni, law and politics."

I almost choked on my drink.

"Yeah." Bella gave me a forgiving smile, curled her feet up into her chair like a cat. "I know who you are. I've been following your brother's case since the girls started disappearing. Most of my courses were online at the time, so I wasn't around, but people were pretty scared. I watched it all on the TV. And then Dad told me you were out here. I mean, wow. Did you have any idea your brother was killing chicks?"

"Bella!" Dez snapped. "Detective Blue doesn't want to discuss her brother's situation. This is supposed to be a friendly dinner."

The girl shrugged.

Dez put out snacks and we made small talk about the town and its various characters. Kash was quiet, staring into his drink. In time Dez cleared the plates and we sat down at the dining table. I could feel Bella's eyes wandering over me while I talked to Snale.

"Do you know much about her brother's case?" Bella asked Snale, leaning around me.

"Bell, really," Snale sighed.

"Hey, everybody's got skeletons in their closet," the girl said, playing with her fork. "I don't think you've got anything to be ashamed of, Harry. Our people slaughtered the Indigenous inhabitants of Last Chance Valley when they settled here. They banished the survivors to the desert. Two centuries later there's only one of them left, loitering out there in the badlands like a stain no one can get out."

Dez sighed at the ceiling. "Do we have to talk about this?"

Bella was watching me carefully, waiting for a reaction.

"People think they called it Last Chance because of all the desert," she said. "Your last chance for food and shelter before the big barren nothingness in all directions. But it's not true. The Destro family turned up, and told the natives to get out. And when they wouldn't, they gave them one last chance before they came down the mountainside with their guns."

"Bella!" Dez thumped the tabletop. "Go into the kitchen and check on the roast."

The girl sauntered away, leaving tension and embarrassment in her wake.

CHAPTER 49

"THIS IS WHAT you get when you send your children to university."
Dez ran a hand over his receding hairline, made a stiff tuft of the dark
orange hair that remained. "They come back *critical thinkers*. Ready to
question everything."

"Is she right?" I asked as Bella brought out some small plates of a
first course. "Did your ancestors kill off the Indigenous population of
the valley?"

"The history is not as concrete as Bella would have you believe," Dez
said. "The Destro people kept diaries and logs, and there are things
we can infer from their letters back and forth to England. But it was
mainly the womenfolk doing the writing, and they didn't note that sort
of thing down. Certainly there were fatalities. But we don't know if
that's because there were accidents when the Indigenous people tried
to help the Destro family settle or what. Jed's ancestors were nomadic,
as I understand it, so I don't see why our people wouldn't have just
moved them on if a disagreement occurred."

"Last Chance Valley is an anomaly out here," Bella said. "As you've likely noticed. The soil is different. It holds water. It's sheltered. The high rock walls make hunting easier. This is the best place for a settlement for hundreds of kilometers around. I wouldn't give it up without a fight, if it were me."

"Well, it's not you, darling." Dez smiled stiffly and patted his daughter's hand. He continued. "Whether some were killed or not, the majority of the Indigenous residents resettled outside the valley and then moved on. Now, only Jed remains. I've tried to bring him back into the fold but he's not interested. He's a stubborn man."

"You tried to enlist him as a tourist attraction," Bella retorted.

"A what?" Snale asked.

"I tried to get his help on the leadership program," Dez said. "Bella is convinced I was being racist."

"You were."

"I run a program every year with kids from the surrounding towns," Dez explained to me. "Anyone can apply for it, and I liaise with the teachers to find out who the best candidates are. Who has the most potential. I take three or four kids out into the desert, and we do exercises. I thought maybe Jed could help me out, with some of his cultural knowledge. As part of the government reconciliation program, Jed's people were given native title for a lot of land out there beyond the town limits. I don't know that he makes much use of it. There's nothing out there. But he legally owns it, and he could exclude us from it if he ever desired. I thought maybe he could take us around, you know? He'd know things. Desert sustenance, for example. The importance of certain landmarks and animals to the Aboriginal people of this area."

"Racist."

"Bella!"

"What? It's racist," she insisted. "You're making a whole host of degrading cultural assumptions. You assume this guy must be some sort of mystical Aboriginal tracker just because he's got Indigenous heritage." She waggled her fingers like she was doing a magic trick. "He'll talk to you about the rainbow serpent and how the kangaroo got its tail and he'll just forget about all the *rape of his native land* stuff. All that unpleasantness is in the past, right?"

Dez covered his eyes.

"Even if this guy did have loads of really interesting cultural knowledge, why would you assume he'd want to share that knowledge with you?"

"Why wouldn't he?" Dez shrugged.

"You're right." Bella sipped her wine. "Of *course* he would. He'd be *so pleased* to be of assistance, to be *invited* to be a part of the town."

"What do you suggest I do with him, then?"

"Don't *do* anything with him," Bella said. "He clearly wants to be left alone. Leave him alone. The guy doesn't want to connect with the people of this town because he doesn't like them. You can't make people like you."

"How could you not like us?" Snale said. "We're lovely."

"Someone's trying to kill you all, Vicky," Bella said. "You can't be that nice."

CHAPTER 50

DEZ STARED AT the ceiling. He seemed to be looking for an escape hatch from his daughter's accusations.

"Let me show you one of our albums," he said. He went to a nearby cabinet and fished out a photo album. I put the book between Snale and me and started flipping through the pictures. Gangly teenagers, all lanky with knobbly knees and big smiles, crouched on rocks before the sheer edge of Last Chance Valley. Some were climbing a huge rock formation in the desert. Some stood pointing toward the horizon. Bright faces, sunburned girls and boys sitting in the light of a fire.

"What sort of leadership stuff do you do with the kids out there?" I asked.

"Navigation, emergency survival techniques, a bit of endurance and adventure training."

Kash had perked up beside me.

"That sounds awesome!" he said. "How'd you develop the program?"

"Oh, I'm an old reservist, myself."

"That's great." Kash downed his Scotch quickly. "I'd love to know what techniques you're using. Do you get them into any self-defense tactics?"

"Well, I would, but I don't have much experience in—"

"Oh, wow." Kash pulled his chair in, sat upright like an obedient German shepherd. "I have some great drills for young people. Leadership stuff, like you're looking for. I got my certification as a recruit trainer a while back. I could definitely assist."

The two fell into conversation. Bella appeared in a couple of the photographs, hanging out at the edge of the frame, fiddling with her bag or staring at the fire. She was watching me from across the table, one leg drawn up so that her elbow rested on her knee, pushing food restlessly around her plate.

"Did you go on many of the expeditions?" I asked.

"A few," she said. "It was usually me behind the camera."

Snale looked at an image of Dez leading a bunch of kids through a search-and-rescue drill, four of them carrying another on a stretcher. Bella seemed the only person not interested in the photos.

"So who killed Theo Campbell?" Bella asked idly, with a mouth full of beans. I had to draw myself away from the adventures before me.

"You tell me," I said.

"I think he was into some tricky stuff." She smiled. "He was starting to get a bit loose with the rules by the time I was ready to leave here for uni last year. Around that time he caught a bunch of us on the south ridge hanging out, smokin' weed."

I looked to Bella's father to see if he'd react to his daughter's admission. But he was busy talking to Kash.

"Chief Campbell didn't do anything," Bella continued. "Didn't even take it off us. Just stopped and chatted for a while. I half expected him to ask for a toke. Guess he was getting old. Didn't care anymore."

"And who exactly were you up there smoking weed with, young lady?" Snale asked.

"You know me, Vicky." Bella tapped the side of her nose. "I'm good with my secrets." Something over my shoulder, through the glass doors to the porch, caught her eye. She leaned sideways, took another spoonful of beans into her mouth.

"Better get your guns out, coppers," she said, seeming amused and nodding toward the doors. "There's trouble out there."

CHAPTER 51

THE SOUND OF footsteps, followed by thumping at the front door. I'd risen from my chair instinctively and dashed down the hall, my gun stupidly still on the coffee table where I'd left it before dinner. Zac Taby was leaning against the door, bashing on it with his hands. He all but fell into my arms as I yanked it open. He was drenched in sweat and shaking.

"They're after me! They're after me!"

"What the hell's going on?"

"Help! They shot at me! They're trying to kill me!"

I went out into the night. It was quiet. On the road in the distance I could see a car stopped, its headlights picking up the evening dust shifting in the gentle breeze, the occasional fluttering of a locust attracted to its beams. I started down the garden path and out of Dez's front gate. Kash was close behind me, actioning his pistol.

"Who is it?"

"Probably Jace Robit and his merry band of meatheads."

"If they fired a shot at that kid, we'll need to bring them all in."

"I'll just talk to them," I said, waving him off. "Stay here. We don't want to present a hostile front."

The car remained idle, the engine humming as I approached. I could see there were four men in it. The elbow hanging out the driver's side indeed belonged to the leathery brown body of Jace Robit. He was watching me approach with a small smile playing about his lips. I knew these men. Though they'd used their truck tonight to chase down a frightened teenager, cracking pot shots off over his head to put the fear of God into him, he wasn't their usual quarry. These were the guys who went out chasing, hunting, gutting bush pigs and kangaroos. The bloodthirsty, bored, angry men of small towns who had too much fire-power and not enough targets to keep them satisfied.

I gained speed as I approached the car, lifted my boot as I got within range and kicked the mirror off the driver's side door. The mirror and its casing smashed into the road, glass sparkling in the dim light.

"Hey! What the fuck!"

Jace shouldered the door open, jumped down and grabbed my shoulder, fingers going for the underside of my arm in a bruising grip. I gave him a half-strength jab to the face, sending him stumbling back, more surprised than injured.

"I told you to leave that kid alone," I said. "You got hearing problems?"

"And I told *you* that we handle things ourselves out here," Jace said. The other men were out of the truck now and all around me. Two were behind me, blocking Kash's advance. My partner was on the road, a hundred meters back and approaching fast, his gun by his side.

"That kid's a danger to our town." Jace pointed at the house. "We want him out. I don't care what you do with him. Take him back to the fucking city with you. Take him into—what d'you call it— protective custody."

"He hasn't done anything wrong."

One of the farmers behind me snorted.

"You're not from around here, sweetheart," Jace sneered. "You've got to understand. There are people who belong here, and people who don't. And the Taby kid doesn't belong. In the bush, you have the native animals, and you have introduced species." He held one palm up, then another, separate. "Like feral cats. They prey on the natives. If you don't squash 'em before they multiply, suddenly you'll be overrun."

"Thanks for the environmental science class," I said. "Truly enlightening. I have a couple of lessons of my own, you know. But you're not going to enjoy them. So I'm telling you just one last time. Get back in that truck and fuck off home, before I decide to start teaching." A ripple of surprise went up through the group of men around me. They looked at each other and laughed. None of them backed down.

"Harry." Kash was at the edge of the gathering now. "Don't."

"Don't what?" Jace sniffed, looked me up and down.

"You heard the man, Elliot," I said, cracking my knuckles. "He said they handle things themselves out here. So let's handle it."

CHAPTER 52

WHEN I FIGHT men, they try to put me on the ground first. They don't want to punch a woman right away. Not until they understand that I'm no ordinary woman. They figure they can grab me and push me into the dirt and I'll realize that I've been playing big boy games and I need to go back to my dolls and stop fooling myself. Jace Robit was a hard man. Wiry strength from years working on farms, burning off fat and loading muscle around uncrackable bones. His big hands came for my shoulders again. I ducked and stepped sideways, gave him a fast uppercut to the ribs, knocking the wind out of him. He stumbled, tried to swing an arm around the back of my neck. I bowed out of it, stepped behind him and kicked him in the arse.

A short, involuntary laugh from the men around him, a sudden betrayal. Jace's fury was rising quickly. Big mistake, fighting angry. I was enjoying this. I wanted them all to jump in at once. This was my therapy. I sidestepped Jace as he came for me again but he saw the move, swung and glanced his knuckles off my ear. I took the pain. Lapped it up gratefully. I stepped forward and faked a left jab, punched him square in the nose with my right.

Blood on the dirt. Exhilaration zapped through me at the sight of it.

"Steady on!" One of the farmers stepped toward us, having had quite enough of my show. He grabbed me from behind and I kicked Jace in the chest, used the backward momentum to shove me into the second attacker, the two of us barreling into the ground. I rolled, righted, stepped on his hand and heard a crunch. The man screamed.

"Grab her," one of them said. "Fucking grab her, John!"

"Yeah, John,"—I beckoned the man with a wave—"come grab me."

The two of them lunged at me at once. Hardly fair, but not unexpected. They thought I'd back up, so I dove instead for John's legs and felt him tumble over me, his own momentum working against him. John's friend came for me and I kicked up at him from the ground, catching him in the chin.

Jace's nose was pouring blood down his face as his friends dragged him to his feet. The men gathered together to reassess the situation. Mentions of a "psycho bitch."

I wasn't done yet. But when I beckoned the men forward again, none of them moved. They just stood there, panting, bewildered by the first devastating round.

"Come on," I urged. My own fury was starting to rise. No one moved. "Oh, for fuck's sake! You pussies!"

I watched the men drive off past Dez's house, standing in the dark beside Kash. My partner had surprisingly little to say at first. We walked back down the dusty road together under the stars. I hadn't even exerted myself enough to break a sweat. The punch in the ear had caused a warm, throbbing pain that wasn't entirely unpleasant. I reached up and held it, relished in the hurt. It would bruise. It'd be hard to sleep on it. That was something, at least. Kash laughed after a while and I looked up at him.

"I thought you said we didn't want to present a hostile front," he said.

"That wasn't hostile," I said. "Hostile would have been arresting them on sight. They wanted us to speak their language. I spoke it. I just wish they'd held out longer."

He didn't reply. I knew how it sounded. My brother was accused of being one of the most vicious, violent people in the nation's history, and here I was, upset that I hadn't been able to beat a bunch of men into unconsciousness. But the words just came out of me before I could stop them. Kash glanced sideways at me and I caught it—the wary look of someone assessing a threat.

The truth was, Kash was right to be wary of me. Most of my life I'd wavered over a very thin line between light and dark sides of my being. There were things in me that were frightening. How quick I was to anger. How much I liked hurting people sometimes. My mind was full of shadowy places where violent fantasies lived, sickening things that sometimes came out in my dreams. Vengeance I played out mentally against bad people from my past. Most of the time, my light half won out, and the shadows and smoke were sent recoiling to where they belonged, not completely driven out, but controlled.

But sometimes, the halves collided. The score came down fifty fifty, and everyone was left guessing what I might do.

Even me.

CHAPTER 53

WHITT HAD DECIDED he wasn't comfortable with Tox Barnes at all. A Sydney colleague had warned him that he'd suffer consequences from associating himself with the shaggy, despondent detective. That a deep, hidden sin in Tox's past, a double murder, some said, meant that he was an enemy within the ranks of the police, and that he was to be avoided at all costs.

It wasn't just that, though. To be in the man's presence felt hazardous, like a journey along a frozen road at night with rain battering the windshield. The man spoke little, laughed almost never, and caused people who didn't even know him to shift out of his path. He was stale-smelling and dusty all the time, as though when he went home at night to wherever in the world that might be, he simply tucked himself into a closet and closed the door. Whitt's own terrible history had caused him to become almost obsessed with freshness and newness, the cleanliness and orderliness of packaged things. He changed his toothbrush on the first of every month. He littered his sock drawer with moisture absorbers. If things weren't exactly right, they were deeply, inexcusably wrong.

Whitt was having those familiar nervous palpitations as he approached Tox on the third floor of the University of Sydney west car park.

"I got the CCTV," Whitt said, drawing a sheet of paper from the folder tucked under his arm. He handed Tox a grainy photograph printed from the security system of a hock shop in Bondi Junction. Whitt had managed to track down footage of the purchase of the video camera found in Sam Blue's apartment, originally stolen from an apartment in Elizabeth Bay. The still showed a man in a cap exiting the front doors of the store.

"It's not a great picture," Whitt said.

"No. It's not." Tox sighed. "Could be Sam Blue. Could be his grandmother."

"I'm going to get it analyzed," Whitt said. "See if we can measure the man's dimensions against the angle of the camera and the doorway. He seems taller than Blue to me."

"You talk to the Simpson girl?"

"Yes."

"Convinced?"

Whitt struggled. "She maintains everything from her last statement. The white van. The screaming. Caitlyn standing there as she ran past."

"We'll soon find out," Tox said.

Whitt took a deep breath and looked around at the car park. They walked to the door to the fire stairs. Was this where Caitlyn McBeal had taken her last breaths of free air?

And if it was, would she ever take any again?

CHAPTER 54

"THIS IS WHERE both girls allegedly entered," Whitt said, walking through the fire-escape door. He glanced down the stairwell. "I suppose the abductor might have seen Linny coming up the stairs. Decided she was his type. Thought he'd stand here, wait for her to come through." He walked back through the door and leaned against the wall, made like he was ready to pounce. "Linny comes through. He grabs her, drags her that way, over to where that white van is sitting."

Whitt pointed to a car space fifty meters away where a white van sat with the side door open. He paused, puzzled at the sight of it sitting there, the very same make and model of vehicle the witness had described in her interviews. Tox had his hands in his pockets. He looked nonchalantly toward the van.

"So what we want to know is," Tox said, "how likely is Linny's story? Why did no one hear her screams and then Caitlyn being abducted? Would the attacker have been able to drag Caitlyn fifty meters to the van? Where and how might he have left traces of the crime if he did?"

Whitt was still puzzled by the van. He looked at Tox.

"That's the same kind of van Linny reported seeing at the abduction," Whitt said.

"Uh-huh." Tox nodded. "It's my van. I brought it here for the purposes of our experiment."

"What experiment?"

Tox didn't answer. He was watching a woman walking toward them up the slope of the ramp, her enormous spike heels clopping like horseshoes on the asphalt. Whitt's first thought was that university students sure dressed differently now to the way they did when he studied. As she got closer, however, Whitt began to notice bruises on her slender white legs, climbing all the way to the hem of the tiny miniskirt. The long blonde ponytail was clearly fake—clipped-in extensions. She put the phone she'd been texting on away in a small faux-fur handbag and smiled broadly at Tox.

"Detective Barnes," she said, hardly glancing at Whitt. "It's been a long time, honey."

"Sure has." Tox looked warm and friendly, Whitt thought. A sudden transformation of his usually dark being. Something was not right. "Whitt, this is Sandy. Sandy, Whitt."

"This is a bit of a weird place for a two-on-one," Sandy smirked uneasily, looking around the car park. "Are we getting out of here, or...?"

"Oh no, we'll play our game right here," Tox said. He checked his watch. There was a strange, tight pause as the man simply stood there, smiling at the girl's face. Whitt opened his mouth to ask what was going on, but before he could Tox lunged at the girl, grabbing her by both arms, yanking her toward him.

"You're coming with me, girly!" Tox snarled.

"Whoa!" Whitt stumbled backwards. "Whoa! Whoa!"

"What are you doing?" Sandy screamed. "What are you doing! Help! Help!"

The girl in Tox's arms suddenly sprang to life, bucking and twisting in his grip. The two of them fell into the side of a parked car.

Whitt launched himself forward, trying to wrestle the girl from Tox's grip as he dragged her toward the van. Her screaming was so loud up close that his eardrums pulsed.

"Please! Stop! Help me!"

"Stop, Tox! Let her go!"

Tox threw his weight sideways, knocking Whitt into another car, sending his glasses skidding across the asphalt. Sandy twisted in Tox's arms, bashed at his head with her forearms. He stopped and adjusted his grip, hugged her to him like a child and loped in the direction of the van with her howling against his chest.

"In you go!" he laughed triumphantly, placing Sandy in the cabin of the van and slamming the door. Sandy was screaming, beating on the door with her fists. Whitt limped toward Tox, his lower back aching from slamming into the side mirror of a nearby Toyota.

"What the hell is wrong with you? Let her out of there!"

"Fifty seconds," Tox said, glancing at his watch. He pushed the door of the van open and Sandy got out. She slapped Tox hard across the side of the head.

"You arsehole!" she panted. "What the fuck is wrong with you?"

"It was just a game, sweetheart." Tox reached out and took her shoulders in his big, calloused hands, smoothed her arms. "That's all. No need to get your pretty feathers all ruffled."

"You're crazy," Sandy huffed and tried to assess the damage the struggle had done to her artificial hair. "You've always been a crazy fuck." She slapped him again, hard, across the face.

Tox peeled a couple of hundreds off a roll he produced from his pocket. Sandy snatched the bills and tucked them into her bra, held her hand out for more. Tox sighed and peeled again. Sandy frowned at Whitt.

"Great load of help you were," she snapped, jutting her chin at Whitt. "Was this your idea? You some kinda freak who likes to watch abductions?"

"No, no," Whitt protested. "I really—"

"What the hell was that all for?"

"I needed a screamer," Tox said. "A real screamer. Not someone faking it. We're being scientists today, darling."

Sandy looked unconvinced. A man in a gray uniform was running up the slope toward them, his hand on his belt.

"What's going on?" He wiped at a sweaty head of black hair. "Who's in trouble?"

"You are," Tox said.

CHAPTER 55

"I'M DETECTIVE INSPECTOR Tate Barnes and this is Detective Inspector Edward Whittacker." Tox paused when he got to Sandy. "And this is... our associate. We're investigating the abduction of Caitlyn McBeal."

"Oh," the man said. He brushed at the front of his gray uniform, fiddled with a name badge that read *Bill Perkins: Security*.

"William Perkins. You're the security guard who gave police a statement about that day, aren't you?" Tox folded his arms.

"Yes."

"Interesting." Tox glanced at the sunshine streaming in through the side of the lot. "Same day of the week. Same hour of the day that Caitlyn was apparently abducted. Wind direction seems to be more or less the same. You hear the screams of a woman, screams that last fifty seconds, and you come running."

"Yes." Bill shifted uncomfortably.

"You were down there in your little security guard's hut on the first floor just now, were you?"

"Uh-huh." Bill cleared his throat.

"That's where you said you were at the time of Caitlyn's alleged abduction."

"Yep."

"So all the variables are the same as they were on that day. But you said in your statement that you didn't hear any screams," Tox said. "You said you heard no screams, no scuffle on the third floor. You said you didn't see a white van exit the driveway anywhere around that time."

The security guard looked intently at Sandy. She was the safe place to look. Whitt and Tox's eyes bored into the man's face, assessing every muscle twitch.

"Were you where you were supposed to be on that day, Mr. Perkins?"

"Yes." Bill straightened. "I was."

"Really?" Whitt raised an eyebrow.

"Yes."

"What if, for example..." Tox mused. "What if I took your head, Bill Perkins, and I put it in the gap of the sliding door of my van here." He gestured to the van. "And I slammed the door closed, over and over?"

Bill swallowed, looked at Whitt for help. There was none.

"Would your answer still be the same?" Tox asked.

Bill started to back up, then turned and ran.

"Answer the question!" Tox called. The security guard put his head down and ran for his life. Tox sighed, pulled a packet of cigarettes from his pocket and lit one.

"He wasn't in the guard hut that day," he exhaled. "I don't know where he was, but he wasn't there."

CHAPTER 56

AFTER SANDY LEFT them, the two men walked to the edge of the car park and leaned on the concrete wall, Tox smoking, Whitt trying to contain his inner horror at his partner's "experiment." They looked over the edge and across a wide, empty netball court to a narrow green lawn where students were filming interviews with handycams, sitting on wooden benches, now and then glancing at written notes as they narrated their works.

"Maybe Bill the Security Idiot was in the bathroom," Tox mused. "Maybe he has a girlfriend on campus he was visiting. Maybe he was listening to music. Whatever the case, it's possible Linny Simpson was telling the truth. Someone did try to abduct her, and she screamed her head off, and no one heard her."

Whitt didn't know if that made him feel better or worse.

"But the van doesn't make sense," Whitt reminded him. "No white van came or went during the time Caitlyn would have been taken."

"Where is she?" Tox growled. "If we could just find her, this would all make sense."

The two men watched the people on the lawn below them.

"What are these chumps up to?" Tox wondered aloud. Whitt looked across the lot at the young people with their cameras.

"Film class, looks like."

"Maybe they have some footage from that day." Tox blew smoke into the wind.

"They'd have heard the screaming though," Whitt said. "Wouldn't they?"

"Not with those headphones on," Tox said.

Whitt followed nervously as Tox descended the concrete stairs to the little garden. The students stopped their filming and assessed Tox as he arrived among them. Four of them were gathered around a single camera, thick headphones clamped to their heads. They took down the headphones.

"S'up?" Tox jutted his chin at the leader of the group, a lanky late-teenager with a shaving rash and long, greasy dreadlocks.

"Nothing much," the boy answered.

"What's this?" Tox gestured to the group, the cameras.

"Film assignment."

"Been doing it long?"

"A few months. It's our major assessment task. It's due next week."

"Hmm." Tox rocked on his heels. "Let me look at it."

"What?"

"I want to look at it."

"Why?"

"Because I said so." Tox shrugged, the gentle, menacing shrug of a dangerous man. "Let me look at it."

Whitt cleared his throat. He understood why Tox was being myste-rious with the youths. If there was footage relevant to the abduction of Caitlyn McBeal, Tox and Whitt would need to confiscate it. And that would take a warrant, and a warrant would take time. A search of the students' footage was technically illegal. Whitt didn't like all the muscling Tox was doing. But he couldn't bring himself to stop what was about to happen. His personal and professional ethics were slowly, slowly degrading.

"We don't have to show you anything," the dreadlocked boy said. Tox didn't reply. He reached out and grabbed the nearest handycam, plucking it from the grip of a young woman with green hair. He stood in the sun and started pushing buttons on the screen, flipping through dates on the digital files. The students exchanged glances, wide-eyed. Whitt held his hand out apologetically to another handycam holder. The young man gave a confused glance to their leader and then handed over the camera.

"Who are these guys?" someone whispered.

"Should we...call someone?"

"What's this all about?" one of the girls asked Whitt. "We've got permits. We're not doing anything wrong."

"We'll just be a minute," Whitt said gently. "I'm really sorry."

"Any footage of drug-taking on those cameras is strictly staged," one of the young people said, eyes on the sky. "We're making a...public awareness film."

"Got it." Tox showed Whitt his camcorder screen. "Ten July. Three pm."

The two men huddled together, watching the students' interview on the tiny screen. The camera faced the car park exit, the driveway at the corner of the image. Anticipation churned in Whitt's chest.

Tox fast-forwarded the footage. The girl on the screen twisted and shivered, her mouth jabbering silently. She was wearing headphones too, doing a sound check. A dark green sedan exited the car park. The footage ended.

The two men exhaled. The students around them seemed to sense that whatever they were looking for was not on their footage. Tox handed the tiny camera back to the girl he'd taken it from.

"Thanks, guys." Whitt smiled. They turned and started wandering away, but after only a few steps he stopped. There was a zinging feeling creeping up from his fingertips. A flush of heat in his throat that even he didn't know the cause of at first. Suddenly, he realized. It all fell into place. He gripped his partner's arm.

CHAPTER 57

"WHAT?" TOX GRUNTED.

Whitt's mind was rushing. He struggled to form words.

"What?" Tox repeated.

"How do we know it was a white van?" Whitt asked.

"Linny Simpson said the guy tried to drag her into a white van."

"But has anyone else ever said that? Has there ever been a white van connected with the other missing girls?"

"Well..." Tox thought about it. "No."

"It's always a white van, isn't it?" Whitt's heart was beginning to race in his chest. "In the movies. People are always abducted into black or white vans. What if Linny Simpson was right about everything that happened to her *except* the vehicle?"

Whitt closed his eyes. Remembered Linny sitting before him at the cafe table.

"She said the van door was closed." He looked at Tox. "When the guy, the abductor, dragged her over to the van, he didn't manage to get her into the back of the vehicle. It was closed. That doesn't make sense."

"Why not?"

"He'd have left it open. Surely he didn't plan to grab her, drag her all the way over to the van, drop her on the ground and expect her to lie there while he pulled the door open."

"How sure was she that the van door was closed?" Tox asked. "She took a blow to the head. She fainted afterward. That's one of the main reasons the police rejected her story, because they think she was confused."

Whitt shrugged helplessly. Tox considered Whitt's words. Then he walked back to the group of students and plucked up the camera again.

"Hey, we need that!" one of the girls cried. "It's due next week!"

"It's worth a shot," Tox said. "Let's get a BOLO on the green sedan. See what turns up."

Whitt was rubbing the bridge of his nose as they ascended the fire stairs, a headache pulsing behind his eyes.

"Oh shit!" he said. "My glasses!"

He jogged up the stairs, remembering the clatter of his glasses as Tox knocked him sideways in the struggle for Sandy. He searched between the cars, bent low and looked under greasy tires. He spotted them deep under a blue Camry. Before he could get down, Tox put a hand on his chest.

"Not in that fancy outfit."

Whitt watched as Tox crawled under the car, dragging himself forward on his belly on the asphalt. He seemed to linger under the vehicle a little too long, the legs of his filthy jeans unmoving.

"You all right under there?"

Tox scrambled out from under the car, threw the glasses at Whitt's chest. He jogged around the back of the Camry, head low and eyes narrowed, like a hound.

"What is it?"

"This channel," Tox said. "This drainage channel."

He pointed to a narrow drainage channel cut into the asphalt, covered with a blackened and oil-covered grille. Tox all but dove under a car two down from where they had stood. Whitt heard the scrape of iron.

Tox reappeared, grinning triumphantly, smeared with grease, and holding a broken phone.

CHAPTER 58

IT WAS TIME to go. Time to risk it all. Caitlyn had tried to bargain with her captor. She'd tried to reason with him. Hell, she'd even tried sympathizing with him, attempting to understand the kind of sickness a mind like his must have. She understood that she had become an animal to him. An inconvenient pet. He didn't speak to her. His eyes hardly ever found hers anymore. He was beginning to feed her only every second day. It was clear to Caitlyn that her captor didn't know what to do with her now. She wouldn't survive waiting for him to decide. This was it. She would have to put everything on the line. Fight or die.

Fighting meant lying as still as she could on her belly in the middle of the floor, the wine bottles smashed all around her. The sour, eggy smell of expired alcohol was making her eyes water. She lay for hours before she heard the footsteps in the corridor. Hesitant, soft. She heard him shifting back the things he used to block the doorway, the scrape and thump of the biggest thing, the rattling and jangling of the smaller things. His hands on the locks. Caitlyn closed her eyes and eased a long breath into her aching lungs, let it slip through her lips. *Softly, softly*, she thought. If she screwed this up, it was all over.

She felt no fear. One way or another, it was about to be over.

CHAPTER 59

I SAT UP in my fold-out bed on Snale's porch, listening to the sounds of the night birds and clicking away at my laptop. I was sending inquiries about Sam's case. Whitt had emailed a list of leads that he and Tox were working on. A green sedan. A broken phone. The fight with Jace Robit's people, and the optimistic tone of Whitt's email, had lit a fire in me. Earlier, I'd managed to get a fifteen-minute phone conversation with Sam, and my brother sounded healthy, and calm despite the catcalls in the background. I sent a request to my chief, Pops, to have the security guard from the car park reinterviewed by Nigel's team. I wanted to get in touch with the detectives in the Gold Coast chasing down sightings of Caitlyn McBeal, to find out if there was any truth to the rumors.

From a thin mattress on the floor beside my bed, Zac Taby spoke up, breaking my concentration.

"So you work on the town's case all day, and you work on your brother's case all night," he said.

"Uh-huh."

"When do you sleep?"

"Sleep is for losers."

"True."

The Taby parents had been mortified first that their son had escaped lockdown at their house, then that he'd been chased like a dog by people from the town. They had been happy to turn him over to us.

"If my typing is keeping you awake, you're welcome to move your mattress away from mine," I told the boy. "No one invited you to sleep this close to me. Frankly, it's weird."

"No way, man," the boy said. "I'm stickin' next to you. You're my guard dog now. You whooped some freakin' arse out there. I'm not leaving your side for nothin'."

I didn't know whether to feel flattered or annoyed by my description as a "guard dog." It had a certain truth to it. I'd have liked to be a guard dog. Unthinking, unquestioning, a loyal hound who followed someone I loved at all hours of the day, searching for threats and receiving treats in return for my service. It seemed a blessedly uncomplicated life.

I heard a grunting, snuffling sound, and Jerry the pig appeared in the doorway to the living room. The huge animal tested the air with its snout a few times as Zac and I watched. Then it lumbered with effort down the single stair onto the porch and took up residence by the teenager's side, crashing to the ground, a mountain of hairy flesh falling. It seemed the coolest place to sleep that night was by my side.

"How much did you say all that gold was worth?" Zac asked, his chin resting on his hands on the pillow. The boy had found the rocks on Snale's kitchen table and marveled at our explanation for them, his mouth hanging open and eyes wide. He'd watched us stash them away behind a handful of books in Snale's living room cabinets.

"About eighty thousand bucks, I think."

"We could just, like...take it." His voice was low, conspiratorial.

"What?"

"Why not?" He rolled onto his side. "You and me. We could split it. Get the fuck outta this lame-ass town."

I laughed aloud. "That's a nice fantasy you've got there, but forty thousand dollars isn't a lot of...money." My words faltered. I was wrong. To some people, it was a lot of money. It was enough for my mother to sell out her only son to the press. To endanger his life, possibly contribute to his eternal damnation, at least in the eyes of the public. It wasn't the kind of money you could run away forever on, though. Or was it? What kind of plans did this young man have? How far was far enough from his miserable life in this loveless town?

"If we stayed together, though, it'd be eighty," he mused, a smile playing about his lips.

"Oh, right," I smirked. "I see. You and me, a dusty old convertible, running away across the country together. Staying in dodgy hotels, escaping our problems in each other's arms."

"Hell yes!"

"Please," I sighed. "I'm old enough to be your mother."

"Isn't that kind of hot, though?"

I slid a leg out from under the blanket and kicked him in the side.

"Shut up, idiot boy."

CHAPTER 60

THE BOY FELL asleep quickly, undisturbed by the pig's snores. I lay on my side in the dark, eyes open, staring at the wall. Soon enough, I sighed and picked up my phone, sent a text.

If you refuse the magazine interview, I'll pay you fifty thousand, I wrote. *I can't let you sabotage Sam's defense.*

I waited. In time, the phone vibrated in my hands and the screen lit my face.

How soon can you get it? my mother asked.

I'll transfer it tomorrow, I wrote.

I'd prefer it in cash, she replied.

I'll bet, I thought.

CHAPTER 61

I DIDN'T KNOW I had fallen asleep until the sound came, a wailing, blaring siren that rang in my skull. I shot up and shoved the laptop and phone aside, almost stumbled over the pig on the ground next to Zac's empty mattress. Kash's bare feet thudded on the polished boards of the living room as he rushed out from the front of the house in only boxer shorts, struggling with his glasses. Lights flickered on.

"What is it?"

"A car horn." He was actioning his pistol.

"Where's Zac?"

"What's happening?" Snale ran out of the bedroom in pink pajamas covered in smiling, dancing pigs.

I sprinted through the house and out the front door, my partners in tow.

Zac was sitting in the driver's seat of Snale's four-wheel drive, leaning on the horn, flashing the high beams. His huge eyes followed me, front teeth locked together.

"What is it?" I called. "What? What?"

I reached for the driver's side door beside him but he screamed before I could pull the handle.

"Don't!" he cried through the glass, hands flat, palms out, surrendered. "Don't touch anything! Look! Look!"

He grabbed a sheet of paper from where it had been stuck with tape to the steering wheel. He pressed the paper against the glass.

The words were handwritten. They read "*DON'T GET OUT.*"

CHAPTER 62

THEY SAT IN Whitt's car on the edge of Parramatta Road, the hammering of rain on the roof the only sound they could hear. Though the engine was off, Tox's hard hands gripped the steering wheel. His head was bent forward and his jaw set, his eyes focused on the patterns the rain made on the windshield. Whitt watched him. He could hardly see the man breathing. His own heart hadn't stopped pounding since they'd stood in the little park inside the university. With the camera in his hands, the sound off, he sat watching the green sedan emerge from the car park driveway at the edge of the footage. There was only a shadow behind the wheel. A pair of white hands pulling the steering wheel sideways calmly, turning the vehicle left toward the science district.

"It could be nothing," Whitt warned. "When the lab traces the phone's serial number they might find it just belongs to some other student. Someone who dumped it there on purpose or dropped it as they were getting out of their car."

"It's Caitlyn McBeal's phone," Tox insisted. "It's broken because she broke it in the struggle as she was being abducted."

Whitt sighed.

"The green sedan," he continued. "It might just be a student leaving for the day."

"It's the killer," Tox said. "Leaving with Caitlyn McBeal."

A search on the green sedan's registration had found it was stolen. Whitt told himself that didn't mean anything. Students could drive stolen cars. Buy them, sell them, steal them, trade them—students and old cars had a checkered relationship. It could just have been a coincidence that the sedan was leaving the lot mere moments after Caitlyn was allegedly abducted. As much as he tried to tell himself they were probably onto nothing, Whitt couldn't help but feel a flutter inside him that maybe that was wrong. When Tox's phone chimed, the two men grabbed for it at the same time.

"They've got the car," Whitt said, motioning for his partner to start the engine. "It's outside the old Pinkerton Hotel. Let's go."

CHAPTER 63

CAITLYN HEARD HIS footsteps near her. Shuffling, despondent, probably relieved that she had finally expired quietly and without mess. He'd won. His game hadn't been a fast, violent, painful end for her but a drawn-out one, one in which she would have had to actually give up, cell by biological cell, and let death take her. Now he had her remains to leave here or dispose of as he pleased.

His foot against her shoulder, shoving experimentally, once, and then again. She was limp. It wasn't hard to relax her limbs completely. Just to stay awake was an effort, had been for weeks. She let the darkness take her, little by little.

She heard him groan as he crouched.

Yes, Caitlyn thought. *A little closer now.*

Hidden between her chest and the ground, Caitlyn clutched the chunky hexagonal fixture at the end of the long, thin steel rod she had extracted from one of the old beer kegs. The weapon was blunt, rusty, but it was all she had. She balled her fist around the handle as she felt his breath on the back of her neck.

CHAPTER 64

"OH MY GOD," I stammered, reading the note in Zac's hand. He pointed desperately to the back seat. I stepped sideways and looked in. There were three huge propane gas bottles sitting like round white passengers strapped into the seatbelts. I put my hands on the glass and Zac put his on the other side, staring into my eyes, terror making his whole body shake.

"I didn't see the note until I got into the car!" he screamed. "I didn't see the gas bottles!"

"I know," I shouted. "I know. It's OK. It's OK."

I looked to my partners. Snale was standing well back, her hands over her mouth. Kash was circling the car, looking in the windows. He dropped to the ground in front of the engine and examined the underside of the car. Both were panting like me, the adrenaline rushing so fast through my veins I could hardly think. My mind split into fragments, thoughts racing in different directions. Three or four times the ludicrous impulse jabbed at me to just open the door and pull the kid out.

"Don't panic!" I called, unable to keep the fear out of my own voice. My mind was begging me now to get away from the car. There was no telling when it would explode, what might cause it to go off. I stopped touching the windows. "Just. Just, uh. Oh God! Just don't panic!"

I looked at Kash, and the expression on his face didn't settle me. The back of his hand was against his mouth like he might be sick. He came to the driver's window, his steps shaky, uneven.

"What happened when you got in?" he shouted.

"I heard a click when I sat down," Zac called, his voice muffled by the glass. "Like a, like a, a sound like things snapping into place!"

"Can you hear anything now? Like a ticking or a whirring? Anything?"

"I don't know! I'm scared! Don't leave me here! Please!"

The boy burst into tears. On the front passenger seat beside him I could see the black plastic and duct-taped package. He'd tried to sneak out with the gold. Tried to take off, into the glorious sunrise, a ridiculous bid for a new life that could cost him his current one.

I backed up a couple of steps with Kash, my hands gripping my hair. "What is it?"

"It could be a number of things." He licked his sweaty upper lip. "We know from the bomb on the hillside that the killer's new at this. So I'm leaning away from complex chemical-reaction devices. It's probably a circuit-breaker. Mercury tilt-switch, maybe."

"What? What the fuck? How do we disarm it?"

"I need to know more about it," he said. The big man before me was trembling gently all over, but his face was hard with focus. "It might be connected to the seat. It might be connected to the doors."

"How much time do we have?"

"There's no telling. We need to find out if there's a timer and what kind."

"You figure that out," I said. "I'm going to do a quick lap around the immediate area. This is a spectacle. There's no way the killer would miss this."

I dashed toward the house, wincing as I heard Zac call out after me.

"Don't leave me!" he screamed. "I don't want to die!"

CHAPTER 65

CAITLYN ROLLED, USING the momentum to push herself up, her shoulder, arm, hand shooting upwards, the metal rod flashing out. There was less resistance than she anticipated. The end of the rod went straight into his eye socket, seemed to shudder as it cleaved through bone and came to rest in his brain.

She got up and staggered back as the man groaned and flopped away from her, limp as a fish. He lay there on his back, the rod sticking grotesquely from his head, bloodless, his mouth agape. Caitlyn shivered, her eyes darting over his ragged clothes and filthy boots, the long thin tendrils of gray and brown hair running from the sides of his otherwise bald scalp.

A homeless man. One of the people who must have come into the hotel and left the trash she'd seen in the hall. She could hear that it was raining hard, now that the door to her prison room was open.

She stumbled, trying not to gag, her stomach rebelling against the sensation now cemented in her memory of the rod going up, the breath coming out of her victim. Fighting her revulsion, there was a white-hot excitement pulsing through her at the sight of the dark gaping doorway. She could feel sobs pushing their way up her throat but couldn't hear them. Her ears were ringing. It seemed an age before her hand finally reached the doorframe and she looked down the long hall.

He was there.

Eyes fixed on the unlocked door, flicking now to her face.

Caitlyn's captor marched toward her.

CHAPTER 66

I DIDN'T WANT to leave Zac. But I knew if I could find the killer, I could force him to tell us how to disarm the bomb. My teeth were gritted as I bolted into the house and grabbed my gun, Snale running after me with the diary from the kitchen table. The rage rippling up through my throat was almost a growl. I was going to find this sick fuck and make him reverse the trap he'd put the child in. If I had to beat him to within an inch of his life to make that happen, I would do it.

I ran across Snale's porch and through the back door into the yard, keeping low so that my silhouette didn't appear against the lights of the house. My gun drawn, I did a sweep, squinting in the dark, then hopped over a fence into the next property. I could still hear Zac's crying from the windswept fields. Around Snale's property, lights were coming on. As the seconds passed, more lights appeared in the distance as residents called each other, panicked, in the night.

"Come on, you fuck." I was seething. "Where are you?"

I rushed across the road and through the property opposite Snale's, making for the tiny house in the center of the barren field. As I leapt up onto the porch a woman emerged, a young mother, small children trailing behind her. She screamed at the sight of me.

"I'm police," I said. "Are you all right? Have you seen anyone in the area?"

"No, no." The woman tried to usher her kids back through the screen door but they resisted, mouths gaping at my gun. "We heard screaming. What's happening?"

"Get inside," I said. "Shut the door."

"It's all gonna come out." She shook her head ruefully, trembling before me, her hands gripping the small children by the shoulders of their pajama shirts like they might run off at any second. "It's all coming to an end."

"What?" I squinted at her. "What's that mean?"

She disappeared inside the house. I kept moving, doing a lap of her house, the next field, sweat sliding down my neck and ribs. When I got back to Snale's house she was on her knees in the light of the doorway, flipping through the diary as Kash tried to get sense out of Zac.

"Did you find anyone?"

"No," I knelt beside Snale. "What did you find?"

"I think it's this." She pointed to a messy diagram in blue and red ink. "I think it's connected to the seat. If he gets up, it'll blow."

I grabbed the diary and took it to Kash, who was standing on his toes with another flashlight, trying to see down the back of Zac's seat.

"Oh Jesus." Zac panted, his sweat-drenched hands squeaking on the other side of the glass, fingers spread, desperate. "Jesus Christ, I think I can hear ticking."

Kash snatched the diary out of my hands, glanced at the diagram. "Thought so. Circuit-breaker. It's linked to the driver's seat. We can open the doors."

"Don't open the doors!" Zac cried. "I don't wanna die! Oh God! Please!"

"Let's go with the front passenger side," Kash said. "Just in case."

We ran to the other side of the car. Kash pushed me back.

"I'll do it."

He eased the handle of the passenger door out. There was a click. My mouth was dry as I cringed, waiting for the blast.

There was none. I rushed forward to the doorway beside Kash, reached out and grabbed Zac's hands.

"It's OK." I squeezed his hot fingers. "Don't move. We're gonna figure this out."

Kash leaned in the doorway, trying not to touch anything, and shone the light quickly around the seats, the console, the back of the cabin.

"Christ," he breathed. "It's all wired up under the seats. I can't get to it from this angle." He stood back, kept his voice low. "I can hear a timer ticking."

"Can you see it?"

"No, it's tucked up underneath. All the wires are. I can't get at it unless I put my hand in there, and we have no idea where the switch is. If I disrupt the connection at the wrong point the thing will blow."

We were walking unconsciously away from the car, taking steps out of the blast zone. Zac sat in the driver's seat, reaching for us, sobbing.

"Please don't go! Don't leave me here!"

"What can we do?"

"We can try to replace his weight on the seat," Kash panted, looking wildly at the house. "It'd have to be at least the same weight as the boy. We don't know how sensitive the switch is. If it's too light it might—"

"I got it." I ran toward the house. In the hall was a backpack hanging on a row of hooks cluttered with hats and coats. I grabbed it and sprinted into the living room, almost slipping on the floorboards, and dumped the contents of the bag on the floor. I grabbed at anything heavy and started shoving. Wine bottles. A huge dictionary. A cast-iron sculpture on a shelf. Things were crashing everywhere as I went along. My hands were shaking so hard I could hardly use them. Zac's screams burned in my ears.

"I'm coming!" I screamed. "I'm coming, Zac! Hold on!"

CHAPTER 67

CAITLYN'S KNEES BUCKLED beneath her. It was the only thing that saved her from his full arm swing, the punch sailing over her head as fear consumed her completely. She flopped against his legs, defeat turning her limbs to jelly. He grabbed her waist, hair, tried to get hold of her. He was standing too close. Stepped back.

"Stupid bitch," he snarled. He flipped her, hands beneath her arms, gripping painfully at the tender flesh. "Get back in there!"

It was the sight of the doorway that awakened the fury again in Caitlyn. The enormous sucking weight of the room beyond it. The hours, days, weeks she had lain awake in that concrete nightmare, dreaming of release. Her limbs suddenly hardened. She lifted her leg and slammed it into the doorframe, shocking him, sending them both staggering backwards.

"No!" she snarled, facing him, her body bent with pain and exhaustion. "Never again!"

She didn't know how to fight. She'd never so much as been in a loud argument with a stranger. It was raw animal terror taking over now. Her hands sprang into claw-shapes, her jaw set and teeth bared. She threw herself at his middle with all her might. They hit the ground hard, his legs coming up and around her waist, arms and hands gripping at her face. She let him pull her into his embrace, bit some part of him hard through his shirt—his shoulder or upper chest. She was blinded, wild, tugging at his face and ears, scratching at his eyes.

He rolled and she was suddenly free, stumbling into the walls. She ran as though through water, trying to pull herself along. His footsteps pounded after her.

CHAPTER 68

I RAN OUT the front door of Snale's house, stumbled, caught myself and rushed to the passenger-side door of the four-wheel drive with my arms full of the bag. Snale was standing on the lawn not far away, her face twisted in anguish. Kash stood dazed, his hands by his sides. The bag in my arms was spewing items. I dumped it on the passenger-side seat. The kid was wide-eyed, teeth chattering, his legs drawn up and arms gripping the ceiling of the car. Shock and terror.

"Zac, slide this between your legs. Don't get up until it's on the seat," I stammered. "I . . . I think it's heavy enough. I think . . ."

I remembered seeing a loose house brick by the front door. Zac grabbed the bag. I turned toward the house, stepped back, already twisting, already seeing the brick in my hand, only meters away.

I heard the timer scream.

CHAPTER 69

HE WAS BEHIND HER. Right behind her—his fingers tangled in the very ends of her hair, yanking some of it free. Caitlyn ran through the labyrinth of halls searching for light, seeing only boarded-up windows and locked and barred doors. What floor were they on? What time of day was it? A part of her frantic brain throbbed with denial that any of this was real. She had dreamed so many times of escape. Part of her wanted to stop pushing her body, lie down, give in, wake again in the cellar room where she belonged. Her whole life outside the room had been a dream. She had no mother, no job, no apartment. She'd been born in these dark depths. She needed to stop fighting.

The exhaustion was hard to push back as she reached the stairs, a mountain of chipped and splintered wood reaching into more dark space. Just as she leapt forward, he grabbed her ankle, yanked her down. Her chin hit the bottom stair hard, cracking her teeth. Caitlyn grabbed one of the banister rails and it snapped free in her hand. It was light, rotten and damp, but she threw it anyway, causing him to release his hold. She hurled herself up the stairs and turned right, no idea where it might lead.

Caitlyn's only terror now was running into a dead end. If she was cornered, she knew she would not be able to fight on. Already her knees and hips were aching, threatening to fail. She could hear him breathing, looked back and saw no one there. She tried a door and found it locked. He must be circling around to find her, using another set of stairs. Caitlyn screamed for help, banging on doors. The rain was leaking through the ceiling here. She shoved hard against a door and fell into the wet street.

The light was blinding. Caitlyn crawled toward the blurry, distant road, trying to find the breath to scream. People were there, walking back and forth, streaks of color in her ruined vision. She called out, but no one turned. Her voice was gone.

She felt a hard hand encircle her arm and yank her backwards.

CHAPTER 70

THE STREET WAS flooded with people. I was aware first of voices shouting and footsteps hammering the earth nearby, hands on my body, dragging me, pulling me, lifting my head. I was trapped in a dream, being ravaged by a mob. I opened my mouth and tried to draw air but my ribs felt flattened.

I lay assessing my injuries. I'd hit the back of my head hard. My left radius was broken. And if I didn't get some air soon, I'd be able to add collapsed lungs to my list. I opened my eyes and watched the stars turning around and around against the blackened sky until Kash's face interrupted them. There was a hose in his hand.

His big hand was on my head. I realized he was hosing me. I could feel the cold water rushing down my shoulders and over the backs of my arms. My clothes were drenched.

"It's only flash burn," he was saying. "Don't worry. You're fine."

"Zac." I coughed. I tried to sit up. The four-wheel drive was on fire. People were standing all around it, their mouths open and eyes wide in the dark, watching the flames four, five meters high. The roof of the vehicle was twisted backwards like the lid of a tin can, the doors nowhere to be seen.

"Don't move." Kash tried to force me down. "You were thrown quite a distance. You could have a spinal injury."

"Is he in there?" I asked. Kash didn't answer. "Did the kid make it out?"

More voices above me. The grass beneath me felt cool, welcoming, its soft green fingers reaching up over my wrists, dragging me down. I let my head loll to the side, looked at the crowd around the car lit by the flames. Gold masks.

At the edge of the gathering, nearest to me, I could make out Jace Robit and a slender woman, his wife, in her nightgown. A tall, shaggy friend of Jace's joined him, and then came the other two and their wives. Jace nudged his friend in the ribs and pointed to the car. Stuck out his hands, as though warming his palms, his face cracking with a grin.

CHAPTER 71

"I'VE GOT YOU," the man growled, heaving Caitlyn up from the ground, a helpless bundle in his thick arms. "I've got you now, love."

Caitlyn was so exhausted. Her head fell back against the man's arm and she looked up at him. Shaggy blond hair, a hard face with dark, tired eyes. He was running with her, glancing back toward the building as he made for the street. "I've got her! Get a medic!"

"Where is he?" she asked. "Is he . . . Is he . . ."

"I don't know," the man said. "But he's not here, and that's all you need to know. I'm police. You're safe with me. We'll get the prick, don't you worry about that."

"I killed a man," Caitlyn whispered. Sleep was pulling at her. There were people all around them now, faces appearing at the man's shoulders as they pushed through. Sirens wailing.

"What?"

"I killed someone," Caitlyn said.

"Yeah?" The blond man gave a crooked smile. "Welcome to the club, sweetheart."

CHAPTER 72

I WAS IN a tiny cubicle lined with pale green curtains, lying stiff as a rod under hot white lights. I jolted as I felt hands around my throat, squeezing, hard fingers against my jaw. I reached up with my good arm and realized it was a plastic neck brace. The pain at the back of my head swelled and I groaned long and low, hoping someone would hear me and bring me drugs. Something was swimming in my system. Probably morphine. My eyes were running tears down my temples. Morphine always makes me cry.

I felt for the Velcro strap at the side of my neck.

"Don't even think about it." Kash's voice. He pulled my hand away. "You haven't had your X-ray yet."

The television in the corner was playing some game show. A plump, middle-aged woman was jumping up and down in excitement, apparently having chosen well from a selection of gold briefcases being exhibited by tanned models.

"Zac."

"He didn't make it," Kash said.

I felt a *whump* of grief in the pit of my stomach, hard as the blow of a fist. Immediately the blame swirled, as it always did, a cacophony of voices roaring between my ears.

You should have known he'd steal the gold.

You should have listened when he told you he was running away.

You should have known Snale's house was a target.

You should have saved him.

You should have saved him.

You should –

"You were pretty lucky, stepping back like that just in time," Kash said. From the corner of my eye I could see he was watching the television. "You've got first-degree burns. They're like a bad sunburn. They'll be gone in a few days."

I lifted my left arm and examined the dark blue cast running from the crook of my elbow to my knuckles. My wrist was shattered. I knew the feeling. Had done it before, taking a swing at someone and hitting a wall instead.

"Where are we?"

"White Cliffs hospital. Four hours out of Last Chance. Medevac picked us up."

"Are you OK? Is Vicky—"

"Everyone's fine," he said. "Except Zac."

I lay sweating in the neck brace, listening to the game show host introducing the rules of the next round. There was forty thousand dollars on the line. A lot of money for some people. Enough to give a life for. Enough to die for. *Three more days, and I'll be home, Sam.* I could last the distance, but not like this. Not lying here, staring at the lights.

I pulled off the neck brace. Kash didn't stop me this time. Probably tired of my bullshit. I sat up and felt the stitches in the back of my skull, the bald patch shaved there.

"What kind of bomb was it?" I asked.

"You shouldn't worry about that right now."

"Just tell me."

"It was a circuit-breaker," Kash sighed. "Like I thought. Forensics have a few pieces of it that they're examining. It was a more sophisticated job than the one that killed Theo Campbell, but not by much. There would have been two triggers. One was a pop-up hinge, like you see on kitchen cabinet doors, the flashy ones without handles. Instead of pulling the door open, you push it, it clicks and when you release it, the door pops open. You have to push again and hear the click for the door to close. The killer would have wired the hinge so that when Zac sat down it clicked and completed the circuit. If he'd have got off the seat, it would have popped open, breaking the circuit, setting off the bomb.

"Looks like the secondary trigger was a plastic kitchen timer that we heard ticking. You can get them at the supermarket for about three bucks. The whole thing would have cost little and been easy to source without raising suspicions."

"Still. Let's check with the store in Last Chance and the surrounding towns and see if any kitchen timers have been bought recently, and by whom."

"The results on the IP searches across the valley have come back. No one teaching themselves to make bombs in the last year. We'll need another warrant to go back further."

"Christ." I rubbed my eyes. "Why didn't I think about someone targeting us? The first victim was the chief of police. Of course it makes sense they'd go after Snale next."

"It mightn't necessarily have been Snale that they were after." Kash shrugged. "Maybe it was you or me. Maybe it actually was Zac."

I lay back against the pillows and watched my partner watching the TV. His mouth was turned down and his eyes were set. He wasn't his usual self. All the bravado, all the heroic puff had left his voice. He seemed drained. When he spoke, I realized why.

"I know you spoke to Tenacity," he said.

CHAPTER 73

I SAID NOTHING. My job as a Sex Crimes detective includes working with the utmost discretion at all times. A good majority of the victims I deal with don't want anyone to know what has happened to them, particularly their families. Confirming or denying that I knew Tenacity at all was completely against the rules. Kash seemed to know, didn't seem to care. He kept talking, turning the wedding ring on his finger around and around.

"You must have dealt with her after the assault," he said. "I know you can't say anything. She thinks I don't know. Her mother told me not long after it happened, said Tenacity didn't want me to know because she thought I'd probably turn it around, make it a part of my obsession. Well, she was right, of course. I just added it to the hatred I was already feeling. It spurred me on. I'd only just come back from a deployment in Afghanistan, and went right back as fast as I could. Stupid. So stupid."

He stretched and settled in the seat, his long legs splayed before him.

The woman on the television screen was dying of joy. She was up to seventy-five thousand dollars.

"That night in Kuta, in Bali," Kash said. "I'd only been out of the bar for about thirty seconds. I walked out to take a phone call from my mum. It was too loud in the bar. I got out the front doors, turned left and went over to stand on the street corner. I felt the pressure wave thump right through the middle of my body. I was actually knocked off my feet by it. I didn't even hear the bomb blast. I felt like I'd been hit by a car."

He ran a hand through his hair. I sat watching, seeing him standing on the corner of the moonlit street hung with neon lights. People screaming.

"And then I look back and the whole place is on fire," he said. "And people are running out of it. Some of them are burning. Some of them were missing pieces. I was a surfer. I'd never seen anything like that. Not even in the movies. It was like I'd died suddenly and I'd awakened in hell. And I knew right away—whoever had caused this, *they* were from hell. They had to have been. Because this wasn't the sort of thing that happened on earth."

The woman on the game show was up to a hundred thousand dollars. A heat rash was creeping up her neck and cheeks. She wiped at her eyes, breathless. Kash watched her.

"From then on, that's how I saw it," he said. "I thought there were evil people, demons, walking around on the earth, plotting to open up the ground and unleash their world on us. I had to fight them. Because if I didn't fight them, what was the point of it all? I dropped everything. I went after them. I devoted my life. It was like my wife and my job and my family and my friends had never existed. I had a clear mission, with clear enemies, and that was all that mattered. And then last night..."

He seemed to drift away. I waited.

"Yesterday I was right back where it all started. Feeling the blast. The pressure wave. Staring at the flames."

"It's not..." I struggled to find the words. "That time hasn't been wasted. You've fought a good fight. There's no way of knowing how many lives you've saved through your work."

"But I wanted to put a stop to the badness," he said. "In my mind, it would have all been over by now. There would be an end, and everything I had sacrificed would have been worth it. But badness is everywhere. There's a little bit of hell on earth, and you never know when you're going to see it next."

CHAPTER 74

"TALK TO TENACITY," I said. I reached over and grabbed his hand. "Call her."

We watched as the woman on the screen battled her emotions, trying to decide whether to risk her hundred grand for what was hidden inside the last briefcase. She was pulling on her neck, tugging her ears down, the weight of the decision seeming to physically force her downward. She picked the mystery briefcase. Animated sad clown faces flitted and flashed across the screen as a ten-dollar note was revealed, taped to a board on the inside of the case.

Kash took out his phone and left me watching the woman crying on the screen.

Hell on earth. I'd seen slivers of that place myself, seen its flames flicker in the eyes of bad men I'd sat across from in the interrogation room, listening to them confess their crimes. I'd seen evil intentions in the eyes of foster fathers who'd welcomed my brother and me into their damp, cluttered homes, television light glaring on the walls, the blank faces of other abandoned children peering from shadowed corners. I understood the realization Kash had experienced as he stood watching Zac Taby's body burn in the driver's seat of Snale's car, a decade and a half after he'd watched his friends burn among the remains of dozens of others on a terrible night in Kuta. Sometimes, it's easy to get caught up in this job, to think that you're getting on top of evil. That in some wonderful distant future there will be no terrorists. No killers. No rapists and fiends. A dream like that is worth sacrificing everything for. Love. Friends. Marriage. Kids. It seems worth the fight.

And then you realize that no matter what you throw on the flames, they keep on burning, mighty and unquenchable. The fight would in fact be eternal. Like Kash, I'd given my life over to my job. I breathed it. I obsessed over it, nurtured it, the way I should perhaps have been nurturing friendships, relationships, maybe children. That sort of stuff hardly occurred to me. And yet it was all other people lived for. Was that what had so strangely drawn me to the baby in Jed Chatt's arms? I'd defied logic, crept close to a man who'd only minutes before held a gun on me, so that I could see a child's eyes. Was something inside me whispering of things I was losing because I refused to believe the world needed to be as bad as it was?

Kash had lost his wife because of his commitment to the eternal fight. He needed to get her back.

I lay in the hospital bed and held my broken arm against my chest and wondered if I'd be happier if I stopped fighting.

I pulled out my IV, pushed aside the blankets and started untying my hospital gown. Two nurses were standing just outside my cubicle, chatting at the counter. As I tied my shoelaces, they wandered on. I snuck past them and made for the car park.

Fighting was all I was good at. I couldn't stop now.

CHAPTER 75

KASH WAS STANDING by a police cruiser loaned from White Cliffs to get us home. He was leaning on the driver's side door, talking gently into the phone. He straightened as he saw me.

"My partner's here," he told the caller. "I gotta go. Love you, too."

"Love you too, huh?" I said.

"Force of habit." He watched me approach. "But it's the first time in a long time there were no raised voices. I'm assuming the nurses have not signed your official release."

"They have not," I said. "So let's quit the small talk and get out of here."

On the road in the darkness, the cruiser sailed over the asphalt between oceans of featureless desert sand. The sun was just beginning to light the horizon. I looked at my phone. There was a text from my mother telling me she'd got the money I'd transferred. No mention of her disappointment that it was not in cash. A call came through as I was looking at the screen. It was an unfamiliar number. I answered with trembling fingers.

"Hello?"

"It's Tox."

"Oh," I said. Tox was notoriously difficult to get on the phone, and even harder to converse with once the connection was made. His already-poor people skills seemed halved by the distance. My heart sank. "What's happened?"

"We found Caitlyn McBeal," he said.

I reeled, absurdly looking to Kash to see if he'd heard the news. My skin was tingling all over, and not just from the burns.

"Is she—"

"She's alive."

"Jesus." I sat bolt upright in my seat. "Jesus! What's she saying?"

"Don't get excited. She's not saying much at all, and what she is saying doesn't sound good for you. She says a guy has been keeping her in a cellar for the last few months. Practically starving her to death. She thinks he's connected to Sam. A partner, maybe."

"What do you mean, she thinks that?"

"I mean that's what she thinks."

"Christ, Tox! Explain what you mean!" I tried not to yell. Every fiber of my being was telling me to scream. "What exactly did she say?"

"She says he didn't touch her the whole time," he grumbled. "Didn't rape her. Didn't torture her. Hardly looked at her. Just seemed to go on standby mode, almost like he didn't know what to do with her. Caitlyn thinks it's because Sam was arrested. She thinks they were a double act, and once Sam was gone, the guy who kept her lost interest."

I shivered in my seat. The drugs were still in my system, making my mind fragmented, twitchy. Again I felt that magnetic pull toward my home. I needed to get back there. Speak to Caitlyn. Convince her that she was wrong. *Three days.* I'd go to her hospital room. Look her in the eyes.

"How...I mean, what did he..."

"I haven't got time to relate it all to you play by play," Tox said. "We're standing outside Caitlyn's hospital room, waiting to go in. Detective Nigel Fuckface is giving us fifteen minutes with her."

"Who's the guy?" I gripped the phone tight. "The guy who abducted Caitlyn. Did you catch him?"

"No, he slipped away," Tox said. "You'll see the sketch on the news in a couple of hours, I reckon."

"But—"

The line went dead.

"Fuck!" I screamed long and loud, looking at the phone screen, Tox's number and the "Call ended" message. He'd hung up on me. "Fuck! FUCK!"

CHAPTER 76

WHITT AND TOX stood side by side, leaning against the wall outside Caitlyn McBeal's hospital room. A few meters down the hall from them, a group of detectives lingered, people from Sex Crimes and Major Crimes, some trauma-trained officers Whitt recognized from the Parramatta headquarters. Beyond them, at the nurses' station, a group of journalists had already assembled, arguing with three beat cops who held them back from the hall.

A photograph of Caitlyn McBeal in her current state would have been worth a lot of money, Whitt thought. It was guaranteed front-page news. Over the four and a bit months she had been held captive, Caitlyn had lost a good ten kilos, and her hair had thinned by half. The girl Tox had carried to the ambulance outside the abandoned Pinkerton Hotel had looked like a cancer patient. Sunken eyes and yellowed teeth, her neck and arms covered in bedsores. Her lips had been dry and cracked and bleeding. Tox had described finding her in the alley outside the hotel, desperately trying to crawl toward the street, the exertion of escaping her captor having reduced her almost to unconsciousness. The doctors were saying that, had the unfortunate homeless man Ronnie Hipwell not stumbled upon her makeshift prison cell and initiated her escape, she would have been mere days from death. It was both a miracle and a tragedy that Hipwell had ventured down to the lower basement level after rain flooding the ground floor had pushed aside the trash that had been obscuring the door leading downstairs. Caitlyn was free. Hipwell was dead.

Detective Nigel Spader emerged from the room and closed the door behind him, eyeing Tox suspiciously as he tucked his notebook into his back pocket.

"Five more minutes," he said.

"You said that an hour ago," Tox said.

"Yeah. Maybe I did. What are you going to do about it?"

"I'm going to go in there." Tox stepped forward, pointed at the door behind his fellow officer. "And if you try to stop me, you'll find yourself downstairs in triage."

"You're lucky you're getting access to the witness at all, Barnes," Nigel spat. "You are not on this task force. Neither of you is. And I can deny an interview any time I want."

It was the first time Whitt had seen Tox almost lose his cool.

"Let me tell you a few things," Tox said, jerking a thumb at Whitt. "This two-man investigation right here, we've got enough to get a mistrial and bail in the very least."

"Bullshit."

"We've traced the camera from Sam Blue's apartment to a hock shop in Bondi." Tox started listing on his fingers. "And we've got video of a man purchasing the camera who digital imaging analysts say is far too tall to be Blue. You yourself admitted that your people muscled Blue to extract the confession. We found Caitlyn McBeal's mobile phone at the crime scene *you guys* released. Your ten-man crack team of task force cockheads is going to look really stupid when the press gets wind of this. You need to fuck off and do some damage control, and leave Caitlyn McBeal to us."

The bigger man had all but backed Nigel into the wall. Nigel shoved Tox's chest.

"Back the fuck up, murderer!"

"There's no need to be so hostile." Whitt came between the two men. "We're cooperating with you, Detective Spader. We let you know as soon as we had a lead on Caitlyn's possible whereabouts so that your officers could be on the scene if she was found. That was a goodwill gesture. Now return the favor and let us have our time with Caitlyn."

"I don't know how good multiple interviews are for her right now," Nigel mused, his eyes never leaving Tox. "She's very fragile."

"You know what else is fragile?" Tox said. "Your neck."

Tox and the much shorter detective stared at each other. The door to Caitlyn's room opened and another officer walked out. Whitt took the opportunity to slip through the gap as the door closed.

CHAPTER 77

THE ROOM WAS full of people. Caitlyn lay against the pillows, talking softly to a police EFIT specialist who sat beside her, scrolling through selections of eyebrows for the composite image of Caitlyn's captor. In the chair on the other side of the bed, Caitlyn's mother sat quietly crying, talking on her phone. Whitt understood Mrs. McBeal had arrived a week earlier to put extra pressure on the investigative team.

"I can't believe it either," she was saying. "No. No. I just can't believe it. I tried to tell them. I tried to tell them all along."

"Caitlyn, I'm Detective Inspector Edward Whittacker," he said, shifting awkwardly between two men standing in the doorway, detectives or counselors, family members, Whitt didn't know. "I'm, uh, I'm part of the team who found you."

"You're Detective Barnes's partner?" Caitlyn looked at him with tired eyes.

"Yes."

"Come here." She patted the bed beside her. Whitt moved around the bed, squeezing between people, and settled on the edge beside the girl. Her strength was incredible. As Whitt looked about the room, he noticed more than half the people here were crying. Though Caitlyn looked exhausted, a tiny fire seemed to be burning in her, brightening her eyes. She was being strong for the people here, her family and friends and those who had been searching for her. They needed to know she was all right.

"I know you've answered a lot of questions already," Whitt said. "But I just need to know anything you can tell me about your captor's connection to Sam Blue. Did the man who kept you ever say anything about Sam? Did he ever say his name?"

"He was very shocked and angry at his arrest," Caitlyn said. "We watched it on the television in the room together that first night. He said they weren't finished yet."

"*They* weren't finished yet?" Whitt swallowed. His mouth was bone dry. "Are you sure those were his exact words?"

Caitlyn reached over and held Whitt's hand. Her fingers were cool and hard, rough from long months in the concrete cell, slowly dying in the darkness.

"He said he needed him. See, he didn't touch me," Caitlyn said. "Not once. He didn't even speak to me. He was just holding me. He didn't know what to do. His partner, Sam, was gone and he didn't know what to do without him."

Whitt tried to breathe. His throat was tight.

"I saw Sam Blue a lot while I was locked up," Caitlyn said. "The TV was my only company. I'd see him walking to court. See footage of him giving evidence. I looked at his eyes. There was a deadness there. It was the same deadness that I saw in the eyes of the man who held me. It was like something inside him had shriveled up and there was only emptiness left."

Whitt felt a chill come over him.

"They killed those girls, Detective," Caitlyn said. "That man and Sam Blue. They're the same kind of monster."

CHAPTER 78

THE SMOKING HUSK of Snale's four-wheel drive had been screened off from the public eye by a white tent. I saw the flashes of the Forensics officers' cameras as we pulled into the driveway, their ghoulish silhouettes augmented by protective suits. All the front windows of Snale's house had blown out. Glass crunched under my feet as I made my way up the drive. Again the townspeople drove by slowly, pressing their faces against their car windows. Others gathered in huddles at a safe distance some meters down the road, to gawk and mutter, some still in their bedclothes.

There was a mustachioed officer talking to Snale as I walked into the house. The guy gave me an odd look as I entered. Snale turned away from him and threw her arms around me.

"Oh, Harry." She squeezed me painfully, smoothed down the sides of my hair. I could see she had been crying. She examined me all over, the cast, my face, the torn remnants of the clothes I'd worn during the blast, still reeking of smoke. "I can't believe you're here. They released you already?"

"The bomb," I said, ignoring her mothering and turning to the Forensics officer. "Any traces? Anything we can use?"

"Nothing biological," he said. "Everything burned to a crisp. Hot and fast, those gas-bottle jobs. Our main concern now is recovering everything we can of the boy for the parents."

My stomach twisted. I must have made a face, because Snale reached up and continued patting my hair.

"Did you speak to them? Zac's parents?" I asked her. "What did they say? Are they OK? We should get them into counseling. On suicide watch, maybe. They'll be fragile. They might—"

"Just give it a break for a while, Harriet," she said. "You look like the walking dead. You smell even worse. Have fifteen minutes off, and then we can get back to it."

CHAPTER 79

I WALKED NUMBLY to the bathroom and stripped, pulling off a bunch of soft layers of skin from my forearms and neck. When I looked in the mirror, half my face appeared badly sunburned, already peeling at my temple. I must have turned away at the last second, put my hands up to try to shield myself from the blast. The tender flesh on the underside of my forearms had taken the worst hit. The edges of my cast rubbed at the irritated skin, causing it to burn anew.

I held my arm up out of the stream of cool water and closed my eyes, raked back my singed hair. Against the back of my eyelids I could see the outline of Zac's mangled corpse in the front seat, the flames twisting around him, flaring out over the roof.

I screamed as something brushed against my leg. The pig had muscled his way into the bathroom and nosed open the shower door.

"Vicky! Vicky, help! Oh God!" I hollered, trying to shove the beast away. It weighed half a ton. Snale rushed into the room, horrified, trying to shield her eyes from my naked form.

"Oh God, I'm sorry!" Despite everything, we were both almost laughing. "He likes to drink the water. I think it's the soap. It tastes different. Oh Jesus, I'm so sorry. Jerry! Jerry! Come here, you idiot!"

The pig was snorting and snuffling at the few centimeters of water at the bottom of the shower. Eventually Snale gave up trying to haul the animal out of the shower with me. I got out and she handed me a towel.

"I'm seeing stuff on the news about Sam," she said. "The girl they found. Caitlyn? Someone got some footage of her being carried to an ambulance. She looked terrible."

"Nothing about us out here?" I asked. "The bombing? Zac?"

"No. No way. We're small fry." She sat on the toilet seat near me.

I wrapped the towel around my body, felt exhausted.

"The girl"—Snale cleared her throat—"she's saying—"

"I know what she's saying," I said. "It isn't true."

Snale shifted uncomfortably.

"Would anything make you believe that it was?" she asked.

I took a comb from the edge of the sink and pulled it through my hair, looked at my own eyes in the mirror. Sam's eyes.

"No," I answered.

CHAPTER 80

KASH WAS IN the living room, looking at the diary, the book pressed flat on the tabletop in front of him. On the left-hand page was a sketch of a body fitted out for a massacre, a faceless dummy strapped with guns and knives. It was a lot like the sketches Dylan Klebold and Eric Harris had made in their own diaries as they planned their assault. They'd envisioned body harnesses in which they could house hand-held pipe bombs, holsters with easy access to knives for hand-to-hand combat should they run out of ammo. The diarist had copied excerpts from Eric's diary into his own.

I must not be sidetracked by my feelings of sympathy, mercy.
I want to burn the world.

In reality, the boys had become bored midway through their killing spree and hadn't used most of the weaponry they'd strapped to themselves. It was the same with Seung-Hui Cho, the Virginia Tech killer.

He seemed to burn out his rage much faster than he went through his ammunition. It was all about buildup with these guys. Anticipation of the terror of their victims.

Maybe that was why the killer had left the note for Zac on the steering wheel, warning him that he was going to die. Otherwise, why not just let the thing activate itself the moment he shifted position? Why give him a chance? Why give him time to escape?

So he could think about it.

So he could know death was coming and be afraid.

"Yow!" Kash yelped, drew a finger to his lips.

"What?"

"I scraped it on the staple." He sucked blood from the tiny cut, examined the injury in the light.

I went to the book, sat down next to him. Indeed, there were two staples in the center of the notebook, holding the pages in place. The bottom fold of one staple was crooked, sticking up slightly, a trap that would catch a careless hand sweeping over it.

I pushed the fold of the staple down. It sprang back up.

Something rushed over me, an electric sensation that made all my injuries come alive at once, my muscles hardening. I snatched the book up and examined it in the light of the living room, tilted it to get the right angle.

"Oh my God," I whispered. "There's a page missing."

CHAPTER 81

"HOW DO YOU know that?" Snale took the diary from me, examined it, squinting.

"The staples are crooked. Someone's bent them outwards to slide the middle page out of the notebook without tearing the paper. They've folded the staples back but they're not completely flat." I took the book from her hands. "Look. Here. I can see the shape of a square indented in the next page. It isn't on the previous page. The missing page has left indentations."

Snale shifted away, her face taut with concentration. She began pulling open drawers and shuffling through them. She found a pencil and a blank sheet of paper and came back to the dining-room table. She flattened the book, laid the blank sheet over it, and began gently shading the pages with the side of the pencil.

"Shouldn't we wait for Forensics?" Kash asked. "Get a carbon scan?"

"We don't have time," I said. "It could easily tell us what's happening next. There was a reason it was removed so carefully." My heart was hammering. Watching Snale shading every millimeter of the paper was painful. She experimented, shading lighter and harder, trying to find the best pressure to reveal the pattern underneath. Lines, squares, arrows pointing and labels. A map was emerging before us. Two rows of blocks, some longer, some short, the same distance apart as they were wide.

"It's the main street," I said. "It's Last Chance Valley."

CHAPTER 82

WHITT SLAMMED THE piece of paper against the prison Plexiglas and pointed at it.

"Who the fuck is this?"

He wasn't usually the type to curse, but his resolve had worn thin. Sitting with Caitlyn McBeal in a room full of people who had all but given up on the idea of ever seeing her again had pushed him over the edge. Whitt's instinct was to bundle her up, feed her, care for her like a newborn babe.

Sam examined the paper Whitt was holding against the glass of the visitors' center, the EFIT image of the man who had almost killed Caitlyn. Sam glanced at Whitt, shrugged.

"I have no idea."

"Enough bullshit." Whitt leaned forward so that his nose was centimeters from the glass. "This is *the guy*. We've got him on CCTV purchasing the camera that was found in your apartment." He shuffled through his papers and extracted the image from the hock shop.

"We've got Caitlyn saying he was desperately upset at your arrest. He's around your age. Slim. Long arms. This guy could be your twin. Who the fuck is he?"

"I don't know!" Sam pleaded. "I've been watching it all morning on the news. I'm telling you, I don't know the guy! I have never seen him before in my life!"

Whitt let the paper slide from the glass, slumped back in his chair.

"I don't believe you," he sighed. "I can't anymore. It's not as though he would tell her you were partners for the benefit of framing you. He didn't expect her to survive."

"He told her we were partners?"

"In a roundabout way."

Sam scratched at his neck then shook his head violently, like he was trying to clear water from his ears.

"How did she survive?" Sam asked.

"She got away."

"Maybe he planned that."

"I doubt it. She killed a homeless man. She fought for her life to get out of that place. When Tox found her, she was crawling on the ground. The experts reckon she had mere days left."

"Look." Sam shifted closer to the glass. "I need you to keep believing in me or I'll never get out of here."

"If you want to get out of here, you better keep looking at this damned picture and figure out who the hell he is." Whitt left the image resting face-up on the counter. He said nothing as he headed past the security guards and into the hall.

Whitt hated to admit it, but he was beginning to wonder if Sam Blue was exactly where he belonged.

CHAPTER 83

IT WAS A massacre plan. As the missing page emerged, my heart sank lower and lower. Before, when the diary had been mainly praise for spree killers, research into bombs and weaponry, I could underestimate the diarist's plans for the people of Last Chance Valley. But I could see now this killer planned to make sure no one survived.

The buildings of the main street made two identical columns down the center of the page, on the right the post office, a hardware store, a tiny cafe and a supermarket, among others. On the left, across the street from the post office, lay Snale's tiny police station, a single-story square with a single interrogation room, a single cell, desk space for two and the armory. Next came the pub with its rear car park, a farming supply store and a mechanic's, also with a wide asphalt parking lot.

Four main buildings, shoulder to shoulder, forming two identical blocks.

Around the buildings, the diarist had marked a dotted line, the path of his plan.

Step one: Kill Officer Snale in police station. Acquire weapons.
Step two: Plant device #1 in the car park behind pub. Set timer.
Step three: Take the semitrailer from the mechanic car park and use it to block off bottom of the main street, creating a U-shape to trap victims.
Step five: Plant devices #2 and #3 in semitrailer. Set timers.
Step four: Get John Destro and secure upper balcony of the post office.

Kash, Snale and I looked over the faint map, following the steps.

"This is terrifying," Snale murmured. A thin sheen of sweat glistened at her hairline.

"You're the tactics guy," I told Kash. "What do you think?"

A brief smile flashed over his features. A truce between us, his mass-casualty expertise finally coming into play.

"It's a single-man operation," he said. "All the steps are sequential. There's nothing here to indicate that there are two people acting simultaneously. Whoever he is, he's pretty confident. Step one—taking out you, Vicky, as you man the police station. That's no mean feat. I don't imagine he's just going to waltz in there and you're going to hand him the keys to the armory."

"Unless he's already got a gun," Snale said. "And he's just going to surprise me and upgrade from whatever he has to one of the semiautomatics."

There was a moment of tense silence. Kash put a finger on the paper and traced the dotted line.

"He then goes and plants what I can only imagine is one of his bombs in the car park behind the pub. He takes a semitrailer and uses that to block off the street, effectively making a trap. This first bomb must be to drive everyone out of the pub, into the street. The truck explodes, blocking off an escape that way. Everyone is herded into this space." He pointed to the center of the map, the U-shape made by the buildings and the burning truck. "They're rounded up like cattle. The road up past the post office is the only way out. And from the balcony, with a semiautomatic, he's ready to pick them off one by one as they run for their lives."

"It's..." Snale was lost for words. She pursed her lips.

"It's very sophisticated," Kash finished for her, looking over the page. "It uses crowd-herding tactics to maximize the death toll. He'd have learned that from the spree killers he's studied. Anticipate where the victims will cluster naturally. Predict their movements when they panic, and channel them into the line of fire by securing the exits. It's interesting, though, that he doesn't channel the survivors of the initial blasts into a final explosion. He wants to shoot them down one at a time."

"It's the same reason he left the note on the steering wheel," I said. "The same reason he was pacing at the site of Theo Campbell's death. He wants to give them time to think about what's happening to them. Time to..." I shrugged. "I don't know. To feel..."

"Sorry," Kash said.

"Sorry for what?" Snale said.

I flipped through the diary. The only thing I could think that united all the spree killers in the diary was their rage. Their desire to be punishers.

I didn't want to die, but I would have no choice. Vengeance is the only path.

I will get you all back.

You could have stopped this.

"You were right, Harry," Kash said. "You were right from the start. It's not terrorism. He's not trying to make a political statement. To get people to act. This is pure vengeance. He wants the people of Last Chance Valley to feel sorry for whatever it is they've done to cause this."

"What *have* we done?" Snale asked. There were tears in her eyes now. She sighed helplessly. I watched her leave the table for the bathroom, swiping at her cheeks.

I turned back to the map. "The plan really seems to be all about maximizing casualties," I said. "So we can assume it'll go off when the most people possible are at the local pub, if the killer hasn't abandoned his plan."

"I don't see why he would have," Kash said. "He knows we have the diary. But he doesn't know we have the plan page. He has no reason to suspect that the plan has been compromised."

"So when are most people down at the pub?"

"Most of the town is there every Saturday night," Snale said from the doorway.

We all looked at the calendar on the wall. We had two days to stop a massacre.

CHAPTER 84

WE CALLED DEZ and asked him to get the word out that people weren't to congregate in the town. Snale left us for Zac Taby's parents' house with a pair of counselors who had flown in from White Cliffs.

I sat in the passenger seat of Kash's car and deleted the many text messages from journalists on my phone, some about Last Chance Valley's deaths, more about Sam. I looked up the EFIT image of the man Caitlyn McBeal was telling the world was my brother's accomplice. I didn't know him. I wanted, so desperately, to feel some spark of recognition. I ran my eyes over his long, straight nose and dark eyes, over the shape of his shaved head. I knew that like most EFIT images, this would be a cleaner, slightly dimmed version of the real man. But there was no trigger in my brain. Not even the softest soundings of alarm.

I looked at the time. In four minutes, Sam would have access to the prison phones. Kash was walking toward the car. I had my finger poised over the answer button.

"My brother's going to call me in a minute."

"Oh. Do you want—"

"No, it's fine. Let's get rolling."

The phone rang. Kash shifted uncomfortably in his seat as he started the car.

"Hi, Sammy," I said.

"*This is a reverse charge call from Silverwater Metropolitan Remand and Reception Center, a division of Silverwater Correctional Complex. If you wish to accept the call, press one.*"

"Urgh. I always forget about the automated message," I sighed. Kash gave an awkward smile.

"Harry?" It was Sam.

"Hi." I could feel myself smiling, despite the heaviness in my heart. "Are you OK?"

"I'm a bit numb, to be honest," he said. "When they said they had a picture of the guy I was so ready for it to be someone I knew. I mean, it would have to be, right? I was ready to be in an absolute rage. But this guy—I don't know him. Do you?"

"No," I said. "Never seen him before in my life."

"This is unbelievable." Sam sounded scared. I sounded scared, too. My voice was coming back to me, half a second later, the recording device used by the prison echoing as it taped us. "Maybe if they catch him, it can all come to an end."

"Whitt and Tox are on it," I said. "I'm going to wrap up here, and then I'll be right there with them."

"I'd rather you weren't," he said. "Harry, he got into my apartment. He can get into yours. What he did to those women. He's an animal. He's smart and he's vicious."

"I'm pretty vicious myself, you know."

Kash smiled beside me as he drove.

"I know you are, but I just don't need anything else to worry about.

If I know you're out there in the desert I can at least pretend you're safe."

Sam was always like that when we were kids. Protective. Worrisome. When we were placed in different homes he would sometimes run away from his placement to find me, even if he had to catch the train from one side of the state to the other. Just to see me in person with his own eyes and confirm I was all right. I felt a powerful yearning to be home with him, to be on the hunt for the man in the picture.

I told Sam we were going to catch this guy. One way or another. I'd spend every dollar I had. I would give up my job, my life, my freedom, if that was what it took.

I sent a text message to Tox Barnes, the beginnings of an idea tingling in the back of my mind.

Something to try, I typed. *Maybe go round my apartment and turn the lights or TV on. If he broke into Sam's place, maybe he'll break into mine. Worth a shot.*

Tox didn't answer. He rarely did. But I knew he would know it was a good trap to set. Whoever this man was, he was obsessed with my brother. Now that Sam was off limits, maybe I could lure him over to me.

CHAPTER 85

KASH HAD WOKEN me from a thin sleep at sunrise by nudging the edge of my bed with his heavy boot. I'd heard him huffing around at 3 am and it seemed he hadn't showered. He smelled of sweat.

"It's all a setup," he said.

"I'm going to need coffee if you're going to be vague," I said. A shimmer of hope went through me that he was talking about Sam's case, but he was holding a laptop, and when he sat down beside me I saw it was full of Qantas ticketing information.

"Jace Robit's crew are making a run for it." Kash pointed to the screen. "An ASIO buddy sent me these after I put in for security checks on Robit and his three mates. In the last six months, all four of them have applied for passports. They've each booked a one-way ticket to Ngurah Rai Airport in Denpasar. All leaving on the same day."

"When?"

"Next week."

"They could be going on a bucks' weekend." I rubbed my eyes.

"John Stieg." Kash brought up a mug shot of Jace's short, thick-bodied friend. "He's closed all his online gaming accounts and cashed in the remaining credit. Frank Scullen's divided his bank accounts with his wife in half and taken his share out in cash. Damien Ponch sold his truck."

"A *big* bucks' weekend."

"One-way tickets, Blue." Kash nudged me. "Focus. I think this whole thing has been a misdirect. An exit strategy. They're not on the offensive. They're trying to hold us off, ensure we only react to the wrong circumstances."

"I don't understand."

"Get your things." He got up and kicked my bag toward me. "I'll explain on the way. Last Chance might be in more danger than we thought."

CHAPTER 86

KASH HAD THE binoculars trained on Jace Robit's house and was slowly adjusting the focus, the dial making a soft clicking as he rolled it with his fingers. The agent had plenty of high-tech equipment in his truck. Beyond the windshield, affixed to the hood of the car, a parabolic microphone was pointed toward the house on the plain. Now and then it picked up voices from inside, the clunking and shuffling of objects.

Robit's three friends were inside with him: Frank Scullen, John Stieg and Damien Ponch. When the heat is on, criminals tend to band together, which isn't clever behavior. Drug dealers call more frequent meetings. Bank robbers organize a late-night rendezvous. Young partygoers who got out of control one weekend and assaulted a girl all come together for a crisis talk to get their stories straight. Kash was muttering reconnaissance to himself like he couldn't help it, marking out distances and wind direction.

"Four confirmed in the interior," he murmured. "None visible on the exterior."

"Yo, General Patton." I slapped his chest. "Tell me what's going on."

"Here's my theory. The gold we found at Chief Campbell's place belonged to these guys," Kash said.

"What makes you suspect that?"

"Think about it. Chief Campbell's got eighty K worth of gold stashed in his house, and his wife doesn't know about it. It's not recorded as evidence at the police station. The very first people Olivia Campbell pointed to as suspects were these guys. She sensed they were a threat to her husband. She asked him what he was up to, and he said it was a drug sting. Well, we know that's not true. There's nothing in the police log about a sting operation. Snale knew nothing about it."

"OK, I'm with you."

"I think these guys acquired that gold from somewhere illegally," Kash said. "I think Theo Campbell found them with it, and he took it off their hands. We know from what Bella Destro said that Chief Campbell didn't always play by the rules. He might have stopped them on the road. Or maybe they were acting weird and he *was* snooping around them for drugs. I don't know. But somehow he discovered them with it, and decided he'd just take it."

"Hmm." I nodded along.

"Now the guys have got a problem. They need to get rid of Theo Campbell. But there are seventy-five people in the town and they're no angels. They're likely to be the first suspects. How do they get rid of Campbell *and* control the circumstances around the investigation?"

"Control the circumstances?"

"I'm talking war tactics." He shook his head. "I'm sorry. In hostile situations, you strategize to control how your enemy thinks and reacts, bait them, feed them false information."

"They constructed the diary," I said. "Used it as bait to make sure we'd connect it with the bombing on the hill. They provided us with the answers before we asked any questions. We went looking for an angry teen."

"Exactly," he said. "We've been totally distracted, looking for vengeful young spree killers in training. Lone-wolf terrorists. They put Zac Taby right under our noses."

"So why kill him? He was a great suspect."

"Maybe they weren't after Taby." He shrugged. "Any of us could have got in that car. Maybe they weren't planning on any of us *actually* getting in. Zac got into the car at night. It was dark. In the daytime, someone would have looked in and seen those gas bottles in the back seat. It's possible they were just trying to scare us. Make us evacuate the town."

"Eighty thousand dollars is a lot of money," I said. "But it's not much shared between four men. And if the whole goal was to get their rocks back, why didn't they take them?"

"Maybe what we found at Campbell's house is just the tip of the iceberg," Kash said. "Maybe there's so much gold they could all start new lives on it. And Theo Campbell was threatening to bring all their grand plans crashing down."

I stared at the house before us. A little fibro shack in the middle of a hole in the middle of nowhere. I could imagine the temptation presented to people like these, scraping out a living from the hard earth. Zac Taby had wanted to run away. Did these men hear the same call of the horizon?

"Remember how the gold was packed?" Kash said. "Wrapped in black plastic. Bound with duct tape. Why wrap it like that? Because you want to store it, disguise it, and ship it."

I sat up and grabbed the criminal record sheets we'd printed out that morning for the crew inside the house.

Jace Robit. Domestic assault. Robbery. Possession of a prohibited substance.

Frank Scullen, assault, grievous bodily harm, theft.

John Stieg and Damien Ponch both had records for fraud. There were also domestic assaults, the complainants their wives.

Kash was right. These men were not the town's most upstanding citizens. They had every reason to want to get away from this life, and the willingness to do it in an underhanded way.

"So what are they going to do?" I said. "They've already killed two people. They think we're well down the wrong track in the investigation. Are they just going to leave quietly?"

"I don't know," Kash said. "It worries me that they removed the massacre plan page. Maybe they just thought it was too much. But maybe they..."

He sighed, his voice uneven.

"Maybe they'll try to go out with a blast," he continued. "A smoke screen. Slip away in the chaos."

The microphone crackled.

"I sure as fuck hope so!" someone shouted. "I hope he suffered bigtime, the little...I tell you what, this place would be better off with a quarter...its inhabitants. Seventy-five was far too...many. Seventy-three now. We're getting closer to perfect."

The microphone crackled and went silent. I thumped the speaker sitting on the console between us.

"This thing is rubbish," I said. "We need to get closer."

"I've already conducted a risk assessment," Kash said. "This is our most effective reconnaissance base. We can do another assessment in forty-seven minutes, if the wind changes, maybe."

I listened quietly to Kash's reasoning, then opened the car door and got out. Kash was behind me by the time I got to the edge of the property, crouching in the bracken.

A handful of locusts, disturbed by my presence, fluttered up and around me. The sun was immediately blazing on my already burned face. I shielded myself against it and crept to the wire fence, to a collection of rusty steel drums.

"Don't get us killed, Harry," Kash murmured as he crept up behind me. "This is Jace's property. If he shoots us he'll have three witnesses to tell the cops it was self-defense."

"What if I kill them?" I said. "What are you gonna say?"

He rolled his eyes at me, shifted forward and signaled for me to wait. His combat tactics would get us up beside the house without being seen. I held on to the back of his belt, waited, sweating, for him to move.

He pointed forward and we rushed into the field toward the house.

CHAPTER 87

THE GRASS WAS waist-high. I huffed with exertion just keeping up with my partner. Though my injuries from the explosion had been mild, it had taken a lot out of me. We flitted across the field and stopped short beneath a window. Kash checked under the house and then flattened on the ground and started crawling underneath on his belly. It was hard to commando-crawl with a broken arm. I dragged myself forward with him, sweat sticking the dust to my cheeks.

The floorboards creaked a meter above our heads. I twisted onto my side and lay in the dirt, watching my partner's face, his glasses fogging with condensation.

"It's not going to be a problem for much longer," someone said. "We get whatever the hell we can over the next couple of days, and then we go."

"Your wife's going to be the one that'll give us trouble, Johnno," someone else said. "Does she have any idea what we're doin'?"

"Nah, mate. No way. She doesn't have a clue. If any of youse touch her, mate, I'll fuckin' stab ya."

"Do as he says," someone said. It sounded like Jace. "Leave her alone. We don't want anyone drawing attention to us until we can get everything into place. After it's done we'll be outta here."

Kash and I stared at the dirt between us, listening to the microsounds as they came through the boards. Someone flipping the cap off a bottle of beer, the hiss of the compressed air escaping. Someone was standing right over us, causing dust to trickle down into our hair.

"I know this probably sounds weird," a voice said. "But do youse ever, I dunno. Have you ever thought about maybe stayin' once it's over?"

"Stayin'? *Here?* Mate, are you nuts? This place is a fuckin' shithole. We're talkin' about changin' *everythin'*. Why the fuck would you want to stay?"

"I guess I feel like I would kinda miss my kids, you know."

There was silence. The men moved around, open and closed doors. There was a horse race playing on a television or radio somewhere. At least two of them fell to cheering the horses on. Groans of joy or sorrow, I couldn't tell, as the race ended.

"What time do you want to go out there tonight, then?" someone said.

Jace Robit replied. "Usual time. Get out there at eight."

Kash and I looked at each other. I saw movement out on the road and twisted slightly, squinted in the light.

"Oh, shit."

"What?"

"Digger. The town dog. Look."

Out on the road, the plump gray mutt was trotting along on its own, tongue waggling limply between its jaws. No clue where it was going, no sign of where it had come from. I knew that if there was one thing that dogs got excited about, other than food, it was humans lying on the ground. If the dog saw us, our risk assessment score would be through the roof.

I squeezed my eyes shut.

"Oh God, don't let it look over here," I breathed. I heard the floor-boards above me creak. "Don't move. Don't look at it. Maybe it won't see us."

As is typical with my luck, I chanced a look at the road just as Digger was glancing over into the shadows beneath the house. The dog stopped short, lifted her head, sniffed the air. I fancied I saw her smile as she began to bound toward us.

"Shit!" Kash seethed. He sprang to his hands and knees, unsure of what to do. "Fucking thing!"

The dog was running at us, barking with joy. I heard the men in the house above us shifting, moving to the front of the house, following the commotion.

CHAPTER 88

"GO," I TOLD Kash. "Get to cover. I'll distract it."

Kash scampered to the back of the house, around the brick foundations, and disappeared between the long grass. Digger slammed into me, a flurry of licking and happy barks.

"What is that thing doing?" I heard Jace sneer from above me. "Fucking dog."

I clamped my hands around the dog's muzzle. She gave a happy growl, tried to play-bite the cast on my arm.

"What's it got?" someone asked from the couch. "A roo?"

"Dunno. I'll go have a look."

I crawled around the foundations, looking for somewhere to hide. If Jace Robit found me down here, he'd know I'd heard their plans to "change everything," to abandon their kids and wives. A group of men fleeing after a dramatic act, whatever it might be. If he found me now...I gripped the bricks, tried to contain the rising panic.

I looked up. There was a narrow gap between the brickwork and one of the wooden beams that crossed the bottom of the house. Just wide enough to snuggle into, just deep enough to hide in. I didn't know if I was strong enough to crawl up into it, to hold myself wedged in the space. But I had to try. I gathered a handful of the dry, powdery dirt from beneath me.

"Sorry, dog," I whispered. I flung the dirt in the dog's eyes. The animal yelped, twisted sideways. I put my feet into the gap beside the bricks and pulled myself upwards.

Digger was blinded and ran out from beneath the house, trying to scrape at its eyes with its paws. Already my broken arm, braced against the wooden beam, was screaming with pain. I closed my eyes and held my stomach in, thought about stone, concrete, solid things. I was a part of the house. I was invisible. I heard Jace Robit walking down the porch stairs mere meters from me.

Something was crawling along my side. Something big. I hoped it was a locust. At least a huntsman spider, those big, hairy but harmless creatures. I prayed silently that it wasn't a red-back. Its needle-like legs were creeping slowly up my armpit, over the top of my shoulder.

"What's wrong with ya? Ya stupid mongrel." Robit's feet appeared beside the dog. He crouched and I tucked my head up against the floorboards. My legs were starting to shake. I shifted my weight from one to the other, pushing hard against the walls of my little hidey-hole with my arms. I could hear the man breathing, feel his gaze wandering over the dirt beneath me. Sweat was rolling down my ribs, collecting in the front of my shirt. The crawling thing walked across my ear and over my temple. I squeezed my eyes shut as it wandered over the bridge of my nose. The urge to scream was all-consuming. Exhale. Scream. Relax. Fall. *Give up, Harry. You can't do this.*

I heard Jace's leather boots creak as he stood.

"Get moving, idiot." He kicked the dog until it began to trot away. Jace sniffed and spat as he climbed the stairs back up to the house.

I collapsed onto the ground with a thud and peeled the spider from my hair, flicking it away. An enormous red-back. It rolled in the dust, oil-black legs wiggling, righted itself and crept away.

CHAPTER 89

WHITT STOOD BY the table at the very back of the police briefing room as the officers assembled in the chairs around him. Tox stood beside him, slowly devouring a Mint Slice cookie, examining the treat closely between bites. It took all of Whitt's resolve not to knock it out of his hand. His nerves were frazzled, and crumbs were falling all over the floor. Whitt needed control, perfection, now more than ever.

He'd learned little more about Tox's deadly reputation, the murders he was supposed to have committed as a child. The man's records were sealed, and rumors of the event varied wildly. It seemed far more fashionable to simply join the masses and hate Tate "Toxic" Barnes than it was to be certain of the facts. Whitt was certain he didn't hate Tox. But he was far too nervous to like him, either.

"All right, listen up," Chief Morris said. The squat old man commanded the attention of the room. Young officers who had been laughing and chatting turned around in their seats. "We'll make this short so you can get back out on the road. We're getting a lot of calls from members of the public who have seen men fitting the EFIT description of McBeal's abductor. You're doing a good job attending to them. We're hoping to hone the search now with some new information we've just received."

Tox seemed to get part of his cookie stuck in his throat. He thumped his chest with his fist. Whitt winced.

"Forensics have done a sweep of the Pinkerton Hotel. Even though we've restricted the analysis to the underground basement where Caitlyn was kept, there are still hundreds and hundreds of prints, and we can't tell which ones are relevant. It's taking time to narrow them down. We've been fast-tracking the prints through the national database and some interesting characters have started turning up. We've shown their pictures to Caitlyn, but she hasn't identified anyone. It's likely some of these guys might have changed their appearance since they were last in contact with police. Some of the photographs are very old."

Six images sprang onto the screen. All white men with the dazed, tired look of inmates appearing for mug shots, their mouths down-turned and eyes distant. Three were bearded. One wore thick-framed red glasses, smiling with missing front teeth.

"Take a good look," Chief Morris said. "Some of these guys are off the grid. Long-term addicts, ex-cons. This one, Regan Banks, has a murder charge from fifteen years ago. This one, Malcolm Donovan, does too. All the others have served time. Robberies, assaults, that sort of thing. But one of them might be our guy. You're going to split into teams and each track one of these guys down, bring them in for questioning."

Chief Morris pushed a button on a nearby laptop and another screen full of dead-eyed men appeared. Someone was walking through the tables handing out printed copies of the faces.

"We need to nab this guy before he does any more damage. This isn't over, people," Chief Morris said. "Not by a long shot."

"I'm gonna split off," Tox said through the remnants of a second cookie. "Gotta go check on Harry's place. You wanna come?"

"No, I'm going to stay here." Whitt rubbed his face, pushed his fingers into his eye sockets and massaged the muscles there. It had been twenty-four solid hours since they found Caitlyn McBeal. Thirty-six or so since he had slept. They had been out most of the day driving around, following operational calls, running in and out of buildings looking for men with shaved heads. His temples were throbbing. "I'm going to put my head down in the coffee room so I can be here if they get a call."

"Right." Tox gave Whitt a slap on the arm and yanked his flak jacket off. He dropped it on the tabletop beside his partner. "I'll be back later."

Whitt watched his partner go without knowing that he wouldn't be back at all.

CHAPTER 90

IT WASN'T OVER for Regan.

He stood by the windows of the discount electronics store and watched the pictures flashing on the huge flat screens, ran a hand over his shaven skull. Twelve men the police wanted to speak to in relation to the abduction of Caitlyn McBeal, and possibly the Georges River killings. In the top right-hand corner of the screen, he saw his own face. Regan was sunken-cheeked and scruffy-haired in the picture, wearing the beard he'd grown in remand to try to make himself look fiercer than he really was. A wide-eyed teen being photographed for intake at Long Bay Correctional. He remembered the corrections officers taking the shot, fifteen years earlier, how terrified he'd been. He'd been able to hear the catcalls down the hall from where he stood. The men, waiting for him.

It had been an apprenticeship in pain. Years learning how to take it, how to experience pain in so many unique and creative ways. When they'd come for him on his last days, Regan had looked at the man in the mirror on the wall of his cell. A master of suffering.

As he'd left the cell block that had been his home, Regan had felt his muscles tightening, hardening. He'd walked through the administration block to collect his belongings and felt his fingers lengthen to talons. Through the transition cages, he'd felt black wings unfurling from his shoulder blades. In the car park where they left him, free to go wherever he pleased, his eyes had begun to burn with bloody, furious tears.

Regan realized that all along, he'd been designed to evolve into the thing he was now, this monster. His time in prison had been a natural steeling process. An incubation period. A thing as hard as him needed to be forged. All goodness needed to be squeezed from it. Empathy. Passion. Weakness. Standing there in the parking lot in the dark, the distant sounds of the waves crashing against the cliffs beyond the prison, he closed his eyes and remembered Sam Blue. All the time he'd been locked away, Regan hadn't dared call his friend's face to his mind. He'd been afraid of the fury that would come. The bloody memories. He remembered Sam, and knew only that he needed to find him.

Regan stood looking at his own face on the television screen now. Inevitably, the news story shifted and there he was. Beautiful Sam, with his downcast eyes and hollow cheeks.

Regan put a hand on the window and bent low, focused on the tiny pixels that made up the man's face.

Sam. His soul mate.

CHAPTER 91

KASH AND I drove back down the main street after our surveillance on the Robit property. There were patrol officers in the town, borrowed from towns all around, talking to people at their fences. Mick the bartender was leaving his house with an armful of towels, watching us roll by, his big belly making a single circle of sweat on his T-shirt where the flesh dipped inward at his navel.

I pulled Kash's arm, gesturing for him to stop. From the street outside the little house across from Victoria Snale's property, I could hear children playing inside. As I went to the door, the young mother I'd seen the night Zac Taby lost his life shouted from somewhere toward the rear of the building.

I knocked and two young ones, maybe three and four years old, ran to the screen door and stared expectantly up at me. I'd seen these golden-haired children that night in their pajamas. The mother was tired when she came to the door, uncomposed, expecting someone else. She remembered me.

"I'm Harriet Blue," I said. "This is my partner, Elliot Kash."

She opened the door. The kids tumbled out, seemingly very impressed with Kash, a thickly muscled superhero towering above them. There was no sign of a dad here.

"Mary Skinner," the mother said, smiling. "You two, get back in here."

The kids giggled and ran into the cool, dark hall. I followed Mary past a wall of framed photographs, backpacks hanging on hooks, a wooden rack inadequately small for the dozens of dusty shoes piled onto it. We went to the kitchen and she didn't offer us coffee. She was uncomfortable. Picking at fingernails split from nibbling.

"You probably know why I'm here," I said.

"The bombings." She glanced toward the door as something crashed in one of the bedrooms. "It's terrifying. Have you got a suspect yet?"

"We've got some leads," I said. "But I think maybe you could lengthen them for me. I don't know if you remember what you said to me two nights ago when I was out there on your porch."

Mary had tucked one arm into her ribs, the other tight against her chest. She opened the fridge to give herself somewhere to look.

"I don't remember anything much except the blast," she said. "I was watching out the window when it happened. I saw you fall. Are you OK? I mean"—she examined my broken arm—"nothing permanent?"

"I'm fine," I said. "You told me that it was 'all gonna come out.' You said, 'It's all coming to an end.'"

Mary looked horrified. Kash was sitting on a stool by the kitchen bench quite near her, measuring the response on her face. She took a bottle of water from the fridge and set it on the counter, turned away from us both.

"I didn't say that," she said quietly.

"Yes, you did."

"Look, I'm alone here." She threw me a hard look, on the edge of snapping. "I lost a child. I lost a husband. I say weird things sometimes that I don't necessarily mean."

The silence that fell was heavy. I could hear the children whispering beyond the door. I looked at them and they squealed and ran away.

"What happened?" I asked.

"My husband left. He's up north. Cairns."

"I mean to your child," I said. "You said you—"

"Brandon overdosed." Mary's gaze was locked on me. "It was an accident. He and his friends had been messing around with stuff brought in by the truckers. He was seventeen, child of my first marriage."

"I'm sorry," I said.

"I don't have anything else for you." Mary shut the fridge door hard, made jars rattle inside it. "That's it. Now, I've got things to do here."

She let us walk ourselves out. The sun seemed somehow closer, more foreboding. I felt I'd disturbed something, shifted a rock off an insect I didn't recognize, something dangerous. Something better left alone.

CHAPTER 92

ALL HIS LIFE, Regan had enjoyed ruining beautiful things. It was a strange sort of instinct, an impulse, the same kind of impulse that drove people to fix pictures hanging crookedly on walls or scrub single greasy fingerprints off of otherwise blessedly clean windowpanes. When new toys came into the youth care facility playroom, he'd break them. Shiny and glossy and smelling of plastic, with their bubbly eyes and stupidly grinning mouths, they seemed painfully perfect. He'd pull out a teddy's eye. Snap off a robot's arm. Cut a doll's hair so that it stuck out of the bulbous rubber scalp in ugly tufts. The broken, dirtied things gave him joy. Maybe he felt they were more like him when they were torn and crooked. He was only small. He couldn't know.

Then he turned his attention to the other boys and girls. It had begun with pretty little Claudia, with her big eyes and golden curls. Claudia would be adopted in a snap. The carers were already talking about it. She was a doll, they said. Regan had snuck in to the kitchen and found a packet of matches. She wasn't so perfect when he was done with her.

Regan became "difficult." The word was mentioned around him in a lot of different ways between foster families and care workers. He listened to them chattering above him like he wasn't there. There had been "difficulties" at his last home. He was "difficult" to place because of his "difficult" behavior. There were other words. Oppositional. Aggressive. Introverted.

Regan was sixteen when he met Sam. He'd been standing by the cake table at one of those pathetic Christmas events the Department of Children's Services ran every year at the town hall. Sam had been a lanky, pale kid, his limp black hair constantly hanging in his eyes. He was the only other teen at the stupid party. Regan had watched him for a long while, bored, until he saw Sam observing the gorgeous Christmas cake someone had baked for the occasion. Perfect edges. Immaculate red and green icing. Sam had reached out when no one was looking and pushed one of the lollies on the top of the cake until it sank into the soft, spongy interior, leaving a gaping hole in the design. Regan had smiled. Sam had seen it.

Regan had found him. His perfect match.

But as always, it wasn't long before that perfection was ruined. Soon there would be blood, and screaming. The adult Regan remembered now as he walked down the empty, dark street, his head low, the baseball cap pulled down over his eyes. Everything was so messy now. So dark, so torn. A beautiful and terrifying time, the very streets seemed awash with new life. Regan came around a corner and a group of young women swirled and ebbed around him. Perfume. He felt the muscles of his shoulders knot, the bones grinding in his neck. Marissa. Elle. Rosetta. His girls. His sacrifices to Sam. The women on the street passed him, a glittering flock of birds. There wasn't time for that now. That part of his life was over.

Regan glanced now and then at the paper in his hand, the numbers on the buildings around him. He reached the pale blue building and looked up to the third-floor windows facing the distant water.

The lights in Harriet Blue's apartment were on.

CHAPTER 93

PEOPLE THINK THAT in the Australian desert there's nowhere to hide. That it makes the perfect hunting ground because for hundreds of kilometers there is no cover. Barren sand oceans, dotted here and there with clumps of thin, dead or dying trees. In truth the desert is full of holes. From where I stood with Kash, Last Chance Valley was almost invisible in the distance, but for a small rise where the rocky rim poked through the horizon. I knew that beyond where we stood, there would be cracks and crevices in the desert, some of them kilometers deep, reaching far enough down into the earth for a person to disappear into. It's a treacherous place. A place not to be wandered into on moonless nights. It does make the perfect hunting ground, but not for its barrenness. It's porous. Full of secrets.

It was here in the depths of the desert that we met the Forensics team. We had spent the day on the ridge, watching Jace Robit's property.

Two men from the team who had dealt with the burned car at Snale's house drove up to our spot in the desert now in a dusty four-wheel drive. The mustached one who had looked at me so strangely in Snale's hallway.

"I'm Glen. This is Wayne." He shook Kash's hand, ignored me. "We just finished up with the vehicle. It's all here." He handed Kash a report.

"I might need you guys to stick around in the town, just be an extra hand if we need it. Something's happening tonight at eight," Kash explained to them. "We've got some interesting suspects moving about. Harry and I will be on this group, and we'll get Snale and some other officers on the town."

Glen gave me another nasty look. I jutted my chin at him, a challenge.

"What's your problem, mate?"

"Nothin'," he said, shrugging.

"Come on. Out with it."

He sighed, gave his offside a look. "I know who you are. I was there at your brother's apartment when they went in after the arrest."

There was a meaningful silence among the men around me. I felt a weight steadily increasing on my shoulders.

"Yeah?" I said. "What's your point?"

"My point is that I saw the evidence, Detective Blue. The duct tape on the bed. The messy sheets. The video camera. It was sick. I have nightmares about what happened in that apartment. I find it mildly infuriating that you've stuck by your brother all this time, that's all."

"*Nothing* happened in that apartment," I said.

"Maybe we should just—" Kash said.

"What's your explanation, then?" Glen said. "I've heard you say your brother is being framed. You must believe he was framed by this guy the police are hunting right now, the shaven-headed guy, the one who abducted Caitlyn McBeal. The guy who *told her* he was Sam's partner.

So, what, this guy abducts these girls right from under your brother's nose and savagely murders them and dumps them like pieces of trash. He waits until Sam goes to work and he says, 'Ha ha! Now's my chance to do it again!' He abducts Caitlyn, and he's all ready to do his nasty business on her, when 'Oh, hot damn! Sam's been arrested! Shit! Holy moly! This wasn't in the script!'"

"Mate"—Kash stepped forward, put a hand out—"just back down."

"So the guy thinks, 'Shit, I'd better high-tail it over to Sam's place and plant that evidence I was going to plant before the police raid the place!'" Glen was waving his hands theatrically now. He waited for me to give him some kind of answer. But no words would come.

"Isn't it more likely," Glen said, "that Sam was going to go home that night and this man with the shaved head was going to be there, and they were going to kill Caitlyn McBeal together? You're violent, Detective. Everybody knows that. Isn't it more likely that your brother is violent, too, rather than the gentle, misunderstood innocent man you say he is? Let's be real!"

There was an old and familiar Harry who would have stepped forward and uppercut the man before me. A swift and hard skyward thrust. But when I called on her, I found her too tired to wake.

I turned and walked toward the car, heard Kash calling after me as I got in. This time, I didn't have the strength to fight, to face my troubles. I ran.

CHAPTER 94

LET'S BE REAL!

I drove through the desert, being real.

Yes, my brother had confessed to the murders of three beautiful young women who studied at the same university he worked at three days a week. They'd disappeared, as Glen the Forensics arsehole had said, from right under my brother's nose. It was "likely" these things had happened because my brother had killed them.

Yes, an awful collection of violent sexual pornography was found in my brother's apartment. It was "likely" this was because Sam himself had acquired that material. Because he liked it. Because he'd used it to fuel his fantasies. Because he was a killer,

Yes, it was "likely" that whoever the man with the shaved head was, he'd told Caitlyn McBeal that he was my brother's partner because he was, indeed, my brother's partner.

Yes, it was "likely" that Sam was violent, because I was violent.

That he had a dark edge, a beast inside, that he could not control. A vicious internal guard dog, identical to the one that had started growing inside me almost from the moment I was born. It was a hellhound, a ferocious thing that I unleashed whenever I needed to. I'd let him free as a child when foster fathers and older brothers crept into my bedroom at night. When kids at new schools ragged on me. When the men I hunted in my job got away with what they'd done to their victims, and someone had to pick up the slack.

My dog was dangerous. It leapt out before I could stop it. Sometimes I could wrangle it back. But the beast had done such a good job over the years protecting me, it was too strong and wild now for me to ever hope to tame.

Did Sam have a beast inside? Had it gone feral on him? Got a taste for blood it couldn't sate?

No. I would never believe that. Could never, ever believe that.

Because if it could happen to him, it could happen to me.

CHAPTER 95

AGAIN I CAME upon Jed Chatt's house without meaning to, and I pulled into the driveway with horror, realizing I'd probably been under the gaze of his rifle for the last kilometer without thinking about it. The crosshairs trained on my face. I wiped at my cheeks and found tears. This wasn't good. I got out and walked up the rocky slope, still arguing with Glen in my mind. Digger the dog burst into a sprint from where she had emerged at the side of the porch, barking happily at me.

"Oh, you." I wiped my nose. The dog jumped and pawed at my waist and I rubbed her furry head. "I'm sorry about before."

Jed Chatt came out the front door of the house and stood watching me, a general look of disapproval on his face.

"I told you to rack off," he said.

"Yeah," I said, leading the dog toward him. "People do that."

He rolled his eyes, weary, and strode back into the house, letting the screen door slap shut. I noticed how remarkably the house had changed. The porch had been swept bare and the old barbecue was gone. The dog followed me inside.

The lanky, long-jawed man was sitting on the faded couch now with an assortment of plastic parts in front of him, tiny screws and brightly colored joints. A baby's play gym half-assembled, some of it still in the shipping box beside him. There must have been so much of this activity in the time since I had seen him last. Gathering up, sorting, squaring away his own things. Making room for the new life that had joined him.

Beside the couch on the floor the infant reclined in a fluffy pale-blue bouncer. Now and then Jed extended his leg and pushed on the bouncer with his big, bare toe, causing the baby to bob gently up and down. The man seemed mildly irritated by my presence, but not curious. I might have stood there an hour without either of us uttering a word.

I didn't fully understand the ease I felt around this man, but I knew then that unconsciously I'd been planning to flee here the moment Glen started attacking me. What was it about this man and this place that compelled me?

"You're a strange one, you," Jed said after a time.

"I get the feeling you might be the same."

I looked at the infant in the bouncer. An awkward, gummy smile playing about perfect lips he couldn't yet control.

"May I?" I asked. Jed said nothing. I extracted the child carefully from his bouncer. He was heavier and warmer than I'd imagined. The baby swiped at my chin, my lips. I kissed his fingers.

"His mother is my niece," Jed said eventually, glancing at the child's chubby hand encircling my finger. "I don't know her that well. Or I didn't. Her parents died some years back, and I never was real good at keeping in touch. She wrote me a couple of months ago. Couldn't call me. I don't have a phone."

Jed left the construction of the mobile and sat back on the couch, rested a bare foot on his knee.

"She grew up over Bandelong way. Even harsher than this, Bandelong. So when she got to the city she was real surprised, and so was everybody else, to tell you the truth. She did her degree, did the extra bits and pieces that come afterward, whatever they are. And then, to top it all off, she got accepted into this…this extra-special legal program. Always wanted to be a lawyer, and this program, she says…There are something like three people in the whole country who get in. Well, she got in. First blackfella in the history of the world to get in. Kind of thing that usually goes to white boys from private schools on the Sydney Harbour there. The other two candidates were just that. They were pretty upset that they were up against her for the position that you get at the end of it. The…partnership, or whatever."

The child had gone to sleep in my arms. Wisps of his soft black hair, finer than cotton, shifted in the breeze from the window.

"Same morning my niece was due to go in and sign her big important contract, she finds out about this one." He nodded at the baby in my arms. "Everybody has a good laugh at her then. The two other candidates, they reckon they're shoo-ins for the partnership at the end of the four-year program. One of the big lawyer types running the thing, he wants her chucked out of the program straightaway unless she gets an abortion. So she writes me asking what she should do. I'm about the last bit of family she's got. And she doesn't know me from a bar of soap. But she needs to talk to someone."

"What did you say?" I asked.

"I told her to do the program. And I told her to have the baby. I'd take him until she was through with it, until she found her feet. And if she never found her feet, well, that was OK. I figured if she'd dropped out, she'd have been all broken up about it. If she'd had an abortion, she'd have been broken up about that, too. This was the only way I could think of that she could get out of it without tearing herself in half."

The infant grizzled. I lifted him higher against my chest and patted his diaper-covered backside. Put my cheek on his head.

"It's not the best place in the world," Jed said, looking at the walls, still stained from years of neglect, the blazing desert sun rolling by the windows. "But it's a solution to a problem."

Jed stood. I guessed it was the signal for me to go. I didn't seem capable, at first, of giving the child back. Some ludicrous part of me saw this place as a solution to my problem. To every problem.

I handed back the child. He held the tiny boy and looked at my eyes. Seemed to know I wanted to stay. Here was a safe place, deliberately constructed on the edge of nowhere, too far into the wild for problems to reach. The kind of place they sang about in sad songs. All the hurt, all the badness, all the worry a person had could be sent here to be swallowed up by this man.

I felt the cruel sense that I belonged here tugging at my chest, even as I headed for the door.

CHAPTER 96

IT HAD ALL happened so quickly. Love stories were like that, so Regan had heard. He'd got chatting to the teenage Sam Blue at the Christmas party and discovered the gangly, shy, black-haired boy was living with a family in Panania, not far from where Regan was in Picnic Point. Their foster parents knew each other. Sam had only just arrived, having been separated from his sister after their last placement fell through. The boy missed her. Regan had listened, marveling quietly at his gentle voice.

There was no way Regan could have told Sam what he felt back then. The obsessive thoughts, the dreams about Sam. He wondered if his friend ever suspected. It was a struggle to stop himself from bringing Sam gifts at the house in Panania, turning up too often, staying too late to talk and giggle in the small blue room his foster parents had put him in. Everything Sam said stuck with Regan. He'd shown Regan a picture of a red racer bike in a catalogue, and Regan had begun to see red bikes everywhere deliciously displayed on street corners and in bike racks, unlocked. Regan closed his eyes sometimes and thought about what

Sam would say if he brought him one of those racers. Imagined him in awe, crying with gratitude, throwing his arms around Regan, the press of his thin, hard body against his own. Bliss. But it was far too risky. Their bond was one perfect thing he wasn't going to ruin. It was pure, untouchable, beautiful.

Joyous months passed. Sam and Regan would meet on the roadway down to the river. Firelight and smoke in the air, the heady scent of dope near the rock wall or on the gray sand. Circles of other kids laughing, whooping. Regan remembered sitting on the edge of the pier with his feet in the water and some nameless girl's face in his crotch, smoothing back her hair as she bobbed up and down on him, looking over and meeting Sam's eye as another girl worked on him. The stab of pleasure deep in his guts, making his legs twitch. They'd lain with the girls afterward, whoever they were. The girls were easy to ignore. Regan closed his eyes and felt Sam's elbow touching his, listened to the other boy's breathing. It could have been just the two of them under the stars. He suddenly felt free.

And then, before he knew it, Child Services was there at the door in Picnic Point. His foster parents had decided to tour Italy and couldn't bring him along. Another placement had been arranged. The couple told Child Services to handle telling Regan, because they were too emotional about it, and they knew he was an emotional boy, too.

They'd meant *difficult*. But they couldn't possibly know that Regan was slowly graduating from difficult to dangerous.

CHAPTER 97

NOW, REGAN STEPPED silently down onto the toilet in Harriet Blue's apartment and turned around, sliding the bathroom window closed behind him. The gentle click as the latch caught was the only sound in the apartment. He stood in the dark looking at the things on her vanity, feeling sick little zings of excitement at the sight of them. Comb. Pill packets. Creams.

He went into the short hallway and gazed at the gold light falling on the polished floorboards from the living room. This was a good apartment. A solid investment for someone who worked hard and spent little on their social life. Regan knew that the place had been sold, probably to fund Sam's legal defense. In mere weeks, all of this would have to be packed up and shipped out. Regan was glad that he could see it as it was, Harry in her natural environment, the girl Sam had talked so much about.

There was no one home. He was sure of it. The lights must have been a tactic by Harriet to appear at home, something to drive away the press or curious gawkers who might try to take advantage and sneak in.

Regan had the distinct sense of her abandonment of the place as he walked into the study. He looked at the work of the Georges River Killer on the corkboard behind the desk. Pictures of his victims, both alive and as he'd left them, lolling dead on the gray sands like washed-up sea creatures. There were forensic reports here. Criminal profiles. Harry's notes. Regan had seen some of these things already in the briefcase he stole from Edward Whittacker. They were close behind him. But it wasn't over yet.

If only it had all gone the way he'd planned. It would have been so perfect. He'd come across Sam for the first time after leaving prison, and it was there that he'd got his idea. Sam had been standing at the edge of the hall outside a computer lab on the Sydney Uni campus, talking to one of his pretty little students, her long chocolate hair awash in sunlight. Regan had followed and watched and realized that Sam was surrounded by these gorgeous creatures. They waved at him from cafe tables and touched his arm as he went by, smiling, asking about some assignment or another. Sam was so happy. Regan could see it in his stride as he walked home, as he climbed the stairs to his neat, bright apartment. Wasn't Sam just the perfect "fuck you" to all those care workers and all those families shuffling him here and there, the raggedy, hollow-eyed urchin Regan knew so well playing tricks in the dark by the riverside. Bad boy. Difficult boy. Unwanted boy. Sam's beautiful world was choreographed as joyously as the opening of a Broadway show. People swinging on lampposts, arms out, soaring voices.

Regan had entered Sam's world like a dark cloud creeping, billowing up over the horizon. He'd wanted to stay longer. It had all been going too well.

He moved out of the study, back into the hall.

And heard a sound in the kitchen.

CHAPTER 98

I PICKED UP Kash. He'd stayed by our surveillance spot, lying on his belly at the edge of the ridge, watching the sun go down, sweeping the valley with his binoculars. He didn't speak as he got into the car. There was an icy feeling in the pit of my stomach, that he'd call me out for walking off instead of standing my ground and defending my brother. But my ability to stand my ground was waning. Two more days and the AVO would be lifted, and I could be by Sam's side again.

"We've got a problem," Kash said, breaking me out of my reverie.

"What?"

"Dez spread the word around town that people aren't to congregate, that we want the pub closed and the main street clear. This seems to have had the opposite effect. People are angry. Defiant. There's talk they're going to gather tonight in the main street as a show of strength."

"Oh, brilliant!" I snapped. "What a fantastic idea! We've told them it's dangerous to gather in groups, and what do they do? They decide to throw a party."

"They're Australians." Kash sighed. "We told them to stay away from their local pub. We might as well have waved a red flag in front of a bull."

There were already people in the main street as we drove through, standing outside shops, talking. Only twelve or thirteen in total, but more would come. There was a strange excitement in the air, the feel of Christmas or New Year's Eve, of community. It didn't seem to matter that someone wanted to kill them all. The mob was stronger than a single killer.

They were wrong. I knew they were wrong.

I spied Mary Skinner, the mother with the young children, walking along the road back toward her house, her two kids running ahead. At least someone was being sensible.

Kash and I parked by the bracken just beyond Jace Robit's property again. At precisely seven-thirty, the man emerged, taking long strides to his ute. Through the growing dark, I could see lights on in Frank Scullen's garage. Headlights swept us as the two men pulled out.

"Come on, fuckers," I said, starting the engine. "Show us your big plan."

CHAPTER 99

WE PLOWED INTO the night. Kash became pointed beside me, squinting into the dark ahead. I left the longest possible distance between Frank's truck and our own, trying not to spook him with my headlights. The trucks disappeared over ridges and hills in the desert.

We were well out of town when the headlights ahead stopped moving. I turned ours off and rolled slowly toward a huge eucalypt surrounded by bush. As Kash and I got out of the car, a group of dingoes somewhere in the vast empty wilderness nearby sent up a howling song.

Here is where I could meet my end, I thought, as I always do when I find myself in situations like this. Rushing into a home where a child is suspected to be in danger, storming the doors of porn studios, dungeons, makeshift brothels. I have plenty of police training to try to combat the dangers of the sniper in the upstairs window, the man with the shotgun behind the door, the tripwire in the hall attached to a grenade. I know to look out for these things. But there's always the chance of a wild card. A new strategy by the bad guys. Cops die every single day. *This could be the day that it's me.*

I jogged behind Kash across the dirt, head low, drawing out my gun.

The trucks were parked at the base of a high cliff, a split in the earth's crust cleaved vertically through the enormous rock shelf, only a meter wide. I knew there was probably a lookout just inside the entrance to the cave. Kash took the other side of the entrance. I crept forward and looked in, saw a pair of stubby legs splayed on the warm earth. John Stieg was just settling into his position, still tapping through his phone, checking the things that needed to be checked and sending the things that needed to be sent before a long stretch of guard duty. I leapt forward before he could look up from the phone, knowing his night vision would be ruined by the bright screen.

He put a hand to the gun sitting on the ground by his hip.

"Don't," I said. I put a hand out. He paused, finger sideways, loose, on the trigger guard.

The man gave in and took his hand off the weapon. He rose reluctantly, rubbing his short beard. Kash's breath was on the back of my neck. It was tight here. Tight enough that in a struggle, I might lose this man. Stieg twisted and I poked him forward with my pistol, away from the gun on the ground, which Kash swept up into the back of his jeans.

"Make a noise, and I'll fire," I said.

We walked through the darkness. Ahead of us there came the clattering and crashing of things being set up, men talking, their voices echoing off the walls of the narrow cave. I spied wires on the ground. My breath was coming in short, hot blasts. Tanks. Cables. The sickly glow of headlamps trying to cut through airborne dust. It was hard not to cough.

The crevice widened and we were suddenly upon the other three,

Jace Robit nearest to me, tugging a cotton mask up over his nose and mouth, a small jackhammer hanging from his fist. I shoved Stieg and he gathered with the rest of them.

"Police!" I shouted, my eardrums pulsing as the sound ricocheted off the close walls. "Tools down! Hands up!"

No one complied. It takes a leader, not a stranger, to get them moving. They all looked at Jace.

"I said hands up, fuckbags!" I kicked the jackhammer out of Jace's hand. It clanked to the ground. The man gave a short, hard laugh, raised his hands and interlocked them at the back of his head. I checked Kash's gun was on them all and lowered mine. I walked around them and looked into the black depths of the crevice beyond where we stood. It seemed to narrow then turn away into pitch blackness.

"Is there anyone else?"

"No," someone said. I kicked the nearest man's knee out. He took the hint and knelt. The others followed. There was a lot of equipment here. Plastic and duct tape, buckets of water. I couldn't get my heartbeat down. My thoughts were racing. Whatever this was, it wasn't bomb-building paraphernalia. That was good. My hands were shaking on my gun. "What the fuck is all this?"

The men didn't answer. Kash kicked over a bucket of rocks near his foot.

"Gold," he said. "They've found a gold deposit."

"Jesus Christ." I glanced at the rock wall beside us, only just now realizing that it was covered in indentations only visible in the light of the headlamps. "This is where it came from. The package we found at Chief Campbell's place. Did he confiscate that gold from you? Did you kill him because he found out what you were doing here?"

Jace Robit was watching me. His eyes were fierce above the hem of the cotton mask covering his nose and mouth. I felt like smashing his face with the butt of my pistol. If there's one thing I can't stand from suspects, it's the silent treatment. But I was working through things in my mind. Trying to fit the pieces together.

"It wasn't drugs you were all into. It was this. Gold. Theo Campbell shook you down. It's just like we said." I looked at Kash. "But he knew there had to be more. So you killed him. You blew him up."

"We didn't kill anybody." Frank Scullen shook his head, glared at me. "This is bullshit. I'm not wearing a fucking murder charge."

"Which one of you wrote the diary?" My voice was quivering. "You wrote the diary to distract us, didn't you?"

"We didn't kill nobody, and we didn't write no fuckin' diary!" John Stieg snapped.

"Then why the secrecy?" I looked at the gold on the ground by Kash's foot.

The men glanced at each other, all but Jace, whose eyes were locked on me.

"Whose land is this?" Kash asked. "Whose land are we on?"

No one answered. Kash pointed at the ground.

"If this land isn't yours, and it isn't public, then this gold is being stolen," he said. "Are we on someone's land right now?"

I heard a click right beside my ear. The unmistakable sound of a hammer drawing back on a revolver.

CHAPTER 100

REGAN GAVE THE corner of the kitchen a wide berth, walked around through the living room and looked in. There was a man standing there, leaning against the counter, his arms folded and his eyes following Regan as he stepped into view. This man looked disordered, crooked, roughed-up somehow. Like the survivor of some kind of natural disaster, emerging from the forest with windswept hair and hard features, dirty clothes, a starved look. He was big. Muscular. Enormous boots. This had indeed been a very big mistake on Regan's part. Who was this man? Was he Harriet's boyfriend? What else didn't he know about Sam's sister? Once again, his plans were being foiled. The game was changing. Regan felt exhilaration rush through him.

"I really hoped you'd come," Tox said.

Regan tried to make sense of the words. He glanced toward the door. Was this a trap? No, of course not. He'd have been knocked to the ground by now, windows bursting in, SWAT teams thumping up the stairs. This man was alone. His black pistol lay on the counter, turned away.

The man in the kitchen looked Regan over, sniffed.

"So you're him," Tox said, eyes roving. "I've seen pictures of you. Seen the imprint of your hand on the bodies of your victims. Your punches. I guess I thought I knew what you'd look like. But you're different."

"Different how?" Regan asked.

The man in the leather jacket shrugged his folded arms.

"I guess I hoped you'd be bigger," he said.

"Bigger?" Regan almost laughed.

"Mmm," Tox said. He sighed. "Stronger." Tox's eyes wandered up Regan's body. "See, I don't like men who hurt women and girls. I really, really don't like 'em. So I hoped that when I finally caught up to you, I'd be able to hurt you for a good while before having to hand you over to police. I've been looking forward to hurting you."

Regan laughed. Oh, what an unexpected gift this was.

"I'm sure I can live up to expectations," Regan said.

The man in the kitchen unfolded his arms, stood poised, his big hands loose by his sides.

"You ready?" Tox asked.

"Oh yes." Regan smiled. "More than ready."

CHAPTER 101

OF COURSE THERE were others. How had I thought something like this might be limited to five men? Theo Campbell, Jace Robit, Frank Scullen, John Stieg and Damien Ponch. Of course it had spread. Small towns aren't equipped for secrets like this, life-changing secrets. Last Chance Valley was an all-consuming hole in the earth. Everyone wanted to escape. A few men had found a way, and the others had been able to smell it on them. Their secret hope. I turned my head slightly and the barrel of the man's gun touched the back of my ear. I caught a glimpse of a fat, bearded man. The bartender from Last Chance. Mick the Prick. I smelled body odor and bourbon.

"Drop it. You too."

Kash and I dropped our guns. Jace's eyes had lost their fierceness now. The man was incredulous, mortified, all his plans crumbling before him.

"Mick," he snapped at the man behind me. "What the fuck!"

"Yeah, exactly," Mick the bartender said, smiling. "What the fuck.

You lot find a fortune and you think you can just pick up and leave with it? You don't think about sharing it around? What a bunch of selfish fucking pricks."

"Don't do anything stupid," I murmured, my hands out by my sides. "We can all walk out of here if everybody just stays calm."

He ignored me. "I wondered what you shitheads were up to," Mick sneered, pushing me forward. I walked slowly toward Kash, turned, trying not to make any sudden movements. Mick kicked the two men nearest to him until they lay on their stomachs on the sand. "I seen you at the pub snickering and whispering like a bunch of old bitches. Knew you had something on the go, so I followed you out here. What a surprise. I thought I'd wait, let you do all the hard work for me. But then I seen these coppers were onto you. I had to swoop in before you got yourselves arrested." He gestured to Kash and me. "You two. On your knees."

We knelt in the dirt. The sweat was rolling down my sides now. Mick went to Kash's back and tugged the second gun out of his jeans, kicked him onto his stomach with the rest of the men.

"You," he pointed at me. "Take those wires over there, tie them up. And don't think you're going to do it loosely. I'll check."

I crawled on my hands and knees to a pile of electrical wire nearby. The men had been drilling, sending charges through the rock wall, exploding bits off to get deeper into the seam. I wondered just how secure this all was, if in the end a collapse from the rock above would bury all of us. A Venus flytrap snapping shut on greedy flies. I looked up. The crack in the earth went all the way up. There were stars up there beyond us all. Maybe there was hope. Mick was muttering to Jace as I crawled over to him and began tying his hands.

"Sure must be a lot of it for you all to have decided you'll just take off and leave everyone behind," Mick was saying. "Let's see. If I wanted to start a new life, I reckon I'd need a hundred grand *minimum.* A hundred grand could see you set yourselves up pretty well in Thailand."

"Fuck off, idiot," Jace snapped, his chin resting in the dirt, teeth together. I moved and tied Frank's hands.

"But then, you guys have been out here for ages, I reckon," Mick mused. "I started to notice you acting weird months back. Let's say it's three months of ferreting the rocks away. Then Soupy Campbell finds you with some. You have to bring him in on it all."

"What's your plan here?" I asked Mick. He'd elected me to bind everyone. He must have some level of trust in me. I tried to keep my voice low, nonthreatening. "You'll leave us all tied up here and then go raid everyone's houses, take the rocks and leave. That's what you'll do, right?"

Mick didn't answer. I'd tied all Jace's men and moved to Kash. His hands were sweaty.

"Because there's really no need to hurt anyone," I continued. "The guys will tell you where the gold is hidden, so you can get away with plenty of time."

"Shut up and finish what you're doing."

"You're talking about theft," I said. "That's all. Leave now. Then if you're caught, you can probably plead out. You do not want to find yourself on the run with six murder charges. When they find us, they'll shut the whole country down to catch who did it."

Mick flicked the gun at the sand. I lay down and felt his bulk shift over me, the sickening press of his crotch against my backside as he pulled my arm behind my back with his free hand.

"Who says they're gonna find you?" Mick asked.

CHAPTER 102

TOX CRACKED HIS knuckles and smiled, and the man smiled, and they rushed at each other.

He was a prison fighter. Tox could tell that right away. You've got to fight fast in prison, before the guards stop you, so Regan faked only once before throwing in his first punch. Tox grabbed the fist as it sailed past his ear, yanked the man forward and hit him hard in the sternum.

Regan spat air, crumpled in half, fell on the coffee table, smashing it to pieces.

Tox grabbed something—a vase or a sculpture or something, he didn't look—and clubbed the man. Once. The second time was blocked.

The kick in the knee was unexpected. Tox backed up into a bookshelf, sent more objects smashing.

Regan was on him. A punch to the jaw that crunched his teeth. Tox blocked the second swing, palmed his attacker in the nose. Blood down the front of Regan's shirt, fast and heavy. The man ignored it. He was a good fighter. Focused, determined under pressure. He'd have been a good killer. Those girls wouldn't have stood a chance.

Tox saw them in his mind, a tiny flash, smiling teeth and bright eyes, beautiful futures. It was what he needed to refocus himself. He leapt forward.

CHAPTER 103

THE PROBLEM WAS tying my wrists with the gun in his spare hand. The cast made things even trickier. He tried, gave up, backed away. I shifted my hands to the ground beside my shoulders, in a push-up position, ready to spring. I didn't know what was going to happen next, but I was the only one with my hands free. It was on me. Sweat was stinging on my burned skin. I planted my toes in the sand, wiggled them down until I felt hard earth. Mick was watching us all. Deciding. I could still talk him out of this. Surely.

"Everybody thinks about getting out," Mick said gently. He rubbed his beard. "I mean, I get it. I grew up here, just like you guys. By the time you're old enough to figure out there's a whole other world out there, you've already grown roots. You stay, or you abandon everything. Everyone. There's no in-between."

He was apologizing. Saying sorry for what he was about to do. My throat was tight with tension. I could barely breathe.

"This was your only chance," Mick said. He pointed the gun at Jace. "It's *my* only chance now."

"No!" I screamed. The gun roared, not once but twice. Mick was a seasoned killer. A country man. He'd shot dogs that got too old, horses that got lame, dingoes that wandered onto his property.

He'd shot Jace in the head and turned and clicked back the hammer and shot the man beside him, Damien, before I even got to my feet. I slammed into him, the image of their bucking heads still shuddering through my mind.

There was screaming. Men screaming. The two surviving men, Frank and John, crawled and cowered against the rock walls. Kash was on his feet, stumbling, trying to rip the wire from his wrists. I struggled with Mick for the pistol. His round belly pushed at my chest as he leaned back, hands high, trying to tug it from my grip.

The third bullet hit the wall above us, dislodged rock and dust. It was in my eyes, in Mick's eyes. I stepped back and kicked him in the crotch before he could take aim again. It was a hard horse-kick with my heel leading. He went down. I grabbed the gun and smashed the butt of it over his nose, crushing bone. I pulled it back and swung again, hammered him in the temple.

Kash's hands were free. He grabbed the gun before I could pound the unconscious man beneath me another time.

Jace and Damien were dead. I went to their bodies, turned their heads, checked for a pulse. Kash was already disappearing through the gap in the rock to call for medical assistance.

I took the wire Kash had stripped from his wrists and flopped Mick onto his belly, started winding it around his wrists. Frank Scullen and John Stieg were watching me, speechless, as I pulled the wire and knotted it over and over again.

"I should make you arseholes free yourselves," I said as I went to untie them.

CHAPTER 104

THE TACTICS WERE dirty. Tox liked that. He'd pinned Regan on the carpet, tugged and twisted him up into a headlock, but the other man had got hold of a shard of the broken vase and jammed it into Tox's forearm.

He stumbled into the kitchen and pulled the shard from the wound, spraying blood on the cupboards. There was a kettle nearby with a curved handle. Tox grabbed it and threw it, listened to it clunk off Regan's head. There was a wine rack by the door to the kitchen. Regan grabbed a bottle and held it by the neck like a club.

He lunged. Tox grabbed the arm before it came down, smashing the bottle against the top edge of the fridge. He got a couple of punches in while Regan was distracted. They fell against the fridge, rattling things inside. Tox went for Regan's throat, his thumbs gripping his windpipe, crushing tendons. Regan's boots slipped in the wine. He was under him, between his legs. Tox grabbed a handful of shirt. Regan grabbed his ankle, brought him down, tried to crawl away while Tox recovered.

Tox steadied himself against the kitchen counter and spied the knife block. Regan was coughing, gurgling, something in his throat broken or bent out of shape. Tox slid a knife from the block. A lean, midsize filleting blade. Razor-sharp. He turned toward his victim. The fantasy of every mother and father with a raped daughter. The beast at your mercy, a sharp blade, his legs splayed. Tox would have to hand Regan over to the police alive. He knew that. But maybe there was something he could do to make sure the man never raped a young woman again.

CHAPTER 105

"HOW MANY SPARE officers have you got?" Kash was in the car, the phone pressed to his ear. I knew he was talking to the command chief of White Cliffs, who had loaned us officers to patrol the main street of Last Chance Valley while the people gathered. "I need at least two to come protect some bodies and take some suspects into custody. Can you redirect your men? No, not the one we've been looking for. Another one. I'll send you the location."

I told Frank and John to lie on the ground, and stood at the entrance to the cave in case Mick woke and tried to come out. I didn't expect him to. I'd knocked him pretty hard. John Stieg was crying, his head on the rocky earth. Kash came and stood by me.

"Do you believe them?" he asked. "About the diary?"

"I do," I admitted.

"So the town's still in danger," he said.

It was a breathless, wordless hour. And then Kash and I were back on the road, Kash driving too fast, smashing over plants and logs as we headed toward the highway. We had come so close to death. I had rushed at a gun without thinking. My mind kept trying to reassure me that I was safe, dumping calming chemicals into my veins, attempting to slow down my pulse. But we hadn't found the diarist. We'd been wrong about Jace Robit and his crew. I only realized I was gripping the seat cushion so hard with my good hand when Kash reached over and touched my arm.

"You're making me nervous."

"Watch the road," I said.

Kash swung the car onto the highway. I shifted in my seat. There was sand all through my shirt and pants, driving me nuts. I pulled my bra away from my body and dumped a load of it onto my stomach. I wriggled in my seat, trying to get it out the bottom of my jeans.

In my left front pocket, another deposit of sand, and a small piece of paper. I pulled out the folded sheet and opened it. Switched on the overhead light. The letters were small and clunky, but I knew the handwriting right away. Had studied it closely.

Dear Oficer Blue,

So sad you didn't want to come away with me. I think we wold have made great partners. I'm sorry for steeling! I know it's wrong. But its a big bad world out there and I'm gonna see it if it kills me. I'm getting out of here finelly! You're a cool chick. See you round some time.

Zac Taby

"What is it?" Kash asked.

"Nothing." I wiped my face, tucked the note away. Zac must have left it before he walked out of Snale's house, toward his doom. I'd failed him. I'd failed him.

"Harry?"

"It's nothing. It's fine. Let's get back to town. If the killer shows his face, I want to be on him like wildfire."

CHAPTER 106

THE TINY TOWN was lit up like a Christmas tree. People wandering toward the center from the dark road out of town, cars parked haphazardly on the dirt. Kash and I drove through slowly, blasting the horn and shining the enormous hunting lights at dazed men in slouch hats carrying bottles of beer.

"Fucking Aussies," I said. "Any excuse to have a piss-up."

Someone was seriously threatening to kill these people, and they were coming out in force to pretend they weren't afraid. Horns beeping, shop fronts open. I leaned over and looked at the back parking lot of the mechanic. There was no semitrailer there. That, at least, was something.

We spied Snale telling off a couple of youths and stopped beside her. Her uniform was patched with sweat.

"It's a madhouse," she panted as Kash rolled down his window. She looked at us, seemed to measure the trauma on our faces. "What happened? Are you two all right?"

"We're OK," I said. "We'll stash the car and come help with crowd control."

Kash drove on. By the edge of town, there was a streak of white in front of the vehicle. Kash slammed on the brakes. It was Bella Destro, in ridiculous high heels beneath her blue jeans, steadying herself against the asphalt with one hand, a beer bottle in the other. I got out of the car and helped her to her feet.

"You're the last person I expected to see out here," I said.

"Woo! Detective Harriet Blue!" She staggered, grinned at me, sweeping back her hair. "Look at all these people! It's a party!"

Kash honked the car horn, scaring us both. I dragged Bella toward the passenger side door.

"I'll drive her home. She's off her head," I told Kash. "You meet up with the other guys, give them a hand. I'll be back in a minute."

I wasn't focused. I was sad and hurt about Zac's letter, about the stupid young lives all around me, kids trying to run off with stolen gold, flopping on the road like wounded animals, cheering and reeking of beer. This was a maddening place. I momentarily felt so beyond rage I could hardly speak.

I was distracted. Not thinking at all as I started driving Bella back the way we'd come, into the dark.

CHAPTER 107

IN THE CAR, she put her head against the window, the cheerful, clumsy girl I'd witnessed on the road gone. I figured she was tired. My mind was not in the car. It was back in the center of town, where a killer was possibly planning on breaking out into a shooting spree.

I ran through the checklist of precautions in my mind. I knew Snale and another officer had separately locked down the armory and the ammunition caches so that even if someone managed to get through their defenses, they'd waste precious time trying to get to any useful weaponry. Snale and the team in town would be doing regular check-ins. I should have taken a radio, got onto their channel. No matter. I'd be back there in minutes. We'd need to charge Stieg and Scullen when this was done. Stealing. Unlicensed mining operations on trespassed property. We needed to arrest Mick, alert the families of the dead. That wasn't important now. I shook my head. What was important was keeping everyone safe for tonight. Even if the killer never showed his face.

I pulled into the Destro property and began driving up the long, lamplit driveway.

"You must feel very alone," Bella said suddenly. I glanced at her. She was sitting with her hands in her lap, facing the house, her expression calm.

"What do you mean?"

"The whole thing with your brother," she said as I came to a stop beside the house. "He's in jail. He's got his own problems to worry about. You're free, out here in the world, wandering around trying to get on with things. No one believes you when you say that he's innocent."

My brother was the last thing I wanted to talk about. I got out of the car. Left my gun right beside her in the center console.

Stupid. Stupid.

"No one believes you," she said again, looking at me as I opened the door for her. "It must be so isolating."

"I don't have time for a deep and meaningful," I said. "Get out. I've got to go. I'm busy."

That was when she pointed the gun at me.

"You're not going anywhere," she said.

CHAPTER 108

I WAS BEWILDERED. At first, my brain told me this was just another inconvenience on what was shaping up to be a horror of a night. I was still cursing myself for not having a radio.

"Don't be stupid," I said. "Put it down."

"Harriet," she said. Trying to wake me up. Bring me back down to earth. "Focus."

Focus. Breathe. I was standing like an idiot in the driveway with my hands by my sides, staring at the gun, the strange, unfamiliar sight of my own weapon pointed toward me and not away. She actioned the weapon expertly, and with that sickening sound I came to.

I looked into her eyes.

"Oh no," I said.

CHAPTER 109

WITH THE GUN at my back I walked numbly up the driveway toward the house, too shocked to offer much resistance. I'd gone into full denial mode, a symptom of my general stress over the case and my emotional detachment after the murders earlier in the night. Cognitive dissonance, the same thing that affects soldiers, sends them wandering into no-man's-land under shellfire like they're going for a Sunday stroll. This was a game. A prank by a strange drunken girl. She was going to be in a whole lot of trouble when she gave me back the gun. I was going to be in a whole lot of trouble if anyone ever found out she'd played with it. Yes, "played." Because she was a girl. A young university student home to study for exams. Her major concerns would be trying to get some proper study time in without wasting the entire vacation watching bad TV and chatting on Facebook.

She showed me into the dining room where just days earlier I had sat with her father and listened to her pick at him about racism in small towns. Dez was sitting in one of the dining-room chairs, as he had been on that day. But he was decidedly less comfortable in the seat than he had been before. A line of duct tape started at his shoulders and wound around and around the chair and his body, over his round belly, now and then splitting to reveal the cloth and buttons of his sweat-drenched shirt. The duct tape around his mouth was so tight his cheeks were swelling purple under the wild eyes that watched me enter the room.

Of course. The massacre plan had said "*Kill* Officer Snale," but "Get John Destro." Snale was only an obstacle. She could be disposed of easily. But this man was the focus. He was the catalyst for it all. He wouldn't be killed right away. Not until he had fulfilled his purpose.

CHAPTER 110

I WAS DRAWN straight to the device around his neck, a clumsy thing secured with more silver duct tape that pulled at the loose skin around his throat. A plastic water bottle turned sideways sat under his chin, sloshing with pale brown, almost tea-colored liquid. I could see wires and fixtures making bumps and veins in the tape around the top and bottom of the bottle. Inside the bottle, awash in the liquid, were more wires crisscrossing each other, tightly wrapped in black electrical tape.

The unprofessional look of the device added to the already deep lack of comprehension I was experiencing. I stood before the man in the chair and looked at the thing around his neck and couldn't believe that it was in any way dangerous. It was so messily constructed, so awkward, that my only concern at that point was the gun on me and the man's rapid breathing, threatening a heart attack.

I looked at the girl with the gun. Of course it had been her all along.

From the moment I met her, she'd been desperate to make me and everyone around her aware of her searing dissatisfaction with the town, its people, her father, everything.

She was more than dissatisfied. She was angry. Over dinner her disgruntlement at her father's racism tumbled off her lips like spittle. Her eyes had implored me from across the table. But I'd been uninterested. And that's the automatic reaction she'd received most of her life, I imagined. A default dismissal of whatever bugged her. Pretty girl. White girl. Student. What could she possibly have to complain about? She flicked the gun toward a nearby chair and I went to it and sat down.

"I decided I wanted to use you for Day Zero when I found out you were in town," Bella began, smoothing her hair down with long, slow strokes. "It was so amazing, you coming, you being right in the middle of all this. I knew it was a sign. I've been watching you and the case with your brother from the beginning. I watched the footage of you going up to the courthouse for the first day of proceedings. You looked so distressed. I remember thinking at the time—you're going to be the victim in this that nobody understands. You're going to be the forgotten one. The forgotten victim."

She glanced at her father. I followed her eyes, watched sweat rolling down his temple.

"There will be people who sympathize with your brother," Bella said. "And there will be people who sympathize with the dead girls. Their families. But right in the middle of it all, there's you. Nobody sympathizes with you. Nobody believes you. I know what that feels like."

She went to the dining-room table and carefully plucked up a tattered yellow envelope, thick as a dictionary. I noticed another gun on the table. Theo Campbell's gun. Bella must have taken it the night she stopped the older officer on the road on the hillside, probably with a ruse similar to the one she'd used on me. Helpless, Bambi-legged. The one who needed management. She tossed the envelope onto the ground at her father's feet. Dez winced. The liquid in the bottle at his throat sloshed.

I took the hint and slowly went to the envelope, picked it up and returned to my chair. Calm movements were essential. Don't antagonize her. Don't challenge her. Just listen, keep alert for something you can use. Something you can bring out, nurture, the key to stopping it all. Because this was a clever young woman. Cunning, manipulative. Not the kind of killer who would have carelessly left her diary full of murderous plans in a blazing red backpack at the local rest stop. That's why the bag was red. Why the bag was otherwise empty. It was a red bag or a fucking neon sign. STOP ME. She wanted to be caught. She wanted to be listened to. She had chosen me to stop her.

I opened the envelope, only now realizing how badly my hands were shaking. The photographs inside were jumbled together, corners sticking out everywhere. I slipped my fingers in, pulled out a handful.

The first picture was of a young boy sitting with his back against a bare rock wall. He couldn't have been older than ten. Naked. Legs splayed. Another young boy had his head resting on the boy's thigh, face turned inwards, just centimeters from his genitals. Both were clearly unconscious.

I let the pictures fall to the floor one at a time. The same faces. Different faces. Boys and girls in their teens. Some youngsters, tweens. Some of them were simply splayed out, on their own, mostly in the light of a fire. On sand. On rock. Curled on their sides on beds of dry grass. Some of them had been entwined awkwardly together. Heads leaning sloppily on bellies and shoulders, gaping mouths in the dark.

A man began appearing in the photographs. His bulging, white, be-speckled belly. His pale thighs. Dez.

A sickness was rising steadily in my stomach, pressing at the back of my throat. I'd seen pictures like this many times in my work.

"What are you going to use me for, Bella?" I said.

"To get my message out." She smiled.

CHAPTER III

THERE WAS A thump at the door, a fist bashing, a shouting voice.

Tox ignored it, stood over Regan as he writhed on a fallen couch cushion, trying to scramble away. Tox stabbed down, got the inside thigh of his jeans, the cushion, some carpet. He put a boot into the man's leg and tried to hold him still. Tox was making this man feel what his victims had felt. It was so good.

The door burst open. A tall, broad figure in a dark polo shirt, hands out. A neighbor on his way home from work, walking past the apartment door, hearing the scuffle within. Tox was distracted for barely a second, and in that time Regan slipped out from beneath him.

A blow to the side of his head, the smash of something porcelain. Tox stumbled. The knife was gone. He twisted, arm up to ward off another blow, but his enemy had risen and encircled him in a tight embrace.

Tox didn't even feel the first entry wound. The knife slid into him like butter. Practiced killer, jamming it under the ribs at the front, into the softness of his abdomen.

Tox gripped Regan, tried to hold him, to make another blow awkward. But the knife came again, sinking deep, pushing the air out of him.

His legs went. Tox hit the floor. His bodily control was gone but his mind was crystal clear. It wasn't over. Couldn't be over. He focused, opened his eyes wide, found the killer moving past him in a dark blue blur of shoes and jeans. He was heading for the good Samaritan in the doorway, a neighbor who'd thought he was breaking up an ordinary everyday domestic scuffle, who had then watched the stabbing, frozen in horror.

Tox reached out with all his strength. Careful now. Don't miss it. The killer's ankle breezed by. Tox grabbed on, under the hem of the jeans, above the low black sock, as Regan bent his knee, exposing the tiny slice of flesh. Tox gripped Regan's ankle. Clamped down with his nails. Held on for as many of the precious passing milliseconds as he could.

Regan hardly noticed the scratch.

The neighbor in the doorway was backing away from him as he advanced.

CHAPTER 112

I PUT THE photographs on the ground. I'd seen enough. Bella was keeping an eye on me as she readied things on the table, duct tape and three small plastic mobile phones, the kind bought at supermarkets for thirty bucks. Dez was watching the floor, his eyes wandering over tiles, trying to distance himself from what was happening.

"It started when I was fourteen," Bella said. "Just after Mum left. For the first couple of leadership camps, he left me at home. But I guess he decided he needed an accomplice, someone to disarm the mothers who didn't want to send their teenage girls away with him into the desert. He had a really good routine going, didn't you, Dad? He'd wait until the second night, after he'd made everyone do the Morse code exercise and report back to their families that they were all having a great time. The second morning starts with a big trek, so by the time we made camp in the evening everyone was always hideously tired and dehydrated. That's when he'd have me spike the water bottles."

Dez squeezed his eyes shut and burst into tears. The stuff in the water bottle at his throat washed back and forth to the rhythm of his sobs.

"It worked so very well with me," Bella said, watching him cry with disinterest. "I was the spectacle. The measuring stick. Everyone would wake up the next day and talk about how dazed and tired they still were. And how they couldn't remember anything after the campfire. I'd be there to reassure them everyone fell asleep so quickly—we all must have been so tired. When we got back to Last Chance Valley I'd prance around and tell all the parents what a great time we had. What choice did I have but to be his accomplice? I was a kid." She looked at her father. "I was a *kid* when he started this."

"Bella," I said, "I can understand your anger."

"Can you?" she asked. She took a seat at the dining-room table, by her little pile of equipment, and looked at me. "I guess you've probably seen stuff like this before, doing what you do. You'll know that sometimes the boys and girls who have been drugged, they start to remember. It's not like they're completely unconscious. You can't give them too much, or you might snuff one of them out. So sometimes they'd recall things. Someone pulling off their pants..." She looked at Dez. Her lip curled in a snarl. "Someone pushing up their training bra."

"Bella—"

"But I was there," she said. "I was the alibi. I'd wrestle the genie back into the bottle. You were dreaming. You were having nightmares. It wasn't real. After a while I got so good at it I'd have them believing they hadn't even dreamed it. Especially the littler ones. You just make them feel ridiculous. And then they never mention it again. Not even to their parents."

I could hear the distant music from the town pub. A bass beat, the occasional cheer. The big windows that looked out onto the fields were

pitch black. What I would have given for someone to arrive unexpectedly, Kash or Snale, someone who would know instantly what to do.
Even if it was just to distract her so that I could grab my gun back. But
she followed my glance, smiled a little, pitying. We both knew no one
was coming.

CHAPTER 113

IT HAD BEEN her plan. All of it. She'd taken great pleasure in the planning, relishing as she counted down the days. Day Seventeen of the countdown to oblivion. Day Ten. Day Zero. Eric Harris and Dylan Klebold had counted down to their Day Zero from more than a year out. They'd woken up on the day of the massacre with the excitement of Christmas morning buzzing in their brains. No one had listened to them before. But they would now.

"The first time I ever told someone outright, it was Chief Campbell," Bella said. "I thought about going to Sergeant Snale first but I didn't think I'd be able to stomach her pity. She'd have been so...*understanding*. So gentle with her questions. You know? I couldn't deal with that. So I marched right into Soupy Campbell's office one day and just told him outright."

"He didn't believe you," I said.

"No, he didn't," Bella said. "And then I knew Snale was off limits, even with all her sickening fucking sympathy. The Chief would have told her to disregard anything I said. She'd have listened. He was her mentor, and he thought I was lying."

Of course he did. She'd picked exactly the wrong person to try her first sexual abuse confession on: an older man in a position of authority, someone who didn't know her, someone obviously more than willing to get involved in serious illegal activity himself. Theo Campbell would have been well versed in the angsty drama of the teenagers in his town. They were trapped. Futureless. And here was the daughter of one of the most upstanding men in town making a ridiculous claim with no evidence and no witnesses. Admitting to having been complicit herself for years. He'd have fobbed her off as the angry daughter of a selfish dad who didn't want to pay her university fees. She was the hot young student who flirted for top grades and made sexual assault claims against her professor when she didn't get them. The girl next door who undressed before open windows, pretending she couldn't see her neighbor watching, until she was caught, pleading ignorance. She was a dangerous temptress, beautiful liar, the scourge of middle-aged men.

I knew her from my work. She was the unbelieved. Shamed and guilted into keeping quiet or hammered quietly with undermining reasoning until she just couldn't believe herself anymore. She was the one who kept quiet. Waited until she couldn't stand it anymore, then wrote a note and killed herself.

But Bella wasn't going to kill herself. Her gesture was going to be on a much grander scale. A spectacle. Terror we would have a good long while to think about before we all died, cut down by her bullets, running for our lives. She was planning a Carrie-style showdown.

And no one would be laughing now.

CHAPTER 114

"I TOLD REBECCA Greene, my old teacher." Bella counted on her fingers. "She promised she was going to do something. A week later she transferred out. Took a posting in Darwin. I never saw her again. When Brandon Skinner overdosed last year, I tried to tell his mother, Mary." She thrust her arm out again, to the north of us. "She insisted it was an accident. Nothing had happened. He was a happy boy."

I lost a child. Mary's words came back to me.

It's all gonna come out.

It's all coming to an end.

"I had no proof. I couldn't find the photographs. He'd hidden them too well. All I had was my story. I told one of the girls who'd been out there with me in the desert on one of the camps." Bella's eyes had glazed over. "Mara. I saw her at uni, in Sydney. We got drunk together. She didn't want to know anything about it. It was too many years ago. She was happy and she didn't want some weird story from back home, about something she didn't even remember and only half believed, ruining her great new life. They were just pictures, right?"

We both looked at Dez. His eyes pleaded with his daughter.

"I believe you, Bella," I said, showing her the photographs at my feet. "I believe you, OK? I can help you. I'll take these photographs and your testimony and we'll prosecute him. We'll send him to prison for a long, long time. And he will suffer in there, I guarantee it." I thought briefly of Sam. The kind of threats a man received when his crime was against women and children.

"I think I've given this town enough chances to stop what's coming," she said. "You read the diary. You know I've been looking into other people who have done what I'm going to do. The consistent thing among all of them is that they gave people chances to turn things around. I left the diary at the fucking rest stop. I was begging you to do something. *Do something!*" She sighed. "And then here you were, sitting with him, lapping up his words over roast fucking chicken. I can't let this go on."

Bella picked up one of the mobile phones on the counter and looked at her father, lazily, the weary teenager tired of Daddy's bullshit.

Dez writhed in the chair.

"It's time to go," Bella said.

She pushed the button.

CHAPTER 115

"OH MY GOD," Whitt said as he walked down the hill from where he'd parked his car haphazardly across an alleyway. The street was blocked by police cars, ambulances, even a fire truck trying to find its way through the mess. Officers were redirecting traffic down a dead-end street and back up the hill toward Kings Cross. There were blockades being put into place. Officers trying to keep the crowds back from the entrance to Harriet's apartment building.

He'd heard the call on the radio—possible sighting of one of the Georges River Killer suspects. *One wounded, one missing, one dead.* When Whitt failed to get Tox on the phone, and then heard the location of the incident come through, he knew. He grabbed his badge from his back pocket and started pushing through the people, approaching the police tape.

Upstairs, a broken window. Glass in the hall. Whitt was charging up the stairs when he was flattened against the wall by paramedics wrestling a stretcher around the tight corner. It was Tox, his blond hair slicked back, wet with blood, an oxygen mask clamped to his face. Blood all over his neck. He looked waxy, gray.

"Get out of the way!" One of the medics shoved at Whitt, leaving a big red handprint on his shirt. "Move!"

"Is he alive? Is he alive? Oh God!"

One wounded, one missing, one dead. Whitt hadn't prayed in many years. But he was praying now that this man, this strange creature he hadn't even been sure he liked, wasn't dead. Because he knew now he had indeed liked him all this time. He was badly behaved, callous, unpredictable. A lot like Harry. Whitt had taken a long time to realize he liked Harry too, and now he'd do anything for her. Further down the hall a big man in a polo shirt was sprawled out on the blood-soaked carpet, two paramedics pumping on his chest.

Whitt ran behind the paramedics carrying Tox's stretcher.

"Tell me if he's alive!"

The paramedics were barking at each other, medical terms, directions. One of them seemed to be wrestling with Tox as they ran along, trying to pull his hands apart. Whitt caught up. Tox was indeed lying with one arm tucked tightly against his chest, the fist closed, holding the arm there with a tight grip on his own wrist. He was alive. Fighting for consciousness, unwilling to let his arm go. Whitt watched, his skin tingling with joy and relief, as Tox's eyes opened, shifted to him briefly before rolling up in his head.

"Sir, I need to get a line into that hand! Let go!"

"Reverence!" Tox moaned, the oxygen mask muffling his words.

"What?" Whitt shoved the paramedic on his side of the stretcher away. "What is it? What did you say?"

"Reverence." Tox was struggling to breathe. He coughed, sprayed the inside of the mask with blood. "Rev. Er. Ence."

"I don't understand," Whitt groaned. "I—"

Tox let his wrist go, reached out and grabbed Whitt by his shirt. The other fist was still balled against his chest. "EVIDENCE!"

Whitt heard the word through the mask that time. He looked at the fist on Tox's chest.

"Oh God. Oh Jesus. OK! I get it! I get it!"

Whitt dashed into the street, wrenched open the door of the nearest patrol car and grabbed an evidence bag. He ran back to the ambulance just as the medics were loading Tox into the back. Whitt jumped into the tiny space.

"Sir, you need to get out of this van! We're trying to save a life here!"

"No way." Whitt took Tox's wrist and slid the evidence bag over his hand. He was passed out now. The wrist was limp.

Whitt grabbed a roll of bandages from the shelf beside him and began winding them around and around his partner's wrist, sealing the bag around his hand. "He's got forensic evidence under his nails. I'm preserving that evidence until we can get it tested."

"How can you be so selfish?" one of the medics snapped as the doors shut behind her and the engine roared to life. "This man is *dying*!"

"Not without reason, he's not," Whitt said.

CHAPTER 116

THERE WAS A *whump* sound, like a fist hitting a taut stomach, and Dez's body bucked backwards in the chair, tipping it onto its hind legs. His head sprayed upwards, a mess of blood and skull and teeth and brain matter lost in a yellow ball of flame that vaporized as quickly as it had ballooned. The headless body rocked forward, taking the chair with it, and collapsed onto the tiles. I hadn't made a sound. I had no voice. The air was trapped in my lungs, and only when Dez fell did it ease out in a short, harsh yelp.

Blood was everywhere. On the ceiling. On the furniture. On my face.

I like to think I'm pretty tough. But nothing I'd ever experienced had hardened me enough to bear this as coldly and emotionlessly as Bella. I went from understanding and sympathizing with her to suddenly being so terrified of her that I could scream. I'd thought I understood. I didn't understand at all.

I watched, frozen with terror, as she took another plastic water bottle from the pile of things on the table.

"Oh God, please. Please don't. Bella, Jesus."

I'd stood. But she had the gun again and was ushering me back down into the chair with the soothing motions of a mother. She took the roll of duct tape and tossed it at my feet.

"Strap up," she said.

CHAPTER 117

WHITT STOOD IN the hospital hallway, motionless. To his left down the stairs was the triage unit where Tox had been taken. The man had died in the ambulance and been resuscitated right in front of him, a pulse lost, a pulse encouraged to return. Whitt supposed that was death. He wasn't sure. A paramedic had clamped another mask over him and sat squeezing a rubber bag, forcing air into his lungs. Another had shone a torch in his eyes, stuck him with needles, strapped things to his limbs. All the while the hand with the evidence bag tied to it remained flopped down by Tox's side, untouchable. Some silent understanding had come over everyone, after the panic of the first moments, that the hand held the evidence of who had done this. Whitt hadn't said anything. He couldn't find the words. But after an hour or so in the emergency room one of the nurses had come out and handed him a glass slide in a little pouch. Whitt had thanked her and run it up to a lab on the third floor. He'd commandeer the lab. Whatever it took. There was no time to waste getting the sample to a police forensic unit.

Now he was in between those two places, the lab where the nail scrapings had gone for testing and the triage department where Tox was fighting for life. He took out his phone and called Harry, but the call rang through.

"Hi," he said after the message tone. He only noticed, at that moment, that his hands were covered in blood. In fact, his clothes were spattered all over with it. People were staring at him as they walked past, alarm in their eyes. "Um. Call me...uh...when you can. We got a DNA sample from the Georges River suspect. It'll be three hours, they think, before they can give us a result. I'm, um, I'm not sure what to do now. Tox is...He's...Just call me back."

He sat down in a plastic chair beside a vending machine filled with high-sugar snacks. He had to focus now. There were units out there in the night searching for the killer, trying to track down the twelve men who'd been identified by their fingerprints at the abandoned hotel. They were now also checking emergency rooms and medical centers for anyone wounded, knowing Tox would have done at least *some* damage to his attacker. The killer wouldn't have been expecting a man at Harry's apartment. He must have seen the lights on, wondered if she might be there. What had he wanted with Harry? The same thing he wanted with the girls he had taken?

None of it made sense. No, it didn't make sense if the theory was that this man was Sam Blue's partner. Because if Sam Blue was his partner, his friend, he'd have no reason to want to hurt Harry. And why go around and break into Harry's apartment if his intentions for her were good? Had he broken in? There was no way of telling. The door had been smashed down, and neighbors in the building were saying they thought the dead man in the hallway had done it. Had he got in another way?

Whitt needed to find this guy. Going to Harry's apartment had been a bold act. Caitlyn McBeal had escaped him. His face had, presumably, been on the television—even if it was buried among the faces of other suspects. Now he was on the run, probably wounded. The killer must be in crisis mode. He would do now what killers in trouble always do. He would go home. Go to where it was safe. Not literally to his place of residence—the police would be covering the houses of the twelve men. He'd go where his heart lived. Where it had all begun.

But where on earth was that?

Whitt stood. He had an idea.

CHAPTER 118

THE LIGHTS OF the town swirled in my vision, the black arms of the cliffs around us. The wind was making me shiver, but I knew it couldn't possibly be as cold as I felt. I tried to walk slowly, to think. The bottle under my chin felt heavy. Bella had rolled the duct tape around and around my neck. It was pulling at my hair. Awkwardly tugging at the skin behind my ear. It was hard to walk with my hands behind my back. The tape there was too tight, jamming my unbroken wrist up against the cast on the other arm. When Bella had asked me to strap up, I'd been pleased with how awkward it was, taping my own hands behind my back. I had started the roll on my good wrist and given myself a little gap between my wrists, hoping she'd think I'd done it by accident. No luck. When Bella had taken over, she'd made sure the bind was nice and secure. My fingers tingled with numbness.

"Speed it up, slowpoke," Bella said, jabbing the pistol into my ribs.

"I'm going to trip if I go any faster."

"I wouldn't if I were you," she said. "You pull one of those wires out of the cap and the thing will blow."

"What is it?"

"It's fertilizer," she said. "Ammonium nitrate and gasoline, a couple of other things. Swimming in the middle is a cheap mobile phone. Well, the guts of one. I pulled apart the phone and isolated the circuit that comes alive when it rings. When I ring the number, the circuit will spark the fuel. And you're dead."

"When?" I stopped walking. Stood before her, looked her in the eyes. "*When* you ring the phone? If you're going to kill me, Bella, you might as well do it right here."

"That's not the plan, honey." She smiled. She waved the gun at me. "It's in your interest to just keep following my directions."

"Why?"

"Because otherwise I'll put a fucking bullet in your leg and you'll have to drag yourself to town. That's why."

She shrugged, the gun in one hand, a phone in the other. I turned and kept walking. Soon we'd come into the reach of the lights. I could see the people standing in the street, hear the clink of glasses.

"Where did you learn to do all this?" I was rambling now, trying to get her talking, even if it was about her devastating plans. I needed to reason with her. She couldn't stay locked in her own irrational mind. "How did you figure out how to build these things?"

"It's all over the internet," she said.

We'd checked the IP addresses and searches of everyone in the town. But Bella didn't live in town anymore. She was visiting.

"You can find a plan for anything you want," she continued. "You don't need complex chemicals or big exciting machines. I killed Zac with the timer from Dad's oven." She sighed, looked up at the stars. A smile crept over her features. "Do you have any idea how wonderful it feels to say that? I killed Zac. I. Killed. Zac."

"He didn't do anything to you. He was never a part of this."

"They're *all* a part of this," she said. "You still don't get it. It's a system. You think bad things happen in the world because a couple of people decide to do them? You're even dumber than I thought, Harry. Bad things happen because a couple of people do them and a bunch of people do nothing about it."

Eric and Dylan. Elliot Rodger. Seung-Hui Cho. Each of them had been willing to take down innocents. People who hadn't wronged them personally. When Day Zero came, it was all about rage. Consuming as many people as possible with it, making the point with suffering, whether those who suffered were innocent or guilty. I shivered. Bella walked close to me. We were two friends taking an evening stroll.

"You think you and your brother got into the mess you're in because of the actions of *a couple of people*?" she asked.

No, I thought. She was right. Someone had killed those girls and set up my brother. I had to believe that. But there were other people who had made the whole situation complete. Nigel and his team had got it wrong and come after him, had squeezed a confession out of him, had locked him up and ignored other leads that had to have been there. Journalists had condemned him and the public had believed those journalists. Our own mother's major concern had been making money from the situation. There was so much rage inside me, and I could share it among so many people. Including myself. I wasn't there. I was in the middle of the road in some shitty town on the edge of nowhere, about to die. I would be just another name in a long list of people who had not been there for Sam.

"I think you want me to stop you, Bella," I said. "I think you left the diary for me to find. You took the plan page out, didn't you? You didn't want it to be too easy. You wanted to be able to carry on if I didn't respond," I said. "But Bella, I'm responding now. You don't have to go through with this."

"Shut up." She kicked me in the small of my back. I struggled not to fall. "The time for talking came and went a long time ago."

CHAPTER 119

THE FIRST PEOPLE to notice us were a group of men I didn't recognize, standing outside the pub, each with a beer glass in hand. They did what so many men do when they're drunk and women come within orbit of them. They pointed and cheered. It must have been the expression on my face that shifted the mood. Cut the cheers short. Maybe it was the gun in Bella's hand. I spied Kash outside the supply store with a pair of patrol officers. His mouth fell open.

People were coming nearer. Absurdly, bizarrely turning from their groups in the street and walking toward us, hypnotized moths attracted to a light. But Bella was nothing like the killer they'd imagined all along with her glittery heels and bright smile, her hair falling perfectly over her shoulders. Kash had his gun up in an instant. Bella waved the mobile phone high in the air. He understood. To the people around us, it was a stunt. A prank. They backed up, murmuring to each other, frowns, the occasional uncomfortable laugh.

I wanted to be sick, to cry out at the visions still flashing before me of Dez's body slumping to the ground. Bella pushed me into the pub. It was crowded here, but quiet, a party ruined. She shoved me to the center of the stage.

"What a perfect place for this," she said. There was a strange self-consciousness to her now. Her plan materializing. How could it be this perfect? Surely something would bring it down. She was so used to her dreams being tugged back to earth. "The pub, huh, Harry? We'll do it here. This is where people come to forget about things, isn't it? This is where we come to be together. Let's all be together for this."

"Get down." Kash was waving people from the tables, directing them away from the stage. He kept his gun trained on Bella, his eyes never leaving her for long. "Stay calm, everyone. Move toward the exits."

"Do *not* move toward the fucking exits," Bella snapped, pointing my weapon at a group of people crouched by the door. "I'm running this show, you pathetic meathead. Get that fucking gun off me before I push this button and end your partner's life."

"That device isn't big enough to hurt anyone here but Harry." Kash pointed at me. "If you kill her, I'll shoot you, and it'll be over."

"Mmm." Bella nodded. Her bravado returned. "See, that's where the plan gets interesting. This isn't the only bomb in town."

CHAPTER 120

WHITT KNEW HE was wrong when he turned the corner and came up against the blockade at the fork in the road. Huge red plastic barriers diverted cars off to the right, away from the river along Henry Lawson Drive. He pulled in slowly behind a driver who was checked and directed away, then flipped his badge open for the patrol cop manning the checkpoint. A light rain was beginning to fall.

"Detective Whittacker," the cop read, shone the torch in Whitt's face. "How can I help?"

"I just want to do a quick check of the riverside. See if he's out and about."

"He's not." The young cop smiled. "We've got it blocked off from here to Timbuktu. They're doing regular sweeps. But you're welcome to go have a look."

Whitt waved and rolled on, disappointed. Of course, someone got the idea before him that the killer might return to the Georges River, a place that obviously meant something to him. He got out and looked down the long, narrow stretch of parkland lining the black water. There were police everywhere, plainclothes and patrollies leaning on trees, looking over maps, shining their flashlights along the muddy sand beyond the gray brick breakwall.

The stretch of river where the bodies of the girls had been found was no more than three hundred meters long. But Whitt thought that didn't necessarily mean only that stretch was important to the killer. Much of the police presence was focused here, where the girls had been laid on the beach. Beyond this part of the river there was more parkland dotted with the occasional clearing where picnic tables and public toilet blocks stood, jungle gyms for the kids, public bins surrounded by thousands of beer-bottle caps and cigarette butts.

What was it about this place that meant so much to the killer? Whitt wondered as he walked in the dark between the trees, beyond the reach of the lights. He thought about critical places in his own life from his home in Perth, places that he could smell when he thought about them. Where the ghost of his child self still played on beaches, huddled into big armchairs in libraries and sifted through the crowded tables of treasures in public markets, his mother's hand in his. Indeed, the only places he could think of that had any deep spiritual meaning for him had cemented themselves in his psyche during his childhood. The Georges River really was a boys' wonderland. Dark forests that stretched for kilometers. Huge sandstone rock formations perfect for clambering on, hiding in and having secret conversations. The park was large enough that wild goats and deer populated its deeper parts, appearing on the road now and then. It would be a haven for teens smoking, making out, lighting fires.

Sam Blue had been fairly nonplussed about the place when Nigel's team had asked him what associations he had with it. He said he'd hung out there now and then as a kid when placed with foster families in the area. He hadn't been back in his adult years. It hadn't struck the investigators as odd that the place where the three bodies of his victims had been found hadn't meant much to their prime suspect. They'd assumed he was lying.

Whitt's phone buzzed and he looked at the screen. A text message from the lab. He opened the image and looked at a face, one of the bearded men from the collection of photographs of suspects from the abandoned hotel. Regan Banks. Number eight. His DNA had matched the samples taken from under Tox's fingernails.

Whitt spied a dark pier ahead reaching out into the water. There was a small boatshed near it. He headed that way, thinking he'd get out of the wind to make a phone call to Pops. He'd lost faith in his idea that the killer might be here at the river, with all the police presence nearby. He was only thinking now of his next angle of attack. The danger lying ahead escaped him.

CHAPTER 121

"SIT HERE, HARRY." Bella smiled, drawing a chair from the edge of the stage. I all but fell into it. My legs were weak, my mind spinning. It wasn't just the bomb strapped to my throat. It was the stage, its height above the people cowering under tables and huddling in corners, unable to look away from me and my captor. We were a grotesque pantomime, a Punch and Judy show. It was all playing out exactly as she had intended it—better, in fact. Her spectacle was drawing people in from the street to the front windows, crowded at the glass, talking to each other, relaying events inside to those behind who couldn't see. She drew another chair close to me, so that our knees were almost touching. I thought about the bomb, and how if it detonated now it would probably injure her grievously, maybe kill her. But like the spree killers she idolized, the girl beside me was probably suicidal. All her mental effort over the last few months, or years, had gone into the planning of this event. There was nothing beyond today, Day Zero, that really mattered. Everything had to go perfectly now.

"It's like we're putting on a show, isn't it?" Bella said, rubbing my leg absurdly. I gripped the back of the chair with my bound hands. "A kind of interview. Harry, why don't you ask me what's going to happen next?"

"What's..." I swallowed. My mouth was bone dry. Kash had cleared a path between the tables and the stage. He'd rush here when he had the chance. But for now he could only hold Bella in the sight of his gun. "What's...?"

"Well, you're going to make a choice," Bella said. She only had eyes for me. "I've chosen you because I think you're the best person to demonstrate my point. I've told you what the people of Last Chance Valley have done. What they've allowed to happen. You know what kind of people they are. I want you to really consider that. Weigh it objectively in your mind. Kind of like a jury member would, you know?" She tapped my temple hard with her index finger, almost knocking me off balance.

"We haven't done anything!" someone yelled from the back of the room. An older woman. "She's crazy! Bella, don't do this!"

"Help!" A young man was crying by the base of the bar, his hands wrapped around his head. "Please! Let us out of here!"

"Stay calm." Kash was inching toward the stage. "Everybody just stay calm."

"There's another bomb," Bella said, ignoring them. "It's somewhere near. Maybe it's here, in this building." She gestured to the audience below us. "Maybe it's out there somewhere. Under someone's house. In someone's kitchen."

"Maybe it's nowhere." I licked my lips. "And you're lying."

She nodded. "I guess you've got to consider that as an option. Look, trust me, it's there. It's the biggest one I've made. I used all my left-overs. All the fertilizer I ground up to make these." She tapped the bottle at my throat, making the liquid slosh against my windpipe. I winced, Dez's death flashing again across the backs of my eyelids. "I'm going to give you a choice. You can save these people. Or you can save yourself."

"Harry." Kash's eyes were desperate. I thought of him in the hospital in White Cliffs. His broken look. He put a hand out. "Don't. Don't do anything."

"I'm going to give you this mobile phone," Bella said. She reached around and put it into my hand. My fingers were numb. I didn't know if I was gripping it too tightly, or not tightly enough. I imagined myself squeezing the phone wrongly, setting off the bomb at my throat before I had time to think. Bella smoothed my arm with her warm hand, stroking my biceps softly. "There's only one button you need to press. The big one. Twice. I've programmed the number of your device into it. It's the only number it has. Push twice, and you die."

Bella looked at the people cowering below us, their stricken faces. This was what she'd wanted. Complete power. Complete control. This was her vengeance. They were listening to her now. And it was too late. Gloriously, hideously too late.

"If you don't push the button, I'll push mine." She lifted another mobile phone and made it do a little dance in the air. "And someone else, maybe many people, will die."

"Harry, listen to me," Kash was saying. "You don't have to do anything right now. We need more time. Bella, you need to give us more time. We need to talk about this."

"The time for talking is over," she said again. Bella stood and stepped back out of the blast zone. I looked at the phone in her hand. Her thumb was poised over the rubber button just below the screen, the biggest button on the phone. Her eyes searched mine. Exhilarated. "What are you going to do?"

I looked at her and pushed the button.

CHAPTER 122

WHITT STOOD IN the doorway of the boatshed, looking at the man on the pier. For a moment he tried to convince himself that the figure sitting there was a pile of ropes, a large barrel with some buoys lying beside it. Anything other than the shape of a man. It was impossible. But as he blinked his vision adjusted to the dark, and he looked at the bright outline of the shaved head, the gentle slope of the broad shoulders beneath the damp T-shirt. He was sitting with his legs crossed under him, his hands on his lap, looking at the water.

Whitt slid his mobile phone out of his pocket and looked at the screen. No reception.

"It's the power station," the man said without turning.

Whitt jolted at the sound of his voice. Around him, ropes hanging from beams shifted gently as the wind raced up the river. He took out his gun and actioned it. The man on the pier breathed in once, then out, coughed a little. He was wounded. Whitt could see that now. He was slightly crooked, favoring his right side.

"The power station," the man went on, waving a hand, "up on the hill. It interferes with phone reception down here on the water sometimes."

"You're Regan Banks," Whitt said. "Sam's . . . Sam's partner."

Regan turned and stood. He was much bigger than Whitt. The detective couldn't know if he was imagining or genuinely remembering it, but he saw a flash of this man in his mind coming up behind him in the car park of his apartment building. The smeared reflection of him in the stainless-steel doors of the elevator. His face was long, pointed. Expressionless. This was the man who had taken those girls. Whitt could smell it on him. The taint of dead dreams. He had none of Samuel Jacob Blue's vitality, his nervous innocence. This was a being who snuffed out lives.

"We're not partners," Regan said.

CHAPTER 123

IF I HAD to make the decision, I wanted it to be quick. Not two pushes quick, but one push quick, something I could do before I thought too much about the pain that was coming. Everything I would lose. The phone beeped. In my hand, I knew, the phone number for the bomb at my throat was listed on the screen, called up from the "Last dialed" list. All I had to do was confirm the call. Send the electrical impulse through the machine, up to a tower, back to the receiver in the bottle at my throat. The people around me were watching, their jaws set, hands covering trembling mouths. My victims, if I wanted it so, if I deemed their lives less important than mine.

The strange thing was, I could see it. I could see me making the decision to save myself. No one is a hero in situations like this. The brain is trained to preserve the body, and as I sat there it was flooded with all the rage I needed to resist the temptation to take my own life in place of theirs. These were people who ignored the helpless in their midst, the man on the edge of their town who lived as though in exile. These were people who refused to believe that a predator walked among them, who ignored or misunderstood a desperate girl when she tried to confide in them. Nothing stays secret in places like these. In small towns, secrets are shared about, held close to hearts. This was a family. They protected their own, no matter how bad the blood.

Bella wanted to make a mark. To be remembered, the way Dylan Klebold and Eric Harris were remembered after the Columbine shooting, monsters on a rampage, cutting through young lives like butter. The way Seung-Hui Cho was remembered by every student who walked onto the Virginia Tech campus. If only one person ever remembered what Elliot Rodger did and altered their behavior because of it, he'd have been happy with that. Bella had said that the time for talking was over. I would be her manifesto.

"I can't do it," I said. Kash was at the edge of the stage now, mere meters from me. If he came any closer, he'd be in my blast zone. "I have to push the button, Elliott. I have to."

"Really?" Bella sneered. "You're really going to die for these idiots?" She looked at Kash, incredulous. "She can't be serious."

"Harry," Kash said. "Just wait. Wait."

"The bomb might be anywhere," I told him. "It might be under Mary Skinner's house. She's in there now with those kids. It might be out there," I looked at the people beyond the windows, huddled together, just as Bella had known they would. "I can't. I can't risk it."

"You don't even know these people," Bella murmured, her eyes pleading with me. Begging me to prove her right. To prove that, like the people of Last Chance, I was only out to protect myself. "Think about everything you have to lose. Think about your brother." There was a smile dancing at the corners of her mouth. This was what she had wanted. A hero laid bare before the undeserving mob. Surely I'd save myself. Surely I was selfish, just like the rest of them.

"I have a lot to lose." I nodded at the girl who would be my killer. I thought about Sam and the tears threatened. "But I didn't take this job to protect myself."

It was the only way I could think to say it. That being a police officer was the one thing about myself that I thought was worthy. From the moment I'd been born, I'd been a problem. An inconvenience. A failure. A burden to be shifted from place to place, only for as long as I avoided causing unacceptable levels of trouble. When I became a cop that feeling went away. Being a cop was my purpose, my penance.

"I'm sorry," I told Kash.

I pushed the button a second time and heard the phone beep.

CHAPTER 124

"YOU...you're *not* partners?" Whitt said. He could hardly talk. The words seemed stuck on the tip of his tongue. The gun in his hand was trembling as excitement coursed through him. A strange, electric joy he knew he had to contain. "You framed him. You framed Sam Blue."

"Yes." Regan nodded, his hands out by his sides, bracing. It seemed he was ready to take the bullet Whitt was threatening him with. "I framed him. Sam is innocent."

Why? Whitt wanted to cry out. But no, he could get the story later. "Put your hands on your head. You're coming with me." Right now, Whitt needed to take this man into custody.

He couldn't believe he'd finally stumbled onto the solution to it all. Here, right before him, stood Sam's freedom. Harry's redemption. Justice for Tox. Whitt felt giddy, off balance. He steeled himself. This was it. He was going to end it all. Save everyone.

"Put your hands on your head," he repeated, stepping forward.

Regan had been waiting for the approach. He reached up, and in a movement so fast that Whitt barely followed it, he lifted the loop of the rope hanging by his side off of a hook on the wall.

Whitt heard a whizzing noise above him. The clunk of the kayak smashing the top of his skull was almost drowned out by the sound of the gun going off in his hand.

CHAPTER 125

THE SOUND OF the beep seemed to echo, to stretch on forever. I found my eyes were squeezed shut, my lips drawn back and teeth bared. I listened for the *whump* sound, expecting pain. But all I heard was the thumping of my heartbeat in my ears, the cracking of my teeth as they ground together. I opened my eyes. A long, low howl escaped my lips as the air rushed out of my lungs. Relief and terror intermingled in one hard, hot knot in my stomach.

By sheer automation, my limbs working at a will of their own, I pushed the button again. And again. The people around me were realizing what was happening, but I wasn't. All I knew was that I should have been dead and was not. No further thoughts would come. My thumb kept plunging down and the phone kept beeping, even as everyone in the room leapt into action.

The people rose to their feet all at once, as though spurred by a starter's gun, making for the doors. Kash threw himself at Bella, who was staggering backwards, knowing he was coming, lifting her phone, the one connected to a bomb somewhere nearby. Her thumb coming down.

Kash grabbed her ankle with one hand and yanked her off her feet. The phone crashed and slid on the boards of the stage away from me. I dropped onto the floor, trying to shift forward on my knees toward it. I had to get it before she did.

I heard Kash and Bella struggling on the ground before the stage, her squeal of rage.

"Get off me!" she roared. "Get off me!"

I lost my balance. Fell on my chest. The duct tape around my wrists seemed impossibly tighter. My phone had failed. There was no way we would be so lucky with Bella's. If she got hold of it, she would detonate the bomb hidden in the town. I was only an arm's length away from the device lying on its side near the back of the stage. I heard Kash cry out. He'd lost his grip on her. The stage shuddered as Bella ran over the top of me, her hands reaching for the phone.

I saw, as if in slow motion, her fingers lifting it from the ground.

I squeezed my eyes shut as the sound of the blast rang through my skull.

CHAPTER 126

THE GUN SLID out of Whitt's hands as he hit the floor of the boatshed, the weight of the kayak that had been slung across the ceiling knocking him into the ground like a nail bent beneath an enormous hammer. The gunshot took Regan in the shoulder, spinning him backwards. Whitt looked up in time to see the man fall, his boots slipping on the wet pier.

Whitt shook off the temptation of unconsciousness and scrambled forward, ignoring the dark shadows at the corners of his vision. He threw himself through the doorway and off the pier, into the cold, rushing water.

Regan was there, an impossibly heavy, impossibly strong monster, reaching up and encircling him in an embrace. They struggled in the thigh-high waves, Whitt's arms and hands seeming sluggish, the blow to the head making him an easy opponent.

Regan's hands came around his throat, and before he could utter a cry Whitt was under the water. The muddy, salty taste of it was at the back of his throat, in his lungs. He bucked and twisted, but in seconds the man had him pinned against the silty bottom. He scratched at the iron hands that held him, grabbed desperately for a rock, a branch, anything to hit him with. Whitt reached for the gunshot wound in the man's shoulder just as the darkness began to close in again.

"Fuck!" Regan cried. Whitt had stuck his thumb into the hole, pushed upward. Whitt rose out of the waves, vomited water. There were lights on the sand. He hadn't realized how far into the water they'd been dragged. The river was sucking at them both, the water waist-high now, pulling on his tired limbs.

"Put your hands up!" someone screamed from the shore. "Put your hands up!"

"No!" Whitt turned, heard Regan's gasp of surprise beside him. He put his arms out. "Don't shoot! Don't shoot!"

The shore lit up with white flashes as they fired. Regan's body jolted once, twice. He sank into the water.

CHAPTER 127

I LAY AS still as possible, my cheek against the floorboards, my whole body aching. Bella's foot was by my face, her heel out of the glittery strap, the ankle tendons relaxed. I looked up and saw the phone lying in her limp hand, her thumb on the button. She hadn't pushed it. The blast I'd heard had come from above. Higher, higher, I lifted my eyes to the second-floor railing, where Officer Victoria Snale was standing with her arms hanging over the polished wooden banister. The rifle in her arms was still smoking from where it had dispensed a single shot straight down into Bella's head.

I shifted up onto my knees, still trying to orient myself. The floor felt like it was tilting beneath me. Kash was there, taking the phone from Bella's dead fingers and setting it aside. He turned to me, plucking at the tape around my wrists.

"Get it off me," I begged. "Get it off."

Someone handed him a pair of scissors and he slipped them between my sweat-soaked neck and the rolls of duct tape beneath my ear. He peeled the bomb from my throat and handed it off to someone. I could hear Vicky crying. I looked up in time to see a young police officer taking the rifle from her hands.

"I killed her." Snale took in a hitching breath that came out of her in sobs. "I've never killed anyone before."

"It's OK," the officer was saying, taking her hand as he led her down the stairs. "It's all OK now."

I sat numbly on the stage by Bella's body and looked at the people around me slowly, uncertainly moving out of the pub, arms around shoulders, some stopping to hug just outside the doorway. In the movies, this would have been the moment for triumphant cheering. For half-humorous one-liners cracked with relief that would lead gently into the credits, the camera panning away from the town and into the night. But the dread wouldn't lift from my shoulders. I couldn't find the strength to move. Kash seemed to sense it and crouched beside me, putting a careful hand on the back of my neck.

"Do you think you can stand?" he asked.

"I have to," I said, gripping onto his shoulder. He slipped an arm around me and brought me to my feet. "I need to get out of here."

"What?" Kash said. "Right now?"

I nodded, let him help me to the door. Something deep inside me was telling me that all was far from OK.

CHAPTER 128

I IGNORED THE instinct still as the sun rose and I pulled the borrowed police cruiser over at the edge of the hillside topped by Jed Chatt's ramshackle house. I shut off the engine. I hadn't turned the radio on. I couldn't bear to hear reports about what had happened in Last Chance only hours before. Neither Whitt nor Tox was answering his phone. As I'd left the town, a couple of people were hounding Vicky as she sat on the edge of an ambulance, drinking water someone had brought her and trying to get over the shock of her first kill. I'd wanted to say something to her, something reassuring about taking a life to save another. That although the memories never leave you, and sometimes late at night the faces of your victims still come, the pain of it dies away in time. I'd killed. It wasn't the worst thing I lived with every day. But instead I'd left Vicky sitting there in the care of a paramedic. She would be all right. She was stronger than me.

I hadn't said goodbye to Kash either. He'd run off almost immediately to evacuate anyone in the town who was still in their house, to see if he could locate the device Bella had hidden out there. Her plan hadn't worked. Her father had been her last victim. As I was loading the car with my belongings, one of Snale's neighbors got word to me that Kash and the other officers had indeed found an explosive device under a house on the edge of town. The bomb had been located right beneath the youngest child's bed, under the floorboards. I knew Kash would deal with it. I had one errand left to run, and then I was going home.

It was my Day Zero. I could finally see my brother.

As I walked up the stairs to the porch of Jed's house, my temples throbbed. I figured I must be getting sick. Just my luck to come down with something the moment I was about to reenter the fight for my brother's life. I knocked on the door and a voice inside told me to come in.

There were more advances in Jed's shack becoming a family home. I looked at the cloth on the table by the window, the newly painted back wall. The tall man was sitting at the far end of the table, shirtless, a pair of checked pajama pants on his long legs. The muscles in his upper shoulders twisted and tightened visibly beneath his golden-brown skin as he screwed the lid back on a jar of PVC glue. There was a wooden toy on a sheet of newspaper before him. A painted duck with a newly reattached wing.

The baby was nowhere to be seen. Too early for him yet. I set the small rock on the table carefully so as not to make too much noise. I knew a sleeping baby was a precious thing.

When Jed spoke, his voice was low.

"What's all this, then?" he asked, looking at the rock.

"This," I said, "is a ten-gram nugget of solid gold."

The outer edge of his left eyebrow twitched briefly. Besides that, he gave no indication of emotion. I picked the rock up again and looked at it, rubbed some of the dirt from its exterior and revealed the mustard-yellow metal beneath.

"There's a lot of it," I said. "Last night, Jace Robit and Damien Ponch were killed in an ambush trying to get the last of it. They found a gold deposit in a cave outside Last Chance Valley, and they've spent months there extracting the metal in secret and stockpiling it. Two of their friends survived the ambush. A couple of patrol officers picked them up and the men are now in custody, being questioned. The guys estimate they have pulled about two and a half million dollars' worth of gold out of the cave over the last few months. They were planning to run off with it all. Start again. A new life overseas."

Jed considered this. We listened to the baby stirring in the next room. After a few seconds the child fell silent again.

"What's it got to do with me?" Jed asked.

"The cave is on land the government handed back to your family," I said. "Rightfully, every ounce of the gold that was extracted belongs to you."

I put the nugget down in front of him. He stared at it, his lips sealed.

"Two and a half million dollars?" he asked eventually.

"It's a rare find," I said. "Almost unheard of. There's probably more in the area that the men were mining. I don't know about these things. An officer will come out and see you, tell you what'll happen next."

"What am I supposed to do?" he said.

"No idea," I answered. I walked toward the door. "Sell the land to a goldmine. Keep it and mine it yourself. Get rich, buy Last Chance Valley and reduce everything in it to ashes. Buy your niece her own law firm. Throw all the gold they found back into the cave and continue on exactly as you are." I laughed. Shrugged. "I don't know."

Jed had forgotten all about the gold on the table. He was looking at me in the doorway. I was frozen there. Something was telling me that if I just stayed here inside the threshold, in the cool of this man's house, everything was going to be OK. This was a safe place.

Jed stood, and his expression made the torn feeling in me all the more real. He looked sad to see me go.

"You don't look right," he said. "Come back in and sit down."

"I can't," I said. "I've got to go."

The baby boy in the other room started crying. We ignored it, watching each other, both wanting to speak. But there was nothing more to say. I made a choice. Perhaps the wrong choice.

I turned and left.

CHAPTER 129

REGAN SHIFTED IN the driver's seat. His wet clothes were sticking to the seat cover, the heat of his body fogging the windows. He had almost passed out in the darkness behind the service station as he sat binding the gunshot wounds in his shoulder and stomach, shoving wadded fabric he'd ripped from a blanket in the back of the car into the blood-soaked flesh. He'd tied pieces of the thin blanket awkwardly in a loop under his arm and around his neck, rolled it tight around his gut. The dizziness, the pain didn't matter. He needed to keep ahead of the road-blocks before they came into place. He'd go to ground later and think about getting his wounds treated. One step at a time. He'd survive. He always survived.

Getting away from the officer in the water had been easier than Regan imagined. He'd felt the impact of the bullets and fallen into the waves, and in the confusion, the rushing people and the bouncing lights, he'd simply slipped away. Dived low, come up shallow, dived again. Let the sucking current take him.

The swirling panic he'd felt as he crawled out of the river on the opposite bank to the police had reminded him of that night long ago. The last time he saw Sam.

It had been a starless night. Low clouds slithering across the sky above the tops of the black pines, reflecting the dull orange glow of the power station. It was almost as though no time had passed at all. He'd been seventeen years old. Sam about the same. Two idiot teens walking in the dark together, talking over each other, trying to get through it all, everything that had passed in the time they'd been separated. There had been so much to say.

Regan had been careful about his words. He didn't want to let slip words he'd never dare say in real life. *I love you, Sam. I've needed you here.*

Hours ago they had come down to the river, to their favorite spot. They'd gone to the hanging tree and swung off the old rotting rope there. Regan was so glad Sam was back, even if it was only for this night. Sam was being bounced through overnight care for stealing his last foster father's car and joyriding through the city. He'd be put in a group home down in Nowra for a few weeks until they could see him through a rehabilitation program and rehome him.

Though Sam would be swiftly out of Regan's life again, it wasn't going to be like last time. They were going to keep in touch. Sam had a mobile phone now. They were going to be together. A year, and they'd be eighteen years old. Legally eligible to be released from state care. They could do what they wanted. Completely and utterly free. Regan had already started counting down the days.

It was Sam who spotted the light that evening. They'd been strolling back along Henry Lawson Drive, about to cut through a park into Revesby Heights. Back to Regan's foster house, before his carers noticed he was gone. The light was at the back door of a small fibro house off the edge of a children's park. The two boys sank onto the rubber seats of a pair of chain swings, twisting this way and that, letting the momentum spin them around.

"Bit late for the vet to be open," Sam had commented, exhaling cigarette smoke.

"Maybe it's a rabbit with a stomach ache." Regan lit his own cigarette, squinting at the door. "A kangaroo with its pouch stuck shut."

"You're weird," Sam had said, pushing off and swinging hard.

Regan snorted. "Lots of money, being a vet."

The two boys swung back and forth, the iron frame squeaking above them. Regan put his feet down eventually and dragged himself to a stop.

"Maybe we should go in." He grinned, watching Sam swing. He took a knife from his back pocket and slipped the blade open with a snap. *"Gimme all your cash or the puppy gets it!"*

Sam laughed.

"I'm serious." Regan slapped his friend. "Come on. Let's go have a look."

"No way." Sam dragged himself to a stop. "We'd get caught."

"As if!"

"They've probably got cameras. Security guards."

"Security guards?" Regan laughed hard. "It's a fucking vet! Who robs a vet?"

"Exactly."

"Exaaaactly." Regan grabbed Sam's arm, felt his biceps beneath the shirt. He squeezed. "The dude won't be expecting it. Let's get what we can and go into the city. This is a great idea!"

"This is a shitty, shitty idea." Sam got off the swing. "I'm not interested. I've got weed at home and it's not gonna smoke itself."

"Come on. Don't be a pussy."

"I'm not a pussy," Sam spat. His fury was surprisingly quick, rising from nowhere. "You're the fucking pussy. Talkin' about sticking up places like a fucking gangster. Who the hell do you think you are?"

"I've stuck up places."

"No you haven't."

"Yes, I have." Regan stood. Something inside him was stirring, turning in his chest. It felt like fingers creeping around his heart, threatening to squeeze. He'd said the wrong thing. He needed to fix it. But the words kept coming. The anger kept rising. He couldn't lose Sam. Not now. "You don't know me. You don't know anything about me, man."

"Whatever." Sam started walking off. Regan was beginning to tremble. He squeezed the knife so hard his knuckles cracked.

"Come back here!" he cried. "Sam!"

Sam walked. Regan shook. He could almost feel something uncurling in his stomach, petal by petal or wing by leathery wing. Sam disappeared around the corner and into the night. The sound of his footsteps faded. Regan tried to swallow but found his throat was blocked.

Pussy.

Regan walked toward the door of the veterinary clinic. The light fell over him, glowed on his fingers as he wrenched the handle down.

CHAPTER 130

THE WOMAN INSIDE the veterinary clinic had been Doctor Rachel Howes, twenty-three years old. A newly registered practitioner in the medical treatment of animals. Beautiful chocolate hair, long and heavy. So much potential. Regan had entered the clinic in what the prosecutors later called a "psychotic state." He'd taken mere seconds to kill her. A dozen dogs and cats watched. He'd retreated to the sound of their howling and barking, $62.75 retrieved from the cash register. Regan's defense lawyer had told him that had it not been for an anonymous call to Crime Stoppers, police would have had little chance of solving the case.

The call had come in only fifteen minutes after Regan entered the clinic.

Sam. Gentle, big-hearted Sam. Of course he had called the police. Sam acted tough, but he didn't want to see an innocent vet robbed of their day's takings any more than the average person did. Sam couldn't possibly have known what viciousness Regan would unleash on the poor, unsuspecting Doctor Howes. Sam had never seen the thing that lived in Regan, growing there behind his eyes, the darkness spreading, waiting for something to finally bring it to life.

Sam hadn't known that Doctor Howes had died. Sam hadn't known that his phone call had got Regan arrested. He hadn't known that Regan went to jail just three months later. That year after year he'd thought of nothing but Sam.

He'd thought only of coming back and finding Sam there in his perfect life. Oh, his beautiful plans, spinning around and around like a fine spider's web, surrounding Sam long before the man knew the invisible strands were there. Regan followed and waited until Sam breezed by one of his pretty-picture girls, and then he snatched them up. Sometimes he was so close, he was sure Sam would turn and see him. Hear the girl scream. The last one, Rosetta. He'd grabbed her out of the mouth of a side street just seconds after Sam passed. He'd been able to smell Sam's cologne as the man moved behind him.

Linny was supposed to have been the last one. He'd decided to make this one different. Take her and set her up at the hotel, splay her out, ready for Sam. Ready for him to see her, so glorious in herself, and yet so incredible as a part of his plan. *This is what I did for you*, Regan had wanted to tell Sam as they stood there before the dying girl. *This is what you made me.*

But Linny had slipped away from him. He'd got Caitlyn instead. No matter. She'd do. And then the terrible news that Sam had escaped him, too.

It was OK. If Regan was anything, he was adaptive. He kind of liked it when things became chaotic, went awry. The little jerk of his heart as the rug slipped out from beneath him.

Now he'd discovered Harry. And his plans for her would put his former work to shame.

Regan was shaken out of his daydreams by the pain. He hugged an arm into his side and re-gripped the wheel, waiting for the spasms to pass. He needed to get off the road soon. It wasn't finished yet. He turned onto the highway heading west and followed the ramp down to the deserted road, picking up speed.

CHAPTER 131

I DRAGGED MY suitcase along the walkway between the plane and the airport terminal, listening to it clunk over the rubber seams in the gray carpet. I knew people were staring. I hadn't showered, changed, fixed my hair or so much as washed my face since the previous morning. There was gray duct-tape glue adhered to the burned skin of my neck. Blood spatter on my shirt. I'd ignored the number on my ticket and gone straight to the back row of the plane, sat there staring out the window and saying nothing until we landed. The flight attendants did not approach me, nor did anyone sit near me. They might have known who I was. Or they might simply have been terrified by my appearance. I didn't know. I was counting the seconds until I got home, and that was all I had the mental strength for.

My phone bleeped as I turned the corner. My mother. I opened the text as I walked.

They just told me about Sam. I'm sorry but I have to keep the money.

I stared at the text, trying to understand what it meant. It didn't matter. I didn't have time for her. My Day Zero was mere minutes away.

As I walked into the terminal, a hand reached out and touched me. I turned and saw Edward Whittacker standing there.

It was all I could do not to cry. He looked as bad as I did. Strangely damp. Blood-soaked. He was steadily working on two black eyes, a blow to the head, it seemed. This was not how I was used to him looking. His shirt was torn. He grabbed my arms before I could throw myself at his chest and held me achingly away from him. His eyes were filled with tears. I didn't get to ask him how he knew what flight I was coming in on. Why he was there. Why he wouldn't let me touch him.

"I need to talk to you before you hear it somewhere else," Whitt said. He glanced at the people around us, many of whom were staring, pretending to stop and adjust their bags. "Tox...Tox found the killer. He fought him. He got injured. He's stable at the moment but it's...it's complicated. He's...not well. He's on the edge. Last night I cornered the killer. Regan Banks. He told me that he set your brother up. He told me Sam is innocent."

I grabbed onto Whitt's shirt. I held on, partly so I didn't fall. Partly so that I could shake him if I needed to. My whole body was afire. He wiped at the tears running down his cheeks.

"He got away," he said. "I let him get away."

"We've got to find him," I said. "We...Where was he last seen? Have there been sightings since? Where's Tox? What hospital is he in?"

"Harry." Whitt held on as I tried to twist away. His grip was hard. Painful. "Word came through from the prison a couple of hours ago. There was an incident early this morning. A fight broke out in Sam's cell block. Harry, your brother's dead."

CHAPTER 132

I STARED UP at Whitt's eyes. The airport around me had been reduced to nothing. No light. No sound. Just a hollow in which this man and I stood. The words tumbled out of him, even as I willed them to stop. Whitt ran a hand through his filthy hair.

"Sam's dead," he said again.

The words rang in my mind, vibrating, the echo of a bell struck hard. I held on to Whitt's shirt. He pulled me into his chest, wrapped an arm around my head, trying to shield me from the on-lookers I could still see over his shoulder. Whitt didn't know what to do. He rubbed my back hard, tried to squeeze the pain out of me even as it began to creep into my blood. I shook my head against his chest. My eyes were wide. I was terrified of closing them, of losing my fragile grip on the room around me. If I could just stay here in this moment, in the airport terminal, if I could just hold on, maybe it wouldn't be real.

No, a voice inside me said. *Please don't take my brother. Please. I don't want to be left here alone. Don't leave me here alone.*

As the tears formed and I closed my eyes, I recognized what I'd been feeling since I left Last Chance. The sickness, the heat, the giddiness. It was Sam.

He was gone.

CHAPTER 133

I FELT THE fabric of Whitt's shirt pull tight as someone tapped him on the arm. "Sir, ma'am? Is everything all right? Can I offer you some assistance?"

Whitt pulled away from me, took in the sight of the flight attendant before him like she was an alien creature, her spotless red blazer and unreal makeup a puzzlement. He spoke to her. Gestured. I didn't listen. I turned and looked at the faces of the men and women who'd gathered around us. I looked from face to face. An elderly lady and her husband clutching their matching suitcase set. A pair of pierced young women lugging backpacks. A family. A group of businessmen. I looked at them, and I didn't recognize them.

Once, I would have thought of these strangers as "civilians." Non-police. Members of the public whose protection was my duty. They were what I woke for. What I breathed for. These strangers standing around me, those walking back and forth beyond them, getting on planes, getting in taxis.

Now they were just faceless people standing in my way.

I felt a rush of warmth over my limbs, an inner surrender. I was no longer a good Harry struggling to control her bad half. A battle had been lost. I felt dark inside. Hollow, dark and empty of goodness.

Because somewhere out there, beyond them all, beyond the terminal and the airport, Regan Banks was waiting. He was my purpose now. He would be what I continued breathing for. There would be time to grieve properly for Sam later, once I had Regan in my hands. I needed to find him, make him confess what he had done, force him to exonerate my brother. I couldn't let the tears fall yet. There wasn't time for that.

Second by second, he was getting away from me. And I was not going to let him escape.

I was not going to let him be caught by my colleagues, by Whitt or Tox, men who would spare his life.

He was going to be mine.

I walked away through the crowd. By the time Whitt noticed I was gone, it was too late.

ABOUT THE AUTHORS

JAMES PATTERSON received the Literarian Award for Outstanding Service to the American Literary Community from the National Book Foundation. He holds the Guinness World Record for the most #1 *New York Times* bestsellers, and his books have sold more than 365 million copies worldwide. A tireless champion of the power of books and reading, Patterson created a children's book imprint, JIMMY Patterson, whose mission is simple: "We want every kid who finishes a JIMMY Book to say, 'PLEASE GIVE ME ANOTHER BOOK.'" He has donated more than one million books to students and soldiers and funds over four hundred Teacher Education Scholarships at twenty-four colleges and universities. He has also donated millions of dollars to independent bookstores and school libraries. Patterson invests proceeds from the sales of JIMMY Patterson Books in pro-reading initiatives.

CANDICE FOX is the author of *Hades,* which won the Ned Kelly Award for best debut novel in 2014. The sequel, *Eden,* won the Ned Kelly Award for best crime novel in 2015, making Candice only the second author to win these accolades back to back. *Fall,* the third Archer and Bennett novel, was released in 2015.

Candice lectures in writing at the University of Notre Dame, Sydney, Australia, while undertaking a PhD in literary censorship and terrorism.

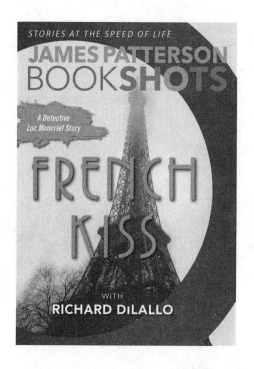

CHAPTER 1

THE WEATHERMAN NAILED IT. "Sticky, hot, and miserable. Highs in the nineties. Stay inside if you can."

I can't. I have to get someplace. Fast.

Jesus Christ, it's hot. Especially if you're running as fast as you can through Central Park *and* you're wearing a dark gray Armani silk suit, a light gray Canali silk shirt, and black Ferragamo shoes.

As you might have guessed, I am late—very, very late. *Très en retard,* as we say in France.

I pick up speed until my legs hurt. I can feel little blisters forming on my toes and heels.

Why did I ever come to New York?

Why, oh why, did I leave Paris?

If I were running like this in Paris, I would be stopping all traffic. I would be the center of attention. Men and women would be shouting for the police.

"A young businessman has gone berserk! He is shoving baby carriages out of his path. He is frightening the old ladies walking their dogs."

But this is not Paris. This is New York.

So forget it. Even the craziest event in New York goes unnoticed. The dog walkers keep on walking their dogs. The teenage lovers kiss. A toddler points to me. His mother glances up. Then she shrugs.

Will even one New Yorker dial 911? Or 311?

Forget about that also. You see, I am part of the police. A French detective now working with the Seventeenth Precinct on my specialty—drug smuggling, drug sales, and drug-related homicides.

My talent for being late has, in a mere two months, become almost legendary with my colleagues in the precinct house. But... oh, *merde*...showing up late for today's meticulously planned stakeout on Madison Avenue and 71st Street will do nothing to help my reputation, a reputation as an uncooperative rich French kid, a rebel with too many causes.

Merde...today of all days I should have known better than to wake my gorgeous girlfriend to say good-bye.

"I cannot be late for this one, Dalia."

"Just one more good-bye squeeze. What if you're shot and I never see you again?"

The good-bye "squeeze" turned out to be significantly longer than I had planned.

Eh. It doesn't matter. I'm where I'm supposed to be now. A mere forty-five minutes late.

CHAPTER 2

MY PARTNER, DETECTIVE Maria Martinez, is seated on the driver's side of an unmarked police car at 71st Street and Madison Avenue.

While keeping her eyes on the surrounding area, Maria unlocks the passenger door. I slide in, drowning in perspiration. She glances at me for a second, then speaks.

"Man. What's the deal? Did you put your suit on first and *then* take your shower?"

"Funny," I say. "Sorry I'm late."

"You should have little business cards with that phrase on it—'Sorry I'm late.'"

I'm certain that Maria Martinez doesn't care whether I'm late. Unlike a lot of my detective colleagues, she doesn't mind that I'm not big on "protocol." I'm late a lot. I do a lot of careless things. I bring ammo for a Glock 22 when I'm packing a Glock 27. I like a glass or two of white wine with lunch…it's a long list. But Maria overlooks most of it.

My other idiosyncrasies she has come to accept, more or less. I must have a proper *déjeuner.* That's lunch. No mere sandwich will do. What's more, a glass or two of good wine never did anything but enhance the flavor of a lunch.

You see, Maria "gets" me. Even better, she knows what I know:

5

together we're a cool combination of her procedure-driven methods and my purely instinct-driven methods.

"So where are we with this bust?" I say.

"We're still sitting on our butts. That's where we are," she says. Then she gives details.

"They got two pairs of cops on the other side of the street, and two other detectives—Imani Williams and Henry Whatever-the-Hell-His-Long-Polish-Name-Is—at the end of the block. That team'll go into the garage.

"Then there's another team behind the garage. They'll hold back and *then* go into the garage.

"Then they got three guys on the roof of the target building."

The target building is a large former town house that's now home to a store called Taylor Antiquities. It's a place filled with the fancy antique pieces lusted after by trust-fund babies and hedge-fund hotshots. Maria and I have already cased Taylor Antiquities a few times. It's a store where you can lay down your Amex Centurion card and walk away with a white jade vase from the Yuan dynasty or purchase the four-poster bed where John and Abigail Adams reportedly conceived little John Quincy.

"And what about us?"

"Our assignment spot is inside the store," she says.

"No. I want to be where the action is," I say.

"Be careful what you wish for," Maria says. "Do what they tell you. We're inside the store. Over and out. Meanwhile, how about watching the street with me?"

Maria Martinez is total cop. At the moment she is heart-and-soul into the surveillance. Her eyes dart from the east side of the street to the west. Every few seconds, she glances into the rearview mirror. Follows it with a quick look into the side-view mirror. Searches straight ahead. Then she does it all over again.

Me? Well, I'm looking around, but I'm also wondering if I can take a minute off to grab a cardboard cup of lousy American coffee.

Don't get me wrong. And don't be put off by what I said about my impatience with "procedure." No. I am very cool with being a detective. In fact, I've wanted to be a detective since I was four years old. I'm also very good at my job. And I've got the résumé to prove it.

Last year in Pigalle, one of the roughest parts of Paris, I solved a drug-related gang homicide and made three on-the-scene arrests. Just me and a twenty-five-year-old traffic cop.

I was happy. I was successful. For a few days I was even famous.

The next morning the name Luc Moncrief was all over the newspapers and the Internet. A rough translation of the headline on the front page of *Le Monde:*

OLDEST PIGALLE DRUG GANG SMASHED BY YOUNGEST PARIS DETECTIVE— LUC MONCRIEF

Underneath was this subhead:

Parisian Heartthrob Hauls in Pigalle Drug Lords

The paparazzi had always been somewhat interested in whom I was dating; after that, they were obsessed. Club owners comped my table with bottles of Perrier-Jouët Champagne. Even my father, the chairman of a giant pharmaceuticals company, gave me one of his rare compliments.

"Very nice job…for a playboy. Now I hope you've got this 'detective thing' out of your system."

I told him thank you, but I did not tell him that "this detective thing" was not out of my system. Or that I enjoyed the very generous monthly allowance that he gave me too much.

So when my *capitaine supérieur* announced that the NYPD wanted to trade one of their art-forgery detectives for one of our Paris drug enforcement detectives for a few months, I jumped at the offer. From my point of view, it was a chance to reconnect with my former lover, Dalia Boaz. From my Parisian *lieutenant* point of view, it was an opportunity to add some needed discipline and learning to my instinctive approach to detective work.

So here I am. On Madison Avenue, my eyes are burning with sweat. I can actually feel the perspiration squishing around in my shoes.

Detective Martinez remains focused completely on the street scene. But God, I need some coffee, some air. I begin speaking.

"Listen. If I could just jump out for a minute and—"

As I'm about to finish the sentence, two vans—one black, one red—turn into the garage next door to Taylor Antiquities.

Our cell phones automatically buzz with a loud sirenlike sound. The doors of the unmarked police cars begin to open.

As Maria and I hit the street, she speaks.

"It looks like our evidence has finally arrived."

CHAPTER 3

MARTINEZ AND I RUSH into Taylor Antiquities. There are no customers. A skinny middle-aged guy sits at a desk in the rear of the store, and a typical debutante—a young blond woman in a white linen skirt and a black shirt—is dusting some small, silver-topped jars.

It is immediately clear to both of them that we're not here to buy an ancient Thai penholder. We are easily identified as two very unpleasant-looking cops, the male foolishly dressed in an expensive waterlogged suit, the woman in too-tight khaki pants. Maria and I are each holding our NYPD IDs in our left hands and our pistols in our right hands.

"You. Freeze!" Maria shouts at the blond woman.

I yell the same thing at the guy at the desk.

"You freeze, too, sir," I say.

From our two pre-bust surveillance visits I recognize the man as Blaise Ansel, the owner of Taylor Antiquities.

Ansel begins walking toward us.

I yell again. "I said freeze, Mr. Ansel. This…is…a…drug…raid."

"This is police-department madness," Ansel says, and now he is almost next to us. The debutante hasn't moved a muscle.

"Cuff him, Luc. He's resisting." Maria is pissed.

Ansel throws his hands into the air. "No. No. I am not resisting anything but the intrusion. I *am* freezing. Look."

Although I have seen him before, I have never heard him speak. His accent is foreign, thick. It's an accent that's easy for anyone to identify. Ansel is a Frenchman. Son of a bitch. One of ours.

As Ansel freezes, three patrol cars, lights flashing, pull up in front of the store. Then I tell the young woman to join us. She doesn't move. She doesn't speak.

"Please join us," Maria says. Now the woman moves to us. Slowly. Cautiously.

"Your name, ma'am?" I ask.

"Monica Ansel," she replies.

Blaise Ansel looks at Martinez and me.

"She's my wife."

There's got to be a twenty-year age difference between the two of them, but Maria and I remain stone-faced. Maria taps on her cell phone and begins reading aloud from the screen.

"To make this clear: we are conducting a drug search based on probable cause. Premises and connected premises are 861 Madison Avenue, New York, New York, in the borough of Manhattan, June 21, 2016. Premises title: Taylor Antiquities, Inc. Chairman and owner: Blaise Martin Ansel. Company president: Blaise Martin Ansel."

Maria taps the screen and pushes another button.

"This is being recorded," she says.

I would never have read the order to search, but Maria is strictly by the book.

"This is preposterous," says Blaise Ansel.

Maria does not address Ansel's comment. She simply says, "I want you to know that detectives and officers are currently positioned in your delivery dock, your garage, and your rooftop. They will be interviewing all parties of interest. It is our assignment to interview both you and the woman you've identified as your wife."

"Drugs? Are you mad?" yells Ansel. "This shop is a museum-quality repository of rare antiques. Look. Look."

Ansel quickly moves to one of the display tables. He holds up a carved mahogany box. "A fifteenth-century tea chest," he says. He lifts the lid of the box. "What do you see inside? Cocaine? Heroin? Marijuana?"

It is obvious that Maria has decided to allow Ansel to continue his slightly crazed demonstration.

"This—this, too," Ansel says as he moves to a pine trunk set on four spindly legs. "An American colonial sugar safe. Nothing inside. No crystal meth, no sugar."

Ansel is about to present two painted Chinese-looking bowls when the rear entrance to the shop opens and Imani Williams enters. Detective Williams is agitated. She is also *très belle*.

"Not a damn thing in those two vans," she says. "Police mechanics are searching the undersides, but there's nothing but a bunch of empty gold cigarette boxes and twelve Iranian silk rugs in the cargo. We tested for drug traces. They all came up negative."

I think I catch an exchange of glances between Monsieur and

Madame Ansel. I *think*. I'm not sure. But the more I think, well, the more sure I become.

"Detective Williams," I say. "Do you think you could fill in for me for a few minutes to assist Detective Martinez with the Ansel interview?"

"Yeah, sure," says Williams. "Where you going?"

"I just need to…I'm not sure…look around."

"Tell the truth, Moncrief. You've been craving a cup of joe since you got here," says Maria Martinez.

"Can't fool you, partner," I say.

I open the shop door. I'm out.

CHAPTER 4

THE SUFFOCATING AIR ON Madison Avenue almost shimmers with heat.

Where have all the beautiful people gone? East Hampton? Bar Harbor? The South of France?

I walk the block. I watch a man polish the handrail alongside the steps of Saint James' Church. I see the tourists line up outside Ladurée, the French *macaron* store.

A young African American man, maybe eighteen years old, walks near me. He is bare-chested. He seems even sweatier than I am. The young man's T-shirt is tied around his neck, and he is guzzling from a quart-size bottle of water.

"Where'd you get that?" I ask.

"A dude like you can go to that fancy-ass cookie store. You got five bills, that'll get you a soda there," he says.

"But where'd you get *that* bottle, the water you're drinking?" I ask again.

"Us poor bros go to Kenny's. You're practically in it right now."

He gestures toward 71st Street between Madison and Park Avenues. As the kid moves away, I figure that the "fancy-ass cookie store" is Ladurée. I am equidistant between a five-dollar soda and a cheaper but larger bottle of water. Why waste Papa's generous allowance on fancy-ass soda?

Kenny's is a tiny storefront, a place you should find closer to Ninth Avenue than Madison Avenue. Behind the counter is a Middle Eastern-type guy. Kenny? He peddles only newspapers, cigarettes, lottery tickets, and, for some reason, Dial soap.

I examine the contents of Kenny's small refrigerated case. It holds many bottles, all of them the same—the no-name water that the shirtless young man was drinking. At the moment that water looks to me like heaven in a bottle.

"I'm going to take two of these bottles," I say.

"One second, please, sir," says the man behind the counter, then he addresses another man who is wheeling four brown cartons of candy into the store. The cartons are printed with the name and logo for Snickers. The man steering the dolly looks very much like the counterman. Is he Kenny? Is anybody Kenny? I consider buying a Snickers bar. No. The wet Armani suit is already growing tighter.

"How many more boxes are there, Hector?" the counterman asks.

"At least fifteen more," comes the response. Then "Kenny" turns to me.

"And you, sir?" the counterman asks.

"No. Nothing," I say. "Sorry."

I leave the tiny store and break into a run. I am around the corner on Madison Avenue. I punch the button on my phone marked 4. Direct connection to Martinez. All I can think is: *What the*

hell? Twenty cartons of candy stored in a shop the size of a closet?
Twenty cartons of Snickers in a store that doesn't even sell candy?

She answers and starts talking immediately. "Williams and I are getting nowhere with these two assholes. This whole thing sucks. Our intelligence is all screwed up. There's nothing here."

I am only slightly breathless, only slightly nervous.

"Listen to me. It's all here, where I am. I know it."

"What the hell are you talking about?" she says.

"A newsstand between Madison and Park. Kenny's. I'm less than two hundred feet away from you guys. Leave one person at Taylor Antiquities and get everyone over here. Now."

"How—?"

"The two vans, the garage…that's all a decoy," I say. "The real shit is being unloaded here…in cartons of candy bars."

"How do you know?"

"Like the case in Pigalle. *I know because I know.*"

CHAPTER 5

ONE MONTH LATER. IT'S another sweltering summer day in Manhattan.

A year ago I was working in the detective room at the precinct on rue Achille-Martinet in Paris. Today I'm working in the detective room at the precinct on East 51st Street in Manhattan.

But the crime is absolutely the same. In both cities, men, women, and children sell drugs, kill for drugs, and all too often die for drugs.

My desk faces Maria Martinez's scruffy desk. She's not in yet. Uh-oh. She may be picking up my bad habits. *Pas possible.* Not Maria.

I drink my coffee and begin reading the blotter reports of last night's arrests. No murders, no drug busts. So much for interesting blotter reports.

I call my coolest, hippest, chicest New York contact—Patrick, one of the doormen at 15 Central Park West, where I live with Dalia. Patrick is trying to score me a dinner reservation at Rao's, the impossible-to-get-into restaurant in East Harlem.

Merde. I am on my cell phone when my boss, Inspector Nick Elliott, the chief inspector for my division, stops by. I hold up my "just a minute" index finger. Since the Taylor Antiquities drug bust I have a little money in the bank with my boss, but it won't last forever, and this hand gesture certainly won't help.

At last I sigh. No tables. Maybe next month. When I hang up the phone I say, "I'm sorry, Inspector. I was just negotiating a favor with a friend who might be able to score me a table at Rao's next week."

Elliott scowls and says, "Far be it from me to interrupt your off-duty life, Moncrief, but you may have noticed that your partner isn't at her desk."

"I noticed. Don't forget, I'm a detective."

He ignores my little joke.

"In case you're wondering, Detective Martinez is on loan to Vice for two days."

"Why didn't you or Detective Martinez tell me this earlier? You must have known before today."

"Yeah, I knew about it yesterday, but I told Martinez to hold off telling you. That it would just piss you off to be left out, and I was in no rush to listen to you get pissed off," Elliott says.

"So why *wasn't* I included?" I ask.

"You weren't necessary. They just needed a woman. Though I don't owe you any explanations about assignments."

The detective room has grown quieter. I'm sure that a few of my colleagues—especially the men—are enjoying seeing Elliott put me in my place.

Fact is, I like Elliott; he's a pretty straight-arrow guy, but I have been developing a small case of paranoia about being excluded from hot assignments.

"What can Maria do that I can't do?" I ask.

"If you can't answer that, then that pretty-boy face of yours isn't doing you much good," Elliott says with a laugh. Then his tone of voice turns serious.

"Anyway, we got something going on up the road a piece. They got a situation at Brioni. That's a fancy men's store just off Fifth Avenue. Get a squad car driver to take you there. Right now."

"Which Brioni?" I ask.

"I just told you—Brioni on Fifth Avenue."

"There are *two* Brionis: 57 East 57th Street and 55 East 52nd Street," I say.

Elliott begins to walk away. He stops. He turns to me. He speaks.

"You *would* know something like that."

CHAPTER 6

WHAT'S THE ONE QUESTION that's guaranteed to piss off any New York City detective or cop?

"Don't you guys have anything better to do with your time?"

If you're a cop who's ever ticketed someone for running a red light; if you're a detective who's ever asked a mother why her child wasn't in school that day, then you've heard it.

I enter the Brioni store, at 57 East 57th Street. My ego is bruised, and my mood is lousy. Frankly, I am usually in Brioni as a customer, not a policeman. Plus, is there nothing more humiliating than an eager detective sent to investigate a shoplifting crime?

I'm in an even lousier mood when the first thing I'm asked is, "Don't you guys have anything better to do with your time?" The suspect doesn't ask this question. No. It comes from one of the arresting officers, a skinny young African American guy who is at the moment cuffing a young African American kid. The minor has been nabbed by store security. He was trying to lift three cashmere sweaters, and now the kid is scared as shit.

"You should know better than to ask that question," I say to the cop. "Meanwhile, take the cuffs off the kid."

The cop does as he's told, but he clearly does not know when to shut up. So he speaks.

"Sorry, Detective. I just meant that it's pretty unusual to send a detective out on an arrest that's so…so…"

He is searching for a word, and I supply it. "Unimportant."

"Yeah, that's it," the young officer says. "Unimportant."

The officer now realizes that the subject is closed. He gives me some details. The kid, age twelve, was brought in for petty robbery this past February. But I'm only half listening. I'm pissed off, and I'm pissed off because the cop is right—it's unimportant. This case is incredibly unimportant, laughably unimportant. It's ridiculous to be sent on such a stupid little errand. Other NYPD detectives are unraveling terrorist plots, going undercover to frame mob bosses. Me, I'm overseeing the arrest of a little kid who stole three cashmere sweaters.

As Maria Martinez has often said to me, "Someone with your handsome face and your expensive suit shouldn't be sent on anything but the most important assignments." Then she'd laugh, and I would stare at her in stony silence…until I also laughed.

"We have the merch all bagged," says the other officer. The name Callahan is on his nameplate. Callahan is a guy with very pink cheeks and an even pinker nose. He looks maybe thirty-five or forty…or whatever age a cop is when he's smart enough not to ask "Don't you have anything better to do with your time?"

"Thanks," I say.

But what I'm really thinking about is: *Who the hell gave me this nauseatingly* petite *assignment?*

I'm sure it's not Elliott. Ah, *oui,* the inspector and I aren't exactly what they call best buds, but he's grown used to me. He thinks he's being funny when he calls me Pretty Boy, but he also trusts me, and, like almost everyone else, he's very pleased with the bust I (almost single-handedly) helped pull off at Taylor Antiquities.

I know that my partner, Maria Martinez, puts out good press on me. As I've said, she and I are simpatico, to say the least. I like her. She likes me. Case closed.

Beyond that, anyone higher than Elliott doesn't know I exist. So I can't assume that one of the assistant commissioners or one of the ADAs is out to get me.

"There's a squad car outside to bring him in," Callahan says.

"Hold on a minute. I want to talk to the kid," I say.

I walk over to the boy. He wears jeans cut off at midcalf, very clean white high-top sneakers, and an equally clean white T-shirt. It's a look I could live without.

"Why'd you try to steal three sweaters? It's the goddamn middle of summer, and you're stealing sweaters. Are you stupid?"

I can tell that if he starts talking he's going to cry.

No answer. He looks away. At the ceiling. At the floor. At the young cop and Callahan.

"How old are you?" I ask.

"Sixteen," he says. My instinct was right. He does start to cry. He squints hard, trying to stem the flow of tears.

"You're a lousy liar *and* a lousy thief. You're twelve. You're in the system. Don't you think the officers checked? You were picked up five months ago. You and a friend tried to hold up a liquor store on East Tremont. They got you then, too. You *are* stupid."

The kid shouts at me. No tears now.

"I ain't stupid. I kinda thought they'd have a buzzer or some shit in the liquor store. And I kinda felt that fat-ass guy here with the ugly-mother brown shoes was a security guy. But I don't know. Both times I decided to try it. I decided…I'm not sure why."

"Listen. Good advice number one. Kids who are assholes turn into grown-ups who are assholes.

"Good advice number two. If you've got smart instincts, *follow them*. You know what? Forget good advice. You've got a feeling? Go with it."

He sort of nods in agreement. So I keep talking.

"Look, asshole. This advice is life advice. I'm not trying to teach you how to be a better thief. I'm just trying to…oh, shit…I don't know what I'm trying to teach you."

A pause. The kid looks down at the floor so intensely that I have to look down there myself. Nothing's there but gray carpet squares.

Then the kid looks at me. He speaks.

"I get you, man," he says.

"Good." A pause. "Now go home. You've got a home?"

"I got a home. I got a grandma."

"Then go."

"What the fu—?"

"Just go."

He runs to the door.

The young officer looks at me. Then he says, "That's just great. They send a detective to the scene. And he lets the suspect go."

I don't smile. I don't answer. I walk to a nearby table where beautiful silk ties and pocket squares are laid out in groups according to color. I focus on the yellow section—yellow with blue stripes, yellow with tiny red dots, yellow paisley, yellow…

My cell phone pings. The message on the screen is big and bold and simple. CD. Cop Down.

No details. Just an address: 655 Park Avenue. Right now.

CHAPTER 7

COPS AND LIGHTS AND miles of yellow tape: POLICE LINE DO NOT CROSS.

Sirens and detectives crowd the blocks between 65th and 67th Streets. Even the mayor's car (license NYC 1) is here.

People from the neighborhood, doormen on break, and students from Hunter College try to catch a glimpse of the scene. Hundreds of people stand on the blocked-off avenue. It's a tragedy and a block party at the same time.

Detective Gabriel Ruggie approaches me. There will be no French-guy jokes, no late-guy jokes, no Pretty Boy jokes. This is serious shit. Ruggie talks.

"Elliott is up there now. The scene is at the seventh floor front. He said to send you up right away."

I walk through the fancy lobby. It's loaded with cops and reporters and detectives. I hear a brief litany of somber "hellos" and "hiyas," most of them followed by various mispronunciations of my name.

Luke. Look. Luck.

Who the hell cares now? This is Cop Down.

Detective Christine Liang is running the elevator along with a plainclothes officer.

"Hey, Moncrief. Let me take you up," Liang says. "The inspector's been asking where you are."

What the hell is the deal? Ten minutes ago I'm supervising New York's dumbest little crime of the day. Now, all of a sudden, the most serious type of crime—officer homicide—requires my attention.

"Good—you're here," Elliott says as I step from the elevator. I feel as if he's been waiting for me. It's the typical chaos of a homicide, with fingerprinting people, computer people, the coroner's people—all the people who are really smart, really thorough; but honestly, none of them ever seem to come up with information that helps solve the case.

I'm scared. I don't mind saying it. Elliott hits his phone and says, "Moncrief is here now."

"Who's that?" I ask.

"Just headquarters. I let them know you were here. They were trying to track you down."

"But you knew where I was. You sent me there," I say, confused.

"Yeah, I know. I know." Elliott seems confused, too.

"What's the deal?" I ask.

"Come with me," Elliott says. The crowd of NYPD people parts for us as if we're celebrities. We walk down a wide hall with black and white marble squares on the floor, two real Warhols on the walls. Suddenly I have a flash of an apartment in Paris—the high ceilings, the carved cornices. But in a moment I've traveled back from boulevard Haussmann to Park Avenue.

At the end of the hallway, an officer stands in front of an open door. Bright lights—floodlights, examination lights—pour from the room into the hallway. The officer moves aside immediately as Elliott and I approach.

Three people are huddled in a group near a window. I catch sight of a body, a woman. Elliott and I walk toward the group. We are still a few feet away when I see her. When my heart leaps up.

Maria Martinez.

A black plastic sheet covers her torso. Her head, blood speckling and staining her hair, is exposed.

Elliott puts a hand on my shoulder. I don't yell or cry or shake. A numbness shoots through me, and then the words tumble out.

"How? How?"

"I told you this morning, she was on loan to Vice. They had her playing the part of a high-class call girl. It seems that…well, whoever she was supposed to meet decided to…well, take a knife to her stomach."

I say nothing. I keep staring at my dead partner. Elliott decides to fill the air with words. I know he means well.

"The owners of this place are at their house in Nantucket. No servants were home…no…"

I've stopped listening. Elliott stops talking. The police photographers keep clicking away. Phil Namanworth, the coroner, is typing furiously on his laptop. Cops and detectives come and go.

Maria is dead. She looks so peaceful. Isn't that what people always say? But it's true. At least in this case it's true. In death there is peace, but there's no peace for those of us left behind.

Elliott looks me straight in the eye.

"Ya know, Moncrief, I'd like to say that in time you'll get over this." He pauses. "But I'd be a liar."

"And a good cop never lies," I say softly.

"Come back to the precinct in my car," Elliott says.

"No, thank you," I answer. "There's someplace I've got to be."

CHAPTER 8

IT'S THE SOUTHWEST CORNER of 177th Street and Fort Washington Avenue. Maria and Joey Martinez's building. I had never been there before, although Maria kept insisting that Dalia and I had to come by some night for "crazy chicken and rice," her mother's recipe.

"You'll taste it, you'll love it, and you won't be able to guess the secret ingredient," she would say.

But we never set a date, and now I am about to visit her apartment while two cops are standing guard outside the building and two detectives are inside questioning neighbors. I was her partner. I've got to see Maria's family.

A short pudgy man opens the apartment door. The living room is noisy, packed. People are crying, yelling, speaking Spanish and English. The big window air conditioner is noisy.

"I'm Maria's brother-in-law," says the man at the door.

"I'm Maria's partner from work," I say.

His face shows no expression. He nods, then says, "Joey and me are about to go downtown. They wouldn't let him—the husband, the actual husband—go to the crime scene. Now they'll let us go see her. In the morgue."

A handsome young Latino man walks quickly toward me. It has

to be Joey Martinez. He is nervous, animated, red-eyed. He grabs me firmly by the shoulders. The room turns silent, like somebody turned an Off switch.

"You're Moncrief. I know you from your pictures. Maria has a million pictures of you on her phone," he says.

"Yeah," I say. "She loves clicking away on that cell phone."

I can't help but notice that he calls me by my last name. I don't know why. Maybe that's how Maria referred to me at home.

I try to move closer to give Joey a hug. But he moves back, blocking any sort of embrace. So I speak.

"I don't know what to say, Joey. This is an incredible tragedy. Your heart must be breaking. I'm so sorry."

"Your heart must be breaking also," Joey says.

"It is," I say. "Maria was the best partner a detective could hope for. Smart. Patient. Tough…" Joey may not be weeping, but I feel myself choking up.

Joey gestures to his brother. It's a "Let's go" toss of his head.

"Look, my brother and I are going down to see Maria. But Moncrief…"

There's that last-name-only thing again. "I need to ask you something."

Now I'm nervous, but I'm not at all sure why. Something is off. The room remains silent. Brother is now standing next to brother.

"Sure," I say. "Ask me. Ask me anything."

Joey Martinez's sad and empty eyes widen. He looks directly at me and speaks slowly. "How do you have the nerve to come to my house?"

I feel confusion, and I'm sure that my face is communicating it. "Because I feel so terrible, so awful, so sad. Maria was my partner. We spent hours and hours together."

Joey continues speaking at the same slow pace. "Yes. I know. Maria loved you."

"And I loved her," I say.

"You don't understand. Or you're a liar. Maria *loved* you. She really loved you."

His words are so crazy and so untrue that I have no idea how to respond. "Joey. Please. You're experiencing a tragedy. You're totally…well…you're totally wrong about Maria, about me."

"She told me," he says. "It's not a misunderstanding. She didn't mean you were just good friends. We talked about it a thousand times. She *loved* you."

Now he pushes his face close to mine. "You think because you're rich and good-looking you can get whatever you want. You think—"

"Joey. Wait. This is insane!" I shout.

He shouts even louder. "Stop it! Just shut up. Just leave!" He shakes his head. The tears are coming fast. "My brother and I gotta go."

CHAPTER 9

WHEN I GET HOME, Dalia is waiting for me in the apartment foyer. Her hug is strong. Her kiss is soft—not sexual per se—just the perfect gentle touch of warmth. The tenderness of Dalia's kiss immediately signals to me that she's already heard about Maria Martinez's death. I'm not surprised. The DA's office has access to all NYPD information, and Dalia knows her way around her job.

Dalia is an ADA for Manhattan district attorney Fletcher Sinclair. She heads up the investigation division. The two qualities that the job requires—brains and persistence—are the two qualities Dalia seems to have in endless supply. Nothing and no one stands in her way when she's hot on an investigation.

Every day at work she tones down her tall and skinny fashion-model look with a ponytail, sensible skirts, and almost no makeup. When Dalia's at her job, she's all about the job. Laser-focused. Don't mess with the ADA.

Some evenings, when Dalia's dressed for some ultrachic charity dinner, even I have a hard time believing that this breathtakingly *belle* woman in her Georgina Chapman gown is one of the toughest lawyers in New York City.

"We got word about Maria at the DA's office late this morning," she says. "I was going to call or text or something, but I didn't want to butt in. I didn't want to nudge you if you didn't need me...."

"You can always nudge me, because I always need you," I say.

"I opened a nice Chilean Chardonnay. You want a glass and we can talk?" she asks.

"Yes," I say. "Mix a glass of wine with a quart of tequila and we'll have a drink that *might* make me forget what a miserable day this has been."

"Maria, Maria, Maria," Dalia says. She shakes her head as she pours the wine into two wineglasses. Then she says, "I hate to ask, but...any ideas yet?"

"I sure don't have any guesses. I don't even have all the details yet. Plus Maria's husband is a crazy mess right now." I decide to skip the details.

"Understandably," Dalia says.

I cannot shake the mental picture of Joey Martinez's hurt and anger as he spat out the words "She *loved* you."

Then Dalia says, "But what about you? How are you feeling?"

"How *can* I feel? Maria was my partner, and she was as good a partner as anyone ever had. She was damn near perfect. As my rugby coach used to say, 'The best combination for any job is the brains of an owl and the skin of an elephant.'"

"What was the name of the genius who came up with that little saying?" Dalia asks.

"Monsieur Pierre LeBec. You must remember him—the fat little man who was always smoking a pipe. He coached boys' rugby and taught geometry," I say. A reminiscence is about to open up.

Dalia and I speak often about the school in Paris we had both attended. We became girlfriend and boyfriend during our second year at Lycée Henri-IV. And we fell in love exactly the way teenagers do—with unstoppable passion. There wasn't enough time in the day for all the laughter and talking and sex that we needed to have. Even when we broke up, just before we both left for university, we did it with excessive passion. Lots of door slamming and yelling and crying and kissing.

Ten years later, when Act II of *The Story of Dalia and Luc* began, it was as if we were teenagers all over again. First of all, we "met cute." Dalia and I reconnected completely accidentally three months ago at one of the rare NYPD social functions—a spring boat ride on the Hudson River. I was standing alone at the starboard railing and must have been turning green. About to heave, I was one seasick sailor.

"You look like a man who needs some Dramamine," came Dalia's voice from behind me. I'd know it anywhere. I turned around.

"Holy shit! It's you," I said. We hugged and immediately agreed that only God himself could have planned this meeting. It may not have been an actual miracle, but it was certainly *une coïncidence grande*. Two former Parisian lovers who end up on a boat and then…

Dalia reminded me that she was not Parisian. She was Israeli, a sabra.

"Okay, then it's a fairy tale," I said. "And in fairy tales you don't pay attention to details."

By the time the boat docked at Chelsea Piers, we were in love again. And—holy shit indeed—had she ever turned from a spectacular-looking teenager into an incredibly spectacular-looking young woman.

She invited me back to her ridiculously large penthouse at 15 Central Park West, the apartment that her father, the film director and producer Menashe Boaz, had paid for. That night was beyond unforgettable. I couldn't imagine my life if that night had never happened.

After the first week, I had most of my clothes sent over.

After the second week, I had my exercise bike and weights sent over.

After a month I hired a company to deliver the three most valuable pieces from my contemporary Chinese art collection: the Zao Wou-Ki, the Zhang Xiaogang, and the Zeng Fanzhi. Dalia refers to them as the Z-name contemporary art collection. She said that when those paintings were hung in her living room, she knew I planned to stay.

But now we have *this* night. The night of Maria's death. A night that's the emotional opposite of that joyful night months ago.

"Will you be hungry later on?" Dalia asks.

"I doubt it," I say. I pour us each another glass of wine. "Anyway, if we get hungry later on, I'll make us some scrambled eggs."

She smiles and says, "An eight-burner Garland range and we're making scrambled eggs."

That statement should be cute and funny. But we both know that nothing can be cute and funny this evening.

"I want to ask you something," I say.

"Yeah, of course," she says. She wrinkles her forehead a tiny bit. As if she's expecting some scary question. I proceed.

"Are you angry that I'm so sad about Maria's murder?"

Dalia pauses. Then she tilts her head to the side. Her face is now soft, tender, caring.

"Oh, Luc," she says. "I would only be angry if you were *not* sad."

I feel that we should kiss. I think Dalia feels the same way. But I also think something inside each of us is telling us that if we did kiss, no matter how chaste the kiss might be, it would be almost disrespectful to Maria.

We sit silently for a long time. We finish the bottle of Chardonnay.

It turns out that we never were hungry enough to scramble some eggs. All we did was wait for the day to end.

CHAPTER 10

THE PERSON RESPONSIBLE FOR whatever skill I have in speaking decent English—very little French accent, pretty good English vocabulary—is Inspector Nick Elliott. No one has mastered the art of plain speaking better than he has.

"Morning, Pretty Boy. Looks like it's going to be a shitty day" is a typical example.

This morning Elliott and a woman I've never seen before appear at my desk. Looks like I'm about to receive an extra lesson in basic communication skills.

"Moncrief, meet Katherine Burke. You two are going to be partners in the Martinez investigation. I don't care to discuss it."

I barely have time to register the woman's face when he adds, "Good luck. Now get the hell to work."

"But sir…" I begin.

"Is there a problem?" Elliott asks, clearly anxious to hit the road.

"Well, no, but…"

"Good. Here's the deal. Katherine Burke is a detective, a *New York* detective, and has been for almost two years. She knows police procedure better than most people know their own names. She can teach you a lot."

I go for the end-run charm play.

"And I've got a lot to learn," I say, a big smile on my face.

He doesn't smile back.

"Don't get me wrong," Elliott says as he turns and speaks to Burke. "Moncrief has the instincts of a good detective. He just needs a little spit and polish."

As he walks away, I look at Katherine Burke. She is not Maria Martinez. So, of course, I immediately hate her.

"Good to meet you," she says.

"Same here." We shake, more like a quick touch of the hands.

My new partner and I study each other quietly, closely. We are like a bride and groom in a prearranged marriage meeting for the first time. This "marriage" means a great deal to me—joy, sorrow, and whether or not I can smoke in the squad car.

So what do I see before me? Burke is thirty-two, I'd guess. Face: pretty. No, actually *très jolie.* Irish; pale; big red lips. A good-looking woman in too-tight khakis. She seems pleasant enough. But I'm not sensing "warm and friendly."

And what does she see? A guy with an expensive haircut, an expensive suit, and—I think she's figured out already—a pretty bad attitude.

This does not bode well.

"Listen," she says. "I know this is tough for you. The inspector told me how much you admired Maria. We can talk about that."

"No," I say. "We can forget about that."

Silence again. Then I speak.

"Look. I apologize. You were trying to be nice, and I was just being…well…"

She fills it in for me: "A rude asshole. It happens to the best of us."

I smile, and I move a step closer. I read the official ID card that hangs from the cord around her neck. It shows her NYPD number and, in the same size type, her title. These are followed by her name in big bold uppercase lettering:

K. BURKE

"So you want to be called K. Burke?" I ask her as we walk back to the detective room.

"No. Katherine, Katie, or Kathy. Any of those are fine," she says.

"Then why do you have 'K. Burke' printed on your ID?"

"That's what they put there when they gave me the ID," she says. "The ID badge wasn't high on my priority list."

"K. Burke. I like it. From now on, that's what I'm going to call you. K. Burke."

She nods. For a few moments we don't speak. Then I say, "But I must be honest with you, K. Burke. I don't think this is going to work out."

She speaks, still seriously.

"You want to know something, Detective Moncrief?"

"What?"

"I think you're right."

And then, for the first time, she smiles.

CHAPTER 11

THE LOBBY OF THE Auberge du Parc Hotel is somebody's idea of elegance. But it sure as hell is not mine.

"Pink marble on the walls *and* the floor *and* the ceiling. If Barbie owned a brothel it would look like this." I share this observation with my new partner as I look out the floor-to-ceiling windows that face Park Avenue.

K. Burke either doesn't get the joke or doesn't like the joke. No laughter.

"We're not here to evaluate the decor," she says. "You know better than I do that Auberge du Parc is right up there with the Plaza and the Carlyle when it comes to expensive hotels for rich people."

"And it affords a magnificent view of the building where Maria Martinez was killed," I say as I gesture to the tall windows.

Burke looks out to the corner of 68th Street and Park Avenue. She nods solemnly. "That's why we're starting the job here."

"The job, you will agree, is fairly stupid?" I ask.

"The job is what Inspector Elliott has assigned us, and I'm not about to second-guess the command," she says.

Elliott wants us to interview prostitutes, streetwalkers, anyone he defines as "high-class lowlife." Enormously upscale hotels like the Auberge often have a lot of illegal sex stuff going on behind their pink marble walls. But asking the devils to tell us their sins? I don't think so.

This approach is ridiculous, to my way of thinking. Solutions come mostly by listening for small surprises—and yes, sometimes by looking for a few intelligent pieces of hard evidence. Looking in the *unlikely* places. Talking to the *least* likely observers.

Burke's theory, which is total NYPD style, is way more traditional: "You accumulate the information," she had said. "You assemble the puzzle piece by piece."

"Absolutely not," I replied. "You sink into the case as if it were a warm bath. You *sense* the situation. You look for the fingerprint of the crime itself." Then I added, "Here's what we'll do: you'll do it your way. I'll do it mine."

"No, not *your* way or *my* way," she had said. "We'll do it the NYPD way."

That discussion was a half hour ago. Now I'm really too disgusted and frustrated to say anything else.

So I stand with my new partner in a pink marble lobby a few hundred yards from where my old partner was murdered.

Okay. I'll be the adult here. I will try to appear cooperative.

We review our plan. I am to go to the lobby bar and talk to the one or two high-priced hookers who are almost always on the prowl there. You've seen them—the girls with the perfect hair falling gently over their shoulders. The delicate pointy noses all supplied by the same plastic surgeon. The women who are drinking in the afternoon while they're dressed for the evening.

Burke will go up to the more elegant, more secluded rooftop bar, Auberge in the Clouds. But of course she'll first stop by the hotel manager's office and tell him what he already knows: the NYPD is here. Procedure, procedure, procedure.

If Maria Martinez is watching all this from some heavenly locale, she is falling on the floor laughing.

After agreeing to meet Burke back in the lobby in forty-five minutes, I walk into the bar. (I once visited Versailles on a high school class trip, and this place would have pleased Marie Antoinette.) The bar itself is a square-shaped ebony box with gold curlicues all over it. It looks like a huge birthday present for a god with no taste.

At the bar sit two pretty ladies, one in a red silk dress, the other in a kind of clingy Diane von Furstenberg green-and-white thing, which is very loose around the top. I don't think von Furstenberg designed it to be so erotic. It takes me about two seconds to realize what these women do for a living.

These girls are precisely the type that Nick Elliott wants us to speak to. Yes, a ridiculous waste of time. And I know just what to do about it.

I walk toward the exit and push through the revolving door.

I'm out. I'm on my own. This is more like it.

CHAPTER 12

K. BURKE THINKS A good New York cop solves a case by putting the pieces together. K. Burke is wrong.

You can't put the pieces together in New York because there are just too goddamn many of them.

One step out the revolving door onto East 68th Street proves my point. It's only midday, but everywhere I look there's chaos and color and confusion.

Bike messengers and homeless people and dowagers and grammar-school students. Two women wheeling a full-size gold harp and two guys pushing a wheelbarrow full of bricks. The Greenpeace recruiter with her clipboard and smile, the crazy half-naked lady waving a broken umbrella, and the teenager selling iPad cases. All this on one block.

The store next to the Auberge bar entrance is called Spa-Roe. According to the sign, it's a place you can visit for facials and massages (the "spa" part) while you sample various caviars (the "roe" part). Just what the world has been waiting for.

Right next to it is a bistro…*pardon*…a bar. It's called Fitzgerald's, as in "F. Scott." I stand in front of it for a few moments and look through the window. It's a re-creation of a 1920s speakeasy. I can see a huge poster that says GOD BLESS JIMMY WALKER. Only one person is seated at the bar, a pretty young blond girl. She's chatting with the much older bartender.

I walk about twenty feet and pass a pet-grooming store. A very unhappy cat is being shampooed. Next door is a "French" dry cleaner, a term I'd never heard before moving to New York. There's an optician who sells *discounted* Tom Ford eyeglass frames for four hundred dollars. There's a place to have your computer fixed and a place that sells nothing but brass buttons. I pause. I smoke a cigarette. The block is busy as hell, but nothing is happening for me.

Until I toss my cigarette on the sidewalk.

CHAPTER 13

A MAN'S VOICE ISN'T ANGRY, just loud. "What's with the littering, mister?"

Littering? That's a new word in my English vocabulary.

The speaker is a white-bearded old man wearing brown work pants and a brown T-shirt. It's the kind of outfit assembled to look like a uniform, but it isn't actually a uniform. The man is barely five feet tall. He holds an industrial-size water hose with a dripping nozzle.

"Littering?" I ask.

The old guy points to the dead cigarette at my feet.

"Your cigarette! They pay me to keep these sidewalks clean."

"I apologize."

"I was making a joke. It's only a joke. Get it? A joke, just a joke."

This man was not completely, uh…mentally competent, but I had to follow one of my major rules: talk to anyone, anywhere, anytime.

"Yes, a joke. Good. Do you live here?" I ask.

"The Bronx," he answers. "Mott Haven. They always call it the south Bronx, but it's not. I don't know why they can't get it right."

"So you just work down here?"

"Yeah. I watch the three buildings. The button place, the animal place, and the eyeglasses place. They call me Danny with the Hose."

"Understandably," I say.

"Good, you understand. Now stand back."

I do as I'm told until my back is up against the optician's doorway. Danny sprays the sidewalk with a fast hard surge of water. Scraps of paper, chunks of dog shit, empty beer cans—they all go flying into the gutter.

"Danny," I say. "A lot of pretty girls around here, huh? What with the fancy hotel right here and the fancy neighborhood."

He shuts off his hose. "Some are pretty. I mind my business."

A young man, no more than twenty-five, comes out of the pet-grooming shop. He has a big dog—a boxer, I think—on a leash. Danny with the Hose and the man with the dog greet each other with a high five. The young man is tall, blond, good-looking. He wears long blue shorts and a pathetic red sleeveless shirt.

"Hey," I say to him. "Danny and I have just been talking about the neighborhood. I'm moving to East 68th Street in a few weeks. With a roommate. A German shepherd."

"Cool," he says, suddenly a lot more interested in talking to me. "If you need a groomer, this place is the best. Take a look at Titan." He pets his dog's shiny coat. "He's handsome enough to be in a *GQ* spread. I've been bringing him here ever since we moved into 655 Park five years ago."

My ears prick up. I go into full acting-class mode now.

"Isn't 655 the place where that lady cop got killed?"

"They say she was a cop pretending to be a hooker. I don't know."

"Luc…Luc Moncrief," I say. We shake.

"Eric," he says. No last name offered. "Well, welcome. I said 'pretending,' but I don't know. Women are not my area of expertise, if you know what I mean. All my info on the local girls comes from one of the doormen in my building. He says all the hookers hang out at the Auberge."

"That's where I'm staying now," I say.

"Well, anyway, Carl—the doorman—says most of the girls who work out of the Auberge bar are clean. Bang, bang, pay your money, over and out. He says the ones to watch out for are the girls who work for the Russians. Younger and prettier, but they'll skin you alive. I dunno. I play on a whole other team."

"Yet you seem to know a great deal about *mine*," I say. "Nice meeting you."

The guy and the dog take off. Danny with the Hose has disappeared, too.

I look at my watch. I should be meeting up with K. Burke.

But first I'll just go on a quick errand.

CHAPTER 14

IF YOU EVER NEED to get some information from a New York doorman, learn from my experience with Carl.

A ten-dollar bill will get you this: "Yeah, I think there's some foreign kind of operation going on at the Auberge. But I'm busy getting taxis for people and helping with packages. So I can't be sure."

I give Carl another ten dollars.

"They got Russians in and outta there. At least I think they're Russian. I'm not that good with accents."

I give him ten more. That's thirty so far, if you're keeping track.

"I heard all this from a friend who works catering at the Auberge. The Russians keep a permanent three-room suite there… where they pimp out the hookers."

Carl gives me a sly smile. It would seem my reaction has given away my motives.

"Oh, I see where you're headed. You wanna know if the Russians had anything to do with the murder on seven. The cops talked to me, like, twenty times. But I wasn't on the door that day. And how the girl got in? No clue."

Perhaps that's true. But I have a feeling Carl might be leading me to some other clues. I give him ten bucks more.

"Strange, though. Those Russians specialize in young, pretty, all-American blondes. You know. Fresh, clean, sort of look like innocent little virgins. Nothing like the woman who got iced. But…there is something else."

I wait for Carl to keep talking, but he doesn't. Instead, he hustles outside the building just as a yellow cab pulls up. He opens the door, and a weary-looking gray-haired man in a gray pin-striped suit emerges. Carl takes the man's briefcase and follows him down a long hallway that leads to an elevator. The old man might as well be *crawling,* he's going so slowly. Finally Carl returns.

"Sorry. Now, what was I saying?"

Damn this sneaky doorman. I know he's playing me, but I'm hoping it's worth it. Because all I've got left is a fifty. I give it to Carl with a soft warning: "This better be worth fifty bucks."

"Well, it's a little thing, and it's from my buddy at the Auberge, and you never know when he's telling the truth, and…"

"Come on. What is it?"

"He says that the girls never wait in the lobby or the suite or the back hallways. The Russian guys keep 'em in the neighborhood somewhere. I don't know where. Like a coffee shop or a private house. Then the girl gets a phone call and a few minutes later one of the blondies is taking the elevator up to the special private suite."

Bingo. I'm ready to roll. And—if you're keeping track—it cost me ninety bucks.

But it was *definitely* worth it.

CHAPTER 15

I WALK INTO THE lobby of the Auberge. Standing there is K. Burke. She's easily identifiable by the smoke coming out of her ears.

"Where have you been?" she demands. "I checked the bar, then the restaurants, then…anyway. What did you find out?"

"Nothing," I say. "And you?"

"Wait a minute. Nothing? How many people did you talk to?"

"*Beaucoup.*"

"And nothing?"

"*Oui. Rien.*"

She shakes her head, but I'm not sure she believes me.

"Well," she says as she gestures me out the front door, "while I was standing around, waiting for a certain someone I won't name, I texted a contact in Vice, who gave me access to some of their files. And I have a theory." Detective Burke begins to speak more quickly now, but she still sounds like a first-grade teacher explaining simple arithmetic to the class.

"There have been three call-girl murders in the past three months, including Maria Martinez. All Vice cops posing as call girls. The first was…"

I cannot keep quiet. We've already looked into this.

"I know," I say. "Valerie Delvecchio. Murdered at a construction site. A *rénovation* of a hotel. The Hotel Chelsea, on 23rd Street and Seventh Avenue. The second cop was Dana Morgan-Schwarz. She was offed in a hotel on 155th and Riverside. A drug-den SRO so bad I wouldn't go there to take a piss."

This does nothing to dampen Burke's enthusiasm for her theory.

"Don't you see, Moncrief? You're not putting the pieces together. This is a pattern. Three Vice cops posing as call girls. All of them murdered. This is—"

"This is ridiculous," I say. "This is *not* a *pattern*. It is at best a *coincidence*. The Chelsea murder is unsolved, yes. But the detective's body was dumped there *after* she was murdered. And Morgan-Schwarz was probably involved in an inside drug deal. No high-class hooker would go to that hotel."

But Burke is simply not listening.

"I set up a meeting for us with Vice this afternoon at four. We're going to get the names, numbers, and websites of *every* expensive call-girl service in New York."

"Good luck with that," I say. "That should only take a few weeks."

"Then we're going to meet all the people who run them. I don't care if it's the Mafia, Brazilian drug lords, Colombian cartels, or other cops. We're going to see every last one."

"Great. That should only take a few *months*."

"You've got a bad goddamn attitude, Moncrief."

I'm not going to explode. I'm not going to explode. I'm not going to explode.

"I will see you at four o'clock for our meeting with Vice," I say calmly.

"Where are you going till then? We've got work to do."

"I'm going to work right now. Want to come along?"

Burke folds her arms and frowns. "You lied to me, didn't you? You did find out something."

"Come with me and see for yourself."

CHAPTER 16

"WELCOME TO THE ROARING Twenties," I say to K. Burke as we enter Fitzgerald's Bar and Grill, on East 68th Street.

"Not much roaring going on," Burke says. The room is empty except for the bartender and one female customer.

The same girl I watched through the window earlier.

The lone woman at the bar is young. She's blond. She's pretty. And after we flash IDs and introduce ourselves as detectives with the NYPD, she's also very frightened.

"Try to relax, miss," says Burke. "There's a problem, but it's nothing for you to worry about. We're just hoping you can help us out."

I'm astonished at the genuine sweetness in Detective Burke's voice. The same voice that was just loud and stern with me is now soothing and gentle with the pretty blonde.

"Could you tell us your name, please?" I ask, trying to imitate Burke's soft style.

"Laura," she says. Her voice has a quiver of fear.

"What about a last name?" Burke asks.

"Jenkins," says the girl. "Laura Jenkins."

"Let's see some ID," I say.

The girl rustles around in her pocketbook and produces a laminated card. Burke doesn't even look at it.

"You're aware, Ms. Jenkins, that in the state of New York, showing a police officer false identification is a class D felony punishable by up to seven years in prison."

Holy shit. I'm in awe of Burke. Sort of.

The girl slips the first card she removed from her purse back into it and hands over a second. It reads: LAURA DELARICO, 21 ARDSLEY ROAD, SCARSDALE, NEW YORK.

"What do you do for a living, Miss Delarico?" I ask.

"I'm a law student. That's the truth. I go to Fordham. Here's my student ID." She holds up a third plastic identity card.

"Do you work?" I ask. "Perhaps part-time?"

"Sometimes I babysit. I do computer filing for one of the professors."

"Look, Miss Delarico," I say, raising my voice now. "This is serious business. Very serious. Detective Burke was being genuine when she said you have nothing to worry about. But that only happens if you help us out. So far, not good. Not good at all."

Laura looks away, then back at me.

"We know that you work for a prostitution ring," I continue. "A group that trades in high-priced call girls. We know it's controlled by a Russian gang."

Laura begins to cry. "But I'm a law student. Really."

"A few days ago a female detective posing as a call girl was murdered. Somebody who meant a lot to me. We need your help."

I pause. Not for dramatic effect but because I feel myself choking up, too.

Laura stops crying long enough to say, "It's just something I'm doing for a little while. For the money. I live with my grandfather, and law school costs so much. If he ever found out…"

A few seconds pass.

Then K. Burke says, "Off the record."

K. Burke is staring deep into Laura's eyes. But Laura is frozen. No response.

"Let me show you something," I say.

Laura looks suspicious. K. Burke looks confused. I reach into my side pocket. Next to my ID, next to the place where I kept the cash for Carl the doorman, are two small photographs. I take them out. One shows Maria Martinez on the police department's Hudson River boat ride. I took that picture. The other shows Maria Martinez dead. It was taken by the coroner.

I show Laura the photos. Then she looks away.

Finally, she says, "Okay."

CHAPTER 17

PROSTITUTES DON'T KEEP traditional hours.

Laura Delarico tells us that she's "on call" at Fitzgerald's for another thirty minutes. She's certain she'll be free by late afternoon. "Even if I do get a client," she says, "I'll be in and out quickly." (No, I don't think she was trying to be funny.)

I suggest that Laura, K. Burke, and I meet at Balthazar, where a person can get a decent *steak frites* and a pleasant glass of house Burgundy. "This will put everyone at ease," I say.

K. Burke suggests that we schedule an interview at the precinct this evening. "This is an investigation, Moncrief, not happy hour. Plus, *I'm* going to that meeting with Vice."

Because proper police procedure always trumps a good idea, at six o'clock the three of us are sitting in an interrogation room at the precinct.

Laura is surprisingly interested in the surroundings. The bile-colored green walls, the battered folding chairs, the crushed empty cans of Diet Coke on the table. I don't think I'm wrong in thinking that Laura is also interested in me.

"So this is, like, where you bring murderers, drug dealers, and…okay, prostitutes?"

"Sometimes," I say. "But today is strictly informal, off the record. No recordings, no cameras, but as much of the cold tan sludge my colleagues call coffee as you can drink."

Laura is wearing a black T-shirt, jeans, and a gold necklace with the name *Laura* on it. She could be a barista at Starbucks or a salesgirl at the Gap or, yes, a law student.

"We're very glad that you agreed to try to help us," K. Burke begins.

Laura interrupts: "Listen. I don't think I want to do this anymore. I think I've changed my mind."

"That would not be a good idea," I say. My goal is not to sound threatening, merely disappointed.

"We're counting on you," K. Burke says. Where does she hide that beautiful soothing voice?

"I don't think there's much I *can* tell you," Laura says. "I get a call. I turn a trick. That's how it goes."

"Tell us anything," I say.

"Anything?" Laura says. Her voice is suddenly loud, suddenly scared. "Like what? What does 'anything' mean? What I ate for lunch? What classes I went to? Anything?"

The conversation needs K. Burke's smooth-as-silk voice. Here it comes.

"Maria Martinez was found murdered on Tuesday," K. Burke says. "Were you working Tuesday morning or Monday night?"

Laura closes her eyes. Her lips curl with disgust. She spits out three little words: "Paulo the Pig."

Burke and I are, of course, confused. I picture a cartoon character in a Spanish children's television program.

But Laura repeats it, this time with even more venom. "Paulo the Pig."

"That's a person, I assume," Burke says.

"A person who deserves his nickname. If you're a girl on call and you get assigned to Paulo the Pig, you never forget it."

Her hands shake a bit. Her eyes begin to water.

"That's where I was the night your friend was murdered. I was with Paulo. Paulo Montes."

"Tell us, Laura," I say. "We need to know what happened that night with you and Paulo. Everything you remember. You're safe with us."

Her story is disgusting.

CHAPTER 18

PAULO MONTES, A BRAZILIAN drug dealer, is usually followed everywhere by two bodyguards. Tonight, however, he sends them away and waits alone for the arrival of his hired girl.

The fat middle-aged man has dressed appropriately for the occasion—a sweat-soaked sleeveless undershirt. Thick curly black hair grows like an unmown lawn over both Paulo's chest and back. The hairs crawl up and down his shoulders and neck. He wears long white silk shorts—longer than boxers, almost long enough to touch his fleshy pink knees. Montes has greased himself up with a nauseating combination of almond oil and lavender cologne. He has used this same overwhelming oil-and-cologne concoction to slick back the greasy hair above his fat round face.

Paulo answers the door himself. "You're much prettier than that dark-haired bitch they sent up an hour ago," he says.

He is speaking to Laura Delarico—tall, slim, blond. With her fine youthful features, Laura is easily Paulo's fantasy come to life— a combination of Texas cheerleader and Italian fashion model. Fresh and clean, lithe and athletic. Just what Paulo is longing for.

He begins quickly, clumsily unbuttoning Laura's white oxford-cloth shirt. "The first one they sent was the kind I could find for ten dollars in an alley in São Paulo. Dark hair, dark skin. Screwing her would be like screwing myself."

Paulo Montes laughs uproariously at his little joke. Laura smiles. She's been taught to smile at a client's jokes.

Paulo pulls her onto the bed. His fingers are fat, and he has become bored with trying to unbutton Laura's shirt. So he pulls it up and over her head. He tugs at Laura's panties, ripping them.

Soon she is naked. Soon Paulo the Pig is naked. Every inch of Laura's flesh is disgusted by him. She feels he might crush her with his weight, but she's skilled at positioning her shoulders and hips in such a way as to minimize all discomfort. She tries to ignore the garlicky alcohol smell as he roughly kisses her face and lips, as he squirms slowly downward to kiss her breasts. He suddenly slaps her face. For some sick reason this makes him laugh. Paulo Montes then pulls hard at her hair.

"Stop it," Laura says. "You're hurting me."

"Like I give a shit," Paulo says. Now he grabs her genitals. His filthy fingernails travel harshly around her vagina. She feels scratching, bleeding. With his other hand he pulls hard at another handful of hair. "I'm paying good money for this!" he yells. "I'm in charge."

He pushes himself back up, again closer to her face. His saliva is dripping onto Laura's cheeks and lips. The kisses begin to feel more like bites. She is certain the skin on her right cheek has been punctured by his teeth. Then more hair pulling. Her vagina is full of pain.

This time Laura screams. "Stop. Slow down!" She pushes at his fat neck.

Then suddenly Paulo makes a huge noise—a kind of explosive grunt. His breathing immediately slows down.

Laura realizes that she doesn't need to protest any longer. It's over. He's finished. He never even entered her. Paulo the Pig begins panting like a tired old horse. He is resting, she thinks. He remains on top of her for a few minutes.

Finally Paulo rolls off and rests at her side.

For a moment, Laura becomes a kind of waitress in a sexual diner. "Can I get you anything else, sir?"

But Paulo Montes merely keeps his heavy breathing pumping. "That was good, very good. Go into the next room. Take what you want. Within reason, of course." He laughs again. What a comedian!

Like all the girls who work for the Russian gang, Laura knows Paulo Montes is one of the most significant importers of what are called travel packages: drugs that are smuggled along strange geographic routes—say, from Ankara to Kiev to Seoul to New York to São Paulo—in order to confuse and evade the narcs.

"No, thank you," Laura says, slipping into her torn underwear, her jeans, and her shirt. She plucks a few of his many sweaty curly hairs from her stomach.

"Don't be ungrateful, bitch," Paulo says. This time he's not sounding funny. He doesn't laugh. "Scag, maybe. I got it in the plastic containers. Or some good China white."

"I just need to use the bathroom," Laura says.

Paulo snaps at her quickly. "Use the maid's bathroom at the end of the hall. You can't use this one. I have personal items in there."

Laura simply says, "Okay." She's tired and frightened and disgusted.

"Now go in the next room and treat yourself. Even something simple. Take a little C. Have a party later with your friends."

To appease him she says, "Do you have some weed? I'll take some weed."

He laughs again, the loudest of all his laughing jags.

"Weed? You're joking. Like Paulo would ever deal low-class shit like that."

She watches Paulo on the bed, naked, laughing.

As Laura leaves the room all she can think of is that line from the Christmas poem: "…a little round belly / That shook when he laughed, like a bowl full of jelly."

CHAPTER 19

LAURA DELARICO HAS FINISHED her story.

"So that's it. The clients don't pay us girls directly. It's all online, I guess. I don't really know. When it was over, I just left."

Burke speaks. "Detective Moncrief and I want to thank you. We know this has been tough."

"I wish I could have helped more," Laura says. "I'm not afraid. I just…well, that's what happened."

"You've helped us more than you can imagine," I say. Sincerely, softly. "What you gave us was big. I'm fairly certain Maria Martinez visited Paulo's room as well."

Burke agrees. "There's a very real possibility she was the dark-haired girl he rejected before you."

"You don't know that for sure," Laura says.

"You're right," I say. "Not yet. But it is a logical deduction. He may have killed her and disposed of her. *Or* he may have put her body in the bathroom."

"The one he wouldn't let me use," she says quietly. "I guess that makes sense."

K. Burke holds up her hand. "Or we may be completely off base. Maybe it was not Maria Martinez. Maybe we've got it all wrong."

I cannot resist. I say, "Ah, K. Burke, ever the jolly optimist."

I reach over and gently touch Laura Delarico's hand. She does not pull away. She is so much less frightened than she was a few hours ago.

"And that is why…" Suddenly, I must stop speaking. Oh, shit. Oh, no.

I feel my throat begin to burn. I'm having trouble breathing. Maria is on my mind, in my heart. Because of Laura's information, we may actually have a shot at solving Maria's murder.

K. Burke senses the emotional hole I've fallen into. She finishes my remarks.

"And that's why…we need you to help us just a little bit more."

CHAPTER 20

LAURA SAYS NOTHING FOR a few long moments.

"Well?" I say.

Laura is suddenly businesslike. Sharp. Composed.

"I know what you'll do if I don't keep helping you," she says.

"You *know* what we'll do?" I ask. "I don't even know what we'll do except ask you to help us."

"No," Laura says. "You'll play the Grandpa card."

"The what?" I ask.

K. Burke is far quicker than I am in this matter.

"Laura thinks we'll tell her grandfather how she's been making money," says Burke.

For the first time I see a toughness in Laura. I am beginning to think that Laura Delarico is not so naive and innocent as I first thought. She'll make a good lawyer someday.

"Believe whatever you want, Laura," I say, "but I promise you with my heart that we will never do such a thing."

"I guess I'll believe you because…well, because I *want* to believe you," Laura says. "I want to help…at least, I think I want to help. Oh, this sucks. This whole thing sucks."

Time for a bottom line. Laura agrees to continue to help. "But just one more time."

Later, after Laura leaves, K. Burke and I walk the dirty gray hallway back to the detective room.

"Nice job," Burke says. "Your performance won her over."

"Did you think that was a performance, K. Burke?" I ask.

"To be honest, I don't know."

Back at our desks, we learn that Paulo Montes will not be in New York for three days. He is on a quick drug trip through San Juan, Havana, and Kingston.

I tell Burke that I'm going to take one of those three days off.

"Impossible!" she exclaims. "Your presence is critical. We have Vice files to examine. We have a reinspection of the murder scene as well as forensics at Montes's suite. I need you to—"

I cut her off immediately. "Hold it," I say sharply. "Here's what I need from *you*. I need you to stop thinking that you're my boss. You're my partner. And I don't mean to throw this in your face, K. Burke, but we would not be progressing if I had not pursued my very *un*professional way of doing things."

K. Burke gives me her version of a sincere smile. Then she says, "Whatever you say, partner."

CHAPTER 21

A MAN KNOWS HE'S in love when he's totally happy just watching his girlfriend do even the simplest things—peeling an apple, combing her hair, fluffing up a bed pillow, laughing.

That is precisely how I'm feeling when I walk into the ridiculously tricked-out media room of Dalia's apartment: the Apologue speakers, the Supernova One screen, the leather Eames chairs. A room that is insanely lavish and almost never used.

As I walk in I see Dalia standing on a stepladder. Her back is to me. She is frantically sorting through the small closet high above the wet bar. She neither sees nor hears me enter. I stand and watch her for a moment. I smile. Dalia is wearing jeans and a turquoise T-shirt. As she stretches, one or two inches of her lower back are exposed.

I walk toward her and kiss her gently on that enticing lower back.

She gives a quick little yell.

"Don't be scared," I say. "It's only me."

She steps off the ladder and we embrace fully. I know a great kiss cannot wash away a bad day, but it surely can make the night seem a little bit brighter.

"When did *this* closet become the junk closet?" she asks as she climbs back up the ladder and begins tossing things down to me.

A plastic bag of poker chips. These are followed by three Scrabble tiles (*W, E,* and the always important *X*). A plastic box containing ivory chess pieces, but no chessboard in sight. And a true relic from the Victorian era: a Game Boy.

"This is for you," she says as she pretends to hit me on the head with a wooden croquet mallet. I add the mallet to the ever-expanding pile of items next to me.

"And you'll like *this,*" she says with a smile. Dalia leans down and hands me a small gold box. I open it. It contains two little bronze balls the size of small marbles. Never saw them before. I shrug.

"Give up?" she asks. "They're those Chinese things they use for sex, for the vagina."

"The vagina?" I say. "Yes. I think I've heard of it." She laughs and punches me lightly on the arm. I decide not to ask where she got them—or how often she used them or with whom.

"Well," she says. "At least we've solved *one* mystery. This closet is not a junk closet. It is obviously a game closet."

"What exactly are you looking for, anyway?" I ask.

"This," she says as she steps down off the ladder. She is holding a slim burgundy leather book. I recognize it immediately. It's the yearbook for our class at Lycée Henri-IV.

She opens it and turns to the page that has her graduation picture. "I was thinking of getting bangs. The last time I had them was when I was a kid. I wanted to see if I was as goofy-looking as I remember." She frowns. "Guess I was."

I say exactly what is expected of a man in this situation. The only difference is that this man means it with all his heart.

"You were beautiful," I say.

"You're mad. Braids on the side and bangs in the front. I look like a goatherd."

I reach toward her and touch her face.

"If so, then you are *la plus belle* goatherd since the beginning of time." I lean in and kiss her. Then I speak. "How about we have something nice to drink?"

"How about a nice warm bath, with lavender perfume?" she says.

"A bath?" I say. "I don't know. I don't think I'm *that* thirsty."

Dalia taps me playfully on my nose. Then she heads toward the bathroom.

CHAPTER 22

Auberge du Parc Hotel
Three days later
1:20 a.m.

LAURA KNOCKS ON THE hotel-room door. Everything feels just as it did the last time she visited Paulo.

She wears a white oxford-cloth shirt. Just as she did the last time. The tiny entrance hall where she waits stinks of liquor and bad cologne. Just as it did the last time. One other thing that's the same, one other thing she cannot deny: she's horribly frightened. Her arm shakes as she knocks on the door again.

Yes, Moncrief and Burke have assured her that everything is set up to keep her perfectly safe. This time, hidden in Paulo's bedroom are two minuscule video surveillance cameras: one is attached to a large bronze lamp on the writing desk, the other to the fake gold-leaf-and-crystal chandelier hanging directly over the king-size bed. The videos play on monitors that are being watched two doors away by five people: Luc Moncrief, K. Burke, Inspector Nick Elliott, and two officers from Vice.

Paulo opens the door and steps back. He smiles at her.

This time Paulo manages to look even more disgusting than

before. Laura Delarico quietly gasps as she takes in the repellent sight: Paulo the Pig is completely naked except for a pair of short brown socks.

"So," he says. "They sent you back like I asked. I'm glad. You're the best."

Laura and the five people watching in the other room realize immediately that Paulo Montes is drunk or drugged or both. He stumbles. He slurs his words. His feeble erection collapses as he lunges toward her, and he begins half spitting and half kissing, half hugging and half groping her.

"Hold on. Come on. Just hold on," Laura says. Then she uses one of the first conversation starters that a woman learns in "prostitute school."

"Let's get to know each other."

Laura wonders how she will ever get Paulo to talk about the dark-haired woman, the woman who may have been Maria Martinez. Laura wafts in and out of that nightmare. She must keep reminding herself she is there to help uncover the truth of the death of a woman she never even knew.

Paulo is even more impatient this time at bat. He tugs hard at Laura's shirt. Two buttons snap off and onto the floor. He pushes his greasy face into her breasts as if he is trying to suck in oxygen from the space between them.

Within a few seconds, he has her on the bed. They are, for the moment, side by side, facing each other. The slobbering. The saliva. The boozy breath.

"So," Laura ventures, trying to cajole him into a calmer, gentler mood. "Just tell me how much more you like me than that dark-haired girl who was here."

Paulo is in no mood for conversation. He is somewhere between crazy drunk and crazy turned on.

"Dark?" he shouts. "Was her hair dark? I don't remember. Does any bitch have the color she's born with? In Brazil they all lie. Lie and dye. That's the joke in Rio and São Paulo. Let's check you. Let's see if you're telling the truth."

Laura fears a harsh inspection of her pubic hair. Instead Montes rolls over and on top of her. He grabs a great chunk of her hair and pulls it hard with his fat heavy hands. She yells for him to stop.

"I have to find the roots!" he screams and laughs simultaneously.

In the surveillance room, Inspector Elliott speaks loudly: "We've got to stop this immediately, Moncrief. We can haul him in right now for aggravated assault."

"I don't want him arrested. I want him to talk," says Moncrief. "I want to get the story on Maria."

"I swear, Moncrief. This whole thing is a half-assed setup. I should never have let it get this far."

"Inspector! Look!" K. Burke says. All five in the surveillance group peer intently at the screen. Paulo Montes is grunting and making animal-like noises as he pinches one of Laura's nipples hard and fiercely bites the other.

"That's it!" yells Elliott.

"Give it five seconds," says Moncrief as he grabs Elliott by the arm to urge him to remain. "The guy might calm down."

Almost as if Montes actually heard Moncrief speak, Paulo begins gently massaging Laura's breasts.

"There, there," Paulo says softly. "You are beautiful. I could love a woman like you."

Paulo gently brushes his lips against Laura's beautiful soft cheeks. He touches her chin and runs his hand down her neck.

"Kiss me," Paulo says. "Kiss me like you love me."

Laura knows her job. She kisses him softly on his lips.

Then suddenly, horribly, Montes slaps Laura violently against her right cheek, so violently that her head snaps to the side. She lets out a scream.

"You are just another dumb bitch," Montes shouts, saliva dripping from his mouth onto Laura's face.

"Get away!" Laura screams. "Get the hell off of me!"

Paulo slaps her again, then holds her down by her wrists. She is fighting as hard as she can. But it's useless.

Again she screams, "Get off! Stop it!"

As Paulo is about to sink his teeth into her, the door to the room swings open.

"NYPD! Freeze!" The voice belongs to Moncrief.

Moncrief, Burke, and both Vice officers are holding guns. They all rush toward the bed.

With the help of one of the Vice cops, Moncrief pulls Montes away from Laura.

Laura quickly rolls away from her attacker. Then she grabs a pillow and holds it up to cover her nakedness. Montes thrashes about in a futile attempt to free himself from Moncrief and the cop. He keeps struggling and manages to push his one free hand under another pillow. He pulls out a pistol. He shoots it once. The bullet hits the TV screen. It shatters into a small mountain of glass pieces. Moncrief pushes his own index and middle fingers into Montes's face. The drunken Montes manages to get off one more shot. The bullet hits a Vice officer's forearm. As Moncrief and the two officers struggle to pull the naked fat man to his feet, Montes struggles to bring his arm around. Montes aims the gun at Laura.

A final shot. It comes from Moncrief's gun.

The bullet goes right into Montes's neck via his Adam's apple.

Laura Delarico is sobbing. K. Burke is on her cell, calling for reinforcements, forensics, the coroner, police attorneys, the DA's office. Nick Elliott closes his eyes and shakes his head back and forth.

When she finishes her phone calls, K. Burke takes a gray jumpsuit from one of the police kits. She walks to Laura and helps her slip into it. For just a moment Burke's eyes meet Moncrief's.

The two of them are thinking the same thing. They are no closer to solving the case of Maria Martinez. And the one person who might have helped them is now dead.

CHAPTER 23

PHOTOGRAPHERS. AND MORE PHOTOGRAPHERS. Detectives and more detectives. Statements are made and then repeated. Hotel guests wander into the hallway.

We go to the precinct. More detectives. Two police attorneys. Everyone agrees: my bullet was justified. The surveillance video verifies what happened. My colleagues can easily rationalize that the world is a better place without Paulo Montes. I want to rationalize it also, but I cannot ignore the fact that I'm the cop who made it happen.

I go home.

"I'm awake," I hear Dalia shout. "Be right out."

I move toward the bedroom.

We meet in the hallway, and we stand directly in front of a black-and-white Léger poster, a drawing of four people artfully intertwined. Dalia and I do not kiss, but we hug each other with all our strength, as if we are afraid that the other person might slip away.

A few minutes later we are seated on a sofa. We watch the city sky slowly brighten. We both sip a snifter of Rémy. I devour a bowl of cashews. I tell her about my evening. Her face fills with horror, her eyes widen when I tell her about the horrific ending.

"Oh, my God, Luc. You must feel…I don't know…I don't know how you must feel."

"I don't think I know, either," I say. "I've never killed anyone."

I find myself remembering the shooting range near Porte de la Chapelle, where I spent so many hours learning how to load and shoot, load and shoot. The paper dummies, the foolishly big ear protectors. One-handed aim, two-handed aim, shoot from a prone position, shoot from a standing position. But shoot, always shoot. You got him. You got him. You missed him. You got him.

My plan for Montes would have worked. I am sure it would have worked.

I take the last gulp of my Cognac. I swipe the inside of the cashew bowl with my index finger. I touch my salty finger to the tip of Dalia's tongue. She smiles. I hold her tightly.

I tell Dalia that all I want to do now is sleep. She understands. We begin walking toward the bedroom. I stop for a moment. So Dalia stops also.

I have an idea. A very good idea. So good I want to share it with someone. But I'd be a fool to share it with Burke and Elliott. What about Dalia? I usually tell her everything, but not this time, not this idea. She'd kill me if she knew.

Dalia looks up at me.

"You're smiling," she says. "What are you thinking about?"

"Just you," I say. And as we fall on the bed, I consider crossing my fingers behind my back.

CHAPTER 24

I CALL GARY KUEHN at Vice. He's one of the few guys in that department who's smart enough to appreciate what he calls my shenanigans.

Shenanigans. English is a wonderful language.

Gary e-mails me a list of names of "superior sex workers" (translation: high-class hookers) and their managers (translation: drug-dealing abusive johns). I specifically request names of girls who regularly service the toniest areas of the Upper East Side.

I tell my new plan to no one—not K. Burke, not Nick Elliott, not even Gary. At midafternoon, I take an Uber car across town and check into a room at the Pierre, on Fifth Avenue at 61st Street. A mere seventeen hundred dollars a night. I silently thank my father for the large allowance that makes this expensive escapade possible.

I arrange for a series of these high-priced call girls to visit my room—one girl every thirty minutes. I do all the scheduling—the phoning and texting and e-mailing—myself.

At three o'clock a girl with incandescent mahogany skin appears. Her skin is so shiny it looks polished. Her hair is short and dark. She smiles. I am sitting in a comfortable blue club chair. She approaches me and touches my face.

"Please have a seat over there," I say, pointing to the identical blue club chair opposite my own. No doubt she thinks we're about to begin a freaky fantasy.

"Here is the first piece of news: I'm not going to touch you, but I will, of course, pay you for this visit." I hand her three hundred-dollar bills. (The agreed-upon price was two fifty.)

"Here is the second piece of news, and perhaps it is not quite so welcome. I am going to ask you some questions."

She smiles. I quickly add, "Nothing uncomfortable—just some simple talking and chatting. I am a detective with the NYPD."

Her face becomes a mask of fear.

"But I promise. You have nothing to worry about."

The questions begin:

Have you ever serviced a client at 655 Park Avenue?

Have you ever serviced a client at the Auberge du Parc Hotel?

Have you ever serviced a client who acted with extreme violence?

A client who hurt you, threatened you, brandished a weapon, a gun, a cane, a stick, a whip? A client who tried to slip a tablet or a powder or a suspicious liquid into a beverage?

Have you ever met with a client who was famous in his field—an actor, a diplomat, a senator, a governor, a foreign leader, a clergyman?

The answers are all no. And the pattern remains the same for every woman who follows.

A few of them tell me about men with some odd habits, but as the woman in the tight yellow jeans says, "A lot of guys have odd habits. That's why they go to prostitutes. Maybe their fancy wives don't want to suck toes or fuck in a tennis skirt or take it up the ass."

Other statements are made.

A tall woman, the only woman I've ever seen who looked beautiful in a Mohawk haircut, says, "Okay, there is this congressman from New Jersey that I see once or twice a month."

A very tan woman in a saronglike outfit says, "Yeah, one guy was *sort of* into whips, but all he wanted was for me to unpin my hair and swing it against his dick."

A woman who shows up in blue shorts cut off at mid-thigh, her shirt tied just above the navel, gives me some hope, but she, too, is a waste of time. "I think I was at 655 Park once. But it was for a woman. I hate working chicks. The few I've done were all, like, just into kissing and touching and petting. They're more work than the guys."

No information of any value. Yes, two of the girls have been slapped—both of them by men who were drunk. Yes, the girl-on-girl prostitute at 655 Park works for the Russian gang, but she knows nothing about the death of Maria Martinez, and she has never even heard of Paulo Montes.

What I am learning from these few hours of wasted interviews is the knowledge that the world is filled with men who are happy to pay to get laid. That's it. That's the deal. Over and out. It is a gross and humiliating way for a girl to make money, but, in most cases, each has made her separate peace with it.

The interviews end. Thousands of dollars later I have nothing to show for my work.

It is definitely time for me to leave the Pierre.

It is definitely time for me to return home to Dalia.

CHAPTER 25

EVERY MORNING AT THE precinct, K. Burke and I have the following dialogue.

Instead of saying the words "Good morning," she looks at me and says sternly, "You're late."

I always respond with a cheery "And good morning to you, *ma belle.*"

It has become a funny little routine between the two of us, the sort of thing two friends might do. Who knows? Maybe K. Burke and I are becoming friends. Sometimes a mutually miserable situation can bring people together.

But this morning it's different. She greets me by saying, "Don't bother sitting down, Moncrief. We have an assignment from Inspector Elliott."

All I know is that unless Elliott has had an unexpected stroke of genius (highly unlikely) I am not interested in the assignment. I must also face the fact that my mood is terrible: interviewing the call girls has led to absolutely nothing, and I can share my frustration with no one. If I were to tell Burke or Elliott about my unapproved tactic they would both be furious.

"Whatever it is the inspector wants, we'll do it later."

"It's already later," Burke says. "It's one o'clock in the afternoon. Let's go."

"Go where? It's lunchtime. I'm thinking that fish restaurant on 49th Street. A bit of sole meunière and a crisp bottle of Chablis…"

"Stop being a Frenchman for just one minute, Moncrief," she says.

I can tell that K. Burke is uncomfortable with what she's about to say, but out it comes: "He wants us to visit some high-class strip clubs. He's even done some of the grunt work for us. He's compiled a list of clubs. Take a look at your phone."

I swipe the screen and click on my assignments folder. I see a page entitled "NYC Club Visits. From: N. Elliott."

Sapphire, 333 East 60th Street
Rick's Cabaret, 50 West 33rd Street
Hustler Club, 641 West 51st Street

Three more places are listed after these.

As a young man in Paris, full of booze and often with a touch of cocaine in my nose, I would occasionally visit the Théâtre Chochotte, in Saint-Germain-des-Prés, with some pals. It was not without its pleasures, but on one such visit I had a very bad experience: I ran into my father and my uncle in the VIP lounge. That was the night I crossed Chochotte and all Parisian strip clubs off my list. Even a son who has a much better relationship than I have with my father does not ever want to end up in a strip joint with the old man.

As for clubs in New York…I am no longer a schoolboy. I am no longer touching my nose with cocaine. And I now have Dalia waiting at home for me.

The fact is that my assignment would be the envy of most of my colleagues. But I am weary and frustrated and pissed off and…it seems impossible for me to believe, but I am growing tired of so much female flesh in my face.

"I won't do it," I say to Burke. "You do it alone. I'll stay here and do some detail analysis."

"No way am I going alone, Moncrief. C'mon."

"I cannot. I will not," I say.

"Then I suggest you tell that to Inspector Elliott."

I feel my whole heart spiraling downward. The entrapment with Laura. The death of Paulo. The futile interviews with the call girls. Now I am expected to go to these sad places, where a glass of cheap vodka costs thirty dollars, and try to talk to women with breast implants who are sliding up and down poles.

"I am sick. I am tired," I tell Burke.

"I know you are," Burke says. And I can tell she means it. "But you need to do it for Maria. This is—"

I snap at her. "I do not need a pep talk. I know you're trying to be helpful, but that kind of thing doesn't work with me."

Burke just stares at me.

"Tell Inspector Elliott we will make these 'visits' tomorrow. Maria will still be dead tomorrow. Right now, I'm going home."

CHAPTER 26

BURKE WILL TELL ELLIOTT that I went home because of illness. And, of course, Elliott won't believe it.

But I think that K. Burke and I are now simpatico enough for her to cover for me.

"Suddenly he's sick?" Elliott will say. "That's pure bullshit."

The answer Burke might produce could go something like, "Well, he was out sick all day yesterday."

It makes no difference. For the moment I am engaged in a very important project: I am in a store on Ninth Avenue selecting two perfect fillets of Dover sole. The cost at Seabreeze Fish Market for a pound of this beautiful fish is one hundred and twenty dollars. I have no trouble spending that much (or more) on a bottle of wine. But—Jesus!—this is fish. In the taxi uptown to Dalia's apartment I hold the package of fish as if it were a newborn infant being brought home from the hospital.

The moment I walk through the door of the apartment I feel lighter, better, stronger. It's as if the air in Dalia's place is purer than the air in the dangerous, depressing crime scenes I frequent.

I place the precious fish in the refrigerator.

I unpack the few other items I've bought and remove my shirt. I'm feeling better already.

In a moment I'll start chopping the shallots, chopping the parsley, and heating the wine for the mustard sauce. This preparation is what trained chefs call the *mise en place*.

I decide to take off my suit pants. I toss them on the chair where my shirt is resting. I am—in my mind—no longer in a professionally equipped kitchen overlooking Central Park. I am in a wonderfully sunny beach house on the Côte d'Azur. I am no longer a gloomy angry detective; I am a young tennis pro away for a week of rest, awaiting the arrival of his luscious girlfriend.

I press a button on the entertainment console. Suddenly the music blares. It is Dalia's newest favorite: Selena Gomez. "Me and the Rhythm." I sing along, creating my own lyrics to badly match whatever Selena is singing.

Ooh, all the rhythm takes you over.

I chop the shallot to the beat of the music. I scrape the chopped pieces into my hand and toss them into a sauté pan.

I am moving my feet and hips. I drop a half pound of Irish butter into the pan, and now I feel almost compelled to dance.

I sing. I dance. When I don't sing I am talking to an imaginary Dalia.

"*Yes,*" I am saying. "*Your favorite. Dover sole.*"

"*Yes, there is a bottle of Dom Pérignon already in the fridge.*"

"*Yes, I left early to make this dinner.*"

"The hell with them. They can fire me, then."

The music beats on. I rhythmically slap away at the parsley leaves with my chef's knife.

In the distance I hear the buzzing of a cell phone. The sound of the phone at first seems to be a part of Selena's song. Then I recognize the tone. It is my police phone. For a moment I consider ignoring it. Then I think that perhaps there is news on Maria Martinez's case. Or it might merely be Nick or K. Burke calling to torment me. But nothing can torment me tonight.

I let the music continue. Whoever my caller is can sing along with me.

I yank my suit jacket from the pile of clothing. I find my phone.

Ooh, all the rhythm takes you over.

"What's up?" I yell loudly above the music.

My prediction is correct. It is Inspector Elliott on the line.

He speaks. I listen. I stop dancing. I drop the phone. I fall to my knees and I scream.

"Noooooooo!"

CHAPTER 27

BUT THE TRUTH IS "yes." There has been another woman stabbed, another woman connected to the New York City police. Only this time the woman is neither an officer nor a detective. This time the woman is also connected to me.

"Who is it, goddamn it?"

Elliott's exact words: "It's Dalia, Moncrief."

A pause and then he adds quietly, *"Dalia is dead."*

I kneel on the gray granite floor and pound it. Tears do not come, but I cannot stop saying "no." If I say the word loudly enough, often enough, it will eradicate the fact of "yes."

For a few moments I actually believe that the call from Nick Elliott never happened. I am on the floor, and I pick up the phone. I observe it as if it were a foreign object—a paperweight, a tiny piece of meteorite, a dead rat. But the caller ID says N/ELLIOTT/NYPD/17PREC.

An overwhelming energy goes through me. Within seconds I am back in my pants and shirt. I slip on my shoes, without socks. I go bounding out the door, and the madness within me makes me certain that running down the back stairs of the apartment building will be faster than calling for the elevator.

Once outside, I see two officers waiting in a patrol car.

"Detective Moncrief. We're here to take you to the crime scene. Take the passenger seat."

I don't even know where the crime scene is. I grab the shoulders of the other cop and shake him violently.

"Where the hell are you taking me? Where is she?" I shout. "Where are we going?"

"To 235 East 20th Street, sir. Please get into the car."

Within moments we are suffocated in midtown rush-hour traffic. How can there be so much traffic when Dalia is dead?

At Seventh Avenue and 45th, the streets are thick with sightseeing buses and cabs. Some people are dressed up as Big Bird and Minnie Mouse. The sidewalks teem with tourists and druggies and strollers and women in saris and schoolchildren on trips and…I tell the driver to unlock the doors. I will walk, run, fly.

"This traffic will break below 34th Street, Detective."

"Unlock the fucking door!" I scream. And so he does, and I am on the sidewalk again. I don't give a shit that I am pushing people aside.

Within minutes I am at Seventh Avenue and 34th Street. The streets remain packed with people and cabs and cars and buses.

I cross against the light at 34th Street, Herald Square, Macy's. Where the hell is Santa Claus when you need him?

Sirens. Cars jostle to clear a route for the vehicle screeching out the sirens.

I am rushing east on 32nd Street. I am midway between Broadway and Fifth Avenue, a block packed almost entirely, crazily, with Korean restaurants. Suddenly the sirens are fiercely loud.

"Get in the car, Moncrief. Get back in the car." It is the same driver of the same patrol car that picked me up earlier. They were right about the traffic, but I am vaguely glad that I propelled myself this far.

In a few minutes we are at 235 East 20th Street. The police academy of the New York City Police Department. The goddamn police academy. Dalia is dead at the police academy. How the hell did she end up here?

"We're here, Detective," says one of the officers.

I turn my head toward the building. K. Burke is walking quickly toward the car. Behind her is Nick Elliott. My chest hurts. My throat burns.

Dalia is dead.

CHAPTER 28

"THIS WAY, LUC," K. Burke says. Both Burke and Nick Elliott guide me by the elbows down a corridor—painted cement blocks, an occasional bulletin board, a fire-alarm box, a fire-extinguisher case.

The usual cast of characters is standing nearby: police officers, forensics, the coroner's people, two firemen, some young people— probably students—carrying laptops and water bottles. A very large sign is taped to a wall at the end of the corridor. It is a photograph of four people: a white male officer, an Asian female officer, a black male officer, a white female officer. Above the big grainy photo are big grainy blue letters:

SERVE WITH DIGNITY. SERVE WITH COURAGE.
THE NEW YORK CITY POLICE DEPARTMENT

Burke and Elliott steer me into a large old-fashioned lecture hall. The stadium seating ends at the bottom with a large table at which a lecturer usually stands. Behind it are a video screen and a green chalkboard. In this teaching pit also stand two officers and two doctors from the chief medical examiner's office. On the side aisles are other officers, other detectives, and, as we descend closer to the bottom of that aisle, a gurney on which a body rests.

K. Burke speaks to me as we reach the gurney. She is saying something to me, but I can't hear her. I am not hearing anything. I am just staring straight ahead as a doctor pulls back the gauzy sheet from Dalia's head and shoulders.

"The wound was in the stomach, sir," she says.

She knows I need no further details at the moment.

Need I say that Dalia looks exquisite? Perfect hair. Perfect eyelashes. A touch of perfect makeup. Perfect. Just perfect. Just fucking unbelievably perfect.

How can she be so beautiful and yet dead?

In my mind I am still screaming "No!" but I say nothing.

I look away from her, and I see the others in the room backing away, looking away, trying to give me privacy in a very public situation.

I must touch Dalia. I should do it gently, of course. I take Dalia's face in both my hands. Her cheeks feel cold, hard. I lean in and brush my lips against her forehead. I pull back a tiny bit to look at her. Then I lean in again to kiss her on the lips.

The room is silent. Deadly silent. I have heard silence before. But the world has never been this quiet.

I will stand here for the rest of my life just looking at her. Yes, that's what I'll do. I'll never move from this spot. I stroke her hair. I touch her shoulders. I stand erect, then turn around.

Nick Elliott is looking at the ground. K. Burke's chin is quivering. Her eyes are wet. I speak, perhaps to Nick or K. Burke or everyone in the room or perhaps I am simply talking to myself.

"Dalia is dead."

CHAPTER 29

"DO YOU WANT TO ride in the ambulance with her?" Elliott asks. And before I can answer he adds, "I'll go with you if you want. We've got to get Dalia to the research area."

The research area. That is the NYPD euphemism for "the morgue." It is what they say to parents whose child has been run over by a drunk driver.

"No," I say. "There's nothing to be done."

K. Burke looks at me and says what everybody says in a situation like this: "I don't know what to say."

And me? I don't know what to say, either—or what to think or feel or do. So I say what comes to mind: "Keep me posted."

I walk quickly through the lineup of colleagues and strangers lining the cement-block hallway. I jump over the giant stone barricades that encircle the police academy in case of attack. I am now running up Third Avenue.

"May I help you, monsieur?" That is the voice I hear. Where have I run? I don't recall a destination. I barely remember running. Did I leave Dalia's dead body behind? I look at the woman who just spoke to me. She used the word *monsieur*. Am I in Paris?

She is joined by a well-dressed man, an older man, a gentleman.

"Can I be of some help, Monsieur Moncrief?"

"*Où suis-je?*" I ask. Where am I?

"*Hermès, Monsieur Moncrief. Bonsoir. Je peux vous aider?*"

The Hermès store on Madison Avenue. It is…was…Dalia's favorite place in the entire world to shop.

"*Non. Merci, Monsieur. Je regarde.*" Just looking.

On the glass shelves is a collection of handbags, purses, and pocketbooks in red and yellow and green. Like Easter and Christmas. I feel calm amid the beauty. It is a museum, a palace, a château. The silk scarves hanging from golden hooks. The glass cases of watches and cufflinks. The shelves of briefcases and leather shopping bags. And then the calm inside me dissipates. I say, "*Bonsoir et merci*" to the sales associate.

I have neither my police phone nor my personal cell. I do not have my watch. I do not know the time. I know I am not crazy. I'm simply crazed.

It's early evening. I walk to Fifth Avenue. The sidewalks are crowded, and the shops are open. I walk down to the Pierre. I was recently inside the Pierre. Was I? I think I was. I continue walking south, toward the Plaza. No water in the fountain? A water shortage, perhaps? I turn east, back toward Madison Avenue, then start north again.

Bottega Veneta. I walk inside. No warm greeting here. A bigger store than Hermès. Instead of a symphony of leather in color, this is a muted place in grays and blacks and many degrees of brown. Calming, calming, calming, until it is calming no longer.

I leave. My next stop is Sherry-Lehmann, the museum of wine. I walk to the rear of the store, where they keep their finest bottles— the Romanée-Conti, Pétrus, Le Pin, Ramonet Montrachet, the thousand-dollar Moët. The bottles should all be displayed under glass, like the diamonds at Tiffany.

I am out on the sidewalk again. I am afraid that if I don't keep moving, I will explode or collapse. It is that extraordinary feeling that nothing good will ever happen again.

A no-brainer: I cannot return to Dalia's apartment at 15 Central Park West. Instead I will go to the loft where I once lived. The place is in the stupidly chic Meatpacking District. I bought the loft before I renewed my life with Dalia. I sometimes lend the place to friends from Europe who are visiting New York. I'm pretty sure it is empty right now.

Will I pick up the pieces? There is no way that will ever happen.

Move on, they will say. Mourn, then move on. I will not do that, because I can't.

Get over it? Never. Someone else? Never.

Nothing will ever be the same.

As I give the address to the cabdriver, I find my chest heaving and hurting. I insist—I don't know why—on holding in the tears. In those few minutes, with my chest shaking and my head aching, I realize what Elliott and Burke and probably others have come to realize: first, my partner, Maria Martinez; then my lover, Dalia Boaz.

Oh, my God. This isn't about prostitutes. This isn't about drugs. This is about me.

Somebody wants to hurt me. And that somebody has succeeded.

CHAPTER 30

A LOFT. A BIG space; bare, barren. Not a handsome space. It is way too basic to be anything but big.

I lived here before Dalia came back into my life. Even when I lived here, I was too compulsive to have allowed it to become a cheesy bachelor pad—no piles of dirty clothing; no accumulation of Chinese-food containers. In fact, no personal touches of any kind. But of course I was spending too many of my waking hours with the NYPD to think about furniture and paint and bathroom fixtures.

I turn the key and walk inside. I am almost startled by the sparseness of it—a gray sofa, a black leather club chair, a glass dining table where no one has ever eaten a meal. Some old files are stacked against a wall. Empty shelves near the sofa. Empty shelves in the kitchen. I have lived most of my New York life with Dalia, at Dalia's home. That was my real home. Where am I now?

I stretch out on the sofa. Fifteen seconds later, I am back on my feet. The room is stuffy, dry, hot. I walk to the thermostat that will turn on the air-conditioning, but I stare at the controls as if I don't quite know how to adjust the temperature. I remember that there is a smooth single-malt Scotch in a cabinet near the entryway, but why bother? I need to use the bathroom, but I just don't have energy enough to walk to the far side of the loft.

Then the buzzer downstairs rings.

At least I think it's the buzzer downstairs. It's been so long since I heard it. I walk to the intercom. The buzz comes again, then once more. Then I remember what I'm expected to say. A phrase that is ridiculously simple.

"Who is it?"

For a split second I stupidly imagine that it will be Dalia. "It was a terrible joke," she will say with a laugh. "Inspector Elliott helped me fool you."

Now a hollow voice comes from the intercom.

"It's K. Burke."

I buzz her inside. Moments later I open the door and let her into the loft.

"How did you know where to find me?" I ask.

"I called your cell twenty times. You never picked up. Then I called Dalia's place twenty times. You weren't there, *or* you weren't picking up. So I found this place listed as the home address in your HR file. If I didn't find you here, I was going to forget it. But I got lucky."

"No, K. Burke. *I got lucky.*"

I have no idea why I said something so sweet. But I think I mean it. Again, an idea that comes and goes in a split second: whoever is trying to destroy me—will he go after K. Burke next?

She gives me a smile. Then she says, "I'm about to say the thing that always annoys me when other people say it."

"And that is…"

"Is there anything I can do for you?"

I take a deep breath.

"You mean like brewing a pot of coffee or bringing me a bag of doughnuts or cleaning my bathroom or finding the son of a bitch who—"

"Okay, I got it," she says. "I understand. But actually, Nick Elliott and I did do something for you."

My forehead wrinkles, and I say, "What?"

"We tracked down Dalia's father. He's in Norway shooting a film."

"I was going to call him soon," I say. "But I was building up courage. Thank you." And just thinking about father and daughter begins to break my already severed heart.

"How did he accept the news?" As if I needed to ask.

"It was awful. He wailed. He screamed. He put his assistant on, and he eventually…well, he sort of composed himself and got back on the line."

My eyes begin filling with tears. My chin quivers. I rub my eyes. I am not trying to hide my emotions. I am merely trying to get through them.

"He sends you his love," K. Burke says. I nod.

"He is as fine a man as Dalia was a woman," I say.

"He asked me to tell you two things."

I can't imagine what Monsieur Boaz wanted to tell me.

"He said, 'Tell Luc that I will come to America tomorrow, but he should bury Dalia as soon as possible. That is the Jewish way.'"

"I understand," I say. Then I ask, "And the other?"

"He said, 'Tell Luc thank you…for taking such good care of my girl.'"

This comment should make me weep, but instead I explode with anger. Not at Menashe Boaz, but at myself.

"That's not true!" I yell. "I did *not* take good care of her."

"Of course it's true," K. Burke says firmly. "You loved her totally. Everybody knows that."

"I…let…her…die."

"That's just stupid, Moncrief. And it smells a little of…" K. Burke abruptly stops talking.

"What? Finish your thought. It smells of what?" I say.

"It smells of…well…self-pity. Dalia was murdered. You could not have prevented it."

I walk to the floor-to-ceiling windows of the loft. I look down at Gansevoort Street. It's this year's chic hot-cool place to be—the expensive restaurants and expensive boutiques, the High Line, the cobblestone streets. It is packed with people. I am disgusted with them because I am disgusted with me. Because Dalia and I will never again be among those people.

I turn and face Detective Burke, and suddenly I am more peaceful. I am truly grateful that she is here. She has stopped by to offer the "personal touch" and I was hesitant at first. Afraid I would feel nervous or embarrassed. But K. Burke has done a good thing.

I walk back toward her and speak slowly, carefully.

"There is one thing we need to discuss very soon. You must realize that these two murders had nothing to do with prostitutes or

Brazilian drug dealers or…well, all the things we have been guessing at."

"I realize that," she says. I continue speaking.

"The first murder, at a rich man's home, was to confuse us. The next murder, at a school where people learn to be police professionals—that was to torment us."

K. Burke nods in simple agreement.

"These murders have to do with *me,*" I say.

"In that case," K. Burke says, "these murders have to do with *us.*"

CHAPTER 31

"WHAT THE HELL IS the story with these two murders?"

This question keeps exploding off the walls of NYPD precincts. It is the commissioner's question. It is Nick Elliott's question. And—obsessively, interminably, awake or asleep—it is my question.

The question is asked a thousand times, and a thousand times the answer comes back the same.

"No idea. Just no goddamn idea."

Forensics brought in nothing. Surveillance cameras showed us nothing. Interviews at the scene turned up nothing.

So it is now time for me to do the only thing left to do: turn inward and rely entirely on my instincts. They have helped me in the past, and they have failed me, too. But instinct is all I have left.

I confront Nick Elliott. I tell him that the answer to the murders is obviously not in New York. The answer must be in Paris.

"Paris?" he shouts.

Then I say, "I need to go to Paris—look around, nose around, see if I can find something there."

Nick Elliott gives it a long pause and then says, "Maybe that's not a bad idea."

Then I tell him that I want to take K. Burke with me.

He pauses again, another long pause. Then he speaks. "Now, *that's* a bad idea."

"Inspector, this is no holiday I'm planning. This is work. K. Burke and I will be examining cases that—"

"Okay, okay, let me think about it," Elliott says. "Maybe it'll help. On the other hand, it might end up being a waste of time and money."

I think quickly and say, "Then it will be a waste of *my* time and *my* money. I'll supply the money for the trip. I only care about getting to the bottom of these murders."

"I guess so," says Elliott.

I say, "I'll take that as a yes."

A minute later I am telling K. Burke to go home and pack.

Her reaction? "I've never been to Paris."

My reaction? "Why am I not surprised?"

CHAPTER 32

K. BURKE AND I are sitting at a steel desk in a small room with bad Internet service at Les Archives de la Préfecture de Police, the dreary building on the periphery of Paris where all the old police records are kept. Here you can examine every recorded police case since the end of the Great War. Here you can discover the names of the French collaborators during the Vichy regime. You can examine the records of the Parisian bakers who have been accused of using tainted yeast in their bread. Here are the records of the thousands of murders, assaults, knife attacks, shootings, and traffic violations that have occurred in the past hundred years in the City of Light.

It is also here that K. Burke and I hope to find some small (or, better yet, large) clue that could connect us to whoever is responsible for the brutal deaths of Maria Martinez and my beloved Dalia.

To find the person who wishes to hurt me so deeply.

"Here," says Detective Burke, pointing to my name on the screen of the archive's computer. *"L. Moncrief était responsable..."*

I translate: "L. Moncrief was responsible for the evidence linking the Algerian diplomat to the cartel posing as Dominican priests in the 15th arrondissement."

I press a computer key and say to Burke, "Listen: after years of being dragged to church by my mother, I know a real priest when I see one, and no *prêtre* I'd ever seen had such a well-groomed beard and mustache. Then I noticed that his shoes…eh, never mind. See what's next."

We study my other cases. Some of those I worked on are ridiculously small—a Citroën stolen because the owner left the keys in the ignition; a lost child who stopped for a free *jus d'orange* on his way home from school; a homeless man arrested for singing loudly in a public library.

Other cases are much more significant. Along with the phony Dominicans, there was the drug bust in Pigalle, the case I built my reputation on. But there was also a gruesome murder in Montmartre, on rue Caulaincourt, during which a pimp's hands and feet were amputated.

In this last case my instincts led me to a pet cemetery in Asnières-sur-Seine. Both the severed hands and feet were found at the grave of the pimp's childhood pet, a spaniel. Instinct.

But nothing in the police archive is resonating with me. I do not feel, either through logic or instinct, any link from these past cases and the awful deaths of my two beloved women.

"I think I need another café au lait, Moncrief," K. Burke says. Her eyelids are covering half her eyes. Jet lag has definitely attacked her.

"What you need is a taxi back to Le Meurice," I say. "It is now *quatorze heures.…*"

K. Burke looks confused.

I translate. "Two o'clock in the afternoon."

"Gotcha," she says.

"Go back to the hotel. Take a nap, and I will come knocking on your door at *dix-sept heures.* Forgive me. I will come knocking at five o'clock."

I add, "Good-bye, K. Burke."

"Au revoir," she says. Her accent makes me cringe, then smile.

"You see?" I add. "You're here just seven hours, and already you're on your way to becoming a true *Parisienne.*"

CHAPTER 33

WE MEET AT FIVE.

"I am not a happy man," I say to K. Burke after I give our destination to the cabdriver. Then I say, "Perhaps I will never be a completely happy man again, but I am *un peu content* when I am in Paris." Burke says nothing for a few seconds.

"Perhaps someday you will be happi*er.*" She speaks with an emphasis on the last syllable. Perhaps someday I will be.

Then I explain to her that because we will have to get back to our investigation tomorrow—"And, like many things, it might come to a frustrating end," I caution—this early evening will be the only chance for me to show her the glory of Paris.

Then I quickly add, "But not the Eiffel Tower or the Louvre or Notre Dame. You can see those on your own. I will show you the special places in Paris. Places that are visited by only the very wise and the very curious."

Detective Burke says, *"Merci, Monsieur Moncrief."*

I smile at her, and then I say to the cabdriver, *"Nous sommes arrivés."* We are here.

Burke reads the sign on the building aloud. Her accent is amusingly American-sounding: "Museé…des…Arts…Forains?"

"It is the circus museum," I say. And soon we are standing in a huge warehouse that holds the forty carousels and games and bright neon signs that a rich man thought were worth preserving.

"I can't decide whether this is a dream or a nightmare," Burke says.

"I think that it is *both*."

We ride a carousel that whirls amazingly fast. "I feel like I'm five again!" shouts K. Burke. We play a game that involves plaster puppets and cloth-covered bulls. K. Burke wins the game. Then we are out and on our way again.

This time out I tell our cabdriver to take us to Paris Descartes University.

"Vous êtes médecin?" the cabdriver asks.

I tell him that my companion and I are doctors of crime, which seems both to surprise and upset him. A few minutes later we are ascending in the lift to view the Musée d'Anatomie Delmas-Orfila-Rouvière. The place is almost crazier than the circus museum. It's a medical museum with hundreds of shelves displaying skulls and skeletons and wax models of diseased human parts. It is at once astonishing and disgusting.

At one point Burke says, "We're the only people here."

"You need special permission to enter."

"Aren't we the lucky ones?" Burke says, with only slight sarcasm.

From there we take another cab ride—to the Pont des Arts, a pedestrian bridge across the Seine. I show her the "love locks," the thousands of small padlocks attached to the rails of the bridge by lovers.

"They are going to relocate some of the locks," I tell Burke. "There are so many that they fear the bridge may collapse."

So much love, I think. And for a moment my heart hurts. But then I hail another cab. I point out the Pitié-Salpêtrière hospital, and we both laugh when I explain that it was once an asylum for "hysterical women."

"Don't get any ideas, Moncrief," Burke says.

Since our bodies are still on American time, it is almost lunchtime for us, and I ask K. Burke if she is hungry.

"*Tu as faim?*" I ask.

"*Très, très* hungry. Famished, in fact."

Ten minutes later, we are in the rough-and-tumble Pigalle area. I tell Detective Burke that she can always dine at the famous Parisian restaurants—Taillevent, Guy Savoy, even the dining room in our hotel. But tonight, I am taking her to my favorite restaurant, Le Petit Canard.

"Isn't this the area where you made your famous drug bust?" Burke asks.

"*C'est vrai,*" I tell her. "You have a good memory."

She is looking out the taxi window. The tourists have disappeared from the streets. The artists must be inside smoking weed. Only vagrants and prostitutes are hanging around.

"Ignore the neighborhood. Le Petit Canard is amazing. I used to come here a great deal when I lived in Paris. With friends, with my father, with…"

She says, "With Dalia, I'm sure." She pauses and says, "I am so sorry for you, Moncrief. So sorry."

Softly, I mutter, "Thank you."

Then I add, "And thank you for allowing me to take you to the crazy tourist sights. It lifted my spirits. It made me feel a little better, Katherine."

Burke appears slightly startled. We both realize that for the first time I have called Detective Burke by her proper first name.

I look closely at Burke's face, a lovely face, a face that goes well with such a lovely evening in such a beautiful city.

"Okay," I say loudly and with great heartiness. "Let me call for the wine list, and we shall begin. We will enjoy a glorious dinner tonight."

I fake an overly serious sad face, a frown. "Because you know that tomorrow…*retour au travail*. Do you know what those three French words mean?"

"I'm afraid so," she says. "'Back to work.'"

CHAPTER 34

MONCRIEF AND K. BURKE return to the hotel. If you were unaware of the details of their relationship, you would assume that they were just another rich and beautiful couple strolling through the ornate lobby of the Meurice.

Much to Moncrief's surprise and pleasure, K. Burke had brought along an outfit that was quite chic—a long white shirt over which hung a gray cashmere sweater. That sweater fell over a black slim skirt. It was finished with short black boots. Burke could *possibly* pass as a fashionable Parisian, and she could *certainly* pass as a fashionable American. Moncrief had told her how "snappy" she looked.

"You look snappy yourself, Moncrief," she had said to him. This was, of course, true: a black Christian Dior suit with a slight sheen to it; a white shirt with a deep burgundy-colored tie.

Moncrief walked K. Burke back to her room and said good night. He listened while Burke locked her door behind her. Then he walked to the end of the hallway, to his own room.

It was a dinner between friends, between colleagues. K. Burke had expected nothing more. In fact, K. Burke *wanted* nothing more. It had been a spectacular day—the odd museums, then the extraordinary dinner: foie-gras ravioli, Muscovy duckling with mango sherbet, those wonderful little chocolates that fancy French restaurants always bring you with your coffee (or so Moncrief told her).

The night had turned out to be soothing and fun and friendly. He referred to Dalia a few times, and it was with nostalgia, sadness. But there was no darkness when he reminisced about his late girlfriend.

Now, as Burke unscrews and removes her tiny diamond studs, she wonders: *Can you have such a wonderful time with a charming, handsome man and not think about romance?*

Of course you can, she tells herself. But then again, it's impossible to put a man and a woman together—the electrician who comes to fix the wiring, the traffic cop who stops you for speeding, the attorney who is updating your will—and not consider the possibilities of *What if…at another time…under different conditions…*

Burke removes her shirt and sweater. She sits on the bench at the white wood dressing table and removes her boots. As she massages her toes she shakes her head slowly; she is ashamed that she is even having such thoughts. Despite the pleasant dinner, she knows that Moncrief has not remotely begun to recover from Dalia's awful, sudden, horrible death. *And yet here I am, selfishly thinking of how great we look together, like one of those beautiful couples in a perfume ad.*

"Enough nonsense." She actually says these two words out loud.

Then she goes into the bathroom, removes her makeup, brushes her teeth, and takes the two antique combs out of her hair. She slips her T-shirt (GO RANGERS) over her head, then she removes her contact lenses and drops them into solution. There is only one more thing to do.

She goes to her pocketbook to do what she does instinctively every night before bed: check the safety on her service weapon. Then she remembers—she doesn't have a gun. The French police said that she and Moncrief were on official business for New York, *not* for Paris. No firearms permits would be issued.

She remembers what Moncrief said to her when she complained.

"Do you feel naked without your gun, K. Burke?"

"No," she had answered. "Just a little underdressed."

CHAPTER 35

THE SAME CRAMPED AND ugly little room. The same primitive air-conditioning. The same stale air. The same inadequate Internet service. But most of all, the same rotten luck in finding "the fingerprint," the instinctive connection between one of my past investigations and the tragedies in New York.

Detective Burke and I keep working. We are once again seated in the police archives building, outside Paris. We have been studying the screen so intently that we decided to invest in a shared bottle of eyedrops.

The screen scrolls through old cases, some of which I had actually forgotten—a molestation case that involved a disgusting pediatrician who was also the father of five children; a case of a government official who, not surprisingly, was collecting significant bribes for issuing false health-inspection reports; a case of race fixing at the Longchamp racecourse.

"This looks bigger than fixing a horse race," she says. "The pages go on forever."

"Print them," I say. "I'll look at them more thoroughly later."

Forty pages come spitting out of the printer. Burke says, "It looks like this was a very complicated case."

"Not really," I say. "No case is ever *that* complicated. Either there's a crime or there isn't. The Longchamp case began with a horse trainer. Marcel Ballard was his name. Not a bad guy, I think, but Ballard was weary of fixing the races. So he fought physically—punching, kicking—with the owner and trainer who were running the fix. *And* Ballard had a knife. *And* Ballard killed the owner and cut the other trainer badly."

K. Burke continues scrolling through the cases on the screen. She does say, "Keep going, Moncrief. I'm listening."

"I met with Ballard's wife. She had a newborn, three months old, their fourth child. So I did her a favor, but not without asking for something in return. I persuaded Ballard to confess to the crime and to help us identify the other trainers who were drugging the horses. He cooperated. So thanks to my intervention—and that of my superiors—he was allowed to plead to a lesser charge. Instead of *homicide volontaire,* he was only charged with—"

"Let me guess," says K. Burke. *"Homicide* in*volontaire."*

"You are both a legal and linguistic genius, K. Burke."

I grab some of the Longchamp papers and go through them quickly. "I'm glad I did what I did," I say. "Madame Ballard is a good woman."

"And the husband? Is he grateful?" K. Burke asks as she continues to study the screen intensely.

"He has written to me many times in gratitude. But one must keep in mind that he did kill a man."

Burke presses a computer key and begins reading about a drug gang working out of Saint-Denis.

"What does this mean, Moncrief? *Logement social.*"

"In New York they call it public housing. A group of heroin dealers had set up a virtual drug supermarket in the basement there. Once I realized that some of our Parisian detectives were involved in the scheme, it was fairly easy—but frightening—to bust."

"How'd you figure out that your own cops were involved?" she asks.

"I simply *felt* it," I say.

"Of course," she says with a bit of sarcasm. "I should have known."

We continue flipping through the cases on the computer. But like the race fixing and murder at Longchamp, like the drug bust in Saint-Denis, all my former cases seem to be a million miles away from New York. No instinct propelled me. No fingerprint arose.

We studied the cold cases also. The kidnapping of the Ugandan ambassador's daughter (unsolved). The rape of an elderly nun at midnight in the Bois de Boulogne (unsolved, but what in hell was an elderly nun doing in that huge park at midnight?). An American woman with whom I had a brief romantic fling, Callie Hansen, who had been abducted for three days by a notorious husband-and-wife team that we were never able to apprehend. Again, nothing clicked.

We come across a street murder near Moulin Rouge. According to the report on the computer screen, one of the witnesses was a woman named Monica Ansel. Aha! Blaise Ansel had been the owner of Taylor Antiquities, the store on East 71st Street. Could

Monica Ansel be his wife? But Monica Ansel, the woman who witnessed the crime at Moulin Rouge, was seventy-one years old.

"Damn!" I say, and I toss the papers from the Longchamp report to the floor. "I have wasted my time and yours, K. Burke. Plus I have wasted a good deal of money. And what do I have to show for it? *De la merde.*"

Even with her limited knowledge of French, K. Burke is able to translate.

"I agree," she says. "Shit."

CHAPTER 36

K. BURKE SITS OUTDOORS at a small bistro table on rue Vieille du Temple. She is alone. Moncrief had asked if he could be by himself for a while. "I must walk. I must think. Perhaps I must mourn. Do you mind?" Moncrief had said.

"I understand," she said, and she did understand. "I don't need a chaperone."

She sips a glass of strong cider and eats a buckwheat crepe stuffed with ham and Gruyère. It is eight o'clock, a fairly early dinner by French standards. At one table sits a family of German tourists—very blond parents with two very beautiful teenage daughters. At another, an older couple (French, Burke suspects) eating and chewing and drinking slowly and carefully. Finally, there are two young Frenchwomen who appear to be…yes, K. Burke is right…very much in love with each other.

Burke's own heart is still breaking for Moncrief, but she must admit that she is enjoying being alone for a few hours.

Back in her hotel room, she takes a warm bath. A healthy dose of lavender bath oils; a natural sea sponge. Afterward, she dries herself off with the thick white bath sheets and douses herself with a nice dose of the accompanying lavender powder.

She slips on her sleep shirt, and she's about to slide under the sheets when her phone buzzes. A text message.

R U Back in yr room? All is well? Mncrf.

She imagines Moncrief in some mysterious part of Paris, at a zinc bar with a big snifter of brandy. She is thankful for his thoughtfulness.

Yes. K. Burke.

But then, for just a moment she considers her own uneasiness. She simply cannot get used to not having a gun to check. So she does the next best thing: she checks that the door is double-locked. She adjusts the air-conditioning, making the temperature low enough for her to happily snuggle under the thick satin comforter. Within a few minutes she is asleep.

Two hours later, she is wide awake. It is barely past midnight, and Burke is afraid that jet lag is playing games with her sleep schedule. Now she may be up for hours. She takes a few deep breaths. The air makes her feel at least a little better. Maybe she will get back to sleep. Maybe she should use the bathroom. Yes, maybe. Or maybe that will prevent her from falling asleep again. On the other hand…

There is a sound in the room. At first she thinks it's the air conditioner kicking back into gear. Perhaps it is the noise from the busy rue de Rivoli below. She sits up in bed. The noise. Again. Burke realizes now that the sound is coming from the door to her hotel room. Some sort of key? What the hell?

"Who's there?" she shouts.

No answer.

"Who's there?"

Goddamn it. Why doesn't she have a gun?

She should have insisted that Moncrief get them guns. He was right. She feels naked without it.

She rolls quickly—catching herself in the thick covers, afraid in the dark—toward the other side of the bed. She drops to the floor and slides beneath the bed just as a shaft of bright light from the hallway pierces the darkness. Someone else is in the room with her. She moves farther underneath the bed. *Jesus Christ,* she thinks. *This is an awful comedy, a French farce—the woman hiding beneath the bed.*

As soon as she hears the door close, the light from the hallway disappears.

"Don't move, Detective!" a muffled, foreign-sounding voice hisses.

Then a gunshot.

The bullet hits the floor about a foot away from her hand. There's a quick loud snapping sound. A spark on the blue carpet. She tries to move farther under the bed. There is no room. It is so unlike her to not know what to do, to not fight back, to not plot an escape. This feeling of fright is foreign to her.

Another bullet. This one spits its way fiercely through the mattress above her. It hits the floor also.

Another bullet. No spark. No connection.

A groan. A quick thud.

Then a voice.

"K. Burke! It is safe. All is well."

CHAPTER 37

HOTEL MANAGEMENT AND GUESTS in their pajamas almost immediately begin gathering in the hall.

K. Burke emerges from under the bed. We embrace each other the way friends do, friends who have successfully come through a horrible experience together.

"You saved…" she begins. She is shaking. She folds her arms in front of herself. She is working to compose herself.

"I know," I say. I pat her on the back. I am like an old soccer coach with an injured player.

Burke pulls away from me. She blinks—on purpose—a few times, and those simple eye gestures seem to clear her head and calm her nerves. She is immediately back to a completely professional state. She has become the efficient K. Burke I am used to. We both look down at the body. She moves to a nearby closet and wraps herself quickly in a Le Meurice terry-cloth bathrobe.

The dead man fell backwards near the foot of the bed. He wears jeans, a white dress shirt, and Adidas sneakers. His bald head lies in a large and ever-growing pool of blood. It forms a kind of scarlet halo around his face.

The crowd in the hallway seems afraid to enter the room. A

man wearing a blue blazer with LE MEURICE embroidered on the breast pocket appears. He pushes through the crowd. He is immediately followed by two men wearing identical blazers.

I briefly explain what happened, planning to give the police a more detailed story when they arrive.

K. Burke then kneels at the man's head. I watch her touch the man's neck. I can tell by the blood loss, by simply looking at him, that she is merely performing an official act. The guy is gone. Burke stands back up.

"Do you know him, Moncrief?" Burke asks.

"I have never seen him before in my life," I say. "Have you?"

"Of course not," she says. She pauses. Then she says, "He was going to kill me."

"You would have been…the third victim."

She nods. "How did you know that this was happening here, that someone was actually going to break in…threaten my life…try to kill me?"

"Instinct. When I texted you I asked if all was well. So I drank my whiskey.

"But fifteen minutes later, when I am walking back to the hotel, I found myself walking faster and faster, until I was actually running…I just had a feeling. I can't explain it."

"You never can," she says.

CHAPTER 38

THE NEXT MORNING.

Eleven o'clock. I meet K. Burke in the lobby of the hotel.

"So here we are," she says. "Everything is back to *ab*normal."

Even I realize that this is a bad play on words. But it does perfectly describe our situation.

"Look," I say. "A mere apology is unsuitable. I am totally responsible for the near tragedy of last night."

"There's nothing to apologize for. It goes with the territory," she says, but I can see from her red eyes that she did not sleep well. I try to say something helpful.

"I suspect what happened a few hours ago is that the enemy saw us together at some point here in Paris and assumed that we were a couple, which of course we are not."

I realize immediately that my words are insulting, as if it would be impossible to consider us a romantic item. So I speak again, this time more quickly.

"Of course, they might have been correct in the assumption. After all, a lovely-looking woman like you could—"

"Turn it off, Moncrief. I was *not* offended."

I smile. Then I hold K. Burke by the shoulders, look into her weary eyes, and speak.

"Listen. Out of something awful that almost happened last evening…something good has come. I believe I have an insight. I think I may now know the fingerprint of this case."

She asks me to share the theory with her.

"I cannot tell you yet. Not for secrecy reasons, but because I must first be sure, in order to keep my own mind clear. *On y va.*"

"Okay," she says. Then she translates: "Let's go."

We walk outside. I speak to one of the doormen.

"Ma voiture, s'il vous plaît," I say.

"Elle est là, Monsieur Moncrief."

"Your car is here?" Burke asks, and as she speaks my incredibly beautiful 1960 Porsche 356B pulls up and the valet gets out.

"C'est magnifique," Burke says.

The Porsche is painted a brilliantly shiny black. Inside is a custom mahogany instrument panel and a pair of plush black leather seats. I explain to Detective Burke that I had been keeping the car at my father's country house, near Avignon.

"But two days ago I had the car brought up to Paris. And so today we shall use it."

I turn right on the rue de Rivoli, and the Porsche heads out of the city.

After the usual mess of too many people and triple-parked cars and thousands of careless bicycle riders, we are outside Paris, on our way south.

K. Burke twists in her seat and faces me.

"Okay, Moncrief. I have a question that's been bugging me all night."

"I hope to have the answer," I say, trying not to sound anxious. "The gun that you used last night. Where did you get it?"

I laugh, and with the wind in our hair and the sun in our eyes I fight the urge to throw my head back like an actor in a movie.

"Oh, the gun. Well, when Papa's driver dropped off the car two days ago, I looked in that little compartment, the one in front of your seat, and voilà! Driving gloves, chewing gum, driver's license, and my beautiful antique Nagant revolver. I thought it might come in handy someday."

In the countryside I pick up speed, a great deal of speed. K. Burke does not seem at all alarmed by fast driving. After a few minutes of silence I tell her that I am taking the country roads instead of the A5 *autoroute* so that she might enjoy the summer scenery.

She does not say a word. She is asleep, and she remains so until I make a somewhat sharp right turn at our destination.

K. Burke blinks, rubs her eyes, and speaks.

"Where are we, Moncrief?"

Ahead of us is a long, low, flat gray building. It is big and gloomy. Not like a haunted house or a lost castle. Just a huge grim pile of concrete. She reads the name of the building, carved into the stone.

PRISON CLAIRVAUX

She does a double take.

"What are we doing here, Moncrief?"

"We are here to meet the killer of Maria Martinez and Dalia Boaz."

CHAPTER 39

A FEW YEARS AGO, a detective with the Paris police described the prison at Clairvaux as "hell, but without any of the fun." I think the detective was being kind.

As K. Burke and I present identification to the entrance guards, I tell her, "Centuries ago this was a Cistercian abbey, a place of monks and prayer and chanting."

"Well," she says as she looks around the stained gray walls. "There isn't a trace of God left here."

Burke and I are scanned with an electronic wand, then we step through an X-ray machine and are finally escorted to a large vacant room—no chairs, no tables, no window. We stand waiting a few minutes. The door opens, and an official-looking man as tall as the six-foot doorway enters. He is thin and old. His left eye is made of glass. His name is Tomas Wren. We shake hands.

"Detective Moncrief, I was delighted to hear your message this morning that you would be paying us a visit."

"Merci," I say. "Thank you for accommodating us on such short notice."

Wren looks at Detective Burke and speaks.

"And you, of course, must be Madame Moncrief."

"*Non, monsieur, je suis Katherine Burke. Je suis la collègue de Monsieur Moncrief.*"

"*Ah, mille pardons,*" Wren says. Then Wren turns to me. He is suddenly all business.

"I have told Ballard that you are coming to see him."

"His reaction?" I ask.

"His face lit up."

"I'm glad to hear that," I say.

"You never know with Ballard. He can be a dangerous customer," says Wren. "But he owes you a great deal."

With a touch of levity, I say, "And I owe him a great deal. Without his help I would never have made the arrests that made my career take off."

Wren shrugs, then says, "I have set aside one of the private meeting rooms for you and Mademoiselle Burke," Wren adds.

We follow him down another stained and gray hallway. The private room is small—perhaps merely a dormitory cell from the days of the Cistercian brothers—but it has four comfortable desk chairs around a small maple table. A bit more uninviting, however, are the *bouton d'urgence*—the emergency button—and two heavy metal clubs.

Wren says that he will be back in a moment. "With Ballard," he says.

As soon as Wren exits, Burke speaks.

"I remember this case from the other day, Moncrief. On the computer. Ballard is the horse trainer who killed some guy and wounded another at the Longchamp racecourse."

"Yes, indeed, Detective."

"But I don't totally get what's going on here now."

"You will," I say.

"If you say so," she answers.

I nod, and as I do I feel myself becoming…quiet…no, the proper word is…frightened. A kind of soft anxiety begins falling over me. No man can ever feel happy being in a prison, even for a visit. It is a citadel of punishment and futility. But this is something way beyond simple unhappiness. Burke senses that something is wrong.

"Are you okay, Moncrief?" she says.

"No, I am not. I am twice a widower of sorts. And now I feel I am in the house where those plans were made. No, Detective. I am not okay. But you know what? I don't ever expect to be okay. Excuse me if that sounds like self-pity."

"No need to apologize. I understand."

CHAPTER 40

A CREAKING SOUND, LIKE one you would hear in an old horror movie, comes from the door. It opens, and a burst of light surges into the bleak room.

Wren has returned, and with him is a young prison guard. The guard escorts the prisoner—Marcel Ballard.

Ballard is ugly. His fat face is scarred on both cheeks. Another scar is embedded on the right side of his neck. The three scars show the marks of crude surgical stitching. Prison fights, perhaps?

His head is completely bald. He is unreasonably heavy for a man who dines only on prison rations; he must be trading something of value for extra food.

The guard removes the handcuffs from Ballard.

Ballard comes rushing toward me. He is shouting.

The guard moves to pull Ballard away from me, but Ballard is too fast for him.

"Moncrief, mon ami, mon pote!" he yells. Then he embraces me in a tight bear hug. In accented English, the guard translates, "My friend! My best friend!"

Then Ballard kisses me on both cheeks.

CHAPTER 41

IT IS BALLARD WHO enlightens K. Burke.

"You wonder why we embrace, mademoiselle?"

"Not really," says K. Burke. "I know about you and the detective. I know that you received a lesser sentence because of *him,* and I know that he received some valuable information because of *you.*"

Ballard smiles. I look away from the two of them.

"Detective Moncrief, you have not told your colleague the entire story of our relationship?" Ballard asks, his eyes almost comically wide.

For a reason I can't explain, I am becoming angry. With a snappish tone I respond, "No. I didn't think it was necessary. I thought it was between the two of us."

"But many others know," Ballard responds. "May I tell her?"

"Do whatever you like," I say. The bleakness of the prison, the memory of the Longchamp arrests, and the indelible pain of Maria and Dalia's deaths all close in on me. I am sinking into a depression. There is no reason why I should be angry that Burke will be hearing the story of Ballard and me. Still, he hesitates.

I try to restore a lighter tone to the conversation. "No, really. If you want to tell her, go right ahead."

After a pause, Ballard tells her, "When I was arrested I was the father of an infant, and I was also the father of three other children, all of them under the age of five years."

He pauses, and with a smile says, "Yes, we are a very Catholic family. Four children in five years." Burke does not smile back.

Then he continues. "Life would have been desperate for my wife, Marlene, without me. The children would have starved. When I was sentenced to the two decades in the prison, I worried and prayed, and my prayers were answered.

"In my second month inside this hell, Marlene writes to me with news. She is receiving a monthly stipend, a generous stipend, from Monsieur Moncrief."

He pauses, then adds, "I was overwhelmed with gratitude for his extreme generosity."

Burke nods at Ballard. Then she turns to me and says, "Good man, Detective."

I do not care to slosh around in sentimentality. I gruffly announce, "Look, Ballard. I am here for a reason. An important reason. You may be able to pay me back for that 'extreme generosity.'"

CHAPTER 42

THE GOSSIP NETWORK IN a prison is long and strong.

Ballard confirms this. "I was overcome with sadness and anger when I heard about your police friend and your girlfriend, Detective. I could not write to you. I could not telephone. I did not know what to say. And, I am ashamed to admit, I was afraid. If the other prisoners found out that I was speaking to a member of the Paris police, I might be in danger."

"I understand," I say. "Besides, Marlene wrote me and expressed her outrage and sympathy."

"*Très bien,*" he says. "Marlene is a good woman."

I am silent. I want to speak, but I cannot. Suddenly everything is rushing back—the sight of Maria in the lavish Park Avenue apartment, the sight of Dalia on the gurney, the crazed run that I made through Hermès and the wine shop.

I think Burke senses that I have wandered off to a deeper, darker place. She keeps a steady gaze on me.

Ballard looks confused. He is waiting for me to say something. My tongue freezes as if it's too big for my mouth. My brain is too big for my head, and my heart is too broken to function.

Ballard reaches across the little table and places his rough hand on mine.

"The heart breaks, Detective."

I remain silent. Ballard speaks.

"What can I do, my friend?"

My head is filling with pain. Then I speak.

"Listen to me, Marcel. I believe that someone being held in this prison arranged for the executions of my partner, Maria, and my lover, Dalia. I think whoever it was also planned to kill my current partner, the person sitting here."

I cannot help but notice that Ballard does not react in any way to what I'm saying. He finally removes his hand from mine. He continues to listen silently. If he is anything, he is afraid, stunned.

"It is pure revenge, Ballard. There are men here in Clairvaux who detest me. They don't blame their crimes for their imprisonment. They blame *me*. They think that by killing the people I am close to...they are killing me...and you know something, Ballard? They are right."

Again silence. A long silence. The minute that feels like an hour.

Ballard interrupts the quiet. He is calm. "*C'est vrai, monsieur le lieutenant.* Someone who hates you is killing the women you love."

"Tell me, Marcel. Tell me if you truly have gratitude for what I've done to help your wife and children: do you have any idea who ordered these murders?"

Ballard looks at Burke. Then he looks at me. Then he looks down at the table. When he looks back up again a few moments later his eyes are wet with tears. He speaks.

"Everyone inside this asylum is cruel. You have to learn to be cruel to survive here."

I am awestruck at Ballard's intensity. He continues.

"But there is only one man who has the power to buy such a horror in the outside world. And I think you know who that is. I think you know without my even saying his name."

And I know the person we should bring in.

CHAPTER 43

BURKE AND I WAIT for Adrien Ramus.

We wait in a smaller, bleaker room than the one in which we met with Ballard. This room is located within the high-security area, where the most treacherous prisoners are kept. It is not solitary confinement, but it is the next worst thing. Isolation, only relieved for food and fifteen minutes of recreation a day in the yard.

The room has no table, no chairs. It is bare except for the emergency button, three clubs, and three mace cartridges that hang on the wall.

The door opens with the same horror-film creak as the door in the previous interview room. Tomas Wren once again accompanies the prisoner, but Ramus apparently warrants *three* guards to keep him under control. What's more, I suspect that the handcuffs behind Ramus's back will not be removed.

Ramus is gaunt, thin as a man with a disease. His nose is too big for his face. His eyes are too small for his face. Yet all his characteristics come together to form a frightening but handsome man. He could be an aging fashion model.

Years ago, during his booking, his trials, and his sentencing,

Ramus spat on the floor whenever he saw me. When this vulgarity earned him a club to the head from a policeman or a prison guard, Ramus didn't care. It was worth a little pain to demonstrate his hatred for the detective who had brought him down.

Ramus does not disappoint this time. Upon seeing me he immediately lobs a small puddle of spittle in my direction.

I sense madness—not only in Ramus but also in myself. I reach across and grab him by the chin. I push his head back as far as it will go without snapping it off. I know the guards probably hate Ramus as much as I do. I know they won't stop me. I could beat Ramus if I wished to.

"My partner! My lover!" I shout. "It was you!"

He just stares at me. He twists his neck forcefully, trying to relieve the pain of my assault. I let go of his chin, then shout again.

"You have sources on the outside who can do such things!"

Now Ramus smiles. Then he speaks. The voice is rough, the words staccato.

"You are a fool, Moncrief. I have sources, yes. But anyone inside this pit of hell can buy influence outside. Put the pieces together, Moncrief. Are you so stupid?"

He spits again. Then he just stares at me. I speak more softly now.

"You will burn in hell...and I cannot wait for that time! I cannot wait for God to burn you. And you will do more than die and burn. You will first *suffer*. And then die and burn. I will see to it."

He says, "When I heard that your two women friends were killed I was happy. I was joyful."

My heart is beating hard. My chest is heaving up and down. Ramus continues.

"Some men are very powerful...sometimes even *more* powerful in the shadows of a prison than they are on the streets of the city."

I feel my hand and both my arms tense up completely. In seconds I will be at him once again. This time I will force my hand around his neck. Then I will force my fingers around his Adam's apple. Then...

He speaks again.

"Believe whatever you want, Moncrief. It is of no meaning to me. As I say, you are a stupid, pathetic fool. When will you learn? Where I am concerned, you are powerless. The boss? He is Ramus."

The tension and strength suddenly drain from my body. My arms fall to my side. I am the victim of a perfect crime.

I bow my head. *I have solved the case, but the women closest to me are gone.*

I try to control my shaking limbs. I try to hold my feelings inside me.

"Get him out of here," I say to the guards.

Ramus says nothing more. They lead him out. It's over.

CHAPTER 44

THE NEXT AFTERNOON K. Burke and I fly back to New York City.

Closure. K. Burke is smart enough and now knows me well enough not to talk about "closure," a glib and wishful concept. Nothing closes. At least not completely.

Friends and colleagues and family will say (and some have said already), "You're lucky. At least you're young and rich and handsome. You'll get over this. You'll find a way to learn to move on."

I will nod affirmatively, but only to stop their chatter. Then my response will be simple: "No. Those qualities—youth, wealth, physical attributes—are randomly distributed. They protect you from very little of life's real agonies."

Menashe Boaz and I speak on the telephone. He is still in Norway with his film—"wrapping in three days." His voice, predictably, is somber. I am one of the few people who knows precisely how he feels. With my complete agreement, he decides that he will send two assistants to New York to oversee clearing out Dalia's apartment. Sad? It is beyond sad. Menashe and I cannot have this conversation without the occasional tear. It is a miracle that we can have the conversation at all.

"I don't want a thing from Dalia's apartment," I tell him. I never want to enter the place again.

Any book I've left there I will never finish reading. Any suit in her closet I will never wear again. The real keepsakes are all inside me. A handful of wonderful photographs are on my phone.

Full of jet lag, fatigue, tension, and sorrow, K. Burke and I speak with Inspector Elliott at the precinct. I describe in broad strokes our time in Paris. Burke describes the same thing, but in much greater detail. I say the words I've been aching to say: "The case is solved."

When our two hours with Elliott are over, I tell K. Burke that her memory is "astonishing. I mean it."

She says, "Almost as good as yours. I mean it."

We return to the detective pool—piles of files, the endless recorded phone messages, the crime blotter. I see that Burke is not her usual ambitious self. She is shuffling papers, typing slowly on her computer.

"Something is troubling you, Detective?" I say.

She looks up at me and speaks. "I'm angry that Ramus has brought us down. I know that's stupid. I know the case is solved. But he *has* committed the perfect crime. He can kill and get away with it. It really pisses me off. I can only imagine how you must feel."

"Life goes on, K. Burke. Who knows? Maybe tomorrow will be a little bit better," I say.

Detective Burke smiles. Then she speaks.

"Exactly. Who knows?"

CHAPTER 45

La maison centrale de Clairvaux

ALL PRISONERS ARE EQUAL in the mess hall. At least that's the way it's supposed to be. Same horrid food, same rancid beverages. But in prison, those who have money also have influence. And those with money and influence live a little better.

Marcel Ballard supplies two kitchen workers with a weekly supply of filtered Gauloises cigarettes. So the workers show their gratitude by heaping larger mounds of instant mashed potatoes on Ballard's plate and by giving him a double serving of the awful industrial cheese that is supplied after the meal. On some lucky occasions, Ballard goes to take a slug of water from his tin cup and finds that a kitchen ally has replaced the water with beer or, better still, a good amount of Pernod.

Adrien Ramus has even more influence than Ballard. Ramus, you see, has even more bribery material at his disposal. Even Tomas Wren has snapped at the bait Ramus dangles. Because he gives Wren the occasional gift of a few grams of cocaine, Ramus has a relatively easy time of it in isolation—a private cell, a radio. Ramus sells many things to many prisoners. He always has a supply of marijuana for those who want to get high and access to local attorneys for those who want to get out.

It is Tuesday's supper. The menu never changes. Sunday is a greasy chicken thigh with canned asparagus spears that smell like socks. Monday is spaghetti in a tasteless oil. And then Tuesday. Tuesday at Clairvaux is always—unalterably, predictably—white beans, gray meat in brown gravy, canned spinach, and a thin slice of cheap unidentifiable white cheese.

Guards patrol the aisles.

No conversation is allowed. But that rule is constantly broken, usually with a shout-out declaring, "This food is shit." Sometimes there's a warning from someone just on the edge of sanity, a "Stop staring at me or I'll slice off your balls" or "You are vomiting on me, *gros trou du cul.*" That charming phrase translates as "you big asshole."

This evening is relatively quiet until one man slashes another man's thigh, and as both victim and abuser are hauled away, most of the other prisoners cheer like small stupid boys watching a game. Two other men fight, then they are separated. Two more men fight, and the guards, for their own amusement, allow the fight to proceed for a few minutes until, finally, one man lies semi-conscious on the floor.

Suppertime, an allotment of twenty minutes, has almost ended. Some men, like Marcel Ballard, have, for a few euros, bought their neighbor's beans or cheese. Ballard stuffs the food into his round mouth.

Other prisoners have not even touched their plates. Most likely they have chocolate bars and bread hidden in their cells; most likely such luxuries have been supplied—for a price, of course—by Adrien Ramus.

Hundreds of years ago this mess hall was the refectory of Clairvaux Abbey. Here the hood-clad monks chanted their *"Benedic, Domine,"* the grace said before meals. The faded image of Saint Robert of Molesme, the founder of the Cistercian order, is barely visible above the doors to the kitchen. Often, when some angry prisoner decides to throw a pile of potatoes, the mess ends up on Saint Robert's faded face.

The men are ordered to pass their individual bowls to the end of each table. Most do so quietly. Others find that this chore gives them the opportunity to call a fellow diner a prick or, sometimes more gently, a bitch.

Lukewarm coffee is passed around in tin pitchers. Nothing is ever served hot. Too dangerous. Boiling soup or steaming coffee could be poured over an enemy inmate's head. Almost everyone pours large amounts of sugar into their cups. Almost everyone drinks the coffee, including one of the most prominent and influential prisoners, who sits silently at the end of a table.

That prisoner takes a gulp of coffee. He then places the cup on the wooden table. Suddenly the man's right hand flies to his neck, his left hand to his belly. He lets out a hoarse and stifled gasp. His head begins shaking, and a putrid green liquid surges from his mouth. The prisoners near him move away. Two guards move in on the victim. As trained, two other guards rush to protect the exit doors. This might easily be a scheme to start an uprising.

This, however, turns out not to be a trick. The stricken prisoner falls forward onto the wooden table. His head bounces twice on the wood. His poisoned coffee spills onto the floor. He is dead.

Prisoners are shouting. Guards are swinging their clubs.

Adrien Ramus remains seated. No smile. No anger. No expression. He is satisfied.

At this exact same time, the rest of the world continues turning.

In Paris, a group of French hotel workers are busy replacing the bullet-scarred carpeting where K. Burke was attacked.

In Norway, Menashe Boaz is calling "Cut" and then saying, "Fifteen-minute break." He must be alone.

In New York, Luc Moncrief, who has just come in from running four miles on the West Side bike path, sits in a big leather chair in his apartment. He is sweaty and tired and sad. But for some unknowable reason he finds that he is suddenly at peace.

CHAPTER 46

"I THOUGHT YOU WERE out today," K. Burke says to me, as crisp and confident as ever. Whatever jet-lag body-clock adjustment she had to make has been made.

"I was," I say. "But I had to see you. I must show you something on the computer."

"What's with you, Moncrief? You sound a little—I don't know…creepy. It's like your energy level is down a few notches."

"Yes, Detective. I am stunned. I am walking in a dream. Maybe half a dream and half a nightmare."

As always, about a dozen other New York City detectives are very interested in our conversation. Everyone is aware of the murders. Now many are aware of the attack on Burke in Paris.

"Interview room 4 is free. I checked. Let's go there," I say.

Perhaps for the benefit of our police colleagues, Burke shrugs her shoulders in that I-dunno-maybe-he's-a-little-crazy way. Then she follows me down the hall to the interview room.

I close the curtain to prevent anyone from spying on us through the two-way mirror. I place my laptop on the table, open it, and tap a few buttons.

"I've read it maybe fifty times," I say. "Now it's your turn. Please read. Then I am going to delete it."

K. Burke looks vaguely frightened, but she is also curious. I can tell. Her eyes widen, then they relax. Then her forehead wrinkles. She begins to read.

Monsieur Moncrief:

I believe that the following information will be of interest to you.

Three hours ago, at 1800 hours Paris, an inmate in my charge died, the direct result of poison administered to his coffee.

He was a man of your acquaintance: Marcel Ballard.

Burke looks away from the screen. She looks directly at me. "Ballard?" she says. "But I thought…no. Not Ballard!"

"Keep reading," I say.

Ballard's death was obviously planned and perpetrated by someone inside La maison centrale de Clairvaux.

I know that it was your belief that the murders of Maria Martinez and Dalia Boaz were ordered by another prisoner, Adrien Ramus.

I must inform you, however, that evidence taken here at this scene after today's murder proves otherwise.

An investigation of Ballard's cell revealed a laptop computer hidden within a broken tile beneath the toilet.

An examination of the laptop's contents showed frequent correspondence between Ballard and two Frenchmen who were in the United States on visitor visas. One of them, Thierry Mondeville, returned to France a few days ago. Mondeville has now been identified as the attacker in the incident involving Katherine Burke and yourself.

Further correspondence indicates Ballard's extreme anger at his imprisonment and the role you played in causing it. Ballard explicitly held you responsible for "destroying my life and destroying my family."

Upon its release by the police I will forward a file containing the complete contents of Ballard's computer as well as the findings and conclusions of the official investigation.

> Je vous prie d'agréer, Monsieur, mes
> respectueuses salutations,
> *Tomas Wren*

Burke and I say nothing for a few moments.

Then she looks at me and speaks. "Do you believe this is true?"

I nod, and, for assurance, I say, "I am certain."

I walk to the other side of the room. I look out the perpetually dirty window. The tops of the brownstones look like figures drawn in charcoal when seen through the dirt on the glass.

"But, Moncrief, you mean…all these years you were helping Ballard, and all these years he was planning to destroy your life?" she says. "You must be amazed at this."

"To be honest, I am not amazed. *I knew.*"

Now Burke is the one who is amazed. She is speechless.

"Ramus is indeed a wretched excuse for a human being. But if he had ordered the executions he would have happily bragged to me about them. He would have told me directly that he was the talent behind the killings. But…he stopped just short of bragging.

"That is why I assaulted him. But I could not drive him to say what he would have been glad to say. He would not admit to being the force behind the killings.

"Then we add the fact that Ballard was so effusive in his thanks to me. Bah! I put him in prison for most of his life. Do you think he cares what happens to his family? Do you think he cares about their welfare? I instinctively knew he was throwing the *connerie,* the bullshit, at me."

I can tell she wants to smile, but this moment is too serious.

"But most important, *I could not have put Ramus in prison if Ballard had not given me information on him.* I knew that someday Ramus would punish Ballard. This was timing *parfait.* Ballard falsely pinned the crimes on Ramus *and* Ballard had previously betrayed him. So, *le poison dans le café.*"

"So the case is solved," she says. But she speaks softly, cautiously.

"I guess so," I say. I know, however, that there is sorrow in my voice.

I walk back to the table where the opened laptop rests. Then I push the button marked DELETE.

CHAPTER 47

I LEAVE THE PRECINCT and head toward Fifth Avenue and 52nd Street. I am standing outside a fabulous shop, Versace. I pause and then walk through the great arched center door.

This was one of Dalia's favorite stores. I can remember almost every single item Dalia ever bought here.

The black skirt. If I looked hard I could see through the tightly woven material and catch a glimpse of Dalia's exquisite legs.

The shoes with thick cork platforms that made Dalia a half inch or so taller than I am. We always laughed at that.

The belts with golden buckles. The black leather shopping totes. The crazy shirts with variously colored geometric shapes that shout at you.

"Signor Moncrief. It has been a thousand years since we have seen you," says the store manager, Giuliana. "Welcome. You have been away, perhaps?" she adds.

"Yes. I've been away. Far away."

Giuliana tilts her head to one side. "I heard of the tragedy of Miss Boaz, of course. We were all so sad."

"Thank you," I say. "I read your condolence note. I read it more than once."

"We liked her so very much," says Giuliana. Then she says, "I will leave you alone. Call on me if I can help you."

"I will," I say. *"Grazie."*

She walks away, and I remain still, moving only my head. I take in the lights from the golden fixtures. The multitude of wallets laid out in their cases in neat overlapping rows.

It is late summer. So they are showing fall coats, fall dresses, fall scarves. Reds and browns and dark yellows. Black jeans and white jeans. And lots and lots of sunglasses. Even the mannequins are wearing sunglasses.

"Sunglasses are always in season," Dalia used to say.

I am about to move deeper into the store. I am calm. Not completely calm, but I am calm.

Then my phone rings. The caller is identified as "K. Burke."

I answer.

"Good afternoon, K. Burke. Don't tell me. There's been a murder."

"How did you know?" she says.

"I just knew. Somehow I just knew."

BOOKS BY JAMES PATTERSON

FEATURING ALEX CROSS

The People vs. Alex Cross • Cross the Line • Cross Justice • Hope to Die • Cross My Heart • Alex Cross, Run • Merry Christmas, Alex Cross • Kill Alex Cross • Cross Fire • I, Alex Cross • Alex Cross's Trial (with Richard DiLallo) • Cross Country • Double Cross • Cross (also published as Alex Cross) • Mary, Mary • London Bridges • The Big Bad Wolf • Four Blind Mice • Violets Are Blue • Roses Are Red • Pop Goes the Weasel • Cat & Mouse • Jack & Jill • Kiss the Girls • Along Came a Spider

THE WOMEN'S MURDER CLUB

16th Seduction (with Maxine Paetro) • 15th Affair (with Maxine Paetro) • 14th Deadly Sin (with Maxine Paetro) • Unlucky 13 (with Maxine Paetro) • 12th of Never (with Maxine Paetro) • 11th Hour (with Maxine Paetro) • 10th Anniversary (with Maxine Paetro) • The 9th Judgment (with Maxine Paetro) • The 8th Confession (with Maxine Paetro) • 7th Heaven (with Maxine Paetro) • The 6th Target (with Maxine Paetro) • The 5th Horseman (with Maxine Paetro) • 4th of July (with Maxine Paetro) • 3rd Degree (with Andrew Gross) • 2nd Chance (with Andrew Gross) • First to Die

FEATURING MICHAEL BENNETT

Haunted (with James O. Born) • Bullseye (with Michael Ledwidge) • Alert (with Michael Ledwidge) • Burn (with Michael Ledwidge) • Gone (with Michael Ledwidge) • I, Michael Bennett (with Michael Ledwidge)

• *Tick Tock* (with Michael Ledwidge) • *Worst Case* (with Michael Ledwidge) • *Run for Your Life* (with Michael Ledwidge) • *Step on a Crack* (with Michael Ledwidge)

THE PRIVATE NOVELS

Count to Ten: A Private Novel (with Ashwin Sanghi) • *Missing: A Private Novel* (with Kathryn Fox) • *The Games* (with Mark Sullivan) • *Private Paris* (with Mark Sullivan) • *Private Vegas* (with Maxine Paetro) • *Private India: City on Fire* (with Ashwin Sanghi) • *Private Down Under* (with Michael White) • *Private L.A.* (with Mark Sullivan) • *Private Berlin* (with Mark Sullivan) • *Private London* (with Mark Pearson) • *Private Games* (with Mark Sullivan) • *Private: #1 Suspect* (with Maxine Paetro) • *Private* (with Maxine Paetro)

NYPD RED NOVELS

Red Alert (with Marshall Karp) • *NYPD Red 4* (with Marshall Karp) • *NYPD Red 3* (with Marshall Karp) • *NYPD Red 2* (with Marshall Karp) • *NYPD Red* (with Marshall Karp)

SUMMER NOVELS

Second Honeymoon (with Howard Roughan) • *Now You See Her* (with Michael Ledwidge) • *Swimsuit* (with Maxine Paetro) • *Sail* (with Howard Roughan) • *Beach Road* (with Peter de Jonge) • *Lifeguard* (with Andrew Gross) • *Honeymoon* (with Howard Roughan) • *The Beach House* (with Peter de Jonge)

STAND-ALONE BOOKS

Fifty Fifty (with Candice Fox) • *The Patriot* (with Alex Abramovich) • *Murder Is Forever* • *The Family Lawyer* (thriller omnibus) • *The Store* (with Richard DiLallo) • *The Moores Are Missing* (thriller omnibus) • *Murder Games* (with Howard Roughan) • *Penguins of America* (with Jack Patterson and Florence Yue) • *Two from the Heart* (with Frank Costantini, Emily Raymond, and Brian Sitts) • *The Black Book* (with David Ellis) • *Humans, Bow Down* (with Emily Raymond) • *Never Never* (with Candice Fox) • *Woman of God* (with Maxine Paetro) • *Filthy Rich* (with John Connolly and Timothy Malloy) • *The Murder House* (with David Ellis) • *Truth or Die* (with Howard Roughan) • *Miracle at Augusta* (with Peter de Jonge) • *Invisible* (with David Ellis) • *First Love* (with Emily Raymond) • *Mistress* (with David Ellis) • *Zoo* (with Michael Ledwidge) • *Guilty Wives* (with David Ellis) • *The Christmas Wedding* (with Richard DiLallo) • *Kill Me If You Can* (with Marshall Karp) • *Toys* (with Neil McMahon) • *Don't Blink* (with Howard Roughan) • *The Postcard Killers* (with Liza Marklund) • *The Murder of King Tut* (with Martin Dugard) • *Against Medical Advice* (with Hal Friedman) • *Sundays at Tiffany's* (with Gabrielle Charbonnet) • *You've Been Warned* (with Howard Roughan) • *The Quickie* (with Michael Ledwidge) • *Judge & Jury* (with Andrew Gross) • *Sam's Letters to Jennifer* • *The Lake House* • *The Jester* (with Andrew Gross) • *Suzanne's Diary for Nicholas* • *Cradle and All* • *When the Wind Blows* • *Miracle on the 17th Green* (with Peter de Jonge) • *Hide & Seek* • *The Midnight Club* • *Black Friday* (originally published as *Black Market*) • *See How They Run* (originally published as *The Jericho Commandment*) • *Season of the Machete* • *The Thomas Berryman Number*

BOOK**SHOTS**

Manhunt (with James O. Born) • *The Exile* (with Alison Joseph) • *The Dolls* (with Kecia Bal) • *The Medical Examiner* (with Maxine Paetro) •

Detective Cross • *Private: Gold* (with Jassy Mackenzie) • *French Twist* (with Richard DiLallo) • *Malicious* (with James O. Born) • *Hidden* (with James O. Born) • *The House Husband* (with Duane Swierczynski) • *Black & Blue* (with Candice Fox) • *Come and Get Us* (with Shan Serafin) • *Private: The Royals* (with Rees Jones) • *The Christmas Mystery* (with Richard DiLallo) • *Killer Chef* (with Jeffrey J. Keyes) • *Taking the Titanic* (with Scott Slaven) • *Kill or Be Killed* (thriller omnibus) • *$10,000,000 Marriage Proposal* (with Hilary Liftin) • *French Kiss* (with Richard DiLallo) • *113 Minutes* (with Max DiLallo) • *Hunted* (with Andrew Holmes) • *Chase* (with Michael Ledwidge) • *Let's Play Make-Believe* (with James O. Born) • *Little Black Dress* (with Emily Raymond) • *The Trial* (with Maxine Paetro) • *Cross Kill* • *Zoo 2* (with Max DiLallo)

BOOKS FOR READERS OF ALL AGES

Maximum Ride

Maximum Ride Forever • *Nevermore: The Final Maximum Ride Adventure* • *Angel: A Maximum Ride Novel* • *Fang: A Maximum Ride Novel* • *Max: A Maximum Ride Novel* • *The Final Warning: A Maximum Ride Novel* • *Saving the World and Other Extreme Sports: A Maximum Ride Novel* • *School's Out—Forever: A Maximum Ride Novel* • *The Angel Experiment: A Maximum Ride Novel*

Daniel X

Daniel X: Lights Out (with Chris Grabenstein) • *Daniel X: Armageddon* (with Chris Grabenstein) • *Daniel X: Game Over* (with Ned Rust) • *Daniel X: Demons & Druids* (with Adam Sadler) • *Daniel X: Watch the Skies* (with Ned Rust) • *The Dangerous Days of Daniel X* (with Michael Ledwidge)

Witch & Wizard

Witch & Wizard: The Lost (with Emily Raymond) • *Witch & Wizard: The Kiss* (with Jill Dembowski) • *Witch & Wizard: The Fire* (with Jill Dembowski) • *Witch & Wizard: The Gift* (with Ned Rust) • *Witch & Wizard* (with Gabrielle Charbonnet)

Middle School

Middle School: Escape to Australia (with Martin Chatterton, illustrated by Daniel Griffo) • *Middle School: Dog's Best Friend* (with Chris Tebbetts, illustrated by Jomike Tejido) • *Middle School: Just My Rotten Luck* (with Chris Tebbetts, illustrated by Laura Park) • *Middle School: Save Rafe* (with Chris Tebbetts, illustrated by Laura Park) • *Middle School: Ultimate Showdown* (with Julia Bergen, illustrated by Alec Longstreth) • *Middle School: How I Survived Bullies, Broccoli, and Snake Hill* (with Chris Tebbetts, illustrated by Laura Park) • *Middle School: Big Fat Liar* (with Lisa Papademetriou, illustrated by Neil Swaab) • *Middle School: Get Me Out of Here!* (with Chris Tebbetts, illustrated by Laura Park) • *Middle School, The Worst Years of My Life* (with Chris Tebbetts, illustrated by Laura Park)

Confessions

Confessions: The Murder of an Angel (with Maxine Paetro) • *Confessions: The Paris Mysteries* (with Maxine Paetro) • *Confessions: The Private School Murders* (with Maxine Paetro) • *Confessions of a Murder Suspect* (with Maxine Paetro)

I Funny

I Funny: School of Laughs (with Chris Grabenstein, illustrated by Jomike Tejido) • *I Funny TV* (with Chris Grabenstein, illustrated by Laura Park) • *I Totally Funniest* (with Chris Grabenstein, illustrated by Laura Park) • *I Even Funnier* (with Chris Grabenstein, illustrated by Laura Park) •

I Funny: A Middle School Story (with Chris Grabenstein, illustrated by Laura Park)

Treasure Hunters

Treasure Hunters: Quest for the City of Gold (with Chris Grabenstein, illustrated by Juliana Neufeld) • *Treasure Hunters: Peril at the Top of the World* (with Chris Grabenstein, illustrated by Juliana Neufeld) • *Treasure Hunters: Secret of the Forbidden City* (with Chris Grabenstein, illustrated by Juliana Neufeld) • *Treasure Hunters: Danger Down the Nile* (with Chris Grabenstein, illustrated by Juliana Neufeld) • *Treasure Hunters* (with Chris Grabenstein, illustrated by Juliana Neufeld)

House of Robots

House of Robots: Robot Revolution (with Chris Grabenstein, illustrated by Juliana Neufeld) • *House of Robots: Robots Go Wild!* (with Chris Grabenstein, illustrated by Juliana Neufeld) • *House of Robots* (with Chris Grabenstein, illustrated by Juliana Neufeld)

OTHER BOOKS FOR READERS OF ALL AGES

Jacky Ha-Ha: My Life Is a Joke (with Chris Grabenstein, illustrated by Kerascoët) • *Give Thank You a Try* • *Expelled* (with Emily Raymond) • *The Candies Save Christmas* (illustrated by Andy Elkerton) • *Big Words for Little Geniuses* (with Susan Patterson, illustrated by Hsinping Pan) • *Laugh Out Loud* (with Chris Grabenstein, illustrated by Stephen Gilpin) • *Pottymouth and Stoopid* (with Chris Grabenstein, illustrated by Stephen Gilpin) • *Crazy House* (with Gabrielle Charbonnet) • *Word of Mouse* (with Chris Grabenstein, illustrated by Joe Sutphin) • *Give Please a Chance* (with Bill O'Reilly) • *Cradle and All* (teen edition) • *Jacky Ha-Ha* (with Chris Grabenstein, illustrated by Kerascoët) •

Public School Superhero (with Chris Tebbetts, illustrated by Cory Thomas) • *Homeroom Diaries* (with Lisa Papademetriou, illustrated by Keino) • *Med Head* (with Hal Friedman) • *santaKid* (illustrated by Michael Garland)

For previews and information about the author, visit JamesPatterson.com or find him on Facebook or at your app store.